I0831868

The characters and events portrayed in this book are fictitious. Any similarity to real persons, living or dead, is coincidental and not intended by the author.

ISBN-13: 9798992918274

Cover design by: Magdalena Pietrzak
(barn-swallow.carrd.co)
Printed in the United States of America

Woefully Damned

Kayla Robinson

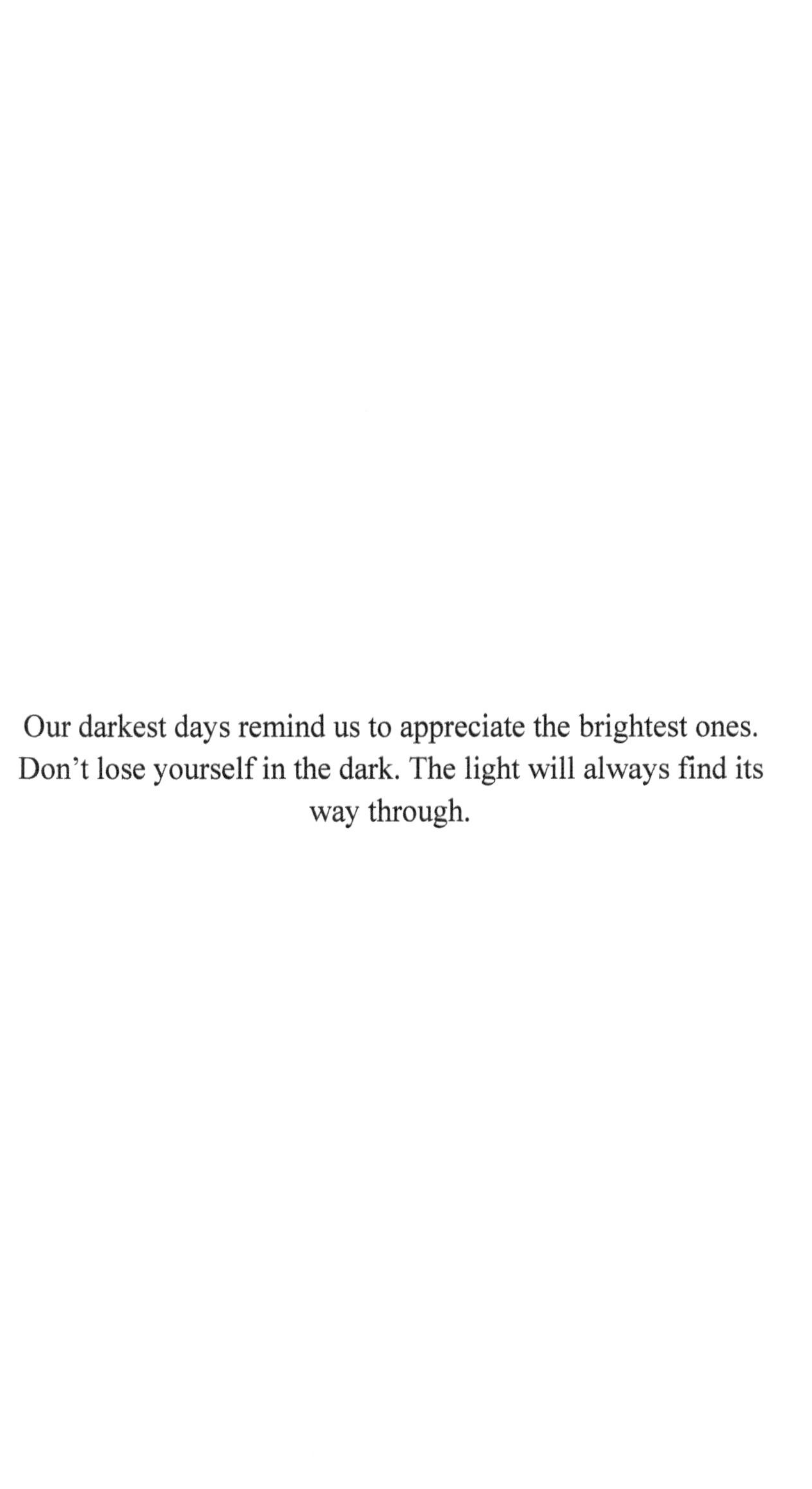

Our darkest days remind us to appreciate the brightest ones. Don’t lose yourself in the dark. The light will always find its way through.

Chapter 1

Mira

"The king is dead." Devlon repeated himself like we hadn't heard him.

We heard him. I think the collective shock that struck us at what he'd said was what left us staring as though he hadn't spoken at all. I blinked and finally shook my head as if that would pull me out of my stupor.

"I heard you." I muttered, while my mind swirled. No, it wasn't a stupor I was stuck in now. It was a spiral. *The king is dead.* The thought rang again in my head while I tried to make sense of it.

We cannot afford for you to panic. Just take a breath. Gaisgeach chose this moment to pop into my head as though his reminder to breathe helped me at all.

"Died in his sleep apparently." Devlon added.

I couldn't stop the halfhearted chuckle that huffed out of me. No, this wasn't funny at all, and yet, I was laughing. Disbelief and horror flooded me now. The laugh was a futile attempt at diffusing my own thoughts. We were *fucked.*

I looked over at Garrick. "I don't think I need to tell you that we're fucked."

His gaze held the same amount of shock, disbelief, and horror that I felt. He was still as death, staring at me now with a question clear on his face. *What do we do?*

I didn't know the answer. I mean, there were certainly obvious ways to handle this, but were they feasible? Were they even reasonable? I didn't know.

"We shouldn't panic." Devlon tried to reason. "Perhaps Ronan will take the throne and just drop his attempts to kill you and capture Adriana. I doubt he has a need for you or her now."

The door swung open and Aris stormed in. "You know damn well that's an absurd thing to say." He snarled at Devlon. "The bastard isn't going to stop coming after her now. He's got a whole gods damned army to do it now."

I was shocked *he* was the one to say it rather than Lazarus or Deiric sitting behind me, but I didn't focus enough to read their thoughts to know why they were so quiet. Perhaps they were just as dumbfounded as me. Aris had likely only found his words because we were all so quiet.

I didn't spare Devlon a glance as I held Garrick's gaze. "Warn *everyone*." I insisted. "Call *all* of our people to the manors if they're in Leinster or send them to the manors in the other territories."

Garrick nodded.

"Mira, we shouldn't panic right away," Devlon placated. It was useless though. I turned and looked at him now letting the full weight of my fear and concern rise to my face.

"You were not *there*." I almost shouted. "You didn't witness the people you loved slaughtered right in front of your fucking eyes while you were basically powerless to help them because you were too much in shock to do anything other than run."

His mouth opened like he might speak, but he shut it again. Yes, he lost someone, but he didn't *witness* it. It was far different if you saw the carnage, the chaos. Aris and I had witnessed it firsthand, and it was brutal. Others had escaped; I'd learned that now. That didn't make me feel any better about it.

"He's going to do something rash. Whether he banishes magic all together or he decides that vampires are to be executed and destroyed, you know it won't be something small." I searched his face for any kind of recognition or understanding but found none. He seemed at a loss for words.

"We will prepare the best we can, and honestly," I looked him up and down a bit dismissively, "you should have everyone in Solas do the same."

"They will not want to run and hide." He mumbled.

I could compel him, I realized. I could *make* him do what I asked, but that wouldn't be right. He needed to come to that conclusion on his own. We operated on trust, and I trusted him thus far to make the right call. I hoped he'd do so now. I looked back toward Garrick.

"Do we have the space to take in *everyone?*"

Garrick's mouth opened and closed, once, then twice, before he finally spoke. "I honestly don't know. We might. I'm not sure that other territories would welcome them either, if I'm honest. It would entirely depend on what Ronan *does* do."

"We'll double up the rooms, fit as many people as we can." I said rather finally, accepting absolutely no discussion on the matter.

Garrick just nodded. "This meeting is over." He glanced at Devlon. "I need to spread the word." Then he was gone.

I turned my gaze back to Devlon again and now he just looked exhausted and frustrated. He wasn't looking at me. He was looking at the table in front of him, his mind far from our discussion. "Do you truly think that even the Solas members aren't safe?"

I sighed. It was denial and fear that had overwhelmed him, whether his face showed it or not. I knew that feeling. "I think that we should prepare for the worst. The gods only know what sort of awful laws or changes he will make under his rule."

His eyes finally met mine. "I will bring this to each magister in this region and let them make the call. I can't force them to call *all* of our members back. There's too many of them to fit in our manors and meeting places anyway."

I nodded. I knew they still vastly outnumbered us. Pulling them all from their homes and lives would be impossible.

"Just letting them have the chance to get out or hide is better than nothing. No matter what happens. We should pull our resources out of the palace immediately."

He gave me a shallow nod and then he rose from the table. "I will let you know if we hear anything else." Then he looked me in the eye again. "How will you tell Adriana?"

I flinched and frowned. "I'm not sure." I said softly as I shifted my gaze down to my hands. I hadn't even thought of that.

I have already told Cairbre. However, I think she'd rather hear it from you. Gaisgeach said.

Devlon walked out of the room, leaving Aris, Lazarus, Deiric, and myself. I stood from the table and turned toward Aris where he stood in the doorway.

"Do we have anyone here from the party last evening that will need somewhere to go?"

Aris nodded. "We had a few nightmages here, but they were sent to Lazarus' manor this morning. We just have one other person who hasn't left yet that would need somewhere to stay."

My stomach twisted when I realized precisely who he meant. "Triss?"

His curt nod confirmed it. I sighed and glanced back at Deiric. He looked up at me with a look that suggested he wasn't getting involved and that it was my call. As much as I didn't really want to have her in our manor, I wasn't going to turn away someone knowing what might come from Ronan when he's crowned.

I knew by now that I needed to heed the feeling in my gut that this wasn't going to go our way. I was rarely wrong. I'd need to strengthen our wards as well, which meant I may need the help of another mage.

"Where is she?" I asked when I made my decision and looked back at Aris.

"Honestly? Probably still sleeping on one of the cots we laid out for the nightmages and anyone who decided to stay after they had too much to drink." He shook his head and let out a less than amused laugh. “She abandoned all sense after she ran into you and Deiric.”

I smiled. At least if I had to go collect her and deliver this shitty news, I could find solace in the fact that she’d likely be miserable about it in more ways than one. I stepped around my chair while Lazarus and Deiric stood to follow me.

“Lead the way.” I gestured to Aris, and he turned to lead us to her.

He led us down the stairs, through the foyer, into one of the large and, normally, mostly empty rooms on the first floor. When we walked in, she was the last remaining person on a cot in the room and lay covering her face with her hand. She barely lifted her head to look at us and let out a disgruntled scoff mixed with a sigh.

“Yes, yes.” She mumbled. “I promise I’m getting up and will be out of your hair in no time.”

I knew from her reaction that she hadn’t really *seen* us. She just noticed that people had walked in and stopped to look at her.

“Actually,” I started, and her head shot up without her hand covering her face this time. “We’re here to invite you to leave with us.”

She stared at me like I’d sprouted six new heads and slowly lifted herself into a seated position. She looked practically green with nausea, and it was clear that she had just collapsed onto the cot without so much as bathing the evening before. She was speechless and stared at us for an uncomfortable amount of time before she finally spoke.

“Why on *earth* would I go anywhere with you?”

Deiric didn’t even try to stifle his chuckle. I shrugged. “Because we’ve just received word that the king is dead and, without giving you the full backstory, let's just say that it is in your best interest to find a manor to run off and hide in. You should also count yourself lucky that we can make room for you."

She stared at me skeptically. "What does the king have to do with me coming back with you?"

"The prince, or rather, the new king will be very likely to want to end our coven or worse." I looked her over before I continued, "And I don't intend to let him harm any member of our coven, no matter how much I might dislike them in general."

She huffed what might've been a slight laugh. "Would you at least give me time to bathe before we head back to wherever it is you're taking me?"

I frowned just slightly. "You can bathe when we get there. I'm in no mood to wait. I have to deliver this news to the princess, and I'd rather not delay that any longer than I need to."

She grumbled under her breath but brought herself to her feet and dusted herself off. "Fine." She walked toward us with a slight frown on her lips.

I ignored her obvious displeasure and turned to face Aris. "Let me know if anyone else needs somewhere to go and you've run out of room. I don't expect anyone to stumble onto our manor by accident."

Aris nodded. "You know, there is *one* other person you could take with you."

I knew exactly what he was implying but wasn't sure that I really wanted to invite my father to our manor so soon. While we had 'made up' at the party last evening, I still didn't know if I wanted to see him on a daily basis just yet.

Then again, if I was inviting my mate's ex-lover to the manor, could it really get any worse?

"Taking him back with you would free up the room for several people." Aris shrugged. "I don't like to make a habit of putting humans with vampires, even if we're in total control of ourselves."

The dig at Deiric and I sleeping together before I'd been turned made me want to hit him, but his slight smile as he finished that sentence told me he was intending it to be a genuine joke. I rolled my eyes.

"Fine."

Deiric nearly choked next to me. "Are you sure?" He asked before he could think the better of it and stop himself.

I glanced back at him. "If I'm bringing *her* to the manor, I really can't justify telling *him* no too."

"Am I missing something here?" Triss grumbled from behind me.

"No." Deiric and I both said in unison.

Her snicker told me that she saw right through that, but she didn't press the issue.

"Have him collect his things and I'll come to collect him later."

Aris nodded again and then turned to head back up the stairs, presumably to deliver the message.

"Who is–" Triss started to ask but was silenced the moment I shifted us to our manor.

"Fuck's sake." She grumbled, putting her hand over her mouth. "A little warning would've been nice."

I glanced over my shoulder at her and shrugged. "Sorry. I told you I wasn't in the mood to wait." It was a half assed apology, and I knew she knew I wasn't truly sorry.

"Please don't puke on the floors." I mumbled as I walked from the foyer into the kitchen where I knew Adriana and the others were likely to be at this time of day. "Liala?"

Liala spun from where she was working at the counter to prepare everyone's lunch. She wiped her hands on her skirt and raised a brow when she met my gaze and saw Triss behind me.

"Could Triss use your bathing room to freshen up while we rearrange and prepare a room for her?"

Liala again glanced around me at Triss, who I could tell had walked with me into the kitchen to avoid being left alone with Deiric out in the Foyer. He and Lazarus began discussing where to put my father, and from the sounds of it, Lazarus was in a losing battle with sharing his room with him.

Liala gave me a pointed look. She didn't want her anywhere near the bathing room she shared with Zane, but I ignored it. She smiled in a strained attempt at pleasantries. "Certainly."

I gave her an apologetic look. "I'll have the room ready by the time she's done. I promise."

The glare Liala sent me said that if I didn't, she might kill me. She walked past me to show Triss to her room. Zane chuckled from where he leaned against the wall between the dining area and the kitchen.

"I'm not sure why she cares. Triss is *anything* but my type."

I looked his way and, seeing Adriana at the table beyond him, I turned to walk in that direction. "I'm guessing she just doesn't like the idea that you might walk in while she's in there." I shrugged. "Maybe stay down here until I have the room ready?"

He just rolled his eyes and shrugged.

I walked over to Adriana with a strained smile on my face. “Adriana?” She stopped mid-sentence and looked up at me. “Can I speak with you, privately?” Her unease was clear in her face, but she nodded, stood up, and followed me up to her room. Probably the only place we’d get even a shred of privacy.

Chapter 2

Deiric

I walked upstairs with Lazarus, listening to him grumble and go on about all of the reasons why having a room with Teron would be an absolute nightmare. It took all the self-control I had not to point out that he *could* return to his own manor. I didn't actually want him to leave. Not with this most recent development.

You'll need him. Don't do anything that would cause him to decide to leave. Fiadh butted into my thoughts.

Well aware. I replied a little annoyed. While I was thankful to have her around again, she occasionally had an uncanny and irritating habit of interrupting my thoughts at the worst times.

I heard that.

I just rolled my eyes.

It wasn't until we reached his room and he halted me outside of the door that I realized his reasoning wasn't because of Teron himself but it was because of the nightmage who had come home with him last night. I'd almost completely forgotten that she'd been here. Mira and I had been so drunk when we came home that I hadn't paid much attention to *anyone* but her.

He peaked in the door to confirm she was clothed before we both walked in.

"You can't be complaining about sharing the room simply because you want to keep *her* here can you?" I asked, glancing over at her.

"No. She'll need to go to my manor anyway for at least a little while." He grumbled.

She looked between the two of us hoping for an explanation.

I wasn't going to point out that we probably could handle another newly turned female vampire here. Mira had handled it just fine. Something told me that any woman who turned would handle the transition better than a man, but that wasn't a thought I wanted to vocalize right now.

"So what's the problem then?" I settled my gaze on him. "Your reasoning so far hasn't been worth my concern."

He leveled a glare at me that likely would've had me withering if I didn't know that I definitely held the upper hand with him now. He might've had age and strength on me, but I had Fiadh, her magic, and was mated to our elder mage. The power had shifted, whether he recognized it or not, and I was starting to realize that myself.

"He absolutely hates me for taking on a role he perceives to be fatherly. Did you not notice how he acted toward me the day that we got him out?"

"I noticed, but it doesn't really matter. If he wants to see Mira, he'll just have to deal with it."

"*I'd* rather not have to deal with it." He snapped.

"Do you have a better idea?"

He glanced at Rosalind and thought for a moment. "What about Leo or Xander?" He asked. "Or, better yet, couldn't he take Eimear's room? She's spent most nights with Renwick anyway."

I looked at him incredulously for even suggesting Eimear's room. "I'm not going to force the woman into Renwick's bed just to empty out a room."

His annoyance was clear as he said, "And Xander or Leo?"

Xander or Leo both likely wouldn't have complained at all if I'd asked or simply demanded that *they* share their rooms. I hadn't considered them because Lazarus' stay was still technically temporary.

It made more sense for *him* to give up his privacy rather than one of my men who would be here far longer than he ever would. After all, we wouldn't need him watching over Mira forever. I hoped anyway.

I sighed and turned to leave. "I'll see what I can do."

Mira slipped out of Adriana's room now, her face solemn and conflicted.

"What's wrong, love?" I asked as I walked up to her. She startled just slightly, like she hadn't heard me approaching. Her troubled eyes rose to meet mine and something told me that her chat with Adriana hadn't gone well.

"She's not terribly upset about the king, but she is *very* concerned for her mother."

I studied her for a moment while I collected my thoughts. “Surely Ronan won’t do any harm to the queen. She’s his mother too.”

She shrugged and glanced down the hallway. “I don’t think he would, but she doesn’t want to leave her in the palace. I suggested that she just wait and see what happens, so I guess time will tell.” She looked back up at me again. “I’m having her ladies maid move into her room with her so that Triss can take that room. How did it go with Lazarus?”

“I think I’ll be talking to Xander or Leo.”

Her face softened and she chuckled. “I’m not surprised.” She turned and started toward the stairs. “I already moved the beds around. Esme is moving her things now. I need a drink.”

I caught up with her in just a few steps. “I’m not sure that drinking is going to help, but I agree.”

“If I’m going to bring my father here, I’m going to need a drink first.”

She had a point. I still couldn’t believe she’d even agreed to it.

*

A few hours later, she shifted the two of us back to Aris’ manor for her father. She left Triss to collect her things on her own, since she was capable of shifting to our manor once she knew where she was shifting to. I was surprised to see him waiting in the foyer, and he didn’t seem to have much with him. To his credit, he didn’t appear the slightest bit annoyed, even though I could tell he’d been expecting us back here hours prior.

Mira looked him up and down. She looked like she was about to ask if he was ready when Devlon appeared at the top of the stairs.

"Wait!" He yelled and sprinted down to stop in front of us. "It seems you were right."

Mira would've probably gloated, if it weren't for the look on his face and the gravity of the situation at hand.

"I wasn't able to get Vivian to leave the palace. She claimed we had nothing to worry about."

"I don't like where this is going." Mira mumbled under her breath.

"They've banned magic entirely. Vampires, mages, and the like. Any vampire that's caught will be killed on sight and anyone who is believed to practice any form of magic outside of the select few people the king has chosen will also be executed."

"Vivian?"

"She communicated that to me mind to mind and I haven't heard from her since."

Mira heaved a heavy sigh. "Are you going to ask for us to go get her?"

He shook his head. "She made her decision. As much as I hate to leave her there, it wouldn't be wise to go in there without a real plan first, and by the time we get there it may very well be too late."

She seemed to consider that and then nodded. "I can try to see if Macha can send some ravens to monitor things for us." She paused, like she was listening to her. "She'll let me know if they see anything."

He nodded his thanks, then glanced between her father and her. "I was a little surprised to hear you're leaving." He smiled at Teron.

"That makes two of us." He didn't look at Devlon. He was solely focused on Mira and me.

"Let's get on with it then." Mira gestured with her head for him to come over to us, even though she didn't need his proximity to shift him with us. She looked back at Devlon before her father got too close.

"Keep me updated with anything you hear. Our doors are open if we need to allow more people to come in. We don't have much space, but I don't want anyone to be executed just for who or what they are."

She shifted us without waiting to see if he replied. She was annoyed, and rightfully so. She'd tried to warn him. Even though she seemed rather indifferent about Vivian, I could tell it bothered her.

Xander was waiting in the foyer when we returned and was leaning against the handrail for the stairs. He only looked slightly annoyed. He arched a brow as he assessed Teron.

"Looks like you'll be bunking with me." He grumbled, shooting me a glare for a half a second before gesturing for Teron to follow him upstairs. "We're all doubling up apparently. Unless you've got a woman sleeping with you." The second sentence was mumbled under his breath.

"You know *precisely* why we're not putting him in our room, asshole." Mira snapped.

"I will sleep *anywhere* but their room." Teron said quickly, his discomfort in the mere idea of that evident in his body language as well as his voice.

Xander just rolled his eyes and started up the stairs. Teron followed without another word, which surprised me to say the least. He didn't even ask for a tour.

"He'll figure it out." Mira mumbled.

Are you sure this was a good idea? Fiadh asked me. She must've blocked out Mira, because she didn't act like she heard it.

No, but it isn't my place to say otherwise.

Mira glanced at me. I didn't hide that I was conversing with Fiadh. I just offered her a shrug of one shoulder. She rolled her eyes and walked off to the kitchen.

First an ex-lover and now her estranged father. This is going to be interesting. She didn't hide the amusement in her voice.

It isn't going to be interesting. Gaisgeach chimed in now. *It's going to be a gods damned disaster.*

He's not wrong. I pointed out. *But they're not exactly estranged. She thought he was dead, he wasn't, and he was just a prick. Family is complicated.*

It shouldn't be. Fiadh grumbled.

Bold statement for someone who was hatched from an egg and didn't even need to know her parents. I snapped at her.

I heard her snort of displeasure, but she quieted down after that.

He has a point. Gaisgeach added, and it took all my self-control not to laugh. He rarely agreed with me on much of anything. Hearing him finally do so was an exciting twist.

Don't get used to it. He grumbled.

Chapter 3

Mira

Adriana informed the mages what happened with the king before I'd come down this morning, which led to a mass panic, a lot of shouting, and demands to leave to find their loved ones. Gerald, who was still with us despite that he could've left some time ago, was the only one who sat quietly, like he couldn't believe what he'd been told. His face was ashen, and he didn't participate in the conversation at all.

"I *need* to go get my parents." Aodh demanded and stood from the table.

"Absolutely not." Deiric snarled. "Sit. Down."

"What if they take them?" Aodh was nearly shouting, waving his arms about incredulously at the fact that Deiric seemed to not care about his family. "They'll be killed!"

"They may have already been taken." I cut in and he shifted his gaze to me. "If they were and they knew they had a son someone might be waiting to take *you* when you rush home to check on them."

"We have to do *something!*" He insisted.

I shook my head. "We need to lay low and wait to see how everything plays out."

"How can you be so okay with doing *nothing*?" Sorcha cut in now, snarling at me like she too needed to go to check on or retrieve her family.

"I never said I was okay with this." I said calmly. "I said it was what we needed to do."

"This is bullshit." Aodh slammed back down in his seat.

"Do you see Gerald's face?" Deiric asked rather coldly and motioned toward the ashen mage who only looked over at us now because he heard his name. "His family was killed in the attacks years ago. His reaction to this should be enough to tell you that you need to listen and lay low."

Gerald looked from Deiric to me, then down at the table. He had been just a child when the attacks occurred. He was saved by one of the other mages who shifted him out before he was killed as well. I'd never asked what he saw that day. I didn't want to bring it up. Now, I was glad I hadn't.

The energy of the entire room shifted as everyone looked at Gerald and took in his face, his body language, and eagerly awaited whatever he might say. He glanced around at them, then locked eyes with Deiric.

"If they've got your parents, you're better off just staying here. If they haven't found them yet, you're still better off staying here." He mumbled, almost too quietly for everyone to hear. "If it's anything like how they did the attacks years ago they kill without mercy. They don't care how old you are, who you are, or what you can do. They kill on sight. It isn't something you want to be near. If they say we are safe here, you should all just stay here and count yourselves lucky."

I heard a light set of footsteps coming down the stairs and recognized it immediately as Triss. Even if her dainty steps hadn't given her away, the striking smell of her jasmine perfume did. It was overwhelming, and a scent I marked on her the moment I met her at the party. She'd worn too much of it then too. Or, perhaps, it was just too overwhelming for my senses. I couldn't be sure.

She quietly took a place in the doorway opposite to where I was standing and leaned against the trim. A few of the mages glanced at her, but none of them gave her the time of day to give a real greeting.

"I'm sure once things settle we'll be able to check around and either make sure your parents made it to a manor or made it out if they're in this country. For now, I *need* you to stay here and be safe. There isn't anything we can do until we see how this pans out, what they do, and how they do it."

A heavier set of footsteps approached behind me now. One I didn't totally recognize but wasn't planning to take my focus off the mages in front of me to address. I didn't pay much attention to how any of the guys walked, except Deiric. It wasn't important anyway.

"And if we don't hear anything from our parents after a few days?" Zemora asked hesitantly.

I opened my mouth to speak but found myself without the words to do so. I didn't have an answer. I couldn't guess what the future held, nor did I have any idea what we might be able to do in that situation. They knew how to weaken us.

How to take us down. Shifting to any of their homes was almost a death sentence. We'd need to get creative.

Deiric stepped closer to me, rested his hand on the small of my back and replied for me. "We don't know." I looked over at him, and he looked as conflicted and frustrated as I felt. "We'll cross that bridge when we come to it."

I didn't have to look back at her to know that tears had started to stream down her face. Or to know that she wasn't the only one that had begun crying. Adriana was still worried about her mother, even though out of all of us I suspected she was the only one who didn't have to worry at all. I finally glanced over my shoulder to see who else had joined our little panic party in the dining room to see my father standing a few steps behind me.

He gave me a knowing and sad look, which told me he caught enough of the conversation to know that none of us could comfort or calm them. This was almost worse than the attack. We didn't see that coming. This was something I'd had a feeling was coming in one way or another, and yet there had been nothing I could really do to prevent it or prepare for it. That killed me.

An ambush was easy that way. You could say you didn't know and it made everything okay. Or, at least, as okay as it could be following something like that. A ban of magic was… all encompassing. Horrifying and finite. It wasn't about our coven this time. It was *everyone*.

If you were caught you were killed. There would be no trial, no questioning. Just death. We trained for something like this, but I hoped I wouldn't have had to see it for many, many mortal lifetimes.

I'd lost both parents, or so I thought. My father had undergone their torture and knew the kind of cruelty they could bring onto people if they chose to. I suspected they'd still be after us. There was something I was sure Ronan still wanted with his sister. Wanted with me. I was afraid to know what that might be.

"What about my mother?" Adriana asked, causing me to shift my attention back to her. Out of all of their families, hers was the one I was most reluctant to deal with.

Triss spoke before I could. "You're the princess, correct?" Her tone was bored, perhaps a little curious, but mostly bored.

Adriana shifted her gaze to Triss and nodded.

"Forgive me for being frank, your highness, but of all of the people in this room, I think your mother's situation is likely the *least* vulnerable."

While I barely knew the woman, and despised her simply for what she was hoping to get from Deiric two nights ago, I suddenly felt like I owed her for her bluntness with Adriana.

Adriana scowled. "You don't know anything about me or my mother."

"All due, respect, dear. I'm pretty sure your mother had no magic in her, which makes it suspicious for how you ended up with anything at all. But," she paused, glanced at me very briefly, and then looked back at Adriana, "I can tell you right now that any one of us would go to rescue their families before we go to rescue your mother. She'll be in the innermost portion of the castle, perfect for an ambush and perfect to lure you back home. Don't be stupid enough to fall for their trap."

"Remember what happened the *last time* we shifted into the castle when we weren't asked there by your father?" Deiric asked.

Adriana frowned and looked away from both of them.

"Dare I ask…" Triss started.

"Don't." Deiric snarled at her with a scowl that had her shrinking and raising her hands in defeat as his arm slid more solidly around my waist.

"He's not my father." Adriana said so softly I was certain that no one but those with enhanced hearing heard her.

"Excuse me?" I asked.

"He wasn't my father." She lifted her gaze back to me again and there was a certainty about her that had me a bit taken aback. I had remembered her calling him 'the king' rather than her father the day after that ambush, but I didn't really think it was *true*.

It made sense though. She barely shed a tear over him before she was freaking out about her mother. I should've picked up on that then.

"How do you know?" Deiric asked.

"I don't know how I know." She shrugged a shoulder. "I just do. He *isn't* my father. He thought he was, but he isn't."

I knew better than to ask her who was. She didn't know. If she had known, she'd surely be asking about him too. I hoped that she was smart enough not to go after her mother. Ronan likely still had one or two former Solas mages working for him. He may have outlawed magic, but he was a hypocritical bastard and I was sure he recognized that he'd need magic wielders to capture and kill us.

"It doesn't matter." I mumbled and all their gazes shifted to me. "You're not going to go try and save your mother. She's safer where she is than here. If *any* of you decide to go try to find your families anyway, we will not be coming to rescue you. You either stay here and stay alive or you're on your own."

The words felt like poison as I said them, but they needed to understand this wasn't a game, nor was it a joke. This was as serious as it was going to get, and while I couldn't stop them I certainly wasn't going to save them either. Even if it killed me to let them go.

Chapter 4

Deiric

I was not surprised to find that Mira was finding anything she could do to avoid Teron the following day. It was absurd, actually. They'd seemed to have reached a mature understanding at the party, but she still didn't want to spend much time near him. I still couldn't believe she'd allowed him to come here with us.

She was determined to proceed as usual for the moment. Magic was outlawed, yes, but we hadn't heard of anyone attempting to storm any manors, nor had we heard of anyone actually getting executed yet. I knew all of our death dealers knew how to hide. I had no concerns for any of them, not even Leo, who was back out keeping an eye on things for me.

Today, I was watching as she worked with Zemora, Stella, and Sorcha. Her focus had been on Adriana for so long that their training had slowed. Now that Adriana was deemed a master, they took the forefront again. She was sparring with the three of them, which was more or less just them throwing attacks at her and her parrying them. She hadn't taken to the offensive yet.

The door opened behind me and Triss stopped next to me. "You certainly picked a good one."

I glanced over at her with a raised brow. "Excuse me?"

"Your wife." She jerked her chin toward Mira. "Or mate." She shrugged. "Whatever it is you call each other."

"And what makes you say that?" I turned back to watch Mira and the mages again. I knew she was listening. She never missed a thing.

"I heard a little bit about the new 'Elder Mage', but I thought she was just as rich and pompous as the rest of the old magisters had been."

I shot her a quick glare and she just huffed a laugh.

"You know it's true. They were all a bunch of pricks."

"Not all of them."

She shrugged. "Whatever. What I'm saying is, I actually kind of like her."

I snorted. A very slight smirk seemed to appear on Mira's lips. "I didn't realize I asked for your opinion."

"Tell her I said thank you for allowing me to come here. I'm sure it bothers her to have me around."

"She can hear you."

As if on cue, Mira spoke up before Triss could say anything else. "Triss?" She barely glanced in her direction. "If you're going to be staying here, you could at least make yourself useful." She didn't miss a beat as she spoke, catching the ball of fire Sorcha threw at her and tossing it back. "I've got three mages here who could use a sparring partner other than me. You're a mage, correct?"

"I am." Triss was both surprised and taken aback by her question.

"Then get down here and spar with one of them." I could hear Triss heave a sigh, but then Mira added, "Please?"

I don't think I'd ever heard her say please, except perhaps when *I* made her beg.

Don't get used to it. I met her gaze in between her parrying Stella and Sorcha's simultaneous attacks. *Just want to get an idea of how useful she might be if we're ever attacked.*

No one should be able to get through the wards.

Triss descended the steps and walked over to the group of them.

"I'll spar with Stella." She offered.

Yes, I'm aware no one should *be able to get through the wards, but I have about as much faith in that as I have faith that the sky will turn purple. Safety is an illusion. If someone wants to kill us, they'll find a way eventually if we don't eliminate them first.*

I didn't know what to say to that. Instead I continued to lean against the pillar and watch as Stella broke off from their circle around Mira and then turned to face Triss.

"What sort of magic do you have?" Stella asked.

"Why don't you attack and find out?" Triss taunted.

"You first."

Triss just shrugged and threw a ball of lightning at Stella. Stella jumped, caught it and threw it back. The excitement that rose to her face was genuine. Mira *could* fight with lightning, but I doubted that Stella had been around anyone other than her with that particular magic. There weren't many of them left.

You just have a thing for unique and powerful women, don't you? Mira pulled me from my thoughts again. There was a playful smirk on her face.

I only have a thing for you, *love.*

She laughed, and I was glad she found this funny rather than wanting to burn Triss again. I doubted Triss would still like her if she threatened her again.

Teron came out now and leaned against the pillar on the other side of the stairs.

"She seems like she's doing well with them."

Of course. Of course he'd want to talk to me.

I heard Fiadh laugh in my head. It was a sound I so seldom heard it nearly startled me.

You actually expected your mate's father wouldn't want to talk to you?

I guess I was avoiding him just as much as her without even realizing it. He and Lazarus were on tentatively civil terms. My men were willing to make small talk, but still haven't warmed up to him much.

I didn't expect him to walk up and start a conversation unprompted.

Fiadh just snorted in amusement.

"She is." I replied.

"She trained the princess entirely by herself?"

"She did."

"Are you ever going to say more than two or three words to me?"

I looked at him now. He was dressed in fighting leathers, as though he'd come out to spar. "You're asking me questions that don't require much more of an answer than that."

He considered that while he studied me, then shrugged. "I'm not really sure what else to ask or say. You've practically been hiding behind her since I got here."

"I haven't been *hiding* behind her. I've been *with* her. Nothing about my normal daily habits have changed since you got here."

"So, you usually watch her train with the mages?"

"Some days, yes. Some days I'm with the dragons."

"The what?" His face screwed up in confusion while he tried to sort out if he'd just heard me wrong or if I was fucking with him.

I was only slightly aware of the faint laugh that escaped Mira. He hadn't seen the dragons yet. Nor had Triss. This was *not* the conversation I wanted to have right now.

Oh, this should be fun. Fiadh seemed far too entertained.

"You heard me. The dragons."

"Have you gone mad?"

Care to fly in and show him I'm not mad? I asked Fiadh.

I'd quite like to see how he'd react to Gaisgeach. Mira thought before Fiadh had the chance to reply.

We're on our way.

"You're about to find out." I smirked.

"Make room." Mira shouted and the mages scrambled toward the manor. Triss looked confused but followed. Mira didn't move, just stood staring at me with an amused smirk on her face.

Their wingbeats prompted Triss and Teron to both look toward the sky like they could see them or had any idea which direction they'd come from.

"Gods." Teron muttered under his breath as Gaisgeach and Fiadh came into view.

Gaisgeach landed first, slamming to the ground behind Mira. Fiadh landed seconds later between Mira and I, but still far enough from the manor that she wouldn't damage it.

They are actually almost ready for you. Fiadh angled her head down so she could look at me.

So eager to save me from this thrilling conversation?

She chuffed but drew her wings into herself so I could run up and get on her.

I walked down the steps while Mira walked around her. I ignored the general confusion and mumblings of awe from both Triss and Teron. Mira could explain to them that we weren't sharing their existence with anyone yet.

I need to stay with the managers. Mira thought when she stopped in front of me. *Don't have too much fun without me.*

I slipped a hand into her hair, rested the other on her hip and pulled her in for a kiss. *I plan to have quite a bit of fun with you when I get back.*

In that case, she pulled back and looked up at me with such a burning gaze that I nearly asked Fiadh to wait so I could take her inside right now. *Don't be gone too long. And* she waved her fingers, and my metal armor appeared on me, *don't forget this.*

I rolled my eyes and stepped around her. *Of course. How could I forget that.*

You can never be too careful. Fiadh cut in.

I ran up and sat on her back. She launched us into the skies. Closely followed by Gaisgeach.

Chapter 5

Mira

It was nearly sunset and Deiric hadn't come back yet. I was sitting in the den quietly reviewing my mother's grimoire and drinking a glass of whiskey when my father wandered in. He sat down in the chair to my right. I glanced over at him as I sipped my drink. He was still wearing his fighting leathers, for whatever reason. I was sure he had other, more comfortable, clothes.

I had changed into a simple blue cotton gown. It still hugged my body snugly down to the waist, but I didn't bother with a corset, opting for comfort over practicality since I had no other plans for the evening. Cairbre had convinced Adriana *not* to go after her mother, so I could relax and enjoy the few quiet minutes I had alone.

Or so I thought.

"You've been avoiding me." My father so astutely pointed out while he watched me sit my glass down.

"I have been busy."

"Hardly."

I looked up from the grimoire and shot him a glare. "I do have mages to train, sparring to do, and a mate who keeps me quite busy."

He scowled. I knew that the last one would hit its mark.

"There's also the dragons, of course."

"You've spoken to your mate's ex-lover more than your own father."

I rolled my eyes. "I let you come to live here. That doesn't mean that I'm suddenly going to go out of my way to talk to you every day. If you annoy me enough, I'll just send you back to Aris."

I heard the slightest huff of laughter from the foyer, and I had no doubt that Lazarus must've overheard that.

"Is that your mother's grimoire?"

I nodded and turned the page.

"Do you have your own yet?"

That made me look up again and really look at him. His tone was soft, lacking the usual bite it had when he was trying to point out a perceived flaw in me. His expression matched it. It was a genuine curiosity. A real attempt at making conversation with me rather than condescending or insulting me.

"No." I flipped the page and glanced down at the next spell in it. "I haven't really had much time to make one, and if I had, there's no sense in doing so because most of what I've done is already in this one."

"There are a few curses in the back."

I looked up at him again, surprised. My mother had never seemed like the type to dabble in anything dark or baneful. Yes, she knew quite a lot about Eldritch magic, but she always seemed so *kind*.

"Curses?"

He nodded. "Not sure how useful any of them are to you, but they're there. If you ever need them."

"She never struck me as the type to work with magic like that."

He smiled now. "You changed her. She was a force to be reckoned with before you were born. She really calmed down after that, unless someone threatened you."

"Why?" The question was out of my mouth before I could think the better of it.

"Why did you change her?" He asked. "I haven't a clue. My best guess is she didn't want *you* dabbling in anything baneful. She was quite good at it though. It was a pity when she stopped. Hexes and curses brought in very good money."

I snorted, thinking of her selling hexes or curses. It was almost too ridiculous to picture. I had no doubts she'd have protected me with the same kind of rage that a mother bear might protect her cubs, but I still couldn't picture her dabbling in dark magic.

The more I thought about it though, the more it made sense. She was always the go to mage for creating the daylight rings. That was still considered 'dark' magic simply for its connection to the vampires. Even before the attacks, she was the only mage I knew of that would do it. Our coven only kept the vampires around for their usefulness in killing the beasts, that much had been very clear until I resurfaced and became what I am now.

The front door opened and Deiric walked into the foyer. I listened as he walked to the dining room first, collected his own glass of whiskey and then came into the den. He walked around the couch and sat down next to me. His right arm rested on the back of the couch behind me.

My father was quiet, just watching the two of us while Deiric took a sip of his whiskey.

"Anything interesting happen today?" I asked a little hesitantly. I knew he was safe with Fiadh, but it made me nervous to know they'd be practicing magic out in the open.

"Not really." He shrugged. "Someone nearly lit me on fire, but I blocked it."

I shot him a look that said that wasn't something to be shrugged off and he just smirked before taking another sip of whiskey.

"Relax. She just pulled a little too much power from her dragon. Fiadh saw it and warned me. She wasn't *aiming* for me."

I sighed and leaned over into him.

"How many dragons *are* there?" My father spoke up and we both looked over at him while Deiric slipped his arm off of the back of the couch to pull me closer to him.

"I'm not sure." Deiric swirled the whiskey around in his glass while he thought. "Probably a hundred or so? They're not all bonded yet."

"And you oversee *all* of them?" There was a hint of pride in my father's voice, which neither of us missed.

"Sort of, yes." Deiric nodded.

"Do either of you have any plans for how we're going to handle this magic ban?"

I looked at Deiric, and he shrugged. "I think we're just waiting to see what Ronan does about it." I shifted my gaze back to my father. "There's no sense in taking a fight to him or starting a war until we see how it all plays out."

"We could always just *leave*." My father suggested.

"The Morrigan said Adriana would be queen. That leads me to believe there's a *lot* more to all of this than any of us are aware of yet."

"The dragons came back because of her too." Deiric added.

"Came back?"

"I was bonded with Fiadh before the dragons left a little over six hundred years ago."

My father arched a brow in surprise but didn't say anything else. We all sat in silence for what felt like an eternity. By the time that Deiric had finished his whiskey my father finally asked, "How do you bond with a dragon?"

Deiric huffed a laugh. "You don't." He said simply. "*They* choose you, and then you either accept or decline. You don't go out and bond with one on your own."

Another surprised look rose to my father's face. It was nice to see him genuinely shocked and at a loss for words. He was always quick to judge or make a smart remark, and we were leaving him without the chance to do so.

I leaned forward and grabbed my whiskey off of the table in front of us. I finished off the last of the glass and leaned back into Deiric. His fingers traced down my side.

You're not wearing a single thing under this dress, are you?

I tried my best but failed to hide the heat that rushed to my cheeks at his tone. I had done that on purpose, but didn't expect him to notice while I sat here with him.

Give me one good reason I should sit here and continue this conversation instead of taking you upstairs and ripping this off of you.

I cleared my throat and shot him a warning look, trying to get him to remember that we were sitting across from my gods damned father. He merely raised a brow and downed the small amount of whiskey left in his own glass. The corner of his mouth quirked up in the slightest smirk. He threw me over his shoulder and had us in our bedroom before I realized where we were going.

"Deiric!" I shrieked. I didn't know where the grimoire I had ended up. The glasses too, he'd taken almost too quickly for me to track.

He sat me down on the bed and untied straps of the dress. "You wore just that dress on purpose." He hooked his finger under my chin and made me look up at him as the top of the dress fell free. His fingers traced up the side of my face and then slipped into my hair. "Did you expect me not to notice?"

I hummed and leaned into his touch. "I didn't expect you to notice right away." I reached up and untucked his shirt, then tugged him closer to me. "But now that you have…" I let my voice trail off as I tugged at his pants next.

He yanked me upright and the dress pooled at my feet. I pulled his shirt up over his head. He took my hand now and kissed it, then twisted his hold on it to turn my arm so he could kiss my wrist.

"Have I ever told you how absolutely stunning you are?" He kissed his way up my arm to my shoulder. "Every. Single. Part. Of. You." He punctuated each word with a kiss, then paused at my neck. "Perfect. In every way."

His breath tickled my neck, making me lean into him, but he moved away just as much.

"How did I ever get so lucky, that fate brought me you?"

I didn't know what to say, so I didn't say anything at all. I found myself silently asking the same question about him. Not once in all of my life before I met him had someone adored me so openly, nor reminded me so frequently. I still didn't quite know what to make of it.

He spun me around, so my back was against his chest and kept a hold on my hand. His other hand rested on my hip. His lips finally brushed against my neck again.

"Do you trust me?" He breathed.

I tried to turn to face him, but he held me still. "Of course I trust you." I said, a little bit confused and startled by the question. "What sort of question is that?"

He released my hand, reached around and pulled a small sliver of black fabric from his pocket. He dangled it in front of me for a few moments, like the sight of it might explain the question. It wasn't until he took the other end of it into his other hand and pulled it over my eyes that I realized just *why* he had asked me that question. I sucked in a breath as he tied a knot behind my head.

"I had to make sure, love." He traced a single finger down my neck. The touch was so featherlight that it was almost not there at all, but the sensation itself was heightened by the fact that I hadn't seen it coming.

"I did tell you once I knew of far more fun things to do blindfolded. Do you remember that?" He whispered into my other ear now. It was frustratingly disorienting and yet surprisingly exciting to be unable to *see* what he was doing or know *where* he was.

He kissed my other shoulder lightly and I tried to lean back into him. He moved away from me but took my hand once again and spun me around. Before I knew what was happening, he'd lifted me up and hooked my legs up onto his hips.

My arms wound around his neck. It was an instinct at this point. At least like this I knew where he was. His movements told me he had crawled onto the bed. Which was confirmed when he placed me down onto the bed with my head on the pillows.

"If you want me to stop, all you have to do is tell me."

I was once again confused, but the reasoning registered when he wound the same material around my wrist and pulled my arm up over my head. He repeated the action with my other wrist and a quick tug told me I wasn't getting out of this unless he let me. Or I used magic.

He traced his fingers down my right arm, then he disappeared again. I tried to listen, to *feel* where he was on the bed, but I couldn't tell. It sent a spike of anxiety through me, or maybe a thrill? I rarely completely left myself vulnerable like this.

The bed shifted next to me and his lips pressed gently against mine. I tried to lift myself up and deepen the kiss, but his hand hooked around my neck and held me in place. I gasped, surprised by how my body seemed to react and crave more.

"So impatient." He chided, his breath tickling my ear now. His grip on my neck remained firm and he trailed kisses down my jaw.

He gripped behind my knee with his other hand and hiked my right leg back up, so my thigh rested against his hip, then he let me go. I let out a whimpering moan when he drug his finger up through the growing wetness between my thighs.

"So eager." I felt his smile against my lips before he claimed me in an absolutely earth shattering kiss.

He circled his finger around my clit lightly. Too lightly for me to handle. I wanted more. I *needed* more. He'd barely touched me and I was already wound so tight I might come. I rocked my hips into his hand, but he moved with me.

Please, I begged, still unable to speak with his mouth over mine. His tongue ravaged me and reminded me just how thoroughly he could feast on other parts of me.

He moved his thumb until it rested over my artery, where my pulse now raced. "Do you know how much I *love* hearing your heart race for me?"

He released my neck. His lips left mine and he drug his teeth down the column of my neck. "It's like music to my ears." He whispered, then his fangs grazed where my neck met my shoulders, and I shuddered underneath him.

"And my gods, the way you smell." He breathed me in, his nose tickling the side of my neck. "It's intoxicating."

He slid one finger into me, his thumb taking its place in circling my clit while he moved his finger in and out of me.

"Deiric." I said his name like a plea, no, like a prayer.

"Say that again." He increased his pace and added a second finger.

His name left my lips in a startled gasp and before I recovered his fangs pierced my neck and a whole new wave of pleasure washed over me. I climaxed with his name on my lips.

That's my girl. He cooed as he worked me through every wave of my orgasm until I didn't physically think I could take anymore, but I couldn't push him away.

He let out a dark chuckle and removed his fingers. He kissed my neck and one of my wrists finally fell free. I reached up to touch him. My hand slid up his side while he untied my other wrist.

When both of my hands were free, I traced them up his body until I could interlace them in his hair. He began kissing his way down my chest, between my breasts, down to my navel, and then lower.

He traced his tongue along the apex of my thigh, and I jerked my hips away from him. I was still far too sensitive and the idea of his mouth being *anywhere* near me was almost too much to bear.

He hooked my legs up over his shoulders and held tightly to both of my hips. *I'm not finished with you yet.*

"I–"

The words died on my tongue when he slid his into me and I moaned. My hips bucked of their own accord, but he didn't let me move, nor did he relent as he ravaged me entirely. I was brought right back to the precipice of pleasure and thrown over the edge so violently that I screamed.

I pulled at his hair like my gods damned life depended on anchoring myself to *something* and I wasn't entirely sure that it didn't.

I should've done this ages *ago.* Satisfaction dripped from his low and sultry voice in my head. My legs shook as the last wave of ecstasy crashed over me and he *finally* pulled away.

I lay limp on the bed, my entire body completely spent. I wasn't sure I could move, let alone steady my breathing.

He was above me again. I could feel his breath against my lips. "Twice just doesn't seem nearly enough." He mused. "I want to see you so sated that you simply can't take anymore."

His lips grazed over mine and I could taste myself on him. It was somehow intoxicating. I lifted my head and deepened the kiss before I pulled his lower lip between my teeth. My fangs nicked him, pulling a single drop of his blood into my mouth and he moaned.

He dropped down onto me and wound one hand into my hair. The weight of him on me was too much and yet not enough at the same time, though I could still feel him bracing up himself on one elbow so as to not completely crush me.

He nudged himself at my entrance and I rocked my hips up to meet him. Waiting any longer would've killed me. I was certain. He thrust into me, all the way to the hilt, and I clawed at his back.

A new wave of energy hit me, and I flipped us over so that I could take control. If it startled him, I couldn't tell. The blindfold still made it so I couldn't see him, but I could *feel* him, and that was all I needed.

I kissed my way down his neck and bit him. The first taste of him nearly sent me over the edge again, but I settled into a mind altering rhythm with my hips that would draw this out as long as I wanted.

One hand pulled at my hair and the other dug into my hip as he rocked his to match the movement of mine. "Fuck, Mira." He breathed.

I moved my hips so I could take him deeper and the moan that escaped him was the most captivating sound I think I'd ever heard. He arched his neck and bit my shoulder.

It sent a shudder through my whole body and this time we both came together. When the tremors of bliss subsided and we both withdrew our fangs I collapsed over him, barely able to hold myself upright.

He chuckled. The *bastard.* I didn't have it in me to grumble a curse at him. Instead, I just lay there silently breathing him in with my face nestled into his neck. He reached up and undid the tie in the blindfold.

When my breathing started to slow, I finally lifted myself off of him and curled up next to him with my head on his chest. It didn't take either of us very long to fall asleep.

Chapter 6

Mira

I was occupying myself with brushing Draga and checking on her field when my father wandered over the next day. He leaned against the fence post closest to where Draga and I were standing. I purposely ignored him and continued brushing her as though he weren't there. Several long awkward minutes of silence stretched between us.

"It seems rather pointless to have horses for a manor full of mages and vampires, doesn't it?" He raised a single brow and looked at me as though the answer should've been obvious.

That earned him a glare, but nothing more while I brushed the dust off her sleek summer coat.

He heaved a heavy sigh and shifted from leaning against the fence post to resting both forearms on the fence so he could lean closer. "What I'm trying to say is I'm wondering why you have them?"

I stopped brushing and sneered at him. "If you wanted me to answer a genuine question, you could've simply asked 'why do you have horses?' rather than making it seem like I'm an idiot for having them." I placed a hand on my hip and gestured toward the manor. "But since you must fucking know, we don't have *all* mages and vampires. Eimear is a witch. She can heal and do simple magic, but she isn't capable of shifting."

"I–" He started, but I cut him off.

"And if that isn't enough for you, we *do* have to blend in now. It would be a little suspicious for people to just *show up* in town without a horse, don't you think? We got them so we could blend in with the humans."

His mouth was still open as though he would've spoken. He closed it and rubbed his hand down his face.

"Look." He grumbled. "I'm just trying to make conversation. You don't exactly make that easy."

"You don't exactly know how to start a conversation that doesn't mildly insult me." I snapped at him.

He stepped back like I'd slapped him. One hand rested on the top fence rail while the other hung loosely at his side.

"Mira, I–"

"No." I snapped, walking around Draga to turn myself to face away from him. "If you're going to provoke me, you're not going to try to placate me and calm me down in the next breath."

He let out another heavy sigh. "I'm sorry. Would you cut me just a *little* slack? Aside from the last month or so I haven't been able to actually interact with anyone aside from my captors and that obviously wasn't very polite."

The guilt sliced right through me, just like I was sure he knew it would. It was hard to talk to him in general when I knew all of his tactics, let alone when I knew that this wasn't even intended to be a *guilt* tactic. It was just the truth. Still, the sting of knowing he knew how to make me feel guilty if he wanted to softened the blow just a little.

"It's hard to cut you any slack when you're only acting the way you always have." I kept my voice cold and angry, even though I knew he was right.

"I can't imagine you'd be spending this much time brushing a single horse if you only had them to blend in." His voice was soft now, tentative even. "Is there another reason you decided to have them? You never learned to ride when you lived with us."

I didn't turn to look at him. I just continued brushing down her back to her rump. "I was alone for a long time."

He didn't interject when I paused, which surprised me enough that I continued.

"This horse, Draga, was with me for nearly nine years before I met Deiric. She was all I had when I was otherwise devoid of all companionship. As soon as the treaty was signed, I tracked her back down. Deiric wasn't really keen on the idea of horses, but they're really not that hard to care for if you have the space."

I shrugged a single shoulder. "I can be very convincing when I want to be, and I won him over eventually. Especially when I told him that I wanted *her*. When we found her, she was with the gray and I offered them an amount of money they couldn't refuse to take them both. I would've hated to bring her back here and then have her spend most of her days and nights alone."

When I was sure I'd brushed all the dirt from her that I could possibly manage to, I stopped and turned to face him. He was looking at me with something akin to a twisted combination of admiration and pity. It was like a war was waging in his eyes.

"Besides." I added with another shrug. "She keeps me calm. I'm not sure how or why, but her presence has always been comforting to me in a way I can't really describe. When I need a few quiet moments to just *be* I come out here to spend time with her."

He cleared his throat and shook his head like that might resolve the war I could tell he was still waging over how to feel about my response. It was odd to see him so disheveled.

"Horses are rather calming animals despite their… excitable nature." He finally mumbled.

I raised a single brow at him but was quickly distracted when Draga turned and nudged me so hard with her head that I nearly fell into the fence that separated us from him. I laughed, full and unfeigned, as I righted myself and spun to give her what she was demanding.

I waved my hand, and a carrot appeared in it, which she greedily chomped on. She'd have taken my fingers with it if I wasn't careful. I knew better than to keep her waiting.

When I turned to look at him again, he was smiling. I wasn't sure at that moment if I'd ever seen him smile so genuinely, like the sight of me nearly getting knocked over by my horse was the best thing he's seen in his entire life.

I gave him a confused smile. "What?"

His brows shot up and he huffed out a breath. "I'm sorry I just realized that I'm not sure I've seen you that winsome in a long time." He shook his head. "Gods, I'd estimate I haven't seen a smile like that on your face since you were barely taller than my waist."

His face took on a sorrowful look. "I wasn't sure I'd ever get to see you like that again. See you at all really."

I frowned and stepped closer to the fence. There were barely more than two steps separating us now, aside from the fence of course.

"I'm sorry. I wasn't trying to ruin your mood." He mumbled as he raised his gaze to meet mine again. "It's just… good to see you like that is all."

I gave him a curt smile. "I guess I can say the same for you. I'm not sure I've ever seen you smile like that at all really."

Something in his gaze shifted and I couldn't quite place it. He cleared his throat uncomfortably and gave me a half smile just as tight as the one I'd given him.

"Perhaps we can see more of that in each other moving forward? If I figure out how to talk to you in a way you won't hate me for, I mean."

I huffed a laugh and looked toward the ground. "Like *that* will happen."

The moment the words left my lips I regretted them. He stiffened, but to my surprise he didn't look angry when I looked up at him again.

"I'm sorry. I–"

"No." He cut me off. "I deserved that."

"There's just…" My voice trailed off while I looked away again, focusing on Draga instead of answering. I wasn't really sure what to say.

“A lot of history.” He finished the sentence I couldn’t find the words to.

I nodded and met his gaze again.

“We’ll figure it out.” A less tense smile rose to his lips now. “Just try not to rip my head off if I fuck up again, will you?”

I smirked. “I’ll try.”

Chapter 7

Mira

I followed Deiric outside, where everyone was gathering to spar the following afternoon. I dressed in my leathers today and hoped to fly with him after. He wasn't going to meet with the other riders, for once, which gave us the freedom to fly wherever we wanted.

Zane, Xander, Renwick, Lazarus, and my father were already outside. Deiric, much to my dismay, called out to Renwick and decided he'd spar with him. Knowing that neither Zane nor Xander would have any interest in sparring with Lazarus or my father, that left me with my choice of the two of them.

They turned toward me, noting that I'd come out in my leathers and had my sword. "I'll sit this one out." Lazarus said with a smirk, then strode off to sit on the front stairs.

Bastard.

I heard Deiric chuckle, and nearly shot the same thought at him until my father caught my attention before I could.

"It's been a while." He smirked. "You sure you could keep up with me?"

I drew my sword and scoffed. "I could ask you the same."

"Don't forget who taught you."

I spun my sword as I walked casually toward him. "Pretty sure Aris had no problem kicking your ass either." That got a chuckle from Lazarus, but a frown from my father. It was almost like he'd forgotten that we never finished our training together.

"On with it then." He impatiently angled his sword skyward before motioning me forward with his free hand.

I wondered if it bothered him that I was about to fight him with his own blade. That he had to get a new one made because I would never have given it back to him had he asked. The sword in his hands was practically a mirror image of the one in mine without the Morrigan's added flair.

I stepped left like I might brace to swing up to the right but then switched my grip to both hands and swung left. He followed my footwork, moving to block a right handed swing and barely adjusted to block me. I smiled.

He swung at me, wide and viscous while he grumbled, "Lucky shot."

I dodged, rather than block the blow. When someone swings with that much effort, you dodge before you block. I learned that the hard way with him several times.

I swung again now, single handed, and he blocked it without a second thought. He studied each movement I made carefully, and I could *hear* him biting his tongue. He'd wanted to point out that I hadn't forgotten when to block and when to dodge, forgetting, of course, that I am half his size and that makes all the difference in most cases. Then he'd wanted to say that I had more power when I gripped with both hands.

It was *killing* him not to try to guide and coach me. It surprised me a little bit that he was actually respecting my boundaries and holding back his comments. They weren't condescending, nor were they judgmental, but he knew I didn't need them.

"You can do better than that." I goaded him. He was moving slower than he used to. He was taking it easy on me.

He arched a brow but picked up his pace. He attacked; I parried. I attacked, he blocked or dodged. We were going back and forth for nearly thirty minutes before he finally paused and smiled.

"I'm not sure what I expected." He made a show of looking me up and down. I wasn't even winded, but he was, just slightly. "I certainly didn't expect to be the one pausing to catch my breath first."

A small and victorious smile rose to my lips. "How about we make this a little more interesting then?"

He raised both brows expectantly and gave me a look that told me to go on.

"Lazarus." I glanced over to where he still sat with an amused expression on his face. "How'd you like to help him out?" My smile grew into a more wicked grin. "Two against one."

He huffed a laugh. "You haven't even sparred with me alone yet, and you want to face both of us?"

I shrugged. "I think you're just worried that I'll kick both of your asses." Okay, maybe I was a little crazy, but I had a gut feeling.

This is incredibly stupid. Gaisgeach cut in.

I think it will be incredibly entertaining. I retorted.

I've gotta see this. Deiric's amused voice hummed in my head.

The clanking of swords behind me quieted as everyone seemed to shift their gazes to the three of us. Lazarus had risen from the stairs and made his way over to stand near my father, sword drawn.

I'm glad I don't *have to watch this shit show.* Gaisgeach snarled. *I bonded with you for your intelligence, and you decide to spar with two elders who are older than your* mate? *Fuck's sake.*

And if I win?

Gaisgeach just chuffed. He had absolutely no faith in me. That stung a little.

"Having second thoughts?" My father mused, spinning his sword around and stepping around me so that he and Lazarus were nearly on either side of me.

"Never." I smirked, lowering into a fighting stance and drawing the dagger from my thigh.

"Interesting choice." Lazarus mused.

"Well, get on with it then." I snarled.

They both lunged for me at once. I spun, deflecting my father's blade with my sword and Lazarus' attack with my dagger. Lazarus was the first to recover, swiping at me again. I dodged out of the way and directly into my father's next swing. I blocked him with both of my blades, sending him flying backward. Something told me they'd fought together many times before.

I heard Lazarus before I saw him in my peripheral. I bent over at the waist and ducked under his sword as it swept above me like he meant to cleave off my head. I spun down onto my knee and kicked his leg out from under him. He stumbled but caught himself while my father swung down at me.

I used the momentum of his swing and a twist of my blade to fling his sword out of his grip. His look of shock was something I committed to memory. I'd never let him live that down. I had less than a second to bask in my glory when Lazarus righted himself and came at me again. This time he meant to stab me. I slid both of my blades along his, directing his sword just to my right. Then I twisted, bringing my knee up into his groin while I held the hilt of his sword between my blades, disarming him as well.

That had given my father just enough time to retrieve his blade and come for me, but my sword was already raised, and he nearly ran into it before he stopped. The tip of the blade was lingering a hair's breadth from his neck. I held my dagger at Lazarus' throat where he still knelt on the ground.

"Well." I smiled. "That was quite fun."

A slow clap sounded from the trees behind me, and I spun around so quickly I nearly gave myself whiplash. A man emerged from the trees. He had short snow white hair and eyes so golden they almost seemed to glow. He wore a dark cloak, despite the early summer heat. I didn't *see* any weapons on him, but the cloak would hide them well.

"Impressive." His deep voice rumbled. "But I must say, your wards could use some work."

My father, Lazarus, and the rest of the guys were on their feet and ready to fight in the blink of an eye. My victory, quickly, meant nothing.

What is going on? Gaisgeach asked.

I don't know yet.

I'm checking for others. Macha's mildly panicked voice told me she hadn't heard or sensed his approach either. It was rare that someone could sneak up on us.

"And who *the fuck* are you?" I snarled at the man.

He chuckled. "You mean you don't see the family resemblance?" He glanced over my shoulder, looking far beyond me. "My daughter is around here somewhere. I hear that she got nearly *all* of my features."

Adriana. Fuck. My face must have betrayed me, because he smiled.

"She is here then." He said rather matter of factly. "Excellent." He started to take another step forward.

"One more step and you'll die where you stand." Lazarus snarled.

The man paused mid-step and then righted himself. He didn't do so out of fear. I didn't get a hint of that from his scent. No, he smelled… odd. Not quite human. I couldn't put my finger on it. He certainly *looked* human. His heartbeat at the same pace as a human.

"I'm here for my daughter." He looked around at all of us and then his eyes settled on me. "Bring her to me, and I'll be on my way."

"Like fucking hell." Deiric snarled behind me.

The man's gaze didn't shift from me. "At least allow me to *see* her."

"First, tell me how the fuck you got through our wards." I kept my voice even, calm, despite that my anxiety rose with every second that I stood here not understanding how he found us in the first place.

He shrugged. "They were childsplay." A wicked smile rose to his lips.

A mage then. If he could sense them and walk through them. Certainly no mage of ours.

"What do you want with her?"

"I've never met her. I'd like to meet her and bring her back home with me."

"Which is where exactly?"

"Emberwyn."

That's in the other realm. Gaisgeach cut in before I could even complete a thought wondering where the fuck that was. *He speaks of a country of mages and magic.*

He's a mage then, I assume?

That seems likely, yes. I could do without Gaisgeach's slightly condescending tone, but at least I knew that for certain. It would explain where Adriana got her magic, since her mother seemed to have none.

"And your only reason for coming here is to see her and see if she'll return with you?" Deiric asked for me.

"Yes." He raised his hands as if to placate us into believing he truly meant no harm. "I'm not here for any trouble."

He had yet to attack, so I was inclined to believe him. Still, something felt off about him. He was, at least, alone.

Macha?

She flew down and perched on my shoulder. *I did not see or sense his approach somehow, but he is in fact alone.*

Are you certain? If you didn't see or sense him, could there not be others?

You are far more adept at seeing things with your shadows than I would be with my eyes. She snapped. *But yes, I am sure.*

She had a point. It would also be pointless and likely senseless to just send him away. He knew where we were now, though I didn't know how he tracked her here.

"I'll see if she'd like to meet you." I gestured to all of the men around me. "Make a single move from that spot before I come back, and they'll kill you without a second thought. Understood?"

He nodded.

Despite that it went against every instinct I had, I turned my back on him and walked around Deiric, Zane, and Xander as I made my way to the front door. Macha flew back up to perch atop the manor. I stalked inside and walked toward the back room where Adriana was helping the other mages with whatever smaller magics and spells Liala was teaching them today.

When I walked through the doors, I was at least breathing a bit easier. I hated to leave them all with him, but I was sure they could kill him before he could be a threat to them, mage or no.

"Adriana?" I called to her, and she looked up at me almost excitedly. "We need to talk." I glanced around at the others, then gestured for her to come with me. "Privately."

Chapter 8

Adriana

I followed Mira out of the training room and into the hallway. She led me into a smaller storage room that I didn't think I'd ever wandered into on my own before. When she shut the door behind us, she put up a sound shield and that made me a little nervous.

Our last conversation about the king had been similar, but this felt more tense somehow. There was no pity in her eyes this time, just uncertainty. I could almost feel her panic given her body language. It might have been missed by everyone else, but I spent far too much time around her to not notice that.

"What is it?" I asked her, very aware of my own nervous tendencies as I began to wring my hands near my waist.

"You've never met your *real* father."

It didn't really come off like a question, given her tone. I nodded anyway.

"So you have no idea where he's from or what he looks like?"

That was more like a question. "My mother never told me anything about someone *other* than the king being my father." I shrugged a single shoulder. "I figured that out on my own. I looked nothing like the king, and he had no magic. I didn't think it was possible for two people without magic to have a child with it."

Mira seemed to consider me for a few breaths before she finally shook her head and continued. "Technically, anyone can have a child with magic regardless of their history. It's unusual, but not unheard of. Sometimes magic will lie dormant for generations before it shows back up again. I didn't question it much with you until you referred to him as 'the king' once instead of 'my father'."

She ran her hand up over her braided hair and seemed even more distressed. Another shake of her head and she began to explain.

"There's a man out front. I don't know how the hell he found our manor or managed to get through the wards, but he claims he's your father." She looked me in the eye now. "The resemblance is hard to deny and he's demanding to see you."

My jaw nearly hit the floor, and I stared at her for far too long before I composed myself.

"Why?" It was the only question I could manage to come up with.

"He wants to meet you and take you home with him." She explained, shifting nervously on her feet. "The other realm."

"By the gods, why the hell would I go anywhere with someone I'd only just met?" I nearly shouted.

"I wasn't suggesting you go with him." She assured me, though there wasn't much fight in her either way. "I pulled you aside to see what you'd want to do."

I didn't answer right away while I thought this all through. Why now? Why did he wait until the king was dead? Oh gods, did *he* kill the king? No. That wouldn't make sense. If he killed him then he would be our new king. He wouldn't have let my idiotic brother take the throne. That made no sense.

"I could just kill him." Mira offered.

I nearly snorted a laugh. She said it so plainly that I wasn't even sure what to say for a few moments.

"No." I laughed again. "Gods, no. I can't have you kill a man I have barely met and don't know whether or not to *trust*, let alone someone who is claiming to be my father."

I didn't miss the frown that appeared on her face. She *wanted* to kill him. It would make things easier for her. Safer, for sure. She'd been through so much hell for *me* and here I was bringing another possibly untrustworthy stranger to her home.

"I'll meet him." I said with far too much finality to it. Even if it made her anxious, or even if he ended up being a bastard we had to kill anyway, I couldn't just kill someone. Or rather, I couldn't just have her kill him.

"If I want you to kill him after I meet him, or if he gives you any reason to think he's a threat, just take him out."

She studied me carefully. "Are you certain?"

"Mira." I let out a nervous laugh. "You were staked because of me. You put yourself in harm's way to train me. If he tries to harm you, *I'll* want to kill him. I'm just not sure I'll be able to."

You are more than capable of killing someone. Cairbre assured me.

"I'm inclined to agree with him." Mira added before I could reply.

"Having the skills to kill someone and actually following through on that are two very different things." I pointed out.

She made a face that suggested I had a point. Although, the idea that she was at any point incapable of killing someone seemed insane to me. She did it so effortlessly that I was sure she'd been this ruthless her whole life.

"I was a child once, you know." She pointed out, sounding only mildly insulted. "I haven't *always* been a killer… I don't even consider myself one now. I only kill for survival or revenge."

I raised a brow.

"The men you watched me kill staked me, Adriana."

"Fair point."

"Let's go then." She turned to remove the sound shield she put up and opened the door. "I'd rather not leave him alone with the guys for too long."

"What if he won't leave after I meet him?"

I followed her toward the front door of the manor.

"Then I'll kill him." She shrugged. "I'm tempted to kill him anyway, simply because he knows where we are now."

I didn't know how to feel about that. I was still processing the fact that my *real* father was here.

Focus. Cairbre's only advice, which I found incredibly unhelpful at the moment. I could've thrown something at him if he'd been in the hallway with us as we made our way out of the house.

When she reached the front door, she walked through without looking to see if I followed. It shouldn't have surprised me how quickly she switched from her nervous demeanor with me to a protector. The masks she put on sometimes were almost terrifying to me with how seamlessly she slipped into them.

Deiric and Xander stepped aside as she walked through. Their gazes remained fixed on my father, who I assumed was standing just ahead of where Mira stopped.

"You wanted to meet her," she said as she stepped aside and gestured toward me with her hand. "Here she is."

I'm not sure what I expected, but he wasn't it, and yet it made sense all the same. I saw Mira's subtle gesture to the men to stand down. They lowered their swords but did not sheath them.

A smile spread across his lips as he looked me over. He began to take a step toward me with an outstretched hand, but Mira stepped in so quickly I didn't even see her movements.

Her sword was out, the point of the blade less than a millimeter from his throat.

"Do *not* take a single step closer to her."

It startled him enough that he nearly stumbled backward before he managed to catch himself. He cleared his throat and brushed invisible dirt from his tunic, which I could now see beyond his slightly open cloak.

"Forgive me. I was only attempting to introduce myself."

"You can do so from where you stand." She snarled at him and did not lower her sword.

She was more protective than my own mother. The woman would've rolled right over and sent me off with this… man? Gods, I didn't even know if he was fully human. There was something just off about him that I couldn't quite place.

"Why are you here?" I cut the tension myself and redirected his attention to me.

He stood a bit taller again as he addressed me. "I came back for your mother, but what I found at the palace was… not what I expected. Now I'm here to collect you."

I scoffed and he bristled. He obviously expected this to go far differently. "Like I'm some piece of property to be traded around?"

Mira continued to stand like a statue, sword hanging in the air level with his throat.

"That's not what I said." He replied calmly.

"That's what you implied."

He looked me over once more. His expression changed just slightly, though I couldn't quite decipher the emotion I was seeing now.

"Clearly we've gotten off on the wrong foot. Allow me to start over." He paused and gave Mira a pointed look.

"Not going to happen." She angled the sword closer to him, pressing it against his throat now. If she pressed any harder, she'd draw blood.

He heaved an irritated sigh. "Fine." He mumbled under his breath. "My name is Azazel," he started, lowering his hand and glancing my way again. "I… was very close with your mother, obviously." He gestured toward me and Mira frowned.

"I didn't know *you* existed, or I would not have been away for so long. I came back for your mother, but she refuses to leave with me without you, and I am not going home without her. Clearly, I cannot stay here with the current state of this…" He hesitated again like he couldn't decide what to call our country.

"Country?" He finally asked.

I nodded.

"Right." He closed his eyes and shook his head while waving his hand dismissively. "Anyway," he met my gaze again. "If you would be willing, I can offer you safe passage back to see your mother and then give you a *safe* place to live in Emberwyn."

I stared at him, desperately trying to keep my surprise from my face while simultaneously battling my need to see my mother and know she was safe with my lack of trust in a stranger I'd never met.

I don't trust him. Cairbre snarled.

Mira was frustratingly quiet. She didn't even so much as look at me, when I would've really appreciated her input right now.

She is silent because she knows you want to see your mother. She's well aware that the offer he's giving you is something you'd be likely to accept, and she doesn't wish to sway your decision with her own.

I wondered how Cairbre knew this.

Dragons do *talk you know.* He scoffed, like that should've been obvious. *She's not blocking her thoughts from Gaisgeach, and he is not holding his back from me.*

And what do you think?

I already stated I don't trust him. However, I can't read his intentions or his thoughts. I don't know whether he's being truthful or not.

"Is he telling the truth?" I asked Mira without taking my eyes off of Azazel. I'd gotten better about shielding my thoughts from her. I could've dropped my shields and thought that question, but then he'd know that she could hear thoughts as well.

"I have not sensed a lie." Her response was curt and emotionless, which is precisely what I expected given what Cairbre explained.

I stood a bit taller. "You can't leave here, now that you know *where* we are, so I will allow you to stay here for a few days and I'll make my decision on the solstice."

Mira's gaze shot to mine now. There was shock, concern, and a little bit of pride there.

"That is an awful idea." Lazarus snarled.

"We should just kill him." Teron offered.

"Enough." Mira snapped at them with so much authority that they both took a step back. "If she doesn't leave with him, she's your future queen and she's made her decision."

"But Mira–" Teron started.

"I said *enough.*" Her glare would've made me turn and run if it were directed my way. "Lazarus." She looked over at him now. "He will stay with you until the solstice. I won't take no for an answer."

To my surprise, the elder didn't so much as blink as though he was shocked by the demand. He merely gave her a curt nod.

Mira looked back at Azazel. "He'll show you to your room. Make one wrong move against anyone in this house and you'll be dead before you even know it's coming. Do you understand?"

He actually looked a *little* bit afraid but nodded.

"Good." Mira lowered her sword and motioned for him to follow Lazarus.

Chapter 9

Deiric

I didn't like the bastard. Mira seemed to have a tentative trust in him. He said all the right things, and his actions suggested he wasn't a threat, but something about him unnerved me. Lazarus agreed to allow him to share his room, which surprised me. I suppose that meant he felt the same way I did.

I was more surprised by Adriana. When he offered for her to go see her mother and give them *both* a safe haven with him I thought she'd jump on it. I wasn't sure why she didn't. She hadn't said anything. Shortly after he'd been shown to his temporary living arrangements, he'd come back out to speak with Adriana again. She informed Mira late last evening that he tracked her here with the ring she wore. It had apparently been her mother's.

Teron appeared next to me. I hadn't even heard him approach. I was too lost in my thoughts. He huffed a laugh when I jumped slightly.

"A little jumpy this evening?" He asked and reached past me to grab a glass from the shelf.

"Apparently."

"I don't like him either." He poured his whiskey and placed the decanter back on the shelf. "Seems like a bastard. No one just blindly wanders into a place like this. Even if the queen told him what he might find."

"Mira seems to trust him." I turned and watched as he walked over to take a seat by the fireplace in one of the two chairs. I leaned back against the cabinet below the bookshelves.

"Mira *wants* to trust him." He corrected. "She cares for that girl like a daughter, and her long lost father just *appeared* like some gift from the gods. While I'd like to say I'd never doubt her judgment, I think it's a little clouded right now."

My immediate reaction would have been to snap at him, because it irked me to no end when he made snide comments about Mira, or even *thought* them, but this time I actually agreed with him. That sort of made me cringe.

He chuckled, like he knew exactly where my mind went, even though I didn't say a word. "You're thinking it too; you just don't want to admit it because I said it."

I looked up from my glass, having not yet taken a single sip.

"You don't like me much, do you?" He took a sip of his whiskey while he studied my reaction to his question.

It was a complicated answer. I didn't hate the man, but I didn't *love* him either. He didn't seem to have much faith in Mira, whether he spoke it audibly or not. That bothered me. He certainly didn't seem to like me much. Being honest with him wouldn't hurt his opinion of me, nor would lying win me any favors.

"No. I don't." I decided on honesty.

He arched a brow, like he couldn't believe I was honest. He leaned back in the chair and sat his arms on the armrests in the most casual position he could. "At least you're honest."

"I imagine I'm not your favorite person either." I finally took a sip of my whiskey. While his thoughts often betrayed his actions with Mira, he rarely spared a thought for me. I wasn't sure if that was good or bad.

"Actually," he smirked, "I've grown to like you."

I huffed a humorless laugh. That seemed like a flat out lie. I rolled my shoulders and my neck before I pushed off the cabinets and walked over to sit on the other chair. I sank down in it casually and crossed my ankle over my knee.

"Why?" A simple question, with a complicated answer, I was sure.

He swirled the whiskey in his glass while he thought about his answer. Finally, he let out a sigh and took another sip. "You support every decision she makes, even if it is… naive or perhaps misguided." He explained and I was already irritated.

"It's clear that you *literally* worship her as though she was the gods' gift to you and that you would step in front of a stake in her stead." It felt like he was staring right through me. "You take care of her, fight for her, and protected her from *me* when she asked for it." He shrugged. "I have to say I respect you for that at least. I don't know what I ever expected for her, but I am glad that she found you."

I couldn't hide the shock from my face. How he could see all of this in me but still looked at her with a bit of disappointment or lack of awe at how absolutely incredible she was, was beyond me. I was nothing compared to her. She was the epitome of strength and perseverance. She was intelligent, strong, and arguably the best swordsman, swords*woman* that I'd ever met.

"I didn't like you at first though." He smirked now. "Can you blame me? I was imprisoned for ten years and came back to find that my daughter had married a vampire I'd never even heard of. *Mated* no less." He huffed a laugh. "You haven't had a child and maybe it's different for everyone, but the idea that she married some no name vampire made my blood boil."

I opened my mouth to snap at him, but he abruptly continued. "I know you aren't that now, of course, but I didn't know that then. And I don't exactly trust Lazarus' judgment on the matter. Whether or not he was once a father, he has no idea what it's like."

I just stared at him. I had no words. I heard a door open and close upstairs, and then faint footsteps. Mira's footsteps.

He leaned in closer to me, resting his elbows on his knees. "Since we're on the same page about the newest house guest, let me be clear. If he even *remotely* seems like a threat to her, I'll kill him without a second thought. I trust you to do the same."

I nodded.

"Good." He rose to his feet and started to leave the den. "Good talk." He said with a smile over his shoulder as Mira started down the stairs.

Mira watched him over her shoulder for a moment as she walked into the den before she turned her gaze to me.

"What was that about?" She walked over to me and casually dropped herself into my lap, draping her legs over one arm of the chair and leaning against the other with her back. She snatched the glass of whiskey from my hand and helped herself to a sip of it.

"I was drinking that." I grumbled and she smiled.

"What, you don't want to share?"

I leaned up and hooked my finger under her chin to pull her into a kiss. "It was nothing, love." I whispered into her lips. "Just sharing a drink with my father in law, is all."

She knew it was more than that. I could see it in her eyes, but she didn't press me for details. "Perhaps I shouldn't have stolen a sip after all."

"Perhaps you should fill the glass back up."

She smiled again and the decanter appeared in her hand. "I'd be happy to." She topped off the glass. "That should do the trick."

"Are you trying to get me drunk?"

She giggled, and it was so genuinely happy that for a moment I forgot all about our newest house guest and pulled her closer. The decanter disappeared and she stole another sip from the glass.

"Maybe I'm trying to get us *both* a little buzzed." She handed the glass back to me, now that I had pulled my arm out from under her legs. She leaned her head onto my shoulder. "We aren't going to tell him about the dragons." She whispered. "I've told everyone else already, but I *wanted* to go flying with you until he got here."

"We still could."

"I'm not leaving Adriana alone here with him."

"She wouldn't be alone, love. She's got Lazarus, your father, Triss, Liala–"

"I know." She cut me off. "But *I* can't leave knowing he's here."

So she didn't fully trust him. At least there was a little bit of doubt in her mind. If I'd had it my way, I would've told him to fuck all the way off and go sleep in the woods for all I cared, but I respected her decision, even if it seemed ridiculous. We only had to put up with him for a couple of days. After that, she'd kick him out or, better yet, kill him and I could stop worrying about what his *real* motives were.

Chapter 10

Mira

"I'll sit this one out today." I announced as we walked outside moments after Adriana. I had Macha on guard duty with her when she was out of sight, but since we were going out to spar anyway it seemed like a good opportunity to keep an eye on things myself.

"Oh come on, I thoroughly enjoyed watching Lazarus get his ass handed to him yesterday." Xander whined.

I rolled my eyes at him. "I guess you'll just have to entertain yourselves today."

"And what are *you* going to do then?" Zane asked.

I glanced over at Adriana and Azazel, who were attempting to have some semblance of privacy on the other side of the clearing in front of the house.

"I'll watch."

Still worried about her? Deiric asked.

I shifted my attention to him while he squared up with Renwick. *I'm not sure I'll ever* not *be worried. I know she can protect herself, but I just don't like it.*

Deiric didn't think anything in response, so I once again placed my attention on Adriana and Azazel. He was describing his home to her. It was a land of mages mostly, which Gaisgeach had already told me, but their mages were different, apparently.

I didn't catch how or even why but did catch that he mentioned several countries and other types of beings I'd never heard of, including something he called fae and elves. It sounded like some kind of fairytale, but I knew now that anything was possible.

Gaisgeach was also frustratingly silent today. I wasn't sure where he was or what the dragons were doing, but he left me to my thoughts while I listened. Adriana was anything but welcoming to Azazel, but she did at least listen to him drag on about where he would take her.

I hoped for a moment that he was sincere. I knew that she wouldn't leave with him, but the idea of sparing even one soul from the hell Ronan was bringing to us was better than none. If she really had an out and things got worse here, it would be well within her right to take it.

He called himself an advisor to the crown of Emberwyn, but something told me that it was a lie. His heart rate didn't change, and there were no other physical changes to suggest as much, but you could twist the truth at times without *lying*. I would've pegged him more for a spymaster.

As though my idea summoned him, Leo appeared at the edge of the trees closest to Adriana and Azazel. He looked alarmed at the sight of them, but then his gaze found mine. He quickly cleared the space between us and stopped next to where I was leaning back against the house.

He only partially blocked my view of Adriana and her 'father'.

"Want to tell me who *that* is?" He gestured toward Azazel.

"His name is Azazel." I shrugged a shoulder. "Apparently he's Adriana's *real* father."

He raised a single brow and leaned his shoulder against the side of the manor. He crossed his arms over his chest. "And we're just letting him stay here?"

"Well, he found Adriana and walked right through the wards so we either let him stay or we killed him." I glanced past him to Adriana once more before I settled my attention back fully on him. "In light of the fact that her pseudo-father just died, I thought it might be nice to at least let her get to know the man before we decide whether or not to kill him."

Leo nearly choked out a laugh and shook his head. "I'm guessing your initial vote was to kill him?"

I smirked. "I mean, that's my initial vote for anyone I don't know and trust, isn't it?"

He jerked his head slightly to the side in a half nod while an amused smile rose to his lips. "I suppose that's true."

"What have you been up to anyway?" I asked him, still half listening in on Adriana's conversation with her father. "Another super secret mission for Deiric?"

His expression turned a little more serious. "I was just wandering around to the neighboring villages, seeing if anything has happened there since the no magic law came about."

"And?"

He glanced over toward where Deiric continued to spar with Renwick. I didn't follow his gaze, but I imagine Deiric nodded at him, so he continued.

"Nothing of note yet. I did witness one of the Solas mages getting drug in by the lord's men, but I didn't see where they took her or what they did with her. There were no public executions, so either they're collecting them all and sending them somewhere else, or they're still deciding whether to go through with executions."

"I don't imagine they'll go against the king's orders and *not* execute people."

He shrugged a shoulder. "I don't know."

"You're sure no one saw you? Obviously you made it back alive, but how much longer do you expect to keep doing this and going unnoticed?"

"No one looks twice at an armed traveler. They assume I'm just a mercenary passing through. It isn't like they've ever caught me before."

I gave him a pointed look. "Do you not recall when you and Aris took me back to Valla?"

He visibly stiffened. "Okay, that was Aris' fault, not mine. I'm very adept at keeping to myself without suspicion." He gestured toward Deiric. "You know he wouldn't send me out otherwise."

Something told me that if it came down to it, he *would* actually still send him out anyway. Deiric was far more militant than I could ever aspire to be. If a job needed done he made someone do it, regardless of the risks. He would say they knew what they were getting into when they signed up for the job and in some ways he wasn't wrong. Still, I couldn't send someone out knowing the danger they'd face.

"Right." I mumbled.

"You doubt your own mate?"

"I know that he knows what needs to be done and will make sure it's done at all costs. It's not about doubting him. It's about worrying about *you.* I care about every last one of you if you didn't notice."

He snorted in distaste. "Right, because you show that so well."

"What? Do you expect me to welcome you back with a hug each time you go out and miraculously don't die?"

"Gods no!" He exclaimed.

"Alright then." I rolled my eyes. "Anything else to report?"

"I suspect that there's a Stryga not far outside of Vellehaven, but I haven't been able to track it and so far the town is unaware."

"That's their problem now. We aren't going to concern ourselves with that."

"I think that's *my* decision, love." Deiric walked over now.

I shifted my gaze to him. "You're actually going to send them out to take care of that when there's a kill on sight order for us?"

"I didn't say that." He responded quickly and shifted his focus to Leo. "Has it attacked humans, or are you just saying you think you *saw* one."

"I saw one. I don't know about any attacks yet."

"We'll leave it be for now then." He decided.

I gave him a look that suggested I was not pleased that *I* couldn't make that call.

"*You* are here to train mages and run the covens. *I* am here to decide which beasts we slay and when. Don't take the one responsibility I actually have."

I snorted and looked back over at Adriana.

You are so deliciously tempting when you're trying to take control of my men.

I gasped, unable to hide my shock, and looked at him incredulously.

"I don't want to know, and I don't want to be involved." Leo put his hands up and headed toward where Renwick stood watching the three of us. "I'll spar with Renwick."

The smirk on Deiric's lips absolutely gave away the comment he made, and the heat in his eyes had me *very* tempted to give up on watching Adriana to take him upstairs instead.

"Have I ever told you how gods damn irritating you can be when you can't keep those sorts of thoughts to yourself when I'm busy?"

He stepped closer to me and slipped his arm around the small of my back. "Have I ever told you that I don't care?"

I stared at him for a few moments, before finally shaking my head and looking back to Adriana and Azazel. "When she's not unattended with him, *then* I'll gladly disappear with you to do whatever you want, but I won't walk away right now."

"Fine." He grumbled and leaned against the wall with me to watch his men spar and help me keep an eye on Adriana.

*

I caught Adriana before Azazel stole her attention the next morning.

"Thank the gods," she mumbled when I pulled her away from the dining room and directed her to walk with me outside instead. "I *really* didn't want to get stuck with him all day today again."

I didn't even glance at her while I guided her out the front door and headed toward the woods. "I wanted to find out what you were thinking of him thus far." I said quietly when we were out of sight of the front door.

I was aware that my father had followed us. I knew Deiric would assign *someone* to keep an eye on me when I was walking beyond the wards, but my father wasn't who I expected. He did however maintain a significant distance, which I was thankful for. Regardless of whether he could hear us anyway or not.

"He doesn't seem awful, but there's just something about him that feels off." Adriana quietly explained. "I can't put my finger on it."

"He seems like he means well." I said, despite my distaste for the man, he didn't seem to be giving me any signs that he *would* be an issue.

"Cairbre doesn't like him." She added.

"Neither do Gaisgeach or Fiadh."

That's putting it mildly.

I rolled my eyes even though he couldn't see me. He loved to interject at the most irritating moments.

"Have you given any thought to his offer?" I asked a little bit hesitantly. I was still torn between getting her out of this disaster of a country and keeping her here to become the queen the Morrigan spoke of.

"I'm not leaving you." Adriana said far more confidently than I expected. "This is my home, and you, Deiric, and the rest of them are my family, whether you intended to be or not. I can't leave you all here to deal with this mess on your own."

"Well, I'm flattered, but I have to point out that letting him leave is not a good idea if we're not sure we can trust him."

"Which means you have to kill him." She seemed so nonchalant about it that I stopped in my tracks and gaped at her.

She made it a few more steps before she realized I was no longer walking and stopped to look back at me.

"What?" Her face contorted in confusion like she hadn't just said very plainly that I'd need to kill her father.

"You're just… okay with that?" I couldn't keep the incredulous tone from my voice. It was so unlike her that I couldn't believe I was talking to the same young girl we'd brought home with us months ago.

"Whether I am or not doesn't make it any less of the truth of the matter. We can't totally trust him so we can't just *assume* he won't go back and turn us in. The last thing I want is to put you, Deiric, and everyone else here in danger."

I stared at her blankly. I didn't know what else to say, but I wasn't going to question her further when her mind seemed made up. It wouldn't have been right.

"You expected me to be upset." It wasn't really a question, but she took a step toward me. She glanced back toward my father, who I knew was standing closer now and listening very intently.

"I'm not sure what I expected, but your blasé acceptance was not what I thought I'd get."

She huffed a slightly amused laugh. "Spend enough time around vampires and I guess death isn't so surprising anymore." She shrugged a shoulder. "I don't have any emotional attachment to him, regardless of the fact that he might be my father by blood. He *appeared* out of thin air. Even if I cared for him, he's done nothing but show up and try to take me away, while you've literally fought for me at every turn and poured all of your energy and time into helping me figure out who I am and how to use my powers over the last few months."

She studied me for a few moments, while I remained silently staring at her and at a loss for words.

"Is it really that hard to believe that I value you over him?"

"I–"

"You'll find that she'll have a hard time believing that anyone values her above someone else. Even if they are her blood relatives or fated mate." My father interjected before I could. "She was treated like nothing more than a weapon for most of her life, and hardly considered of value by half of the coven. Her reaction shouldn't be surprising at all actually."

I spun around so fast to look at my father that I nearly stumbled. I didn't miss the slightly amused smirk that ghosted his lips for a fraction of a second. His face returned to something more neutral and contemplative like that slight flicker of amusement hadn't existed in the first place.

He laid out the most miserable and frustrating parts of my life like they were yesterday's news, then seemed amused that I couldn't believe *he* noticed. I could've slapped him, if I weren't so gods damned shocked at what he'd said. The truth the words held, and how absolutely bare it seemed to strip me in front of Adriana, who barely had a glimpse into my past.

"Well," Adriana said with an air of finality. "On that incredibly depressing note I think we should get back before daddy dearest comes looking for me."

I turned and looked at her as my jaw nearly hit the floor.

She chuckled. "It is sort of fun to see you shocked for once."

I huffed a laugh and cracked a slight smile. "Don't get used to it."

*

Later that afternoon I began to casually eavesdrop on their conversation when Triss walked into the dining room. She turned toward the kitchen and walked over to collect lunch for herself. She finally noticed me when she turned around and approached the dining room table.

"You alright?" She asked, studying me as she passed me. She took a seat at the head of the table, just a few steps from where I was leaning against the wall. I was staring out the door, across the foyer, and into the den where Adriana sat with Esme.

I shifted my gaze to her and nodded. "I'm fine."

"Eavesdropping then, I take it."

It wasn't really a question, but I nodded.

"I can see what the queen saw in him."

I scrunched my face up in confusion. I couldn't picture how she could even find him remotely attractive, given that she'd once been fucking Deiric, but clearly we didn't *always* have the same taste.

She snorted. "He might not be *your* type, but he's attractive. I'm sure he was far more attractive than the king."

"I'm not really sure I paid enough attention to what the king looked like to be able to speak to that."

Eimear chuckled. "I'm not sure you'd find anyone but Deiric attractive. I've never even seen you take notice of anyone else as long as I've known you." I'd forgotten she, Zemora, and Stella were even at the table, but I scowled at her.

"I've found *plenty* of people attractive other than Deiric."

"And who might *they* be?" She asked.

"If you recall, I had a thing for quite a few bards *before* we met."

"Oh, did one of them happen to be that adorable bard at the party the other night?" Triss interjected. "He was *delicious*."

"One of them was." Deiric walked in with a smirk on his face. "The woman too, apparently. What was her name again, love?" He stopped next to me and leaned his shoulder against the wall while he gave me a mocking smile. "Beitris, I think?"

I opened my mouth to reply with a slight smile rising to my lips when Triss chuckled. "Oh *and* she goes both ways. I like this one, Deiric."

I shot her a glare, but then Deiric slipped his arm around me. "I don't recall asking for input, but thanks, I guess."

"If you ever–" Triss started.

"No." Deiric and I said in unison.

Triss put up her hands in defeat, then went back to eating her lunch.

"Gross." Zemora mumbled under her breath.

"Seriously." Stella added.

They're telling me. I thought.

Deiric tried and failed to stifle a chuckle, then looked over toward the den. "That seems to be going… well enough I guess."

"She doesn't seem to care much about whether he lives or dies, which I find a little surprising."

"I don't think he's going to win her over." Deiric looked back at me again. "When do we kick him out?"

Now would be nice. Gaisgeach butted in.

Yesterday would've been better. Fiadh added.

I can't just tell him to fuck off if Adriana wanted *to get to know him at least a little bit. I did leave it up to her.*

Actually, you can, and you should have. Fiadh spoke before Gaisgeach had the chance. *Anyone from that realm is dangerous.*

He has yet to threaten any of us or even display a spec of magic. Deiric thought.

Don't defend your mate's irresponsible choices just to stay in her good graces. You agree with me. I'm not stupid. Fiadh snapped.

I raised a brow at Deiric, and he shrugged.

I do kind of agree with her, but I can admit that he hasn't been a threat yet.

Humans. Gaisgeach's voice was nothing short of exasperated.

We're vampires, actually. I pointed out.

He chuffed. *Right now, you're acting like two idiotic humans.*

Thanks for the vote of confidence. I snapped at him. *We'll give him until the solstice. Then we'll kill him if she decides she's not interested in leaving with him.*

Fine. Gaisgeach and Fiadh grumbled at the same time.

It was only two days. We could deal with his presence for two more days.

Chapter 11

Deiric

It had become abundantly clear that Adriana had no intention to leave with Azazel. I wasn't sure how he ever thought he'd win her over in just a few short days, but he seemed entirely too at ease despite her obvious lack of interest in leaving with him.

He currently stood in the kitchen watching while Adriana helped Mira set the table for the ridiculous feast that Liala and Eimear were preparing. We certainly had enough people here to eat all of the food, but it still felt absurd to me.

I was looking forward to finally getting rid of him. He barely spoke to the rest of us. Adriana was the only one he even looked slightly comfortable being around. No one seemed to notice save for Teron, Lazarus, and I though. If Adriana noticed that, she didn't ever mention it.

I still don't like him. Fiadh cut through my thoughts.

I don't either.

Perhaps I could just eat him.

I don't think you want to do that.

I would enjoy that very much actually.

I sighed and shook my head. *You can't eat him.*

Last I checked, I wasn't asking for permission.

Fiadh. Gaisgeach snarled. *Adriana and Mira would not be pleased.*

I could hear her sigh and practically *feel* her eyes roll. Part of me thought Mira actually wouldn't care one way or the other, but I imagine Adriana wouldn't want him to die *that* way.

Lazarus walked in the front door, bringing me back to what was unfolding in front of me. I was leaning against the threshold between the dining room and foyer. I glanced over my shoulder at him.

"The pyre is ready." He glanced in at Mira and Adriana before his gaze shifted to Azazel leaning against the wall across from me. He narrowed his eyes like he didn't trust the fact that he was lingering so close to the kitchen. "He leaves tomorrow, correct?" He lowered his voice so no one but I could hear him.

I nodded, keeping up the ruse he was leaving in case he was able to hear us. "First thing tomorrow morning"

"Good."

Mira slipped away from the table and wandered past us toward the study. "Having a roommate is really that awful?" She mumbled as she strode past, but didn't wait for an answer before she disappeared around the corner to grab the whiskey and bring it over to the dining room.

"Yes. It is." Lazarus growled when she strode past again. She gave him a rather dismissive look before she grabbed a glass for herself and poured.

"It's a little early for a drink, isn't it?" Azazel asked. There was an edge to his voice that made me acutely uncomfortable.

Mira narrowed her eyes at him and leaned back into the buffet table behind her. "It's never too early for a drink on the solstice."

The ghost of a frown flashed across Azazel's otherwise blank expression, but he didn't reply.

Mira lifted her glass and smiled at him, entertained by his discomfort in her willingness to have a drink already. She tipped the glass as though she'd clink it with another. "Cheers."

She brought the glass to her lips and took a sip, only to immediately begin to choke as if she'd swallowed hot coals. The glass fell from her hand as she began to crumble to the floor. Before Lazarus or myself made a move to catch her, Azazel was next to her.

Then they were gone.

What just happened? Gaisgeach growled. Adriana cursed, Liala and Eimear stared in disbelief, and Lazarus and I nearly exploded with rage.

Lazarus poured some of the whiskey into a glass, brought it to his nose, and sniffed as though he'd smell whatever might've been in it. He dipped a finger into the whiskey and hissed.

"Vervain." He snarled. "He put vervain into the fucking whiskey, and a shitload of it at that. No wonder she fucking choked on it."

She's gone. I explained to both dragons. *It looks like Azazel tried to drug us all, but she drank first. He took her.*

I think everyone heard his roar. I spun around to find Triss walking up behind me to see what the fuss was about.

"What's going on?"

"Azazel put vervain in the whiskey. Mira drank it, and he disappeared with her. Is there some kind of locator spell you can do?"

Her mouth gaped open, and it took her a few seconds to take in the room behind me to fully grasp what I said. "I mean, we have spells to locate and track people, yes, but they're rather limited and don't always work."

I realized then that it was a stupid question anyway. She was shielded from any of that by the Morrigan. *Fuck.*

What can we do? Fiadh asked, I assumed because Gaisgeach was too pissed to think straight.

We have to find her. Have Gaisgeach fly around until he can sense her. You can do that right?

Yes. Fiadh replied. *He can do that. We will do that.*

I'm coming with you.

No. She snapped. *He knows where* all *of you are now. He could lead others here. You need to get everyone out of here. You don't know what his plans were.*

Macha flew in the window and landed on my shoulder, squawking like she was either panicked or trying to tell me something I couldn't understand. I wished I could hear her like Mira could.

I turned and rubbed a hand over my face, then looked at Triss again. She still stared at me like she was waiting for me to tell her what to do.

"Forget the locator spell. It won't work anyway, and I don't have time to explain. We need to get everyone out of here *now*."

It seemed like something clicked in her mind, because the look in her eye changed from fear and shock to cold determination. "I'll get the mages moving."

The whole manor became a fluster of movement then. Everyone was running around, gathering supplies, clothing, and anything we might need before we were shifted away. I was sure we had plenty of time. The bastard surely couldn't shift a whole army here, but the gods only knew what he'd do if he came back anytime soon.

Triss was barking orders at the mages at the top of the steps. I slipped past her into my bedroom to gather clothes for myself and for Mira. We would find her. I didn't care what it took. We'd bring her home. *I* would bring her home.

"Deiric." Triss was in the doorway now, watching me frantically pack as much as I could into a large satchel.

"What?" I snarled as I glanced over at her.

She didn't even flinch. "Where are we going to go? Aris doesn't have room."

I paused and looked away while I thought through our options. Devlon. He would know where we could go. "We go to Aris' manor, find Devlon, and go from there." I said when I met her gaze again. "We don't need to know where we're staying permanently right this second. We just can't be *here*."

She didn't look convinced, knowing that Devlon was with Solas, but she gave me a curt nod.

I went back to focusing on packing, grabbed another satchel, and packed it with as much of her clothing as I could fit. I grabbed both of her swords, attached them to my belt, and headed back into the hallway.

*

We all arrived at Aris' manor together, thanks to the mages helping with shifting. We were all a bit frazzled though. Triss shifted Lazarus' men back to his manor before meeting us in the foyer. Aris came rushing up to us. Teron had been surprisingly quiet during our frantic packing. I wasn't sure if he was just too shocked, or if he was quiet when he was pissed.

"What's going on?" Aris asked, surveying the large group of us now filling up half his foyer.

"Azazel drugged and took Mira." Adriana said before I could explain. "We need somewhere to go. He's likely to come back to the manor with a lot more manpower, and he clearly had no problem getting through the wards."

Aris gaped at her. "Who the fuck is Azazel?"

"My father, apparently." Adriana grumbled. "Where's Devlon?"

Aris disappeared in the blink of an eye, presumably to get Devlon. My assumption was proven correct when Devlon appeared before us seconds later, looking us all over in disbelief.

"They took her?" He looked at me. "They took Mira?"

I nodded and he let out a slew of curses that would've made most people blush.

"I'll take you to the castle. It's the biggest and safest place for you all. I don't know if he'll figure out the wards there, but it's better than nothing and there is room for all of you there."

I opened my mouth to thank him, but he'd shifted several of us before I had the chance. We now stood in the office where we'd met with Tellus a few times.

Tellus spun around from where he stood looking out the windows beyond his desk and looked at us with raised brows.

"What the fuck?"

"Explain it to him." Devlon demanded and then he was gone.

I glanced around me. Adriana, Lazarus, Triss, and Teron stood behind me. I settled my gaze back on Tellus, who was both startled and confused, and walked him through everything that had happened over the last several days.

He muttered a similar string of curses to what Devlon had, and then quickly strode around his desk, past us, and through the door into the hallway.

"We'll get you set up in some rooms here." He said as he turned right and headed down the hall. "Do you have any idea where he might've taken her?"

"No." Lazarus' voice was as sharp as a blade.

Tellus only glanced over his shoulder for a half a second before shifting his focus to where we walked. "We'll find her."

We followed him through several halls, and down two floors before he showed us into rooms. The others had arrived in this hall, it seemed, because Devlon was there to meet us when we finally reached it.

Fiadh, can you hear me?

Yes.

We're at the Solas castle. Will you be able to find me?

We will come there once Gaisgeach either finds her, or is willing to rest for the night.

I nodded, even though she couldn't see me. Macha, who'd been silent and still on my shoulder since the moment she flew in after Mira was taken, flew off into the room Devlon opened for me.

"This should do for the two of you, when we find her." He said quietly. "Do you need any additional clothing? Need to make a trip back for any other belongings in the meantime?"

I stepped into the room and tossed both satchels off my shoulder and onto the clean and made bed. "No." I spun around to face him. "I mean, yes, I could use more clothing, but that's the least of my concerns right now."

He stared at me warily, like he half expected me to lose my mind at any moment. I couldn't say I blamed him. I was on the brink.

"We *will* find her. I'll get all of the magisters on it, all of our best mages, as well as yours. I've already sent word to Garrick."

"And what do we do until then?" I snarled. "What do I tell them," I motioned to the rest of the mages and my men still being ushered into rooms in the hall.

"You tell them that they're safe here, and that we'll find her and get her out as soon as we can." He paused, glanced over at Macha who now perched on the windowsill. "Will she be any help?"

"I can't understand her, and she flew to me when she was taken, so I'm guessing not."

He muttered another curse under his breath. "Do you know if he's working with Ronan?"

I shrugged. "We didn't exactly interrogate the bastard. He claimed to be Adriana's father, and the resemblance was there." I removed Mira's swords and walked over to place them on one of the dressers. "He seemed harmless enough, until he wasn't."

"If he's working with Ronan, it would stand to reason she might be in the palace dungeons."

I nodded. "I'll tell the dragons to go there."

His brows raised, and he looked at me incredulously. "I'm sorry, the what?"

"Fuck." I mumbled.

"Did you say *dragons?"*

I managed to huff a laugh. "I guess you'd have found out the moment they got *here.* But yes, the dragons. Mira and I have bonded dragons."

"And when the *fuck* were you going to tell us about that?"

I shrugged a shoulder. "When the timing seemed right."

He shook his head. "Where are they now?"

"Searching for her."

He sighed, glanced behind himself down the hall, then looked back at me. "We need to know everything about them. Once you're all settled, meet me in Tellus' office."

I nodded and he turned to help Tellus get the others set up with their rooms. I didn't plan to tell him *everything*. But I could at least give him the same explanation and lesson as the mages.

Adriana ran up to me. "I left the ring at the manor."

I just stared down at her.

She sighed and shook her head. "Shit. Sorry." She grumbled. "Remember, the ring that he tracked me to *your* manor with?"

Right. He'd mentioned that. At least she thought ahead enough to leave that behind.

“Is there anything else your mother gave you that might be tracked?”

She shrugged. “I left all my jewelry at the manor. I only brought the clothing I acquired since living with you.”

“Good.” I looked down the hall to where the rest of the mages were being shown to rooms by Tellus. “Help them get settled, and then you’re coming with me to talk to Tellus.”

She nodded and ran back down the hall to them.

Chapter 12

Deiric

An hour later we were sitting across from Tellus and Devlon at his desk in his office. Devlon was pacing behind Tellus. Tellus sat with his elbows on the table and his head resting on his hands.

"Dragons?" It was Tellus who finally broke the silence.

I was too distracted waiting for any word from Fiadh or Gaisgeach to start the conversation myself. Adriana sat silently next to me, staring at the floor in front of her and wringing her hands like that might resolve the anxiety and anger we were all feeling at the moment.

"Yes." I stopped watching Devlon pace and focused on Tellus instead. "Dragons."

"You realize how crazy you sound." Tellus leaned back in his chair, placing one elbow on the armrest to prop his head on his hand and letting his other arm fall to his lap.

"If you don't believe me, they'll be arriving here eventually, and you can see for yourself." I glanced at Adriana. "Where is your dragon anyway?"

"Fuck's sake." Devlon stopped in his tracks and looked back and forth between the two of us. "She has a dragon too?"

Adriana didn't answer. She continued to stare at the floor.

"Adriana." I snapped, perhaps a little too harshly because she nearly jumped out of her skin.

"Sorry, what?" She mumbled as she looked at me.

"Where is Cairbre?" I said as calmly as I could.

"I'm not sure. Wherever he usually is when we aren't with them I guess." Her hands stilled in her lap at least, but I could see the anxiety still welling up within her.

"You haven't spoken to him since she disappeared?" I raised a brow.

"I have, but I don't ask him where he is." Her response was a little clipped and I realized I must've hit a nerve.

I sighed and shifted my focus back to Tellus. "Her dragon is more likely to be here before Fiadh and Gaisgeach. They're out searching for Mira."

"And you can talk to them?" Tellus seemed more intrigued now than stunned. Devlon resumed his nervous pacing.

"Yes. We communicate mentally with them."

Do not share all of our secrets with him, or I'll kill you myself. Fiadh snarled.

Well-the fuck-aware.

A threatening growl was the only response she gave me. Apparently, I was pushing everyone's buttons today.

"Which means that her dragon should be able to find her quickly?" Tellus raised a brow and seemed to perk up some. Devlon once again stopped where he was and looked at me eagerly for an answer.

"I'm afraid it's not that simple." I leaned back in the chair I was sitting in and rubbed a hand down my face. "They drugged her, which means she's unconscious. He can't communicate with her when she's unconscious, and we have no idea what vervain would do to the connection we have with the dragons, given that it blocks magic."

"Fuck." Devlon grumbled, resuming his pacing once more. I was convinced if this conversation didn't end soon he might wear a gods damned hole in the floor. I was pissed, but at least I was capable of sitting still for the moment.

"So why are they flying around?"

"Hypothetically, he should at least be able to sense her presence if he flies close enough. I don't know how that works when she's unconscious either. We've never encountered that before."

Now would be a great time for you to chime in if you have any answers. I grumbled at Fiadh.

I don't have answers for you. We don't know either.

Is it not the same when we're asleep?

No. He can't feel a connection with her at all right now.

It was my turn to mumble a curse.

"I assume that means your dragons have just confirmed what you told me?"

I looked back up at Tellus. "Yes. Unfortunately."

"Then we'll have to do this the old fashioned way. I can do a locator spell. It's not always accurate but–"

"It won't work. She's cloaked by the Morrigan so that *no one* can find her. It isn't even worth the effort."

You never thought to mention that to me? Fiadh snapped. *That could very well be why he can't sense her. When she's conscious there's an open window into her mind which probably supersedes that cloaking, but when she's unconscious there's nothing at all.*

I opted to ignore her. I could deal with her wrath later.

"There are less than a hundred dragons. Some are bonded to a rider and some are not. I've been training all the riders we've come across so far. A handful are vampires, while the rest are all human." It seemed better to just carry on with explaining the dragons than to wallow in what wouldn't work for Mira.

"So there are more than just you three." Tellus wasn't looking at me. He was staring off at a corner of his desk while he processed what I told him.

"We planned to keep them a secret until absolutely necessary, but like I told Devlon, you'd know when Gaisgeach and Fiadh arrived here after they gave up the search for the night. Assuming that they *do* come here to rest at some point."

"While I'm a little offended you don't seem to trust us completely, I understand the need for secrecy in this case. We won't share it with anyone beyond this group or whomever might run into them while they're here."

"Thank you."

"So there's nothing else we can do for Mira right now?" Adriana asked hesitantly.

I looked over at her and she was looking back and forth between the three of us.

"There's got to be something. Some way we can track her, right?" Her gaze fell on me.

"Not really, no." I grumbled. "We can't just run to the palace and check the dungeons. If he is working with Ronan and took her there, they would be likely to set up a trap for us. While we *should* have magic users capable of handling that, it's obvious that they have Azazel, and he could be just as skilled with shadow magic as Mira."

She shuddered as the realization that it could mean he could simply have misted all of us at the manor like Mira had demonstrated doing several times with plants. Something told me if he were capable of that kind of magic he likely would've just done that at the time, so either he didn't know of it or he had other motives. I couldn't be sure what the hell he'd been planning.

I let myself go down that thought process. If he drugged all of the vampires, he'd still have to fight off Triss, Eimear, and all of the mages. I doubted they'd spring into action quickly, so I was still lost on his thought process there, unless he didn't think any of them were a threat. Was the goal to drug us and just take Adriana against her will? He could have done that at any moment during his time with her, so that didn't seem likely.

Was the goal to drug us and take one or two of us as captives to convince Adriana to do what Ronan wanted if they were working together? Gods. I had no idea what their motives were. Even Ronan. I knew he hated magic users and vampires, but to what end and why? Would he try to end us all, or was he just trying to get us to leave the country? And what fucking purpose would having Adriana do at that point?

I shook my head.

"You seem just as confused as I feel." Tellus commented and I looked up at him again. "It doesn't make sense right? Why would he drug her? Or presumably all of you? Obviously he wanted Adriana to go with him, but to what end?"

"Exactly." I mumbled.

"We'll find her." Adriana said a little bit more confidently now. "We have to."

"We have to." I repeated.

Chapter 13

Mira

I felt like my body was dead weight. I could hardly open my eyes. I smelled nothing but mildew and dirt. I was in a cell, that much was obvious. The shackles around my wrists were more than enough of an indicator to confirm that. Except this time Deiric likely wasn't going to be here to rescue me.

Alesmira? Gaisgeach appeared in my head before I even had the chance to think about anything else.

I'm awake.

Azazel took you.

Obviously. I grumbled.

I assume then you also know you were dosed with vervain. His tone was surprisingly patient despite my grumbled and angry responses.

Yes. That was blatantly obvious when I nearly choked on the gods damned whiskey.

Well, something you wouldn't *know is that it blocks your innate magic, but it shouldn't block mine.*

What?

You are a conduit for my magic. He explained. *All you do is act as the channel for it, so you could try to pull from me to help you escape.*

Where even am I?

I am not sure yet. He replied. *I am close enough to communicate with you, but I'm still figuring that out.*

"Is she awake yet?" Azazel. That fucking bastard.

I was too busy talking to Gaisgeach. I didn't hear his footsteps as he approached. I heard someone shuffle on their feet, followed by the sliding of metal on metal.

"She doesn't appear to be." A male voice replied. Then metal on metal slid again before whoever it was shuffled away from my cell.

"How heavily did you dose her?" Ronan asked.

"I just poured what you gave me into the whiskey." Azazel said in response.

"Fuck's sake. All of it?"

"Was I not supposed to use all of it?"

"Fuck no." Ronan grumbled. "Gods. She could be out for days."

"More explicit instructions would be far more useful next time."

"Yeah, and maybe a little better fucking planning on your part. You need to find Adriana *and* the rest of them.

You were supposed to dose them when they *all* would be drinking it."

"I *did* but the bitch took a drink first and choked on it."

"Of course she choked on it. You used the whole gods damned bottle of vervain. It probably burned the shit out of her mouth. Fucking idiot."

There was a snarl. "We don't have vampires like them in my realm. Forgive me if I don't know the details of how much of this fucking poison takes one down."

"Let us know when she wakes." Ronan said.

"Of course, your majesty." The guard outside of my door replied. I heard their footsteps as they walked away, then the cell was silent again.

I think I'm in the palace dungeons. I said to Gaisgeach.

Are you certain?

No, but if Ronan and *that fucking asshole are here, I would guess I'm somewhere close to him. He wouldn't travel far.*

I will fly that way and see if I can find you. Then Gaisgeach went radio silent.

I wanted to focus on drawing magic from him, but the silence, combined with laying still with my eyes closed, left me quickly fading again. I hated the way the effects of vervain lingered when I couldn't feed and negate them right away.

Mira. Gaisgeach snarled. *I need you to stay with me. I can't find you when you're unconscious.*

I'm trying.

Try harder.

If I moved, they would hear me. I tried to flutter my eyes open, but my eyelids felt like dead weight.

Mira.

I'm sorry I barely managed to say before I faded out again.

*

I woke to the sound of approaching footsteps. I began pulling on Gaisgeach's power almost immediately.

You're awake.

Obviously.

I listened as the footsteps grew louder, but wasn't able to figure out who it was. I couldn't catch a scent on the approaching person either.

I'm going to try to get out.

I wasn't able to determine where you were. Don't move until I tell you to. I'll have Deiric and Fiadh come to meet us.

No. I snarled, trying to focus on pulling in his power, and feeling overwhelmingly hot as I did so. It reminded me of a fever, while I was still half human, but far worse.

You're pulling too much. You'll burn yourself up.

I'm fine. I snapped. *Do* not *come to the palace and risk yourself or Deiric. I'll get out and I'll come to you.*

You can hardly keep yourself conscious.

It took everything I had not to audibly sigh. The footsteps stopped in front of my cell. *I'll make it out and find you. Stay close but out of sight.*

He didn't reply, and I half expected him to disobey my request.

"Still unconscious?" Azazel asked.

"Yes, sir." The guard replied. "She hasn't moved an inch."

There was an exasperated sigh, presumably from Azazel, before he said, "It's time to wake her up." I didn't know how he thought he'd accomplish that, but I wasn't waiting around to find out.

There was a jangling of keys, and then I heard the lock on the cell door turning. This was my chance.

Alesmira! Gaisgeach shouted in my head in warning as I pulled even more of his magic into me. I was sweating and it felt like there was a ball of fire within me.

The moment the door swung open I erupted. Fire burst out from my entire body, and I flung it at Azazel and the guard at the door. It hit them with such force that they flew back into the wall behind them. They remained burning as I stumbled to my feet and began to drag myself out. The chains had melted the moment the fire left me.

I was dizzy, disoriented, and completely spent. It took everything I had just to keep myself upright as I inched along, using the wall for support. I moved my feet as quickly as my exhausted body would allow.

I glanced behind me to confirm that they were still unconscious, thanking the gods that I hadn't encountered others yet, and then rounded the corner.

There was a sharp piercing pain in my chest, and I turned my head to see that I'd just run straight into Ronan and his outstretched dagger. It missed my heart, but barely. A wicked and horrifying smile rose to his lips as he looked down at me.

"Going somewhere?"

Mira! Gaisgeach's voice was now filled with worry and rage. I had no doubt he could feel that I'd been stabbed.

I grabbed onto Ronan. His dagger and my grip on his arms were the only thing holding me upright. His smile only grew when he twisted the dagger, and I let out a muffled cry of pain before dropping to the floor in front of him when he shoved me off the blade.

Blood pooled around me as he leaned down and whispered, "I underestimated you. That won't happen again."

He stepped over me and one of the guards with him knelt down before a blow to the back of my head knocked me out again.

Chapter 14

Deiric

I was sparring outside with Lazarus. It was the only thing that kept my mind off of searching for Mira. Fiadh was with me today while Gaisgeach still flew around trying to find her. He said he should be able to sense her presence the moment she woke. I didn't know if that would be possible with only the gods knew how much vervain was in her system, but I wasn't going to question him. It had been two days since she disappeared with him, and we had yet to make any progress finding her ourselves.

She's awake. Fiadh said suddenly, and I spun around to look at her, nearly dropping my sword.

"What?"

Lazarus stopped advancing on me the moment he saw my attention shift to Fiadh.

He said she's awake. He can feel her.

"What is it?" Teron asked from somewhere behind me.

"She's awake." I kept watching Fiadh, who was looking in our direction, but her eyes were distant, like she was focusing far too hard on hearing whatever Gaisgeach was communicating. I had no idea how far they could stretch their communication, nor how far he'd flown.

He's instructing her on how to use his *magic. He hasn't located her specifically yet.*

Teron and Lazarus stood on either side of me now as I stared at Fiadh and waited for an update. I kicked myself for not forcing her to learn with the rest of the riders.

"Has she said anything helpful?" Teron asked.

Fiadh snarled at him, and he took a step back. His fear of her brought me more joy than it should have, given the situation.

"She is waiting on Gaisgeach."

He lost her.

I took a step forward, the rage and frustration returning in full force now. *What do you mean he* lost *her?*

I mean, she's unconscious again. He wasn't even able to get remotely close to finding her. All he said was she confirmed she was in a dungeon, and Ronan and Azazel were there.

"Fuck."

"What?" Lazarus and Teron asked in unison.

"He lost her."

"Lost her?" Teron snarled. "How the fuck does he *lose* her?"

"She's unconscious again."

"What, like they've dosed her again?" Lazarus growled. He was just as quick to violence as Teron. His temper knew no bounds.

"No." I shook my head. "Like she probably came to long enough to communicate with him but passed out again. She was in and out of consciousness the first time she was drugged with vervain. It wouldn't surprise me if the heavy dose she got this time affected her the same."

"Now what are we supposed to do?" Teron glared at Fiadh. I didn't have the wherewithal to tell him that it was not a good idea to glare at a dragon he wasn't bonded to. Quite frankly, I didn't care enough.

"We wait." It killed me to say it, but we couldn't plan a rescue when we didn't know where she was, and we certainly couldn't go rushing into the palace dungeons if she might be elsewhere. We'd likely be dead if we didn't have her awake and ready to help us.

*

He's felt her again.

Fiadh's voice was barely a whisper. She was flying with him today. I was sitting in the dining area of the castle with Lazarus and Leo. We were going over what Leo and some of our other spymasters had managed to discover about Ronan and his army, which seemed to be gathering for *something*. Macha rested on my shoulder. She stayed close to me nearly all the time now.

I sat straighter in the chair I was in, which drew Leo and Lazarus' attention, though they didn't ask any questions and kept discussing the men he'd seen.

Where are you?

Gaisgeach has insisted we stay close to the palace. She's not in *the palace. We're circling behind it, and he believes she's somewhere underground. We can't get low enough to be sure without alerting the archers on the towers.*

"She's in the dungeons near the palace." I shot to my feet. "Where's Tellus?"

"I'll find him." Leo ran off before I could say another word.

"Are you sure?" Lazarus asked.

"Fiadh said they're circling behind the palace, and Gaisgeach had confirmed with her she was in a dungeon or cell of some kind the last time he communicated with her."

Lazarus nodded. "We're not taking Teron."

"Why?"

"He'll be more of a problem than a help. He's not going to be able to stop himself from just *killing* them and we might need one of them alive for questioning."

I was surprised he wasn't telling *me* to stay behind. I wasn't sure that I would fare any better.

She's going to try to get out. You need to hurry.

I can't just infiltrate the dungeons without a plan. Tell her to wait. It could be a trap.

You know how well she listens to any of us.

"Fuck."

"What now?"

"She's going to try to get out on her own."

"Fuck's sake."

Tellus appeared in front of us. "You've found her?"

"We think she's in a dungeon near the palace." I explained.

"We can't just barge in then." He seemed to think for a moment. "Gather a group to go in with us, and we'll make a plan. I think we have some older maps of the dungeons somewhere. I'll look for them. Meet me in my office when you're ready."

He disappeared before I could tell him that we needed to hurry. Without him or a mage that could shift us there we weren't going to be able to get there quickly anyway, so I had no choice but to do as he said.

We ran to Triss first. She was with Liala, Eimear, Adriana, and the other mages. At the moment, she was assisting Zemora with continuing to practice fighting with her magic in the courtyard.

Triss barely spared us a glance until I announced that they'd found her and said we needed her help.

"I'm helping too." Adriana insisted, running up to us with Triss.

"Absolutely not." I glared down at her. "Mira would kill me if I let you come with us."

"You're out of your gods damned mind if you think that I'm staying behind."

Princess. Cairbre snarled. *You will stay here.*

She whirled around to snarl right back at him, but the steam he huffed from his nostrils suggested she should learn how to listen, and she just crossed her arms and stomped instead. "Bastards."

"I'll help." Aodh ran over from where he'd been sitting along the wall and watching Sorcha and Stella spar. "I'm a master, surely that counts for something."

"Fine." I looked back at Triss. "We're supposed to meet Tellus in his office to create a plan. Shift us there?"

She nodded and shifted us.

Devlon was already there, along with Garrick and Liam. How they'd summoned all three of them so quickly was beyond me, but I wasn't about to ask questions. They were staring at maps they'd laid out over Tellus' desk.

"Do we know what *part* of the dungeons she's in?" Devlon asked, looking at me.

I shook my head and stepped up to the desk to look at the maps myself. "They just know she's not in the part that's beneath the palace."

He frowned, then went back to sifting through the maps. "There are many levels and caverns that make up the dungeons. It's designed that way to make it hard for anyone to escape even if they manage to get out of their cell."

"So you're saying that we could end up lost in there ourselves before we even come close to her?"

"Yes." Tellus answered for him.

She got out, but she didn't get far. Fiadh cut through my thoughts, still sounding incredibly quiet given how far away she was.

Is she alright?

No. Not based on what Gaisgeach felt before he lost her again.

I growled another curse and slammed both of my fists on the table in front of me hard enough that everyone seemed to step back and look at me a bit warily.

"What?" Lazarus was the only one who dared speak. "What is it now?"

"She tried to get out on her own, but didn't make it far. By the sounds of it, she went down again and she's not in good shape."

"Well, we know where she is now." Devlon said, stepping back up to the maps. "We just need to find a way in. You two will stay with one of us so we can shift you back out. They can't pin us down if we can shift."

"If they're using vervain soaked weapons they can." Garrick pointed out, pulling a map closer to his side of the desk so he could review it.

"It's a chance we'll have to take." Triss said as she stepped back up to the table. "You two seem most familiar with this. What do you recommend?" She gestured toward Tellus and Devlon. Devlon was leaning on the table with one hand, scouring over the maps while Tellus stood next to him gazing around at everything on the table in front of them.

"The easiest way to get in is here." Devlon pointed to an entrance far from the palace. "Obviously, we can shift in anywhere, but we don't know what we're shifting into. We should probably shift into one of the less used areas first unless you're comfortable fighting our way in."

"No." Garrick stepped closer now and leaned over to see where Devlon was pointing. "We shift in, *quietly*. We try to sneak around as best we can until we find her. Then we shift out. Communicate mind to mind while we split up to search for her."

"And if we can't find her?" Aodh asked.

Everyone turned to look at him.

"What?" He looked shocked that we'd not even considered it. "If she just tried to escape on her own, it stands to reason that they're going to move her. What if they move her before we go to collect her?"

"We check *every last cell.*" Devlon said more calmly but coldly than I've ever heard him. "If she's not there, we come back here and we keep looking the same way we have been."

*

Lazarus, Triss, and I shifted into the final hallway of cells. We agreed that we'd all split up and go in groups of three. The moment we appeared at the end of the hall the smell of burning flesh bombarded my senses, combined with the smell of *her.* Specifically, the smell of her blood.

Lazarus and I exchanged glances, before we charged down the corridor without looking to see if Triss followed. We had our swords drawn before we'd even made it two steps. It was surprisingly empty. Triss caught up with us quickly, but was furious that we just took off.

"What's going on?" She whispered, though we were making no effort to be quiet.

"We can smell her." I said over my shoulder as we rounded a corner.

We all stopped in our tracks at the sight before us. A body lay charred in front of an open cell door. It was hardly recognizable, but clearly male.

"Holy gods." Triss breathed, covering her mouth and nose with her hands. I was certain she'd never smelled anything quiet so pungent and awful.

"This must've been Mira." I stepped around him and into the cell. "She was here." It looked like she'd melted her way through the chains that held her, seeing the solid drips of metal around the cell.

"We should keep moving." Lazarus said from where he was kneeling next to the body. "I can smell blood from *her* that way." He pointed further down the hall.

I stepped out and around him to head further into the dungeons. They both followed close behind me. We moved more quietly now, expecting to run into guards at any moment.

We rounded a corner in the corridor to find a maid on her hands and knees scrubbing blood from the floor. She jumped when she saw us and cowered back into the wall with her hands raised.

"Where is she?" I growled at her. The blood was Mira's. I would recognize her scent anywhere. There was so much of it that I had no doubt it was more than just a small cut.

"I– I don't know who you're asking about." The woman stammered. I hesitate to call her a *woman*. She looked barely older than eighteen. She was practically still a child.

"The mage." I stepped closer to her, stepping into the soapy and bloody mess on the floor in front of her. "The vampire," I bared my fangs at her as I spoke, "That caused this mess."

She scurried further away from us, flattening herself against the wall. "I– I'm sorry, s– sir." She stammered. "I– I don't know. I was just asked to clean this up. The king disappeared with that shadow man nearly an hour ago. He– He said if I didn't clean this up before he came back that he'd kill me."

I knew he was a ruthless bastard, but threatening a *human* like that? One so gods damned young. It made me sick.

Garrick and Liam appeared beyond her, coming from the other corridor of cells. "Anything?" Garrick asked, looking down at the woman between us.

"She was here." I gestured toward the blood at my feet. "She went down here. They left an hour ago."

"You're sure she's not here?" Liam asked.

I shook my head. "We'll check *every cell* until we're sure."

"Fuck." Garrick muttered then turned to head to the next hall. "Let's keep looking. Have you run into any guards?"

"No." Lazarus answered for me as we all stepped around the cowering maid and walked toward the next corridor with them. "I would've expected to find at least one."

"Something isn't right." Triss whispered. "It's like they were expecting us."

"Or." I said coldly. "They didn't want anyone to know they had her. I'm sure that they don't regularly guard the empty cells." I didn't get a hint of any other scents in these halls. Not human or otherwise, like they hadn't been used in years.

We wound our way through the halls of the dungeon. It was like a labyrinth, and I struggled to understand why there were so many. I didn't take this kingdom for the type to keep quite so many prisoners so close to the palace. When we caught up with Tellus and Devlon, they had a mage cornered near the last row of cells. There were still no guards, and there were no other prisoners around either.

The mage's eyes fell to me, and he smiled. The look in his eye combined with that far too triumphant grin snapped something in me and I shot forward, past Tellus and Devlon. I slammed him back into the stone wall behind him and held my sword to his throat. His grin didn't falter.

"Where. The Fuck. Is She?" I ground out, ready to rip his throat out with my fucking teeth.

He laughed. Actually fucking *laughed* at me.

I pressed my sword into his throat until it drew blood, and he had to breathe more cautiously so I didn't slit his throat. "Tell me where she is."

"Even if I knew, I wouldn't tell you." He scowled down at me now. "That stupid bitch deserves–"

His words died on his tongue, quite literally, as I removed his head from his shoulders with a single swipe of my sword.

"We could have questioned him further," Tellus started, but stopped the moment I spun around to face him, and he saw the state I was in.

I didn't give a fuck what else they could've gotten out of him. All that mattered to me was finding my *mate.* I would kill anyone who got in my way.

Chapter 15

Mira

An acrid smell jolted me awake. I jerked away from it, surprised to find that I was nearly immediately overwhelmed with the urge to feed. I wasn't given much time to wonder how long I'd been out though, as I realized that I was strung up on a wall. My wrists and ankles were bound in metal shackles, and my arms were restrained out on either side of me to hold me up.

My hair had come slightly undone from the braid, leaving long tendrils down in front of my face. I lifted my head and stared through the hair blocking my vision to see Azazel and Ronan standing before me with a handful of guards behind them. Just beyond the guards stood another man. One I recognized from the day we fought against Solas. Kieran.

I smiled when I saw the visible scarring from the burns I'd given Azazel. I let out a humorless laugh and made a show of looking him over.

"What a pity. You survived." I spat. "Sorry about your poor face."

He backhanded me, hard enough that my head nearly blew back into the wall behind me. My bottom lip smashed into my fangs and blood filled my mouth.

I laughed again and spit the blood filling my mouth in his face. "Is that the best you've got?" I lifted my head. I grinned, large enough to display my fangs and hopefully unnerve the guards at the very least. "Pathetic."

The blow to the pit of my stomach came quickly. A cheap shot, and one I was not even slightly surprised by. Despite expecting it, I couldn't swallow the grunt that escaped me when all the breath left me.

I tried to laugh that off again too, summoning all the bravado I was capable of. "Typical. Beating a woman while she's down."

"You're an abomination." Ronan snapped. "Not a woman."

I snorted. "Perhaps to you." I lifted my head once more and glared at him. "You know nothing about me. You perceive me as a monster simply because I need blood to survive."

Azazel's hand was around my throat almost as soon as I finished speaking. "Enough." He snarled, leaning closer than he probably should have.

I jerked against his grip on me, trying to reach for any part of him that my fangs could connect with before his grip tightened and nearly cut off my airway completely.

"You won't get to bite me." He smiled, leaning even closer now, and pressing me back against the stone behind me. I couldn't move. Not in my weakened state. It didn't take a genius to determine that they'd pumped so much vervain into me that I was effectively human.

Azazel was probably the only person in this room I *could* feed from lest I risk drinking more vervain anyway. I was certain they'd have anyone that came near me drink it so if I fed from them I wouldn't get far.

"Where is my sister?" Ronan asked, stepping a little bit closer to me, once he was satisfied that my restraints were holding me.

I opened my mouth to speak but being unable to draw in any air left me unable to answer. Azazel's grip on my neck loosened enough that I could draw a real breath.

I smiled at Ronan. "What, did you run back to my manor after you took me, and she wasn't there?" I snorted, and the grip around my neck tightened once more. I fought against it managing to choke out, "How– the fuck– am I supposed to– know where she is?"

"Where would they run to?" Ronan asked now.

I managed a shrug, despite my bindings.

"She knows. I'm sure of it." Azazel snarled.

I glared at him, but Ronan just asked a new question. "Can she summon creatures from other realms?"

I shrugged again. Azazel withdrew his hand from my neck and swung at me. His fist collided with my temple with such force that it flung my head back into the stone behind me. I let myself hang loosely from my bindings while stars swirled around my vision. I hadn't seen that coming, though I shouldn't have been surprised.

"You *will* answer me." Ronan snarled.

I didn't look up at him. "Go fuck yourself."

A blow to my ribs came next, and I was certain one had broken. Still, I said nothing. I gritted my teeth to hold back any grunts or cries in pain. I wouldn't give them the satisfaction.

"Get her to talk." Ronan said, before he strode from the room. "By any means necessary. When she decides that she's willing to talk, send for me."

So I wasn't in the palace anymore. At least I knew that. I also wasn't anywhere close to wherever Gaisgeach and Fiadh were, because I couldn't hear him in my head at all. That, or where I was it was impossible for him to feel or find me. Neither were good. I was alone. *Completely* alone, and entirely at Azazel's mercy.

Azazel let out a sadistic chuckle. "Oh, we're going to have so much fun together."

"Somehow, I doubt that." I didn't look up at him. I didn't need to. I could hear him as he walked around the room.

"Where is my daughter?"

I looked up now and smiled. "Oh, you know," I drawled. "Somewhere between 'go fuck yourself' and 'you'll never fucking break me you sadistic fuck'."

When I met his eyes, there was nothing but cold resolve in them. I lowered my gaze to his hand, where he held a torch. He didn't give me a moment to regret my words before he shoved the burning end of the torch against my chest. I couldn't stop the scream that time.

*

I jolted awake as pain shot up my right leg and another shrill scream wrestled its way up my throat. I didn't know how I *could* still scream. He'd been at this for hours. There wasn't a part of me that he hadn't burned, cut, or broken. I'd passed out again when he drove the knife into my shoulder, shredding the ligaments and making my left arm completely useless. Now, he'd stabbed me in the thigh.

"Ready to talk yet?" He mused a far too pleasant smile on his face for what he'd been doing.

I knew my fangs were bared. It was an instinct, and I couldn't seem to calm myself enough to withdraw them anymore. I'd stopped replying entirely hours ago. I didn't quite know how much more I could take. He wouldn't break me, but I didn't think he could keep me going like this. Surely I'd pass out and *stay* that way eventually, right?

"Very well." He said it as though we were having a very casual conversation. He dug his dagger into my knee.

I screamed and thrashed against him, despite the pain that it caused in my already shredded shoulder. He still pushed his dagger deeper, trying to shred my knee just as he'd shredded my shoulder. It didn't take long before I blacked out again.

*

I woke up whole again, but groggy. There wasn't a single trace of pain in my entire body. At first, I thought it had all been a dream, but then I moved and felt the shackles still snug around my wrists and ankles.

Someone had healed me. I guessed it had to be Azazel. I doubted that Ronan had other mages or witches working for him. Let alone mages that would be willing to partake in *this*. He likely only tolerated Azazel because they had a mutual interest in Adriana.

My clothes were still shredded and caked with blood. *My* blood. I was so thirsty and still so disoriented it took me a few moments before I picked up on the scent of other *human* blood nearby. I opened my eyes.

I was laying on the ground toward the back of the cell, laying where most of my blood from the torture session had pooled. There was a small wooden cup in front of me, close enough to reach despite my chains. It smelled of stale human blood.

I lurched forward to take it and my head spun from the sudden movement. I was still drugged. I still only moved as quickly as a human would. I grabbed the cup and nearly had it to my lips when a realization hit me. It was likely laced with vervain too. They wouldn't give me blood knowing that it would rejuvenate me enough to fight them.

My cell door opened, and Azazel stood in the threshold smiling at me. "Go ahead and drink it." The sinister look in his eye told me everything I needed to know. "Wouldn't want you to go completely feral if you starve."

I chucked the cup at him fighting against all my instincts that were demanding I drink it anyway. The blood splattered all over the far too fine looking clothing he was wearing.

He chuckled. "You'll regret that."

Shadows circled my throat and tightened, cutting off my air while simultaneously lifting me up to my feet and sending me flying back into the wall. I grasped helplessly at my neck, as though that would help me. I knew better. I'd used this on countless enemies before.

Guards came in and grabbed my wrists. They pulled them to either side of me and latched the chains to restraints on the wall, so I was once again held up by my arms.

"Ready for another session?" He didn't wait for my reply before he released the shadows from my neck and struck me across the face. Several more blows to my ribs and abdomen followed before he finally stepped back to ask a question.

"Now." He smiled. "Where is Adriana?"

"What the fuck do you want with her anyway?"

"I'm taking both her *and* her mother home with me."

I laughed. I'm not even sure why. She'd never go with him anywhere and Ronan would never let her go. "You think Ronan will let you leave with her?"

There was a shred of doubt in his face. Just enough that I saw it for a split second before he schooled his features back into neutrality.

"He won't have a choice."

I snorted.

"But, if I have to choose one, I'll just take her mother."

"So it's a trade then?" I lifted my head and met his gaze. "Your daughter for, what? The woman you fucked once?" I forced out another crazed laugh. "You're even more of an idiot than I thought."

He charged toward me, grabbed a handful of my hair and yanked my head to the side before putting his blade against my throat. "You have *no* idea what you're talking about."

The threat of the blade on my throat was useless. He'd done far worse. I smiled. "About what? Your useless royal whore or the daughter you don't give a rat's ass about?"

The blade disappeared from my throat and then he stabbed me, right between my already battered ribs. Missing my heart on purpose, but sinking deep enough to send a searing pain up my side. Just like I hoped he would.

The vervain was wearing off. I had *some* of my speed and strength. I took the moment he thought he'd won by stabbing me to lurch forward and sink my teeth into his neck. He'd fallen *right* into my goading trap. His blood tasted… odd. I couldn't quite place it. Sweeter than human blood. Perhaps it was because he wasn't from this realm.

He cursed and thrashed away from me, ripping a hole in his throat in the process. His free hand covered his neck while he slung out a string of curses and healed himself.

"You wretched bitch." He glared at me.

The wound on my side started to stitch itself back together. Even the smallest amount of blood brought me closer to normal now. I yanked against the chains at my wrists. They didn't break, but the anchors in the wall seemed to budge a little. I yanked again before shadow restraints tightened around me once more.

"I don't think so" Azazel stalked closer once again, now that I couldn't lunge at him. "There's plenty more vervain where that came from." He gestured toward the blood I'd splattered on him. "Now, where were we?" Another lit torch appeared in his hand.

Chapter 16

Deiric

There was a knock on my door. I had spent the last two hours staring at maps, plotting *everywhere* we knew that they could keep her near the palace. I took a sip of my whiskey and grumbled at whoever was at the door to enter. I didn't have any interest in talking to anyone at the moment. Finding her was all I cared about.

Leo appeared beside me less than a second later. "Deiric."

I didn't look up at him. I was going over the map for probably the third time today and was trying to decide where to stop first.

"Deiric." He said again, more earnestly this time.

"Whatever you've come to tell me had better be fucking important." I snapped and looked over at him.

He narrowed his eyes at me. I guess he had a right to be annoyed. I never spoke to any of them like that, but I couldn't think straight. I'd been on a short fuse since she'd been taken. Even Fiadh treaded lightly these days.

"I think I have a lead on where they might be keeping her." He gestured toward the map. "I overheard some of the lord's guards in Eldevere talking about a dark haired mage they were holding. It's a long shot, but it *could* be her."

"Do you really think they'd trust her to one of their lord's guards?"

"I don't think we should ignore it."

You shouldn't. Fiadh's voice was closer than I expected.

I thought you were flying with Gaisgeach?

He couldn't find her. It's like she's disappeared completely. Like she isn't even in this realm. He could feel her faintly before. He can't feel her at all now.

You don't really think–

No. He wouldn't have taken her out of this realm. He's smarter than that.

That should have relieved me, but it only made me more frustrated. She was alive. I was certain of that because Gaisgeach was still alive, but also because I was certain I would be able to feel if she weren't.

"Fine." I said to Leo. "Where are they holding this mage?"

He stepped closer to the map and pointed to Eldevere, then to an area just to the north of the town. "There's a larger stone building right about *here* that they had several guards watching day and night. I assume that's where they're keeping all of their prisoners."

He stepped back and looked me over again before continuing. "You shouldn't go alone. I think they have them underground. If you go alone you'll risk getting cornered down there."

"I have a fucking dragon. *Two* dragons actually. I'm pretty sure I'll be able to handle it."

Don't be an idiot.

I scowled at her comment, as though she could see me.

"And by the look on your face I assume your dragon told you to listen to me." He smirked.

"*You* don't have armor. You're not going with me."

"I can at least serve as a lookout. Bring Lazarus if you want someone with armor."

"Find him. We'll leave in a few minutes."

"You can't be serious," Leo started. "You've been drinking."

I spun on him and bared my fangs, barely keeping the primal rage that seemed to be overwhelming me daily in check. "I am not going to waste a single fucking minute if there's a chance we can find her."

He stepped back, stunned, then sprinted from the room. I downed the rest of my whiskey and walked to the dresser to grab my armor.

How exactly are you planning to get there?

Can you carry the two of them?

She scoffed. *I'm sure they'll be thrilled by that, but yes I can carry them.*

Good. We'll meet you in the courtyard.

I slipped the armor on, grabbed my sword, and walked out to find Lazarus and Leo in the hallway.

“I assume he’s filled you in.” I said, walking past Lazarus and heading toward the stairs.

“I don’t suppose you have a plan?” Lazarus turned and walked with me as I passed. Leo followed suit.

“My plan is to get there, see what the fuck we’re dealing with, and kill anyone who gets in my way.”

“Right.” Lazarus seemed less than amused. I couldn’t have cared less. They had my mate. They were all as good as dead in my eyes, whether they knew who she was or not.

Teron stepped out and I nearly walked right into him. “Where are you–”

“Not right now.” I snarled as we walked past. I could hear his mind racing. He knew we were going out to look for her, but likely hadn’t overheard the details.

“I could help you.”

I sighed, stopped, and glanced over my shoulder at him with a glare. “You don’t have armor. If something happens to you, she may very well kill me for allowing you to come along.”

“You have Leo. He doesn’t–”

“This isn’t up for debate.” I turned and continued on toward the courtyard. I heard Lazarus thinking that I wasn’t giving Teron any reason to like me by shutting him out. I didn’t care. He didn’t need to like me right now. He just needed to stay the fuck out of my way.

“How are we getting there anyway?” Lazarus asked, seconds before Fiadh slammed down on the cobblestones in front of me.

“We’re flying.” I ran up her leg and positioned myself on her shoulders.

“You’ve got to be–” I didn’t hear another word after Fiadh snatched them off the ground and took to the skies. I did, however, hear all the awful things they called me in their thoughts.

*

Fiadh and Gaisgeach dropped us as close to the town as they dared to go while still having some cover from the trees.

"Lead the way." I told Leo, who was still dusting himself off and looked like he might be sick.

"I should kill you for that." He muttered, then brushed his hair back out of his face and began walking toward the town. "We should be able to skirt around the town and just creep up behind that building. I think it's a meeting hall of some kind."

"And they're keeping prisoners there?" Lazarus didn't seem convinced that we even had the right location. Honestly, I wasn't either, but any lead was better than none.

"Yes." Leo lowered his voice as we crept closer. "I told you; I heard them talking about a mage." He stopped and held his hand up signaling for us to do the same. "There." He pointed. "That's the building they're holding them in. Looks like there's two guards at the front door and one at each corner around the back."

"That's not many guards for a prisoner like her." Lazarus pointed out.

"They wouldn't want to draw attention to it." I didn't even fully believe what I was saying, but that small shred of hope was all I had. "You take the one on the left and I'll take the one on the right. We'll slip in through the bars in the middle and fight our way out if we have to."

"That's a shit plan." Lazarus stepped up next to me.

"Do you have a better one?"

"You haven't really given me much time to think of one, no."

I drew my sword. "Don't tell me you're afraid of fighting a few humans."

"I'm afraid of what will happen to us if Azazel is in there."

"Kill first." I smiled, baring my fangs and preparing for bloodshed. "Ask questions later."

Lazarus merely raised a brow at me, before he drew his sword as well.

"If we're not back in five minutes, get to Fiadh and get backup."

"This is a horrible idea." Leo grumbled, but stepped out of the way to allow us to pass between the trees and move forward with our plan.

I sprung forward, clearing the distance between our place in the woods and the guard on the right corner of the building in the blink of an eye. I snapped the guard's neck. The lack of a scream from the other guard told me Lazarus had moved just as quickly as me.

We knelt down in front of the barred window at the base of the building. I pulled the bars apart so we could slip between them. It was hardly a quiet task, but nothing seemed to stir inside. I shimmied myself through, feet first, and landed in a dark and damp cellar.

A single torch lit up the space from the bottom of a stairwell toward the front. The cellar was wide open, with six pillars supporting the two beams holding the wood floor above our heads.

Chains and shackles were mounted to each pillar with a few more sets attached to the stone walls of the foundation.

There were four women chained along the right wall, mostly concealed by shadows. They all smelled distinctly human and *none* of them were her.

The creak of metal hinges told us that someone was coming down here. We both slipped behind a pillar on either side of the cellar to quietly observe. I was certain the women saw us, even though I hadn't glanced at their faces, but they didn't utter a word.

Two sets of footsteps came down the stone staircase. "Dinner time." A male voice mused, and I heard the clatter of a metal tray hitting the floor. "Enjoy."

I peeked around the edge of the pillar I stood behind to see that it was one single tray, containing two loaves of bread and two cups of water, which had now toppled over. The man who dropped it to the ground was smiling in a way that made my skin crawl, and the other man just looked bored.

Before they could turn to leave, I flew from my hiding spot. Lazarus did the same, and we had each of them in a headlock before they could even register that we were there.

"I'm told you were holding a mage with dark hair here." I snarled, my fangs aching to sink into this bastard's neck. I chose the one who dropped the tray. Regardless of whether he had the information I wanted; I would take joy in ripping his fucking throat out. "Where is she?"

The man fought against me until he caught sight of my fangs, then he nearly went limp in my arms. "She's that one." He pointed to the dark haired woman chained closest to the stairs.

I looked in her direction, and she just looked shocked. She was filthy, her dark brown hair was messy, about shoulder length, and she wore a tattered dress that had seen better days. She could've been with Solas or Oíche. I didn't particularly care which one, but I wasn't going to leave *any* of them here.

I moved us closer to the stairs and slammed the bastard into the wall. I held him up by his throat, holding tight enough that he didn't struggle against me, but not tight enough that he couldn't breathe. Not yet.

"There's a mage with black hair that's being held prisoner by your king. *Where is she?*" Each word was laced with violence. The man soiled himself while he stared at me. Fear wafted from both of them in intoxicating waves. It took all the self-control I had to wait for his answer and not drain him immediately.

"I–" He stammered. "I don't know of a mage with black hair. We only have these mages. They are being held until we're told what to do with them. King's orders." He started shaking under my grasp. "Please." He begged. "I don't know anything else, I swear."

Useless. Both of these men were fucking useless. Unfortunately, I wasn't sure if *they* had consumed vervain, and it wasn't a chance I was interested in taking.

"Fine." I snarled. "You're of no use to me then." As I'd done with the guard outside, I snapped his neck.

I spun around and examined the man Lazarus held now.

"There was talk of a black haired mage being held at the palace." The man started, as if having my attention on him loosened his tongue a bit. "Really powerful, someone said. The King pulled some of our men to the palace to help reinforce his guard in the palace."

"Is that so?"

He nodded fervently, despite the head lock Lazarus held him in.

I smiled, and he shrunk back into Lazarus even further. I knew how wicked I must look with my fangs still exposed.

"Tell me," I stepped closer to him, pulling back my fangs and locking eyes with him long enough to compel him. "Have you been drinking or eating vervain?"

"N– No." He shook his head. "The vervain is only for the mages, to keep them from using their magic."

"Excellent." Lazarus released him and shoved him toward me. "Because I'm famished."

His eyes widened, but that was the only reaction he was able to make before I sank my fangs into his neck. He fought against me, which did nothing but tear his neck to shreds while I drank. When he finally slumped over into me I dropped him to the floor.

Blood dripped down my chin as I turned to look at the women chained to the wall.

"You could have at least *shared* him." Lazarus grumbled when he stepped over the corpse and stood beside me.

"You didn't ask." I shrugged. "You're all mages?" I asked the women. There was no need to compel them. If they were with Oíche, they'd know we were here to help them. If they were with Solas, they were probably terrified, but hopefully came to the same conclusion.

They glanced between one another and then nodded.

"Solas or Oíche?"

Two of each, if I could pick apart their simultaneous responses. I snatched the keys from the first dead guard's belt, unlocked each of their shackles, and was back standing next to Lazarus before they could even register what I'd done.

"You're coming with us."

*

Gaisgeach and Fiadh slammed down onto the cobblestones outside of the Solas castle. Gaisgeach had carried all the women back, two in each claw. They were absolutely petrified, and still shaking when he sat them down on the stones.

Leo and Lazarus walked over to them immediately to lead them into the castle and up to Tellus, where we'd figure out what to do with them. Teron was leaning against the exterior wall of the castle, looking up at me with a slight glare.

"I take it you didn't find her?"

I swung my leg over Fiadh's back and slid down her leg. "What do you think?" I snarled.

"Well, judging by your still foul mood, I'm guessing you didn't. Did you get any information on where she might be?"

"No." I walked toward the door that Lazarus, Leo, and the women had disappeared through.

"And are you going to let me help you on these bat shit crazy missions, or are you going to keep me in the dark?"

I stopped, turned toward him and growled. "Are you going to find someone to make you armor and then make sure you don't get in my fucking way?"

He pushed off the wall and took a step further away from me. "I am glad you care about her so much, but you could lay off the primal 'get the fuck out of my way' bullshit and allow us to help you."

"If I let you come with you and you get yourself killed she may very well kill me when I *do* find her for letting you come along when you don't have any fucking armor." I stepped closer to him until we were nearly chest to chest. He wasn't quite meeting my challenge, but he no longer backed away.

"I will point out *again* that Leo didn't have armor."

"*Leo* is *my* fucking spymaster. He is not my mate's *father.*"

"So you'd sacrifice him to find your mate?"

"I told him not to go."

"Interesting." He stepped around me and began to walk toward the door. "If there's anything you'll *allow* me to do, please let me know." He walked into the palace without another word.

You should be careful threatening her father. Fiadh suggested.

I glared at her.

I'm just saying you need to calm down.

"Would you be calm if your mate was being held captive by some shadow mage and a king who has wanted to kill her from the moment you met him?" I snapped, advancing a few steps toward her.

Her silence spoke volumes. Her condescending look only angered me further. I shook my head and turned to walk inside.

*

By the fourth dungeon we raided, I was fed up with the lack of answers I was getting. I stopped focusing on just those that Leo seemed to find references to a dark haired mage in and started just going after every stronghold he found. Today's raid was at a town less than a day's ride, on horseback, from the capital.

Lazarus and I crept up toward the outside of the building. Unlike the others we raided, this one just looked like a house. I was almost certain she wouldn't be in here, but I would leave no stone unturned.

This was far less guarded than the last dungeon we raided. I crept up to the side of the house and peered into the window. Lazarus stood behind me with his back against the wall.

"Well?" He whispered.

"This is an office." I explained, flattening myself against the wall next to the window. "There's no one inside. Just a desk littered with papers and bookshelves along the walls."

"That's not very promising. Was Leo *sure* this was another prison?"

"He claimed to be."

Lazarus' answering scoff was enough to tell me he was over this process already. I knew he wouldn't complain though. He wanted to find her just as badly as I did, but with a little less blood rage to go with it.

We ducked under the window and snuck along the edge of the building until we reached another window. I peered in and this time found what we were here for. Three chained prisoners sat on the wood floors of an otherwise empty room. They were shackled together and secured to the floor. Some of them looked barely conscious.

Vervain was their drug of choice, it seemed, but it shouldn't knock out humans like it did vampires. It was hard to tell if this was a drugged stupor or if they were merely exhausted from a lack of food and water. If it was the former, they were upgrading to use more than just vervain.

Mira, of course, was not in the room. I wasn't surprised, nor was I disappointed. At least I could free these people. That would make her happy if she were here.

I wedged my dagger up under the window and used it as a lever to push it open, snapping the lock in the process. The amount of noise it made would've just sounded like one of the prisoners had moved. No one would notice a thing.

Once the window was open, I pulled myself in. Lazarus followed quietly.

The woman closest to the window stirred and looked at us like we were idiots for breaking into the building. Lazarus immediately got to work freeing them of their chains while I stalked toward the door to the room, expecting a guard to burst through at all the noise.

Sure enough, as soon as the first woman was free and Lazarus moved onto the man next to her, the door burst open. Two guards came rushing in.

I shut the door behind them, and had them both pinned to the wall by their throats before they could even see how many people they were up against.

I leaned into the first guard. "You will not resist. You will stand here quietly while we remove the restraints from these prisoners." He nodded. No vervain. *Excellent.*

I shifted my gaze and leaned toward the other guard, a dark haired man who was young, lean, and glaring at me. He scoffed. "You can't compel me, demon."

I smiled at him. If I couldn't compel him, that meant he knew more than the rest of them. *He* would've been close to *her.* I released the first guard, but leaned in to compel him again.

"You will answer all of my questions truthfully. Do you understand?"

He nodded.

"Has this guard," I gestured to the dark haired one, "been in contact with the black haired vampire the king is holding?"

"He bragged for days after he assisted in guarding her at the palace."

A growl escaped me before I could tamp down my temper. "Do you know where they've taken her?"

He shook his head.

"Do you know what was done to her?"

He looked at the guard I was still holding. "She was drugged, then moved when she tried to escape."

"Do you know anything else about her?"

He shook his head again. "He might."

I laughed at his offer. He thought it might save his life. He thought wrong.

"Are there any other prisoners in this building? Any other people?"

He shook his head.

Lazarus was next to me now. I nodded and he snapped his neck. The guard I was holding visibly flinched. I smiled at him next. "Feel like talking yet?"

"Fuck you."

I shrugged. "In that case, you're coming with me."

"What?"

Lazarus handed me chains, which I promptly wrapped him in. I called up fire to my hands, and threw it at the door they'd come through. I couldn't burn the other dungeons, but I could burn this one.

I drug the man with me while Lazarus helped the three mages out through the window. I threw him through, then stepped out myself just as the fire really caught in the room and smoke started to billow out the window. It wouldn't take them long to notice it, but they certainly wouldn't get it out in time to save the building.

We ran into the woods with the mages. As per usual, Gaisgeach flew the mages back, but this time also took Leo. Lazarus and the guard were carried by Fiadh.

*

Tellus was waiting for us when we returned. We'd gotten into a bit of a routine with our raids now. He waited each evening to collect the mages we found, get them clean clothes, and find them somewhere to stay. In most cases, he sent them off to manors outside of Leinster.

He appeared surprised that we brought a prisoner of our own this time. "Who is that?"

I shrugged. "Does it matter? He has been taking vervain, so I can't compel him. I need to interrogate him."

An emotion I couldn't quite place flashed across Tellus' face, but then he gave me a terse nod. "The dungeons are available to you. Just try not to make a mess."

"Of course." I smiled.

Lazarus and I walked with the guard down to the lower levels of the castle and threw him into one of the cells. I told Tellus' guards to find somewhere else to be until we came for them. They looked at me nervously, but did as I asked.

I stepped into the cell and closed the door behind me, making sure it wasn't locked. When I turned to face Lazarus and the guard the color had drained from the man's face. Lazarus unchained him and stepped back.

He glanced between us a few times before he finally snarled, "Get on with it then."

He was trying so hard to appear unbothered by being cornered with two vampires. It was almost comical. I stepped closer to him and in a movement too fast for his eyes to track, I broke his right forearm.

He screeched in pain.

"Ready to talk yet?"

"Fuck you," he growled through gritted teeth.

I shrugged. "Have it your way then." I broke his other forearm. He managed to stifle the scream this time, but couldn't hide the agony from his face.

"Where have they taken her?"

"Even if I knew, I wouldn't tell you."

"Not good enough." I broke his clavicle with one well placed punch. "Where is she?"

He was barely holding himself together. His breathing was ragged and shallow. He looked like he might fall to his knees. When he didn't answer, I decided to help him there by breaking his femur.

"I'm getting tired of this game already." I mused. "Tell me where they've taken her and what state she's in or I'll break the other leg."

"I don't know." He started, pausing to take a breath. "Please. I don't know where they took her."

"What did she look like the last time you saw her?"

"She–" He tried to pull in a deep breath through the pain. "She was unconscious. The King… stabbed her in the chest… with his dagger. She collapsed." Hard and short breaths punctuated each pause. "We were excused after that… and other guards shuffled in." He looked up at me. "Please. That's all I know."

"Then you're no longer of use to me." I ripped his still beating heart straight out of his chest and set fire to it, until it was nothing but ash in my hand.

Lazarus let out an exasperated sigh. "Tellus specifically asked you *not* to make a mess."

I glared at him. "Tellus should be glad this is the *only* mess I've made."

Chapter 17

Mira

I woke this time to the sound of footsteps approaching my cell. It was rare that I woke *before* the torture began. I was laying in a heap on the floor, discarded like yesterday's trash. I suppose that's all I was to them. Trash.

I wasn't what they wanted. They wanted Adriana. They had to give up at some point. I was sure of it. There was no sense in continuing to torture me when I had no plans to talk.

The cell door creaked open and a pair of boots I'd become far too familiar with walked up to me. I was awake, but there was no fight left in me. I let the guards that followed him lift me up and chain me to the wall again. They were all dosed with vervain anyway. There was no point in trying to escape anymore.

"She's awake." One of them mumbled as they walked past him. I wasn't sure how he could tell. I did my best to be dead weight for them.

"Good." Azazel mused and walked closer. After I bit him, the chains were tightened to a point where I could hardly move each time they strung me up. He could stand right in front of me, and I couldn't reach him.

"You're becoming nothing more than a thorn in my side compared to that vengeful mate of yours."

My stomach flipped at the mention of Deiric coming from his lips. He couldn't have him here. I would know. I was sure of it. He would parade him in here as leverage. Or kill him.

"He's been raiding every single prison around the palace looking for you. I have no doubt he was the one who killed Finn. It's a pity, honestly. He was an excellent asset to the King."

So many emotions hit me at once it was hard to decipher. Part of me wanted to be relieved. That confirmed he wasn't here. He was out there looking for me. Another part of me wanted to scream. He was putting himself in danger to find me. I could never live with myself if he died trying to free me. I fought to keep my emotions hidden and kept my eyes on the floor. On the bastard's boots.

He grabbed my jaw possessively and lifted my face to force me to look at him. "Look me in the eye when I'm speaking to you *witch*."

I channeled every ounce of rage I had into my eyes as I stared at him. I was given no other choice now. I couldn't fight against his grasp even if I wanted to. I was too tired. Too weak. But I couldn't let him know that. Even the starvation slowly eating away at me ebbed when I was this exhausted. No primal instinct in me could force me to move now.

"He burned down the prison closest to the palace with our guards in it." He snarled. "At least, I assume it was him. Last I checked vermin like you don't normally have magic, but you *do* have fire mages, don't you?" His smile made my stomach turn. "Sorcha, was it? Oh, and Aodh. Perhaps I should kill them when we find them."

My expression didn't falter, even though the idea of him getting anywhere near them made me want to scream. All I could do was stay here and take this. So long as he was here torturing me, he hadn't found them, and he wasn't out looking.

I just wanted to get this over with. We'd be at this for hours. The sooner he got started, the sooner it ended. I spit in his face.

He released me but quickly swung and blasted me in the face with his fist. Stars fluttered around my vision. I swore each time we did this, it took less to make me pass out. I shouldn't have been surprised. I felt more human by the day.

"You bitch." He snarled. Several more blows came in quick succession. "Tell me where my daughter is."

Nothing but silence answered his demands. I wouldn't speak. I didn't even swear at him anymore. I'd effectively gone mute. I wasn't even sure if I *could* speak with how frequently I screamed. I was certain my throat and vocal cords were destroyed.

The fire and the knives came next, until the world faded to black again.

Chapter 18

Deiric

Two weeks. It had been *two fucking weeks* since she'd been taken, and we still weren't any closer to finding her. I raided several more dungeons with Lazarus, Leo, Fiadh, and Gaisgeach searching for her, leaving several bodies in our wake each time.

She wasn't in any of them, and none of the guards knew anything. I was preparing to go out and fly around to see if Gaisgeach could sense her when Macha stopped me from walking out the door. She flew in through the open window, backing me away from the door by fluttering frantically in front of my face and diving at me until I was almost at the bed.

"What?" I snapped, swatting at her. "What the fuck is it?"

I'd lost my patience more times than not when someone tried to stop me from going out flying, so no one bothered to stand in my way anymore.

She swooped around and landed on the dresser where I sat Mira's weapons. Specifically, she landed on her sword. The one blessed by the Morrigan. She stared at me, unblinking.

"I don't understand."

She pecked at the sheath on the blade, hopping excitedly like I'd understand what she was signaling. I didn't.

She shook out her whole body, then took flight again, swooped to my left hand and grabbed it with her beak before swooping back to the sword again.

"An offering?"

She cawed at me.

"You want me to make an offering to the Morrigan?"

She cawed again and hopped up and down on the sword.

"It's the dark moon, isn't it?"

Another caw.

Good. At least we'd established our communication skills.

"Will the Morrigan help us find her?"

She just stared at me. Her head cocked to the side, but otherwise, she didn't move.

"Was that a no?"

Silence.

"You're not sure?"

She cawed.

I sighed. "Fine. I'll do an offering tonight."

She seemed satisfied and flew back out the window.

Fiadh.

Yes?

Is the Morrigan's temple still standing?

I'm not sure. We can fly that way.

We should.

I walked over to the dresser, took Mira's sword and attached it to my belt. I wasn't sure that I *needed* to go to her temple, but it felt like the right thing to do.

I opened the door and was about to step into the hallway when Adriana appeared before me.

"You're making an offering to the Morrigan?"

I looked her up and down and narrowed my eyes. "Are *you* able to communicate with Macha?"

"No." She said quickly. "Cairbre mentioned you asked Fiadh about her temple, and given that tonight is the dark moon I was able to connect the dots."

"Right." I looked her up and down one last time before trying to step around her to walk down the hall.

She stepped in front of me again and blocked my path. "I'd like to go with you, assuming that the temple is still intact and safe."

I rolled my eyes and gestured for her to move. "Fine, but get out of my way. We need to keep searching for Mira."

She smirked. "That's the other thing. I'm going with you today."

"Why?" I glared down at her.

She shrugged. "I haven't really flown much lately and if you find her I'm helping you. Cairbre didn't say no this time."

He might not have, but I wanted to. Mira would still kill me if I put her in harm's way on purpose.

"Fine." I found myself agreeing simply to get her out of my way. She smiled and stepped to the side. I pulled my bedroom door shut as I slipped past her down the hall and she turned to follow me.

*

"Are you alright?" Adriana asked as we walked into the Morrigan's temple. It was somehow still entirely untouched despite the laws banning magic. No one had come to destroy or damage it, though I doubted it was visited often prior to all of this anyway.

I stepped around her when we cleared the threshold and headed toward the altar. "I'm fine."

"You haven't done anything other than fly with the dragons or spar." She quickened her pace until she was walking next to me. "You barely talk to anyone unless it's absolutely necessary. You hardly seem *fine*."

Was this what Mira felt like after she recovered from their last ambush when she wouldn't stop asking if she was alright? It was far more annoying than I expected.

"How *should* I be acting?" I glanced at her when I stopped at the altar. "My *mate* is in the hands of a magic hating sadist, who clearly isn't opposed to torture. I found a puddle of her blood when we tried to go rescue her and it's been two weeks since she was taken. Eleven days since I thought we'd find her."

She looked surprised, like she hadn't expected me to have been counting, or she hadn't expected me to give her an honest reply for once.

"I'm not saying that you should be acting differently." She said, taking a step back to really look at me. "I'm just pointing out that you're *not* fine, but you can talk to me if you need to."

"There's nothing to talk about."

"Bullshit."

I glared at her. "We're here to give the Morrigan an offering. I imagine we shouldn't be arguing in her temple."

She huffed, but crossed her arms. "Fine, but this conversation isn't over."

"It is." I drew Mira's sword and held my hand out over the bowl on the altar. "Do you remember the prayers she said to her?"

"I do."

"Good. We'll both say them." I sliced my palm over the bowl, and let my blood drip down the blade. When I felt like I'd given enough, I removed the blade from my palm and handed it to Adriana.

She did the same, before healing her hand and handing the sword back to me. We both quietly mumbled the prayers Mira would usually say. There were a few seconds of silence afterward and then a gust of wind blew through the space. I looked up to find a cloaked figure shrouded in shadows standing just beyond the altar.

Adriana didn't say anything, nor did she react, which led me to believe she didn't see it.

"You haven't found her yet." Her voice was calm, contemplative. It had an otherworldly tone to it that was unnerving.

"We haven't."

Adriana looked at me now, confused, confirming that she didn't see her.

"You will." She stepped closer to me, until nothing but the altar itself separated us. "She will need you. More than you realize."

"What does that–" She was gone before I could finish my question. What the fuck did that mean?

"You saw her?" Adriana asked immediately. "What did she look like?"

I was still gaping at the empty space in front of me. I shook my head and looked down at her. "I don't know."

"You were looking at *something.*"

"She was cloaked and shrouded in shadow. I couldn't have seen what she looked like if I tried."

Adriana frowned, then turned to walk back outside. "We should get back."

I sighed and followed her out. I wasn't sure why the Morrigan revealed herself to me. The message itself was so cryptic it almost seemed useless, but it gave me the little bit of hope I needed.

The Morrigan was all knowing, said to know everything that would happen from now until the end of time. She said I would find her. I just hoped that when I did, she wouldn't be completely broken.

Chapter 19

Mira

I woke on the cell floor, covered in fresh blood. I had started to occasionally wake before they'd healed me, but it was never long before I was injected with vervain. I was also never conscious enough to make any effort to fight back.

This time, however, I was wide awake. By this point I was numb to the pain from the injuries so long as I didn't move. It was like my body had forgotten how to feel. Footsteps sounded outside of my cell. The same footsteps I'd become accustomed to hearing before the vervain hit again.

I never saw *who* it was, but they were surprisingly gentle as far as I could tell in my barely lucid state. The door opened and they walked into the cell.

Kieran. I recognized his scent. I was surprised I could even pick it up, but I saw my way out. I wasn't sure I could take this any longer. I silently thanked the gods that one of my shoulders had not been shredded this time.

He knelt down next to me and brushed the hair away from my neck to administer the vervain. I flung my eyes open and grabbed his tunic, moving surprisingly fast for how weak I was. I was shocked too, that my grip was as strong as it seemed. It was almost like the vervain was losing its effectiveness.

"I know you have wanted to kill me for months now." I whispered. I barely recognized my own voice, and it was almost painful to speak.

He stared at me in both confusion and pity.

"Stake me." My grip on him faltered, the shred of energy I had summoned to grab him must've been the last my body had left. I searched his face for any indication that he would obey me.

"Please." I begged, desperation leaking its way into my voice.

"I'm sorry," He mumbled with a sincerity that only made me even more desolate. I didn't even flinch when he jabbed me with the needle and injected the vervain. It only took seconds for everything to fade to black as I fell limp onto the stone floor again.

Chapter 20

Deiric

Lazarus and I were sparring, mostly to get some of my anger out. I couldn't seem to keep it under wraps lately given that I *still* wasn't any closer to finding Mira. Lazarus, at least, could keep up with me. None of my men would've.

Macha's loud and angry cawing as she dove down toward the courtyard snapped me out of focus on the fight I was losing myself in. She circled around me, then around Gaisgeach and Fiadh, who were sitting not far from us at the edge of the space.

The raven insists that we fly today. Fiadh glanced my way. *She says that we'll find her and is demanding we follow her.*

"Want to clue the rest of us in on what all the commotion is about?" Teron asked.

I turned to see that everyone else had stopped what they'd been doing too to watch just as I had.

"Macha wants us to follow her. She thinks she can find Mira." Macha dove for me and nearly speared my face with her beak if I hadn't been fast enough to move out of her way. An angry ear piercing screech was her only response.

"I don't think she will take no for an answer." Lazarus observed.

I sheathed my sword and walked toward Fiadh. *Do as the raven says. If anyone can find her it would be Macha.*

Gaisgeach let out a disgruntled snarl, but launched to the sky. Fiadh followed as soon as I found my seat. I prayed that the raven was correct. We'd spent the last three days and nights searching. I finally agreed to give them a day off to rest and now we were going out again.

Macha didn't fly as fast as the dragons could, so our progress was slow even with her going as fast as she was physically capable. After what felt like an eternity, she swooped up, let out a shrill cry, and dove down into the trees.

Gaisgeach and Fiadh followed suit.

She's here. Gaisgeach's relief was palpable, until we got closer and landed.

A man I only vaguely recognized from far above was carrying her. When Fiadh landed and I slid off her back I was horrified by what I saw. An animalistic growl left me before I had the chance to consider what effect that might have on the man holding her.

Kieran. I recognized him now that I was closer. One of the magisters she took the magic from. He flinched backward and nearly dropped her, but I was there to catch her in the blink of an eye.

"I was helping her," He nearly shouted at me, the plea for mercy obvious before he even had to say more. "Please. I was trying to get her out."

I glanced at Gaisgeach, who had landed behind the man, and he huffed hot steam onto the former magister's back.

He jolted forward toward me again. "She's been starved. She could wake up at any moment and she'd likely kill me, but I couldn't let her down there for another day."

Grab him. I demanded of Gaisgeach before I carried her limp body back toward Fiadh. She was alive, thank the gods. Her breathing, however, was shallow and far too slow. Her heartbeat was even weaker.

Fiadh crouched to make it easier for me to climb back onto her with Mira in my arms.

Let's get her home.

Without any further discussion Fiadh flapped her wings and launched us back into the air. I didn't look to confirm whether or not Gaisgeach grabbed Kieran. Nor did I pay attention to whether Macha followed. Part of me didn't even care if Kieran came with us or not, but I had a feeling he'd at least be helpful in figuring out what their plans were, or what had happened to Mira in the time she'd been gone.

I looked down at my mate. She was so broken and battered that she was barely recognizable. One eye was swollen shut and dark bruises covered most of her face and neck. The rest of her was covered in both dried and fresh blood. Her shoulder looked like someone had done a number on it, and her chest was riddled with burns.

What little was left of what she'd been wearing was shredded to bits and barely covered her. I was almost certain I didn't want to know what had been done to her. I didn't think

I would recover from the blood rage it would inevitably cause in me.

I knew one thing for certain. Azazel was going to meet a very untimely and miserable end, along with Ronan, even if it was the last thing I ever did.

When we descended upon the courtyard several minutes later Lazarus, Teron, Leo, Devlon, and Tellus were there to meet us. I should've expected as much, and part of me wanted to thank the gods for it.

I slid off of Fiadh at the same moment that Gaisgeach less than gently placed Kieran on the ground in front of him.

"By the fucking gods." Lazarus breathed, taking in the sight of what was left of Mira.

Teron seemed to be rendered speechless, and I'd never seen the man so pale.

"Kieran apparently got her out." I gestured toward him with my head. "Leo, take him somewhere secure so we can question him later."

Devlon and Tellus mumbled curses under their breath as I walked closer to them.

"She's been starved." I told Lazarus as he came up beside me.

He looked over at Tellus and Devlon. "Do you have anyone… *expendable* in the dungeons?"

"Excuse me?" Devlon gasped.

"Expendable." Teron snapped. "Meaning someone, or multiple someones, that we can let her drink from without caring whether they survive it or not?"

Devlon's face paled, but Tellus nodded. "Several, actually." He glanced between Teron and me. "We have the three men who were trying to find Adriana a few months ago. Do you need more than that?"

"That should be fine." Lazarus answered for both of us.

"I'll arrange to have them all moved to one cell." Tellus turned and headed inside. Devlon quietly and quickly followed him.

"Are you sure that doing this in a cell will be good for her?" Teron mumbled to Lazarus.

"I'm sure that doing it in a cell will be the best to keep her contained if she completely loses her control. I'm more worried about that than her mental stability otherwise at the moment."

"I'm going in with her." I interrupted their quiet discussion as I followed them down to the dungeons.

"I assumed as much." Lazarus pulled a dagger from his bandolier across his chest and handed it to me. "We will guard the door in case she makes it past you."

"I doubt she'll be that out of control." Teron offered, attempting to be at least slightly optimistic.

"She's a fledgling." Lazarus grumbled. "Regardless of the impressive control she's shown thus far, she's never gone this long without feeding. She'd be likely to tear through all of us if she's completely overtaken by bloodlust when she wakes up."

I prayed that he was wrong.

We transcended several halls and staircases before we finally reached the depths of the castle and entered the dungeons. The smell of mildew and other less than pleasant scents overtook us. Tellus had shifted down here ahead of us and shoved the last man into a cell a few meters ahead.

"That's the last one." He motioned for me to carry her in. "Is there anything else you need?"

"Have Leo make sure that the halls are clear to our room, then have him get Xander to stand guard and wait for us."

Tellus eyed me cautiously, his thoughts giving his opinion away, but he nodded and headed in the direction of the other exit to the dungeons that led back to the living areas of the castle. He thought both requests were overkill, but he'd never witnessed a fledgling lost to bloodlust. Even if she regained her composure, I didn't want to run into anyone before I got her cleaned up and confirmed she was in fact mentally stable.

I walked into the cell and Lazarus pulled the door shut behind me as he wished me luck. The men all crowded into the furthest corner of the cell. It was obvious that Tellus hadn't told them why they'd been brought in here. I didn't particularly care to inform them either.

I crossed the room in the blink of an eye and compelled the first one to give me his arm and stay still. This was easier if at least the first one cooperated. The fear and confusion of the others would drive her to feed from them even if her conscience kicked in and said she shouldn't.

I knelt down with her, and he followed suit. I slid the dagger across his forearm, and he hissed in pain. I lifted it to her lips. It didn't take more than a few seconds for her eyes to snap open and for her to take a hold of him instead.

He didn't even cry out, to my surprise. The remaining two men, on the other hand, began to scream and bang on the door to be let out.

Mira was up off the ground now, leaving the first man dead at her feet. She cleared the space between her and the door in the span of a single heartbeat. She grabbed one man's hair and pulled his head back. She ripped into his throat without a shred of remorse.

She tossed him to the side when he was drained and descended upon the last one, who now cowered in a corner and begged for mercy. It was quite something to watch her be so unhinged. She was a beautiful and deadly weapon when she needed to be.

When he finally stopped fighting, and she dropped his lifeless body to the ground she spun to face me. I couldn't read the emotion on her face for a few moments. Not until her eyes returned to their normal violet and her legs seemed to give out on her.

I caught her right before her knees hit the ground. Her arms reflexively wound up around my neck and she melted into me as she sobbed.

"You're safe now." I whispered to her. "It's okay, love."

I continued to murmur reassurances and gently stroked her back as she cried. Nothing I said seemed to console her. Not that I expected it to. Given how she looked when we found her, I couldn't imagine what they'd put her through.

Lazarus, Leo, and Teron came in to pull out the bodies while I held her. When her tears finally seemed to dry up I slid my arm under her knees and lifted her up with me as I stood.

"Let's get you cleaned up." I said softly. She gave me the faintest nod, but continued to cling to me like her life depended on it.

Lazarus opened the door for me again. Teron led the way to our room while Lazarus followed behind. I didn't think at this point that she was a danger to anyone, but we all knew she wouldn't want anyone to see her like this.

Xander opened the door for us as I walked up, giving me a slight nod before closing it behind me. I placed my hand on the wall and set up a ward that would block all sound from both sides. I walked into the adjoined bathroom.

"I'm going to set you down now, love."

She gave me another barely perceptible nod and I slowly lowered her feet to the floor. She released my neck and took a single step back. Her eyes remained lowered, like she couldn't bring herself to lift her head and look up at me.

I stepped around her to undo what was left of the laces on her corset. It dropped to the floor as soon as I loosened it. I spun around, turned on the water, and let it start filling the tub.

When I turned to face her again she'd removed the rest of her clothes. Other than being covered in dirt and blood, most of which I assumed was her own, she had fully healed. Thank the gods.

"Would you like me to stay and help you, or do you want me to step out?" I would never have questioned it before, but she had yet to say a single word to me and I couldn't read her thoughts either.

"Please stay." Her voice was raspy and sounded awful.

I nodded and stepped out of the way. She stepped into the tub and let out a relieved sigh as she lowered herself into the water.

I turned off the faucet and stepped around the tub to begin to work on undoing the mangled braid that still hung behind her back. When I finally had it undone I took the soap and began to wash her hair. While she didn't specifically ask for help, she didn't fight me either.

"Do you want to talk about it?"

"No." Her response was firm and finite. It almost made me not want to ask her anything else.

"Are you alright?"

"No." This time it was softer, like she was almost afraid to say it.

She leaned her head back to rinse out her hair when I asked her to, and otherwise cleaned herself up in silence. When she was finished I grabbed a towel and held it out for her. She stepped out of the tub, took the towel and quickly dried herself off before those beautiful violet eyes met and held mine.

She cleared the space between us, slipped her hands up into my hair and pulled my head down until her lips crashed into mine.

By the gods I missed you. The sound of her voice in my head again was like a gods damned siren song and I had forgotten just how beautiful she sounded.

My arms wrapped around her waist, and I pulled her against me.

I missed you too, love. More than words can even express.

I slid both of my hands into her hair, holding her close to me while I kissed her. She kissed me like she wasn't just starved of blood, but starved of me too. She kissed me like I was the very air she needed to breathe. I returned the same passion, the same need.

She yanked at my leathers, desperate to remove them. I helped her pull them away, and take my tunic up over my head. She kissed down my jaw and my neck. I scooped her up and wrapped her legs around my waist, leaving the towel forgotten on the floor.

Her fangs grazed my neck for a heartbeat before she bit me. The relief and pleasure that flooded me was so sudden it nearly made my knees buckle. I moaned and carried her to the bed.

I leaned down and laid her on the bed. She withdrew her fangs and kissed her way back up my neck until her lips met mine. I pulled away only long enough to remove my pants and then climbed in bed with her, situating myself over her.

I slipped my hand between her thighs and ran my fingers over her. She was already absolutely drenched. Her breath caught when I brushed against her clit.

"I want you. *All* of you, now." She breathed against my lips. "No teasing or taunting."

"You don't have to tell me twice." I could feel her smile as I spoke.

I nudged at her entrance and then slowly, oh so slowly, slid into her. She clawed at my shoulders and let out the most beautiful moan I think I'd ever heard. I had forgotten how good she felt. How well we fit together. And gods, I missed it.

I settled into a steady and slow rhythm, determined to make this last as long as I possibly could. Every little noise she made was like music to my ears. She nipped at my lower lip again, her fangs grazing it as she did so. I moaned and thrust into her harder. I sped up the rhythm as she rocked her hips up to meet mine.

I kissed down her neck, nipping lightly as I went. "Bite me." She breathed. "Please."

I hadn't intended to. I didn't need to feed from her, but I wasn't going to tell her no. I sank my fangs into her neck and she gasped. I could feel her tighten around me, and her moans told me that she was nearing her climax.

It took all of my self-control not to feed from her like I would normally, but I kept slowly and barely drinking as I worked her through her orgasm. She came with my name on her lips, and that was nearly enough to drive me there as well.

Then she moved and spun us so I was lying on my back and she was on top of me. The move was so abrupt that I hadn't expected it and I was left staring up at her with my mouth gaping.

She smiled down at me. "I love you," she breathed before she took over and started to grind her hips on me.

"Fuck." I called out before her lips met mine again.

Easy, love. She thought. *Unless you set up wards to soundproof this room, we wouldn't want anyone else to hear you.*

Gods. I don't know if I ever remember her calling *me* love, but that was so hot. I sat up into her and kissed down her neck again, then her chest. My mouth closed over her nipple and it sent a quake through her whole body.

She was close again already. I could feel it. She pulled at my hair and my hands slid down to her hips. I rocked her hips harder into me until her legs shook. She let out another breathy moan before I dropped back down onto the bed and she followed.

Her fangs sank into my neck again and with each movement she made I rocked my hips up into her. She rode me through her orgasm, with my help, and brought me to my own release as I called out her name.

She collapsed onto me when she withdrew her fangs and we both laid there for a few moments trying to steady our breaths.

"Gods I missed you." She gasped out.

I chuckled and she finally lifted herself off of me to lay next to me. I flipped her around so her back was against my chest and kissed down her neck and shoulder. "I missed you too, love."

We laid like that for a while. Her breathing steadied and slowed. It didn't take her long to doze off.

When I was sure she was completely asleep, I slipped away as quietly as possible. She didn't seem to stir, even while I dressed. I snuck out, nodded at Xander who still stood guard at our door, and headed down the hall.

We were to have a coven meeting today, but I imagined it would be a much larger meeting than it was normally and she didn't need to deal with that right now. Truthfully, I wasn't sure if she *could.* And I wasn't about to let this meeting happen without one of us there. Perhaps this is what the Morrigan meant when she said she'd need me.

When I reached the meeting hall, everyone else was already there. The meeting today was more casual than usual. All of my men were there, Liala, Triss, and Eimear as well. Silas, Elias, and Aris were there too, much to my surprise.

Half of them were standing around or leaning against the wall. Only a handful sat at the large table we usually used. I came a few feet inside the door and just stopped to stand. I wasn't going to be able to sit still and not worry about her waking up while I was out here.

They'd already gotten started with general updates. A few of them acknowledged my presence, but otherwise they kept moving along as though I hadn't walked in at all. I was here to speak for Mira, so they should've waited for me, but I let it slide. She almost never contributed to this part of the meeting anyway.

When they got to Tellus, he filled them all in on what they'd learned Mira had been through. It took all the self-control I had not to explode when I heard the things that sadistic fuck did to her. He also explained that we were holding Kieran here.

When it got to Garrick, he mentioned that they got word public executions were beginning, which tracked with what Kieran had told them. Apparently, the first set was to take place in two days in a town close to Silas' manor. The town I frequented when I used to train his men to compel and read people's minds.

"We shouldn't interfere." Devlon cautioned. "They're undoubtedly going to be on high alert, especially since she escaped. We can't risk anyone to save the handful of lives that will be lost that day."

"Mira's not going to like that." Silas and I said practically in unison.

"She doesn't."

I nearly jumped out of my skin hearing her voice behind me. Several of the others around the table were startled as well. I hadn't heard or scented her approach. I twisted around to see her standing in the threshold now, with one hand against the wall where I guessed she'd been leaning in the shadows just moments before.

She wore a loose fitting floor length indigo gown that tied up behind her neck. Her hair was unbound, and she hadn't even bothered to put on her boots, which told me she hadn't intended to reveal that she followed me down here.

"Mira." Quinn breathed in a voice laced with pity and sorrow. Mira frowned and I watched as she looked around the room and her eyes snagged on a handful of people. When I followed her gaze I saw that Triss, Eimear, and Liala had left their places in the group and were walking toward her.

I turned back to face her, and she waved her hand dismissively. "Do go on." She mumbled. "You were doing just fine without me. Sorry to interrupt." She spun and walked back down the hallway with the three women in tow.

"That doesn't bode well." Silas commented and I turned around to face them all again.

Teron stepped out around Lazarus and headed toward the hallway. I shot him a questioning look and he shrugged. "Apparently I'm being summoned too." He disappeared down the hallway.

Devlon rose from his seat to follow her. "No, it doesn't bode well at all."

I stepped in front of him and blocked the hallway. I didn't know what she was up to, but I didn't want anyone she hadn't asked for following her. "I'll handle it. We should get back to the meeting."

Devlon looked like he might protest, but when he saw the promise of violence in my eyes if he went after her anyway he backed down and returned to his seat at the table. Several of the magisters continued to look after her down the hallway for several minutes with a combination of relief and sorrow on their faces before their focus returned to the task at hand.

Chapter 21

Mira

The moment Deiric moved, I woke up. I didn't move though. I did my best to keep my breathing as even as I could. I'd gotten quite good at that lately anyway. He slipped silently out the door. I immediately got out of bed and began to rummage through the drawers to find any clothes he might've brought here for me.

I settled on a plain floor length dress and pulled it on quickly. When I cracked open the door I was surprised to be met by Xander on the other side.

He jolted and turned to look at me with nothing but concern in his eyes. "Mira," he breathed. "Are you alright?"

I studied him for a few seconds, then looked beyond him and glanced down the hall. "Deiric–"

"There's a coven meeting." He interrupted me quickly. "He assumed you wouldn't be up to attending."

"And you're… guarding me?"

He opened his mouth to reply, but then hesitated after he drew in a breath. "I'm…" his voice trailed off as he glanced to the left to think of a better answer.

"Guarding me." I finished for him when he couldn't seem to come up with anything.

"Yes." He finally reluctantly said.

"Take me to him."

"He'll have my head if I–"

"I just spent the gods know how fucking long chained up in a dungeon. You will take me to him, or *I* will have your head in a fucking second." I snapped, perhaps harsher than I intended, but it got the point across.

He stepped back and gestured for me to go right down the hallway. "Of course."

Shadows pooled out around me, silencing our already quiet footsteps as he led me down corridor after corridor and up two staircases. I started to hear the discussion happening ahead of us and paused just before the light from the meeting room lit up the hallway.

I listened as they went around and gave their updates. Most of which didn't really interest me. They were the same updates I'd heard at the last meeting before I–

Wait. The last meeting was one of the last things I remembered doing before I was taken. *Fuck*. I was gone for nearly a month. Time had lost all meaning. No wonder Deiric had Xander guarding me. I'd been starved and tortured for far longer than I thought.

I was drawn from my spiraling thoughts when someone mentioned that the first execution was finally scheduled to take place.

"We shouldn't interfere." Devlon cautioned. "They're undoubtedly going to be on high alert, especially since she escaped. We can't risk anyone to save the handful of lives that will be lost that day."

My heart nearly seized in my chest. There was no way I would stand by and let people die. Not after what I just went through.

"Mira's not going to like that." Silas and Deiric said practically in unison.

I didn't really have time to process that Silas was also here. I moved before I even thought about what I was doing. The shadows hiding Xander and I from sight dropped and I stepped into the light.

"She doesn't." I mumbled.

Everyone's gaze shot to me, including Deiric who looked like I'd nearly given him a heart attack by emerging and speaking up.

"Mira." Quinn breathed and the sorrow and pity that filled her voice nearly made me want to scream. I didn't need her pity. I glanced around the room, locking eyes with Eimear, Triss, and Liala.

I need your help with something. Could you come with me? I spoke into each of their minds, and they quickly rose to their feet to follow me out of the room.

I waved my hand as I said, "Do go on. You were doing just fine without me. Sorry to interrupt." I spun on my heel and walked back down the hallway with Xander at my side and the rest of them in tow.

I sent a mental message to my father too. I'd need him if I was going to pull off the plan I had. I ignored whatever continued discussion was happening in the meeting room.

"Kieran got me out?" I asked Xander. It was what I had managed to find out from what Tellus was telling them at the meeting. I could have gone without him explaining what all was done to me even if it lacked much detail.

"Yes." The answer came from my father as he caught up with us. "He's being held here."

"Where?" I asked without looking back at him.

"Why?" Xander jumped in again.

"I've got my own questions for him." And I wanted to make sure he didn't share the moment he knew I broke. The moment I begged him to stake me.

He hasn't spoken much about your time in that dungeon, but I know of the moment you're thinking of. Gaisgeach, who had been silent from the moment I woke, finally spoke up. It was such a relief to hear his voice that I nearly stumbled. *He only shared that they tortured you and then healed you to begin the process again. If Deiric knew of that moment, he would be... well, he'd likely demand to go find Azazel now and kill him himself.*

Please don't tell him.

I haven't even told Fiadh.

There was something about him keeping this secret from even Fiadh that made me feel a bit conflicted. I shoved that feeling away to deal with at another time.

"What kind of questions?" My father caught up with me now and walked to my left, while Xander remained on my right.

"Are you going to take me to him or not?" I snarled.

My father glanced at me, his gaze filled with both concern and confusion, but he finally grumbled a yes and led the way.

When we reached the room they were holding him in I was surprised to see it wasn't a cell, but rather just a less extravagant bedroom which was guarded by a mage I had yet to meet.

"We have some questions for him." My father's tone left little room for discussion. The blond mage glanced between my father and me before nodding and stepping to the side.

I pushed open the door and walked in without knocking. In hindsight, that probably wasn't the best idea, but I found him lying, fully clothed, on the still made bed and staring up at the ceiling.

"I was wondering when you'd come by." He said by way of greeting.

"Save it." I snapped. "You drugged me, repeatedly. Was it *just* vervain?"

He pushed himself up, so he was sitting cross legged on the bed. He looked around at everyone who was with me and then finally settled his gaze on me.

"Yes."

"Is there an antidote?"

He glanced at my father, then at Xander, before he once again locked eyes with me.

"Not that I know of no."

"Did you even look for one when you realized it also nullified the magic of *anyone*?"

"No." He shrugged a shoulder. "It just nullifies magic in humans. It only completely disables vampires. Or, in your case dhampirs too."

I mumbled a curse under my breath. "Everyone out." I glanced between Xander and my father. "I need a minute alone with him."

"You can't kill him." The male mage outside the door nearly shouted.

"I'm not going to kill him." I turned around and shot him a glare. "I'm asking for a minute *alone*. I have other questions no one else needs to hear."

To my surprise, everyone obeyed. When the door was shut behind us I erected a small soundproof shield around us.

"How many times?" I snarled through gritted teeth.

"How many times what? Were you healed, tortured, or drugged?"

"All of the above."

"Nineteen, twenty, and twenty five. In that order."

The look on my face must've shown my confusion, because he continued unprompted.

"Toward the end the vervain was wearing off more quickly. I don't know if you were getting used to it, or what was happening, but I had to stand by while they healed you with more just in case."

"How did they find me?" I could've asked Deiric, or even Gaisgeach but I had to hear it from him.

"I couldn't stand by and watch them torture you any longer. I was already bothered by it, but the day you asked me to stake you I couldn't take it anymore. The first moment I could safely get you out after that I took down the guards and carried you out."

"Why?" The question had been burning in me from the moment I heard them explain what had happened in the meeting. It didn't make sense. He had every right to hate me and *want* me to suffer. Hell, he'd had the chance to stake me and didn't take it.

"You weren't going to talk, or you didn't know the answers to the questions he was asking. Contrary to what you might think, I'm not a monster. Yes, at one time I wanted power. I wanted to rule this land and all of the mages in it, but I am not cruel enough to stand by while that sadistic fuck rips you to pieces every gods damned day."

"You held and tortured my father." I snarled at him.

"I can assure you that the inconvenient torture he went through was absolutely nothing in comparison to what that monster did to you. I *clearly* was not trained in real torture. That was barbaric."

I scoffed, hardly convinced, but there wasn't much else for me to say.

"If anyone asks–"

"I won't tell them the final straw that led to me getting you out. You have my word, for whatever that is worth to you."

"Thank you." I lowered the sound shield. "But that's not all."

He raised a brow at me.

"You're going to help us find an antidote, or better yet, a way to prevent the vervain from affecting anyone at all."

He seemed to consider me for a few more moments before the door opened again. "There may not be anything that *will* do that."

"You'll help us search until we've checked every possible herbal combination."

He nodded and I turned to face the door.

"That's what you needed us for?" Liala asked gently.

"Yes. I want the mages involved too."

They all seemed surprised I was already working on this. I had assumed I was dying in that cell after a while, but that didn't mean I didn't make many other plans before I'd given in to my inevitable death.

I pointed at Triss and my father. "I need the two of you for something else though."

They exchanged a look, then followed me as I walked back out of the room and left the mage to guard the door again. I paused a few steps into the hallway when I realized I had no idea how to get back to my room.

Xander, seeming to realize that, stepped in front of me and led the way. At some point, Eimear and Liala branched off from our group. When we reached my room Xander stood outside while Triss and my father walked in with me.

The moment the door was closed I spun around and sat on the bed.

"We're stopping that execution."

"Absolutely not." My father snapped almost as soon as the words left my lips.

"We can't let those people die." Triss interjected for me. She turned to look at me. "What's your plan?"

"He will have to distract Deiric. I'm certain he's not going to let me out of his sight." I gestured to my father.

"You're not going to tell him?" Triss gasped. "He'll be furious."

"He's not going to let me do it."

This is an awful idea. Gaisgeach interjected.

I didn't ask you. I snapped right back.

"We'll have Adriana help. The three of us will sneak into the crowd. When they've got all of the people lined up on the platform, you'll strike every single one of the guards down with lightning."

Triss' face paled. My father, to my surprise, gave me an approving smirk and raised a brow.

"Then we'll shift them all back here and find them somewhere safe to go."

While the idea is impressive, not telling your mate is a recipe for disaster. Gaisgeach sounded proud, but the edge to his voice said that he wasn't going to keep *this* secret from his mate.

You and Fiadh will go with us. We just need to distract Deiric in a way that he won't know what's going on. So convince her not to tell him either.

That's not going to happen.

I guess you've got some decisions to make. So go do that instead of criticizing me or I'll just go without you both.

A disgruntled snarl was the only response he gave me.

The dragon is correct. Macha's voice appeared in my head for the first time since I'd been taken.

I also didn't ask you. I snapped back.

I didn't say it wasn't possible. I think the plan is solid, but not telling your mate will not end well.

I rolled my eyes.

"I assume your dragon is just as horrified by this as I am." Triss observed.

"He's not thrilled, but finds the idea to be solid at least."

"Deiric will kill me for helping you." Triss insisted.

"I won't let him." I looked at my father. "Are you in, or not?"

"I don't like the idea of you putting yourself in danger not even two days after you *finally* escaped their dungeon, but if you're confident the plan will go well then I'll play along. Just make sure he doesn't kill *me* either."

I nodded. "He won't. He won't even know you're involved if you find a solid distraction."

He nodded. "I'll think of something." He turned to leave the room. "I'll let you two discuss the details alone. It's probably better that Deiric doesn't come back here and see *me* with you, or he'll know I was involved."

"Good point."

He slipped out silently, mumbling something to Xander about going down to help with Kieran and the search for an antidote. At least he was already covering his involvement there.

Triss eyed me cautiously. "Are you sure you're–"

"I'm thinking clear enough. I had a *lot* of time to think down there, trust me. If you can produce enough lightning to take them all out, we won't have any issues. I can shift many people without touching them. Adriana can too, and I can promise you she won't want to sit this out. You'll have to tell her the plan though. Deiric will be back–"

The door opened and Deiric slipped into the room. He glanced between us like he couldn't believe we were conversing so calmly without him.

Triss cleared her throat. "Right, well… have a good evening then." She gave me a half smile that was anything but inconspicuous and then quickly left the room.

"Do I want to know what that was about?" Deiric asked.

"No." I answered plainly.

"You're angry." It wasn't a question, yet he raised a brow as he walked across the room toward me.

"You waited until I fell asleep to slip away. Of course I'm angry."

"I'm sorry, love. I didn't think you'd be up for the meeting, and I couldn't just sit it out. I went there to speak for you."

"And yet you allowed them to decide that we weren't going to interfere with the executions." I raised a brow and took on a more accusatory tone with him. Maybe it was too soon, but I *was* angry about that.

He came closer and held my face in his hands as he kneeled before me. "I just got you back. You were *tortured* for weeks. Forgive me if the thought of taking you anywhere but this heavily warded castle is out of the question right now."

I sighed. "Just don't leave me while I'm sleeping again, please."

"Never again, love."

"Could we go outside?"

He blinked in surprise and studied me for a few moments.

"I haven't seen the sun in… well I don't know how long."

Understanding washed over his features, and he stood up. He let his hands fall from my face and held out a hand for me to take to follow him outside. "Of course, love. It's almost dusk though."

"I'd even be happy to see the moon at this point." I mumbled as I let him pull me to my feet and lead me to the door.

He dismissed Xander when we walked out into the hallway and then we made our way through several hallways and staircases before we walked through a door that led into a courtyard.

The crisp evening air nearly took my breath away. I forgot how wonderful it felt mid-summer. The various scents from the garden hit me next. There were roses, violets, orchids, and many others I couldn't identify that smelled just as sweet. Even the simple smell of grass and earth hit me harder than I expected.

The feeling of the sun on my face, even if it was quickly disappearing beyond the horizon, was grounding in a way that I'd never noticed before. I hadn't even realized that I'd stopped until Deiric released my hand and came to stand behind me so I could take it all in.

I also hadn't noticed until I finally looked around us that Lazarus, my father, Zane, and Leo had been out here too. Their conversation must've ceased the moment Deiric opened the door, and they now stood quietly observing us.

Lazarus cleared his throat and then turned to shuffle the others away. They didn't *have* to leave, but I appreciated the privacy all the same. I shifted my attention to the far end of the open courtyard, where Gaisgeach and Fiadh were lying curled up against one another. Their heads rested on the ground while they slept quietly within the safety of the wards.

I committed every single piece of each of them to memory as though I'd never see them again, just as I did with every other aspect of this place. It was so calm and peaceful that it felt odd to stand in it after everything that had happened over the last few weeks.

Deiric was a solid and steady presence behind me, resting one hand on my hip while I watched the sun set. I had begun to notice how much more I felt his emotions along with mine lately, but in this moment he felt just as calm as I was. Like everything had finally fallen back into place again. Like we could breathe without worry for the first time in the gods knew how long.

While I realized that I had several other problems to deal with, I refused to break the peace we had now with talks of what we needed to do tomorrow. I earned just one night of peace before I got back to business again.

Chapter 22

Mira

I woke up the next morning tangled in Deiric's arms. Judging by the light from the small window in our room, it had to be midmorning, but he seemed to still be asleep. I wondered if he even slept during the weeks that I was gone. If I'd been in his shoes I know I wouldn't have. He hadn't appeared exhausted yesterday, but some of that could be hidden if he fed enough.

I had barely moved at all when I heard his breathing shift and knew he'd woken up.

"Good morning, love." His voice was still groggy with sleep.

I rolled so I was facing him and wrapped my arms around his neck. "Good morning."

"How are you feeling?"

I tilted my head up to look at him. "I'm feeling like I'd like to be outside. See the sun again, maybe see if Gaisgeach and Fiadh want to fly."

He huffed a laugh and toyed with my hair. "I have a feeling Gaisgeach and Fiadh would rather have a day off, but I'm sure if you asked they'd be happy to go out with us."

I would rather rest, but I will gladly fly you around for a while if you'd like.

Deiric gave me a look that said 'see' and I just smiled. *If you need a day off, Gaisgeach, I can wait till tomorrow.*

He made a chuffing noise, but didn't reply. I knew why, and I didn't push it. I leaned up and kissed Deiric before I propped myself on my elbow next to him. "I do actually need to collect a few grimoires today."

Deiric narrowed his eyes at me. "For what, exactly?"

"As lavish as this room and I'm sure the rest of this castle is, I'd like to go home."

He looked more concerned now, perhaps even a little frustrated.

"I know there's a much stronger way to ward a manor, or ward anywhere for that matter. I've heard my mother talk about it before." I traced circles on Deiric's chest with my fingers. "I'm wondering if there also might be a way to make a talisman of some kind to prevent any kind of poisoning, like vervain, from affecting someone. I'm sure there's all kinds of things in the old grimoires at Aris' manor."

"One of those was at our manor." He said cautiously. "You can't be suggesting going back there now."

"No." I said quickly. "I already know that one doesn't have what I need, but there are lots of others at Aris' manor that would probably have what I'm looking for."

He sighed. "If you insist."

"I insist on getting back to normal as soon as possible. I'll even join in on some sparring today, if they'll have me."

I could tell he wanted to say no. He wanted to tell me to take a few days. I wouldn't be taking a few days. I spent three weeks lying on the floor of a cell or getting ripped to shreds by a fucking maniac. I wasn't going to lay around more and be unhelpful while people were literally dying by the hands of our new fucked up king.

Something in my eyes must have told him as such, or maybe he heard my thoughts, but either way he shrugged. "Fine." He grumbled. "We should get up and get dressed then. I'm sure we could even find someone willing to let you feed from them at Aris' manor too."

I almost began to protest before Gaisgeach snarled at me. *You are weak and still too thin. You will feed on whoever decides to let you. You may be unbreakable, but you are not invincible.*

"You know better than to disobey a dragon." Deiric smiled over his shoulder while he put on his fighting leathers.

I slowly rose from the bed and made my way to the other dresser and rummaged through it to find a pair of leathers for myself.

*

After we collected the grimoires we returned to the castle and I insisted that we spar. Lazarus, Leo, Renwick, Zane, Xander, and my father were all already sparring in the courtyard that Deiric took me to last night. Gaisgeach and Fiadh were sunning themselves in the far corners of the open gardens. I was still surprised there was even enough space for them to lay out like they were without smashing anything.

Gaisgeach shot me a withering look. Fiadh seemed entertained by that thought. My attention shifted back to Lazarus and my father when they stopped sparring to look over at us.

"Mira." Lazarus looked at me cautiously. "Shouldn't you be… resting?"

I opened my mouth to reply, but Deiric did before I had the chance. "She asked to spar."

Lazarus shot him a less than amused look. My father didn't seem to be bothered by my presence, but just watched me warily, like he still wasn't sure how to interact with me. I wanted to assure him I wasn't as fragile as I'm sure they all thought, but no one was going to listen to me. Honestly, I wouldn't listen to me. They were right, but I wouldn't admit it.

Lazarus' gaze shifted back to me. "Are you sure you're feeling alright enough to spar?" Gaisgeach snarled. Lazarus glanced over his shoulder at him, but apparently took the hint. "Sorry." He muttered. "I just wanted to be sure."

"I'm fine." I drew my sword. "Everyone can also stop answering *for* me." I shot both Gaisgeach and Deiric a glare. "I'm perfectly capable of answering for myself."

"She's sparring with *me*," Deiric said, placing his hand on the small of my back and guiding me over to the open space closer to Gaisgeach and Fiadh. I knew the look on his face conveyed that he was going to take it easy on me, and that was the only reason that Lazarus dropped it and went back to sparring with my father. Still, that irked me.

You know I'm perfectly capable of sparring with any of them. I snarled at Deiric.

I don't actually. He said gently. *You were locked up for three weeks, Mira. Whether you fed and regained your strength or not, you were literally torn apart repeatedly and are out of practice.*

And I will continue to be out of practice if you don't stop scolding me and start sparring with me. I pointed out as I lowered into a fighting stance and spun my sword. As reluctant as I was to admit it, it did feel oddly foreign in my hand at the moment.

Deiric sighed, and lunged at me. He swung his sword at my side. I blocked him without much effort. He spun and swung for my other side, forcing me to jump backwards to dodge his blade. Normally, I could've blocked that.

He arched a brow as if to say, 'I told you so', but I swung at him now. I just had to find my flow again. Get used to the weight of the blade again. *Yes*, I had lost a good bit of weight, and with it a fair amount of muscle, but I wasn't completely helpless.

We continued for several minutes. He would swing for me, and I would block or dodge. It was far from my best. I could feel the others watching occasionally. Especially Lazarus and my father.

Don't worry about them, love. Deiric thought, as I swung for him again and he blocked with his usual ease. *Just focus on me.*

I'm focusing on you. I snapped. I wasn't frustrated with him. I was frustrated with myself.

Deiric was taking it easy on me, far more than I thought he would. I knew it. If he came at me with everything he had right now he'd either actually cut me or he'd have disarmed me already. The thought of that had me trying even harder.

He returned my newfound determination with a little more effort of his own. I barely kept up with his advances as he backed me toward the courtyard wall. I was at least *stopping* each of his blows, even though I was losing ground.

He threw in a couple of quick movements that had my back actually hitting the wall, then he knocked my sword off to the right, grabbed my wrist and held it above my head while he rested his sword arm across my chest.

The sudden move left me pinned, and the panic that rose up within me was like nothing I'd ever experienced. The magic that flew out of me was all reflex, rather than a real thought out blow.

Deiric went flying backward, taking a hard hit to the chest with a burst of shadow magic that I wasn't even totally in control of. He bounced and rolled halfway across the courtyard, while his sword ended up skittering across the ground toward Lazarus.

I dropped my own sword and fell to my hands and knees. My breathing was quick and shallow as the panic consumed me. I rocked back on my heels and lifted my trembling hands from the ground.

Deiric was there a second later.

"I– I'm so–"

"I'm sorry." He said quickly, interrupting my attempted apology. "I shouldn't have pushed you."

He pulled me into his arms and murmured several other reassurances, reminding me to breathe as the panic attack took over.

Chapter 23

Adriana

I came outside to check on Mira. Triss told me she was sparring with Deiric, despite that she thought that was an absurd idea. I had yet to see her since she returned yesterday and I was desperate to make sure she was alright. They wouldn't tell me what had happened to her, but Cairbre told me he knew she was tortured and in very rough shape when Deiric found her.

When I walked into the courtyard I found Lazarus and Teron watching while she and Deiric sparred. She wasn't keeping up with Deiric's advances like she used to and that alone spoke volumes.

Gaisgeach and Fiadh watched them move toward the courtyard wall. Mira was responding more violently to Deiric's advances. Perhaps that was a good thing. I didn't know what someone might need after an experience like that, but getting back to 'normal' seemed like a good idea.

Then she hit the wall and exploded. I'd never seen her react in such a way to an advancing attack. But then again, when they sparred with swords instead of magic she was never allowed to use her magic. This was all reaction, with no real thought to how the magic was thrown.

Deiric went tumbling back nearly halfway across the courtyard and took a few seconds to pick himself up. She'd knocked the wind out of him and I didn't miss the few minor wounds he'd sustained in that short burst of movement.

Mira had fallen to the ground, and she was shaking like a leaf that was moments from falling in the wind. Deiric was back in front of her in seconds and began to comfort her, but she was almost inconsolable.

Watching the most powerful woman I'd ever met break like that fractured something in me that I couldn't even explain.

"I knew it was too soon." Lazarus mumbled as he turned to walk back inside.

"Try telling her that." Teron commented as he watched the two of them with more than a little bit of pity on his face. "She's far too stubborn to be told no."

"You're telling me." Lazarus commented as he walked through the door back into the castle. Teron watched for a few more seconds before he too disappeared back into the castle.

I couldn't leave. Couldn't take my eyes off of the two of them until she seemed to calm down enough that she could breathe normally again. It felt like I was violating her privacy by watching, but I couldn't bring myself to look away. I had to make sure she was alright.

Deiric helped her to her feet, collected both of their swords and guided her toward me and the door that led back inside. She was too lost in her own turmoil to notice I was standing there even as they walked right past me. Deiric gave me a knowing look, but then walked right past me, pulling her along with him.

What did they do to her? I found myself asking Cairbre.

I was not privy to the details. Gaisgeach knows everything, but all he would share was that she was tortured. Even Fiadh knows nothing more than that. I've asked.

That proved to me how bad it was, that even my dragon was concerned. I doubted they usually concerned themselves with anyone but their own riders, but this was… different somehow. She was the most powerful among us. It didn't look all that great if the most powerful rider was a shattered shell of herself.

I need to find out. I wasn't going to be brushed to the side while the 'adults' knew what had happened. Some of them saw her when she arrived. Even just that alone meant they knew more about what had been done to her than I would. And I knew they would never tell me. They were protecting me.

You're still quite young, Adriana. Cairbre pointed out. *They'll try to shelter you from the worst parts of the world until you're at least an adult.*

They can't shelter me forever. If I'm going to be a queen I need to know everything.

I'm not saying you're wrong, but you're going to have a hard time telling them that.

I scoffed, then marched back into the castle myself.

Deiric would want to know what happened to her, and I was certain he didn't know everything yet. He could compel Kieran to talk. I just needed to find a way to pull him away from Mira long enough to go talk to the bastard.

That bastard got her out. Cairbre reminded me.

At what cost? He waited far too long.

His responding chuff told me he no longer disagreed with my name for the man.

*

I waited in the hallway for far longer than I probably should have, but eventually Deiric emerged from their room *alone*. Thank the gods. He glanced left and then right, when his eyes landed on me.

"Can I help you?" His voice had an edge to it that told me he would absolutely remove me from the hallway if he thought I was looking for Mira.

"Actually yes." I motioned for him to follow me further down the hallway.

I was surprised when he glanced at the door behind him, but actually listened and walked toward me. I turned and walked down the hall in the direction of the stairs that would take us to where Kieran was being held. Teron had told me his location earlier when I pinned him down.

"I want you to compel Kieran to answer all of my questions." I said confidently after we were far enough away from their door.

"Excuse me?" He sputtered, glancing at me like he hardly recognized me and was surprised I was trying to give him an order.

"You heard me correctly. I'm tired of being left in the dark. I want to know precisely what happened to her. It'll help me decide what to *do* with my father when we inevitably catch up with him."

I could see the incredulous look on his face out of the corner of my eye, but I kept walking down the hall and didn't give him the time of day to look his way and acknowledge it.

"I don't think you actually want to know." He finally mumbled, but kept following me anyway.

"You do though. I'm not stupid."

A disgruntled snarl left his lips, but he didn't reply otherwise.

"See." I shrugged a shoulder. "So you're going to go down there with me and compel him to tell me everything."

"Something tells me this isn't really going to be as helpful as you think."

I turned and headed down the stairs. He followed just a step behind me.

"Maybe not, but if anything it will at least help us understand why she's *that* broken." I took a few more steps in silence before I stopped at the bottom and turned to face him. "I saw what happened in the courtyard. Torture is one thing, I'm sure, but she's been shattered and barely pieced back together. I suspect it's far worse than any of us thought."

He stopped one step above me and frowned down at me. "You didn't see her when I found her, Adriana." He shook his head. "I can assure you that I'm already aware of just how bad it likely was."

"Regardless." I spun on my heel and turned down the hallway Kieran was being held in. "You're still following me, which means you don't plan on telling me no."

He was silent aside from the sound of his footsteps as he kept pace with me. This certainly wasn't going to be pleasant, but at least then I'd have a better understanding of what she went through and maybe, just *maybe*, that would help me help her.

I stopped in front of James; the blond mage I'd met a few times while wandering around the castle. He offered me a half smile.

"Can I help you princess?" He insisted on calling me princess, which bothered me to no end, but his flirting and general polite company was a welcome change so I let it slide.

"We're here to talk to Kieran." I gestured to Deiric behind me.

His gaze shifted between the two of us before he finally shook his head. "I'm not sure what else there is to ask–"

"Step aside." Deiric demanded. His tone left no room for discussion.

James startled a little, but nodded and stepped out of the way. I reached forward, spun the knob and stepped into the space.

"You know, you all could knock." Kieran grumbled and looked up from the book he was reading. He was sitting with his back against the wall and his legs spread out across the bed in front of him. "I swear no one here has any understanding of boundaries and basic manners."

"Enough." Deiric snarled. "Adriana would like to ask you some questions. I'm just here to make sure you answer them."

Kieran looked at him with a raised brow. He closed the book, sat it beside him and then pushed himself forward until he was sitting right at the edge of the bed.

"And what exactly are you going to do to make sure I *do* answer them?"

Deiric was in front of him before I could reply. He leaned down so they were eye to eye.

"You're going to answer all her questions, and do everything she asks of you. Is that clear?"

Kieran, seemingly in a bit of a daze, nodded. Deiric moved to the side and motioned for me to get on with it. Kieran blinked and shook his head. I heard him mumble a curse under his breath, but ignored it.

"I'd like to *see* what happened down there. Were you involved in her torture or involved in holding her?"

He swallowed, but nodded.

"What role did you play?"

"At first, not much at all, but when we relocated her to another dungeon with far more wards and safeguards in place I was in charge of drugging her after every torture session."

I raised a brow, but he stopped talking. He technically did answer my question, so at least the compulsion is working.

"Show me." I held out my hand to him. The request was obvious. I wanted to *see* his memories. While he didn't have the magic to share them anymore, I could use mine to peruse them. It was a trick that Mira had taught me not long before she decided I'd mastered my magic. At the time, I didn't understand what the need would be for it. Now I was thankful I had learned.

He eyed my hand cautiously. "Are you sure–"

"Yes." I demanded before he could finish his question. I held out my hand to Deiric. "And I'm going to share it with him too."

He swallowed nervously again, but then reached out and took my hand.

"How much do you want to see?"

"All of it." I looked him over. "Every single memory you have of her time with them."

He cringed, and I wasn't sure why, but then he opened his mind up to me and the memories flashed in front of my eyes like a horrifying dream that I couldn't walk away from.

I watched the day of her attempted escape when she walked directly into Ronan's outstretched dagger, then fell to the floor. They scooped her up and took her to the secondary location and chained her up while she was still unconscious and bleeding.

The next thing I saw was her being woken up for the first interrogation. She was feral, her fangs on full display and nothing but fiery resolve to fight them at every turn. Even just the first few blows had me wishing I could stop watching, but it only got worse.

Then I watched as Kieran drugged her and the process started again… and again… and again. With each passing session she got less fiery. She stopped fighting altogether. Then Azazel mentioned Deiric, and she barely moved. She hung limp from the wall while he talked. The only noises she made toward the end were screams or grunts in pain that she wasn't strong enough to stifle anymore.

I watched one final time as he walked in to drug her. This time, she lurched forward and grabbed ahold of him. She begged him to stake her. To end her suffering. Why she thought he would help her was beyond me, but it was this memory where he finally made a move to get her out.

He still drugged her, but when he stepped out the door and saw the healers weren't there, he knocked out both guards, unlocked the shackles, and carried her out. The memory faded when the dragons slammed down in front of and behind him.

I yanked my hand from his and gasped, the full weight of what I'd seen nearly sending me to the bathroom to puke. Deiric was as pale as a ghost. His expression was contorted in horror, and he couldn't seem to lift his gaze from the floor in front of him.

"I couldn't leave her in there. I had wanted to end it long before that day, but I hadn't had the chance. I saw the opportunity and I took it. I don't know how much longer she would've lasted." He shook his head. "She never broke though. She refused to talk no matter what he did."

"She broke." Deiric's voice was barely audible. "She just didn't break in the way that they hoped she would." He turned and walked toward the door. "Unless you have more questions for him, I'd like to get back to Mira."

I shook my head and turned to leave with him. "I don't want to know anything else."

I told you it wasn't good. There was a reason they weren't telling you. Cairbre grumbled.

He wasn't wrong.

.

Chapter 24

Mira

I jolted upright gasping for air. I thanked the gods that it was only a nightmare, but of all the nightmares I'd experienced in my lifetime, this one was hands down the worst so far. Deiric didn't immediately jump up with me, but I knew I'd woken him.

I slipped out of bed before he could say anything and shut myself in the bathroom. I didn't *want* to be alone, but he'd already comforted me through one panic attack in the last twenty four hours. I didn't need him to lose sleep helping me through this too.

I turned on the sink and splashed cold water on my face, as though that would wash away the horrifying images that I couldn't get out of my mind. Or like it might push away the pain and misery I felt down to my very bones. It didn't work, but after several minutes of holding onto the counter for dear life I finally got myself calmed down and my breathing under control.

I opened the door and tiptoed back into the bedroom, hoping that maybe Deiric had fallen back asleep. When I slipped under the sheets next to him he pulled me back against his chest.

"Do you want to talk about it?" His breath tickled my neck in a way that *shouldn't* have sent shivers down my spine, but it did.

"No." I breathed, fully relaxing back into him.

"How can I help?" He whispered and gently kissed the side of my neck.

I sighed and angled my head away to give him better access to my neck. "I could use a distraction."

He hummed a low growl and moved so I was lying on my back with him looming over me. "Do you want a distraction, or a reminder of just how thoroughly you deserve to be worshiped like the goddess you are."

He trailed his fangs down the column of my throat, and I traced my hands down his chest. My breath left me in a gasp when he nipped the base of my neck.

"The second option." I barely managed to breathe when he continued moving down my body and stopped for a moment to suck on and bite my breast. I let out a gasp and soft moan. He knew precisely how to get me going, and it never took much.

With pleasure. He hummed into my mind. He continued to kiss his way down until he settled himself between my legs and smiled up at me.

The first stroke of his tongue set me on fire. His hum of delight reverberated through me as he fully descended upon me and devoured me with a fervor that left me desperately gripping at the sheets and calling out his name far sooner than I even thought possible.

He sent me rolling from one orgasm to the next. Between his teeth, his tongue, and his fingers. I lost track of the number of times he sent me over the edge.

When his lips finally met mine once more I flipped us over before he could stop me. I straddled him and brought my hand to his throat, holding his jaw firmly while I kissed my way down his neck.

I'm supposed to be worshipping you. He said breathlessly. *This is not–*

I sank my fangs into his neck and his protest was cut short, replaced by a moan that set my soul on fire instead. His hands left my hair and slid down my body. One cupped my breast and massaged it while the other found its way to my ass.

I lowered myself onto him slowly, and his breathy moan told me I had him entirely at my mercy.

Mira. He breathed into my mind.

Shhhh. I cooed. *It's my turn now.*

I moved my hips in a rhythm that I knew would drive him mad. He mumbled a curse, desperate to move his hips in a way that would meet mine and push him toward the pleasure he so desperately craved.

Unfortunately for me, the pace I set quickly brought me to the precipice of pleasure again, and his assistance sent me flying over the edge before I could reign myself in.

He chuckled darkly as he flipped us again and took over. I withdrew my fangs from his neck and met his lips with mine again.

You just can't control yourself can you.

Fuck you. I gasped, and his smile against my lips was telling.

You already are, love.

His lips left mine and trailed down my face to my jaw, then my neck. He settled the heel of his palm below my jawline, forcing my face up and allowing him free access to my neck without putting any pressure on it.

His fangs sank into me and I arched my back into him as pleasure pulsed through me.

That's my girl. He crooned, and that alone sent me over the edge again. My nails dug into his back as he kept up a pace that left me writhing and moaning with pleasure until he reached his own climax and we collapsed onto the bed together, breathless and euphoric.

"I love you." I said softly, burrowing my head into the crook of his neck as he held me close.

He sighed softly and gave me a light squeeze. "Love is too simple of a word to describe how I feel about you." He began to run his fingers through my hair and held me so I couldn't pull back to look up at him.

"You are the anchor that keeps me grounded. The very axis that my world spins around. The other half of my soul. I couldn't imagine living in a world without you in it. Don't ever forget that, love."

He let me pull away to look up at him and rested his forehead against mine. "I will spend every day for the rest of our immortal lives proving that to you."

I didn't have the words to eloquently explain my feelings for him at that moment. I wasn't sure I ever would. He seemed to understand that and mumbled, "I know," before he shifted so my head was resting against his chest and he held me until I fell into a dreamless and peaceful sleep again.

Chapter 25

Mira

Deiric and I woke very late the following morning, which felt odd given that we'd once kept such a consistent schedule. Everything felt odd now though. I couldn't figure out what normal was anymore. My body itself felt entirely foreign at times, which I assumed was because of the weight and muscle I'd lost while rotting on the cell floor.

By the time my father knocked on our door, it was nearly time for the executions to begin. I knew that my father's distraction wouldn't last long, so I had done my best to keep Deiric distracted and with me until I couldn't anymore. It seemed without me saying so my father had noticed my part of the plan and played along.

I was finishing my braid when Deiric opened the door.

"Forgive the intrusion," my father began rather formally. "Silas needs to speak with you." He met Deiric's gaze with an unwavering determination that said he wasn't going to take no for an answer.

"Silas?" Deiric questioned. I saw him glance at me out of the corner of my eye. "What could Silas possibly need? He was just here two days ago."

My father shrugged. I tied off my braid and walked up behind Deiric. I rested my hand on the small of his back while I peered around him at my father.

"I don't know what he wants, but he said it was important."

Deiric muttered several curses under his breath, then looked over at me.

"I'll be fine. Go ahead." I urged him.

He looked more suspicious than anything. He opened his mouth presumably to suggest I went with him, but I cut him off.

"I need to help Triss, Liala, and Eimear. Go and deal with whatever Silas wants. I'll be fine."

It was like everything in him demanded he not leave my side, despite his willingness to do so just last evening when he needed to check in with Leo. Triss appeared right on time, standing just to the left of the door a few steps from my father.

"She'll be with me." She smiled, glancing between us. "Go deal with the uptight prick and we'll research some herbs with the mages." She even started to shoo him with her hands. "I promise to look after her, though I seriously doubt she needs it."

Guilt welled up within me as he finally relented and followed my father down the hall. I'd felt the guilt even last night when he professed his love for me, but this was even worse. I hoped he'd forgive me.

"Come on." Triss said when she was sure he was far enough away. "I have Adriana just down the hall. We're running out of time."

This is still an awful idea. Gaisgeach's voice was very quiet in my head. He was already flying close to the town we were going to shift to, which was a significant distance from here.

I'm not denying that.

It will take time, but he will *forgive you.* Fiadh's equally soft voice came through now. Gaisgeach must have filled her in. I was certain that she wasn't privy to my every thought.

She's not. He confirmed before I could worry too much about that.

"Alright." I grabbed my cloak, flung it around my shoulders, and shut the bedroom door behind me. "Let's go."

*

Triss had very carefully crafted the enchantments for each of us, and we'd all very thoroughly discussed the plan, as well as any of our backup plans. We would slip into the crowd, evaluate the situation, and then make our move.

We all wandered into the chaos of the crowd that had gathered from various different locations outside of the town. I was relieved to find I was correct in my assumption that there'd be plenty of people eager to watch this spectacle. We were not the only cloaked figures, especially with the light rain that was falling.

Are you in place? I checked in with Gaisgeach, just to be sure.

Yes. Hovering above the clouds and keeping an eye on things. Bless Gaisgeach and his enhanced sight. He could watch us from just about anywhere.

I slowly made my way to the front of the crowd while the women and men were led onto the platform. They were soaked through their clothes, which told me they'd likely been out here in the weather for some time.

Several of them had bruises and marks all over what I could see of their skin like they'd been stoned or beaten. My money was on the former. Their faces were concealed with burlap sacks for the moment. None looked familiar to me by clothing or body type.

Adriana, are you in place? I spoke into her mind.

Almost. Her response was distant. We hadn't practiced mind speaking much. All mages were capable but it wasn't often utilized.

Triss? Are you ready?

Waiting for your mark.

The burlap sacks were removed, and it was then that just a few meters ahead of me a little girl started shrieking and crying. I'd thought I'd heard a faint cry moments ago, but didn't think much of it. A woman on the wooden platform was also near sobbing as the noose was placed around her neck. Something about her felt familiar.

I looked back at the child, and it hit me. It was the little girl I'd shown my magic to in that tavern months ago. Her mother wasn't even a witch, let alone a mage, and yet she was on this gods damned platform with a noose around her neck. It was then that I confirmed I'd absolutely made the right decision by intervening.

Ronan and Azazel were not here. I would have scented them if they had been. This was just a public execution, one they didn't need to travel for. The first of many, I was sure.

I moved closer to the sobbing little girl. She appeared to be entirely alone, like no one could bother to care for her after her mother had been taken. She looked like she'd spent a few days on the street too. I forced myself to look back at the lineup. They'd just finished putting the final noose around the last man's neck.

Now Triss.

Lightning streaked across the sky. I had to shut my eyes against the light that filled the square. She'd hit her marks. Every last one of them. When the light dissipated, and the crackle of thunder shook the ground all of the guards were dead.

I scooped the child up into my arms and we all shifted back to the castle, directly into the meeting room, where I knew we'd have enough space to hold everyone. Triss was right next to me.

The people who'd been seconds from execution were lined up in front of us, with Adriana at the far end of the line. Deiric, my father, and Silas stood near the hall leading out of the room. The same hall I'd listened in on the meeting from.

Tellus and Elias were quietly chatting in the corner across from Deiric and the others. Everyone stopped their chatter and turned to face us as soon as we appeared.

I removed the ring from my finger so that my enchantment would drop and they could see who I was. I felt Deiric's rage as well as the betrayal. He spun on my father and Silas and I *knew* I had to get over there or he might very well decide to kill them. He'd been suspicious earlier. He knew something wasn't right and now he knew precisely what that was.

I sat the girl on the ground and shifted before I could confirm she was heading for her mother. I was in front of Deiric just as he was about to snarl at them and undoubtedly say something he'd regret.

"Deiric." I cautioned, but he didn't look down at me.

"You *knew*." He growled. I didn't miss the fact that Silas actually took a step back behind me. I grabbed him and shifted us to our bedroom. This was not a meltdown he should have with an audience and it surely was not a discussion *I* wanted to have an audience for either.

When we were alone his gaze finally fell to me and the weight of the anger and betrayal hit me like a blow to the chest.

"They *knew*. They *lied* to me."

"Because I asked them to." I said carefully, not removing my hands from his biceps, thinking that just that small touch might be enough to ground him.

"You could have *died*." He snarled, but his voice had a broken and pained edge to it. "They *let* you leave the safety of this gods forsaken castle and for *what*? A handful of mages you saved from death?"

"A handful of innocent humans and mages alike."

That single fact managed to ebb some of his rage, though it was fleeting. "What?" He sputtered.

"Do you recall the woman and the small child we ran into months ago? You were teaching Alastor–"

"Yes, I remember them." He snapped, the anger returning in full force.

"Then you should recall that neither held any magic what-so-ever. They were both glaringly *human*."

"I fail to see how that is relevant–"

I cut him off again before he could finish his thought, since we were both in the habit of interrupting each other now. "The woman was one of the people on the platform to be executed. If I hadn't intervened they wouldn't have just killed mages. They would've killed *humans* too and left a child an orphan."

He blinked at me, which was the only evidence of his surprise.

"I'm sorry." I said quietly, stepping closer to him and cupping my hands around either side of his face. "I'm so fucking sorry that I didn't tell you, but you never would've allowed me to leave and I couldn't just stand by and allow this to happen." I paused, searching his face for any flicker of forgiveness before I continued.

"I hated not telling you. I hated having to drag my father into this to help me, but I knew he would listen to me, and do as I asked, for no reason other than that he's desperate to rekindle a relationship with me and he has been beaten into submission with questioning me lately."

And there it was, a flicker of acknowledgement that I was telling him the truth, and the realization that he knew I couldn't have lived with myself if this had happened, and I didn't intervene. It wasn't forgiveness, but it was at least understanding.

I rose up onto my toes and gently brushed my lips against his in the shadow of a kiss before I rested my forehead on his.

"I am so sorry, but please don't take it out on Silas and my father. My father hated the idea and I'm sure Silas was not all that thrilled to go along with it. I didn't even know he was involved until this morning."

Deiric was silent for several moments, before he finally sighed heavily and placed his hands on my hips.

"You could've been killed, or worse."

"I know." I said before he could say anything else. "I knew the risks, but I went anyway."

"If I lost you…" His voice trailed off.

"I know." I whispered. "I'm sorry."

"You've said that nearly five times now. It doesn't make it any better." He lifted his head and rested his chin atop mine while he pulled me in closer to him. I slid my arms around his neck.

"You're going to make a habit of this, aren't you?" He sounded defeated, perhaps even a little depressed, but at least the rage was gone. Though the betrayal he was feeling still stung.

"I won't keep it from you again if you'll at least allow me to do it."

"You will not be going without me." His tone left no room for argument, but there wasn't any argument in me. Not after I already felt guilty before we'd even begun the charade this morning.

"We need to get back." I said softly, pulling away and instead resting my hands on his chest. "They'll need to figure out what to do with all of the people we just rescued, and I'm sure that they'll want an explanation."

He just nodded and I shifted us back to where we'd been when we left. To my surprise, Silas and my father were still standing just behind me.

Chapter 26

Deiric

"I assume by the fact that you're back here that he's not going to kill us?" Silas mused, though I didn't miss the slight hesitation in his tone.

Mira didn't respond to him and merely slipped quietly around me to head back over toward where I could hear Triss and Adriana trying to organize everyone with Tellus. Elias walked over to us now.

"I'd still like to kill you for lying to me." I hoped I said it quietly enough that Mira didn't hear me, although something told me I was wrong. I turned and stepped to the side, so I was standing next to Silas and observing the chaos that ensued behind me.

"She knew you wouldn't go along with it." Teron whispered. "I wasn't exactly given much choice in my involvement."

"So I've heard." I shot him a glare, but returned my focus to the people surrounding my mate, none of whom I had any trust in at the moment.

I quickly identified the woman we'd both seen in that tavern months ago. The little girl that had approached Mira was less than a step behind her and practically clinging to her leg.

The woman threw her arms around Mira in a hug, which immediately left Mira going as stiff as a board and freezing in place. Despite recognizing that it wasn't a threat, Mira didn't soften until the woman finally released her, murmuring her appreciation the entire time.

"Is she alright?" Silas asked almost too quietly for me to hear.

"No." I replied quickly and sharply. "Not even remotely, but she'd like to act as though she is."

"I figured as much." He observed her nearly as closely as I did. "Did you ever get details about what happened to her from Kieran? Other than the vague details they shared in the meeting, I mean."

I shuddered, wholly unable to keep that in as I recalled the memories that Adriana had played back for me from the bastard still held in a bedroom a few halls and floors away.

"Unfortunately." I muttered.

"I haven't seen much that could affect you so obviously." Silas commented, a hint of pity in his voice. "I'm not sure I want to know, in that case."

"You don't." My response once again was clipped and devoid of all emotion. It took everything I had in me to keep myself from snapping at him. While I expected no loyalty from Teron, I would've at least liked to think Silas wouldn't have gone behind my back to help her hide something like this from me.

I gathered by Tellus' tone with Mira that he was not thrilled, but Triss stepped in and handled it far better than I would've expected. It was a situation that Mira normally would've handled herself, but she seemed content for someone else to lead the conversation.

Once there was some direction and Tellus had control of the situation, Mira walked to the far wall of the meeting room and began to walk down the stairs that led outside. I followed her without even thinking twice about it.

I saw the shift in her mood. The moment that she realized she was far too overwhelmed to remain in the room. I didn't understand why she didn't shift away, but I didn't take the time to think of reasons as I followed her outside.

It was pouring now, far more so than it had been earlier in the morning. She was already a bit wet, though her cloak was doing at least a half decent job of keeping her dry underneath it.

She pushed through the doors a handful of steps ahead of me and walked right out into the rain without a care in the world about it. I followed her through the door, but hesitated under the small section of the wall that stuck out far enough to prevent the rain from falling on me.

Her hood was down, but she didn't bother to put it back on her head. She tilted her head back and closed her eyes as she looked toward the sky. A soft sigh escaped her, and she stood there silently like the rain might wash away all of the incredibly twisted up emotions I could feel from her.

I knew she knew I was with her, but she made no effort to acknowledge me. It reminded me of the time I'd found her lying on the ground outside staring at the moon and I suddenly felt like I was intruding.

I have no reason to think she's bothered by your presence. Fiadh's voice fluttered into my mind. I didn't know where they were today, but I imagined laying in the open courtyard in the rain was not on their list of favorite activities.

And you would know? I asked hesitantly. Fiadh was not privy to her emotions or thoughts like Gaisgeach would be.

He's been keeping a close eye on her, whether it is obvious or not to her. She's calm now.

I'm not sure calm is how I'd describe what I'm feeling from her.

One can be calm while still brimming with a million emotions. Calmness is a state of mind. You can ground yourself to return to a sense of calm while you process the emotions at war within yourself. That's precisely what your mate is doing. One does not simply brush off trauma like what she's experienced in a matter of days.

I understand that. My tone was a little more defensive than I intended, but Fiadh didn't give me any indication it offended her. *I just wish I knew how to help her, and wish she didn't feel obligated to hide things from me.*

I imagine she felt like she was protecting you. You wouldn't have allowed her to go, and the lack of interference on her part would've eaten her alive. She's too fragile to give herself any more reason to fall apart.

I had forgotten how much I appreciated her wisdom at times. Even if it didn't help the emotions *I* was struggling with. I was still upset with her, but the part of me that worried about her outweighed that.

I stepped out into the rain and walked up behind her.

"Would you like some company, or would you rather be alone?" I gently placed my hand on her left hip, resting on her completely soaked cloak.

She didn't open her eyes, nor did she look my way. She took a deep breath, then stepped closer to me. Her right hand slipped out of her cloak, found mine, and she intertwined our fingers.

It didn't take long for the rain to soak completely through my leathers, but I would have stood with her there until the world ended if she'd wanted me to.

Chapter 27

Mira

I stood in the rain until I was frozen to my very bones. The cold, generally, didn't affect me as much since I'd turned, but that immunity only went so far. After an absurdly hot soak in the tub, which Deiric inevitably joined me for, I made my way down to the rather large library Solas had in this castle.

I had never appreciated its size. We'd come here numerous times for meetings, and a handful of other times when we brought prisoners here, but I had never paid much attention to the halls we walked down or the rooms that branched off of them. It was excessive in its extravagance, but that was something I absolutely took for granted at the moment.

The study was the perfect place to review some of the grimoires I found, and Tellus had assured me that they'd be safe in this room. He had his librarian secure an entire section just for us and had someone ensure that the grimoires from our coven were entirely off limits to anyone else who might browse the library during our time here.

Deiric had told me he would meet me down here, so I sat with Adriana in companionable silence while the two of us were reading and reviewing various resources. In her case, she was reviewing another large book of herbs. I had other motives though. In addition to finding the spell for a different form of warding, I also wanted a curse.

This was not a fact I shared with anyone. Not yet.

Deiric snuck up behind me and slipped his arm around me as he sat down next to me.

"Finding what you're looking for?" He asked, reading over my shoulder while he sat a steaming cup of tea on the table next to the large leather bound book. "Fuck's sake." He leaned in. "That's… barbaric."

The grimoire I was sifting through now was very old, probably older than Lazarus, actually. I nearly laughed at the thought. This was *truly* dark magic as well as blood magic. This sort of thing involved sacrifices in some cases.

I was reading through a hex, which traditionally were some of the darkest castings we would do. They weren't exactly outlawed, but they also weren't really acceptable anymore either.

"I suppose it is." I mumbled dismissively as I turned the page. "I'll bet that the original spell that created vampires is in here somewhere."

"And you're reviewing this for what again?"

I shrugged. "A more powerful ward. Something that will keep *everyone* out but those that I allow in."

"Wouldn't that be problematic for teaching new mages?"

"No. There are ways to allow people in."

"You know that and yet you don't know the spell?"

I shot him a withering look and he shrunk back slightly into his seat.

"I'm just asking if you've *seen* the spell before, or if it's something you heard of. If you know enough about it that you could describe it to me I could help you look."

I snorted, then looked back at the grimoire in front of me. "And miss out on reviewing all these spells?" I skimmed over the one on the page now, which turned the unfortunate soul it was cast on into a cat. "This one could prove useful. You never know."

Deiric leaned in again, read it, and then muttered a curse under his breath. "Remind me to never piss you off."

I smiled and flipped the page. "You could never piss me off enough that I'd need one of these spells, I assure you." I raised a brow and glanced at him before I reviewed the next page. "I do, however, have a lot planned for our least favorite shadow wielder and I'm sure that will only get worse when I reach the end of this grimoire."

"In that case," he reached over to grab another grimoire from the pile next to us. "I'll look at this one and bookmark the worst ones I find."

I didn't miss his attempt to be both helpful and humorous, as though he felt he needed to lighten the mood. I had already looked through the one he grabbed, but it didn't hurt to have an extra set of eyes, and I found myself far too curious to see what he might find to be worse than what I'd already been reading in this one.

"Mira?" I looked up to see Adriana had spun around in her chair to look at us. "I think I found something."

I marked my place in the grimoire with a blank shred of paper and then both Deiric and I walked over to where Adriana sat.

"Have you *tried* any remedies?" She looked up at us when we reached the table.

"No." I leaned in so I could read over her shoulder. "I was the only one it would have really been used on at that time, and we didn't have time to work through a bunch of testing before we had to fight Solas."

She pointed to an herb on the page. "Mugwort." She mumbled. "It is claimed to both prevent and counteract poisoning." I skimmed the paragraph over her shoulder while she spoke. "It's not a talisman, like you hoped, but it is something. We can test it with the mages tomorrow."

"Good. That's something. We'll keep looking for a talisman or some kind of protection though. Something tells me we'll need it."

She nodded and went back to reviewing the book. Deiric and I walked over to sit down with the grimoire I'd been reviewing again.

"So, you're experimenting on the mages?"

I glanced at him, and he looked more than a little concerned. "Sort of, yes. But they are willing volunteers, and I won't give them enough vervain to harm them." I opened the grimoire again. "Or, I guess I should say *Triss* won't give them enough to harm them."

"That will only block their magic though. How will you know what would help us, or you, for that matter?" He asked while he flipped the page in the grimoire he was looking at. He not so subtly pushed the mug he'd brought closer to me.

I glanced at the mug, then back to the pages in front of me. "I'll have to *experiment* on your men at some point too."

"*Our* men." He corrected me.

"Right." I mumbled and turned the page again. I was sure I could find something worse, but subtle to cast on Azazel. I needed something that wouldn't be obvious and would torture him over time. I *wanted* to take my time with him for all the misery he put me through.

A few quiet minutes passed before Deiric's hand brushed against the small of my back. "Do you not want the tea, love?"

I pulled my attention from the curse I was getting hopeful about and lifted my gaze to meet his. "If it's the same tea you gave me before all this happened, I'm not so sure it's going to help."

All it had done before was help me sleep and calm me. I didn't know that was really what I needed anymore.

"It can't hurt." He offered; his concern written all over his face.

I supposed he was right, although it didn't make me anymore eager to drink it. It *might* help prevent some of the nightmares. I knew he expected them. I wasn't sure *why* he'd suddenly seemed even more attentive and protective than when he'd first found me, but something had changed.

I hadn't the slightest idea what though.

*

Deiric and I ended up at the same table the following afternoon doing precisely the same thing. He had spent every single minute with me since I'd snuck off to stop the executions with the exception of when he slipped away to get me tea yesterday.

He spent the morning working with me on sparring in a much less brutal way. I was immensely thankful for his patience while we worked through several sets of the same movements to help me retrain my body into the motions I had done so fluidly before.

It still felt awkward. Yes, I had the supernatural strength that came with our immortality, but that was not nearly the same as having the muscle memory and *real* muscle to back up that strength. My father avoided assisting, I assumed because he couldn't help himself with coaching and didn't want to break the fragile foundation we were rebuilding our relationship on.

Now I found myself staring at yet another grimoire, but this one was not full of curses. It was full of helpful spells and wards. They varied greatly in effectiveness and power. None of what I'd read so far would have been any better than the wards we had before.

"Is this it?" Deiric asked, practically shoving the grimoire he was reading over to me.

I pushed the one I had out of the way and pulled his over. He sounded far too excited for it to be nothing, and I hadn't given him nearly enough credit with finding a suitable curse last night.

I skimmed through the ingredient list, then read the details of the ward. It was *exactly* what I'd remembered someone describing to me. A ward bound by the blood of the homeowners, or in this case, all of the vampires that lived there.

It was perfect. Down to the inclusion of a handful of keys to allow others to enter. There was of course the concern that one of those could fall into the wrong hands, but I was confident that we'd be able to make that work.

It was not something that one could just *break* like Azazel had done with our previous wards. No one could merely walk through it, and when done correctly it was probably the most solid warding we had at our disposal.

"This is *exactly* what I wanted." I smiled and lifted my gaze to his.

He looked far more hopeful than I think I'd seen him since I'd come home. It was an excitement that I didn't even realize either of us were capable of. I couldn't help but be a little bit thrilled that he was the one who found it. My very vague description hadn't given him much to go on, but it was enough, apparently.

"The full moon is this Friday, is it not?" I asked, starting to stand from the table to get Triss and confirm we'd have the ingredients necessary.

"It is." He raised a brow and watched as I started to walk away from the table. "You can't mean to do this that soon, can you?"

"Is there any reason to wait?" I halted mid-step and turned to face him again. Triss was just a few shelves over, but it felt inappropriate to shout in the library.

"I could think of several." He stood and stepped over the bench. "I just don't see the rush to get back is all. We're perfectly safe here."

"This isn't *home*." I said too quietly for anyone but him to hear. "I want to go *home*."

He sighed and walked up until he was directly in front of me. He cupped my face with his hand. "We don't even know what's left of *home*. We haven't gone back since you were taken."

"Gaisgeach has flown over and confirmed the manor is still standing."

The corner of his mouth turned down in the hint of a frown. I didn't understand why *he* was so insistent that we stay here. Yes, it was safe, but it was still unfamiliar, and I got lost several times already in the handful of times I'd attempted to wander off on my own. I felt like I was trapped in a maze.

"And what if we go to set up the ward and the inside of the manor is in shambles?" He traced his thumb over my cheek.

"Then we'll fix it." I said simply, trying to ignore how desperately he searched my face for any shred of doubt. He wouldn't find it. I was fully committed to going home, no matter what it took to get there.

He closed his eyes, leaned his forehead against mine, and let out a soft sigh. "You're impossible, love."

"Give me one good reason we can't go home if we have a strong enough ward in place." I demanded, defiantly fighting against the idea of staying here for any longer than was absolutely necessary. Something about the far too generous hospitality Solas was extending to us just didn't feel right to me.

He was silent. I could tell he was desperately trying to come up with something he would convince me with and falling short. "I don't know." He finally mumbled.

"Good. Then we'll move forward with setting up the wards and we can go home."

He finally opened his eyes and there was a hint of amusement in them despite his best attempts to hide it under a mask of frustration.

"At least you haven't lost your will to fight, I suppose." He released my face and walked back toward the grimoire. "Go find Triss. I'll mark the page and set this one aside."

"Thank you." I said softly, and darted off to give Triss the good news.

Chapter 28

Mira

Silas and Aris met us at the castle Friday evening, completing the group that would go with me to create the wards. I didn't fully explain this process to Adriana, but told her she was to stay where she was safe until the ward was in place.

They wanted *her,* not me and I couldn't risk her by taking her with us while the wards were down. She wasn't thrilled, but Cairbre agreed with me. While I was arguably just as important as she was, we needed her more.

Silas and Aris were a little bit annoyed at being summoned without much explanation, but waited with everyone else while I gathered all of my supplies and the grimoire to do the spell.

I shifted the twelve of us to the manor after confirming with Gaisgeach and Fiadh that there didn't appear to be anyone there. I was more surprised to find the place in one piece and not torn to bits from a search than to discover it was in fact empty. It stood to reason that we wouldn't have left any indication for where we went in a book or in our dresser drawers, but it still seemed odd. Even the horses were left in their field, entirely untouched and seemingly absolutely fine thanks to the summer grass and stream that ran through their pasture.

I walked into the dining room to find the shattered glass from my drink that day still scattered on the floor. The food that had been prepared sat on the counters, molding and rotting with how much time had passed. I hesitated in the doorway. Deiric was beside me almost instantly and placed a reassuring hand on my back.

I took a deep breath and then gestured for everyone to follow me into the dining room. I didn't look back to see if they followed as I sat my supplies down and lit a few candles to illuminate the space.

"This ward will prevent anyone who isn't blood bound to it from entering without a key." They all filed into the space and looked at me expectantly. "These crystals will become the keys. You're all here because you'll be blood bound to it."

Eimear looked around, then settled her gaze on me. "I'm the only witch here. Did you intend to only make this blood bound to vampires and have me help you with the spell?"

"No." She raised a brow. "You'll be blood bound to it too." I shrugged a shoulder and flipped open the grimoire in front of me. "Call it a gut feeling." I glanced behind her at Renwick, then back to her, before I waved my hand to summon one of our cauldrons from the back room.

"I'll be right back." I shifted to the side of the mountain close to the manor where I knew edelweiss grew. I pulled the plant out entirely, including the roots. It was oddly convenient timing, if I was honest. The spell required me to pull this out on the Friday of the full moon, and tonight *was* a full moon. If that wasn't a sign that this was the right thing to do, I wasn't sure what was. When I shifted back to the manor there was a spark of annoyance in Deiric's eyes. I hadn't even thought of taking him with me, but I should've at least told him, I supposed.

I wrapped the edelweiss in a white cloth and placed that into the cauldron first, leaving the extra fabric laying over the edge of the top of the cauldron for when I would burn the mixture later. The next ingredient was mugwort, which I tossed into the cauldron after grinding it into a fine powder.

I repeated that process with the garlic and sprinkled that in. The last ingredient the spell called for was vervain. One of the down sides of *being* a vampire now was that I couldn't handle the vervain without it burning me.

I had Triss collect some and put it into a cup for me, which I had carefully covered with a piece of cloth and twine. I pulled the cloth and twine away before pouring the vervain into the cauldron. The spell also called for our blood. Each person who would be permitted entry needed to bleed into the cauldron. I, however, really wanted to give this spell a nice kick. I had a small satchel of chili pepper seeds which I tossed in as well.

I drew my sword now. I could have used a dagger, but using the sword that was blessed by the Morrigan just felt right. I needed all the extra backup I could get. I sliced the blade across my palm and held it there until I was satisfied with the amount of blood I'd contributed. I looked up from the cauldron at the group before me.

"Who would like to go next?"

Deiric stepped forward without hesitation, took the blade from me, drew my sword over his palm, and bled into the cauldron until I nodded. Silas stepped forward next. He had been surprisingly quiet outside of his mumbled complaints at being summoned so soon *again*. Eimear was the last to step forward and was still a bit confused and apprehensive as to her participation.

I stirred the blood and herbs, with the exception of the whole plant wrapped in cloth, with the seven iron stakes that I brought to act as the perimeter of the ward. Finally, I took the thirteen quartz crystals I collected to be our keys for others to enter and dropped them into the cauldron.

I held my hands over it and began to mutter the enchantments from the grimoire.

Chapter 29

Deiric

I watched her do a handful of spells since we met, and had watched several other witches and mages over the years do many as well, but nothing was quite as detailed and intense as this seemed to be. Everyone stood around her silently while she focused and mumbled the enchantments.

She finished one sentence, and I noticed her take a sharp intake of breath as though something had startled her. The room began to darken, like the night itself had swept in early. The few candles she lit barely illuminated her workspace and left most of the rest of the room in shadow. She was speaking in a language none of us understood now.

Her eyes and tattoos seemed to begin to glow, and a dark aura built around her. It resembled a cloak, but seemed to be made of shadows that whirled and spun around her.

It took me longer than it should have to recognize that energy. It was the same one I felt when I'd done my offering to the Morrigan. It seemed odd and out of the blue that she would suddenly be helpful, but she had made a deal with Mira that related to shielding, so I assumed maybe this was just an extension of that.

The white cloth hanging over the edge of the cauldron caught fire, and the candles seemed to burn brighter, higher, and hotter the more she spoke in that unfamiliar language. The caws of several ravens echoed around the exterior of the manor.

None of us dared to speak. We didn't want to break her concentration, but I heard the sound of several of them shuffling behind me. Their thoughts all raced, and it was hard to pick them apart to hear each of them individually.

Mira drew her hands up, and the stakes floated out of the cauldron with them. They were still dripping blood when she splayed her fingers out and they flew outward toward where she'd decided the boundaries would be. The magic that took them through the walls without causing damage was both incredible and unnerving.

The cauldron burst into flames then, larger and brighter than just the burning of the cloth, and the entire room went black. It was like the sun and moon both suddenly ceased to exist. While the sun had been setting when she began, I knew we hadn't been standing here long enough for it to have fully set before she completed the spell.

As quickly as the darkness came, it dissipated as though it had never been, leaving blood red crystals as the only items remaining in the cauldron.

Mira's legs seemed to buckle, and her arms flung toward the table. I was there to catch her before she crumbled, though she did manage to catch herself on the table with her hands at least.

"Fuck." She breathed. While she seemed to steady herself on her feet once more, I didn't release my gentle hold on her waist.

"What the *fuck* was that?" Teron asked. Mira lifted her gaze to him with a smile that unnerved even me.

"*That* was an extra twist to the spell thanks to the Morrigan. These crystals will let others come within the perimeter, but if they mean us any harm, they'll just spontaneously combust."

"They'll *what?"* Silas' face was ghostly pale, like he himself had to worry that would happen to him.

Mira laughed. "They'll just," she wiggled her fingers, "poof. Burst into flames and burn until they're nothing but ash." She seemed far too excited about that detail, but I couldn't say I blamed her. Still, something about her seemed darker since she came back.

"Fuck's sake." Silas breathed.

Mira shrugged. "It's effective." She grabbed a crystal and tossed it to Silas. He caught it, but held it like it was going to explode in his hand. "Keep that safe. Give it to Elias, or whoever you intend to use to shift you here if you need us." She picked up another and tossed it to Aris who caught it similarly to Silas. "Same goes for you."

"How exactly are they supposed to wear them?" Silas asked.

Mira shrugged once more. "However makes sense. Put it on a string, make it into a bracelet or necklace, it doesn't matter really. If they take it off while they're within the perimeter though, they'll just get teleported out."

She waved her hand, and the now empty cauldron disappeared. "To the outside world, this manor essentially doesn't exist. People will walk up to it and then walk around it without knowing why. You won't even be able to see it from outside of the warding."

"Why don't more of the manors implement this?" Zane asked.

Mira looked his way. "Because it would be a royal pain in the ass to do this for a manor that wasn't run by vampires. In case you forgot, all other members of our coven *will* die eventually. They'd have to refresh this kind of spell far more often than would be deemed practical."

"Right." Zane mumbled.

"I'll shift you all back to the castle to collect your things." Mira mumbled.

"Are you sure you should–" I started, but she cut me off with a glare.

"I'm fine. It was just more than I was expecting."

I shot her an unconvinced look and she just rolled her eyes and grumbled something under her breath that even I couldn't hear or decipher.

She shifted everyone before I could protest again. She swayed on her feet.

"You are in no condition to shift us back tonight. We can go home *tomorrow*."

She spun toward me, which resulted in her almost falling over. It didn't ebb the fire in her eyes though as she snarled at me. "I did *not* put up the ward to sleep here for one more gods damned night."

"If you like living, I'd suggest you let her do what she wants." Teron suggested with a slight smirk as he walked past us toward the hallway that led to his room. "She doesn't seem like she's going to take no for an answer today."

"Best of luck with that." Silas added with a smirk before Elias shifted both him and Aris away.

I met her gaze once more and that unfaltering stubbornness rose up behind it. "Look," I started, searching her face for any chance I might be able to talk her out of this. "If you absolutely *insist* on going back tonight, at least let someone else shift everyone there, including us?"

She opened her mouth to protest, but I stopped her with a quick kiss. "Please, love. You don't need to burn yourself out, and I know that you're going to fight me if I demand you feed to replenish your strength before we leave so just let Triss shift us."

She searched my face for a few moments and, presumably, not finding what she was hoping for she sighed and relented.

"Fine." She grumbled. She tried to pull from my grip to walk toward our room.

I slipped my arm around her waist while I spun around to walk us toward the same hallway Teron had just disappeared down. Everyone else dispersed slowly, either walking ahead of us or falling in line behind us.

"I'm perfectly capable of walking on my own." Her voice was barely audible even to me.

"I'm aware, but you don't need to."

When we finally walked through the door to our room and were alone, I let her go.

"You don't have to tend to my every need you know." She said softly while she walked far too slowly to the dresser that held the small amount of clothing I'd brought for her. "I'm sure you're still upset with me for lying to you earlier this week and you've been through your own version of hell this past month."

I walked toward the dresser with my things, grabbed my satchel, and began to pack them up.

"I have, but that doesn't mean I can just stop worrying about you."

"And yet I've done nothing for you."

I stopped and turned to look at her. She was staring down at the dresser, her hand stopped midway through putting one of her dresses in her satchel. She looked like she might cry, which was so at odds with the borderline feral look in her eye not even ten minutes ago.

"You don't need to do *anything* for me." I mumbled, shifting my attention back to the task at hand. "I can handle myself just fine."

The soft sound of rustling fabric told me she'd begun to do the same.

"You deserve to have someone that is just as willing to care for you as you are for them. I've hardly even considered what you might've been through until now. I'm not sure why. It feels selfish."

I stopped abruptly and turned to face her again. She was still quietly filling her satchel.

"Mira." I said softly, walking over to brush my hand against her shoulder gently while she stuffed the last piece of clothing into her pack. "You were literally ripped to shreds for a sadist's entertainment. I was driven mad with worry, but the two situations are hardly the same. You shouldn't worry yourself with *my* emotions right now."

She turned to face me and did not look convinced, but conceded the fight just as quickly as she'd started it. I knew she wouldn't have the energy to push much, but even this was unusual for her.

"I'm sorry."

I moved my hand from her shoulder to her cheek. "You have nothing to be sorry for, love."

"I'm sorry for not telling you about my plans the other day. Whether you feel I need to apologize for anything else, I absolutely need to apologize for that."

"You've already done so," I glanced away in a show of thinking it over. "Probably about a dozen times already, actually." I offered her a small smile. "I've also already forgiven you at least a handful of times as well."

She opened her mouth to speak again, but was interrupted by a knock on the door. I sighed, dropped my hand from her cheek and returned to my dresser to toss the last two items into my satchel.

Mira answered the door. Triss stood in the hallway with a pack strung over her shoulder.

"Lazarus mentioned that you would need me to shift the two of you home. He also mentioned that I needed to get crystals to the mages and get one for myself if I wanted to be able to even get to the manor." She looked Mira up and down expectantly.

Mira opened the small leather pouch on her belt and handed over enough crystals for the mages and Triss.

"I haven't crafted them into a necklace or bracelet yet, but all they need to do is keep this on them somehow. We can work on crafting them into a necklace one by one at a later time. I have extras."

Triss raised a brow. "I imagine we'll need to do *something* immediately because I'm sure they won't be able to keep them on them in their sleep otherwise."

Mira appeared surprised. It was odd for her to have not thought the entire plan through, but given the events of the evening she likely had forgotten.

"Right." She said softly. "We can work on that as soon as we get home."

Triss eyed her carefully. "I will have the mages work on it when we get there. You look like hell."

Mira scoffed, but it was halfhearted. "Gee, thanks."

"It's just the truth." Triss shrugged a shoulder dismissively. "Give me a moment to pass these out and then I'll come to collect you."

She turned and walked down the hallway.

Mira sighed as I walked up beside her and urged her out the door.

"I can't believe I forgot that."

"It wasn't like you had time." I reasoned, then slipped my arms around her waist and pulled her closer to me. "I am sure you didn't anticipate the Morrigan swooping in and pulling all of your energy out of you."

She slipped her arms up and around my neck, then rested her head on my chest. "I suppose you're right."

Triss appeared next to us. "Right, well then. Let's get on with it." She grumbled, and shifted us to the foyer of our manor. "The others will be here momentarily."

She wrinkled her nose and turned to face the dining room. "Gods, that smells rancid." She spun back to face us. "You couldn't have at least cleaned up the mess while you were creating the wards?"

"She didn't exactly have the chance." I snarled at her. She looked like she might be sick, which felt like overkill given that not even any of us had been so bothered by it.

"Right." She grumbled, pinching her nose between her fingers. "I'll take care of it." She waved her hand at me. "Go take her to bed. She looks like she's about to fall asleep on her feet."

Mira lifted her head briefly to shoot a glare at Triss as she walked away. I scooped her up into my arms and started to walk toward the stairs.

"I absolutely can walk to our room myself." Mira protested.

I smirked. "I'm sure you can love, but I'm going to carry you anyway."

She let out a disgruntled growl, which I promptly ignored as I walked into our bedroom and placed her gently on the bed. I pulled the satchel off her shoulder and placed it back on her dresser.

"We can worry about these later." I walked over and shut the door. I wasn't sure if the sound shield she'd put up was still around the room, so I also took the time to put up a new one with *my* magic just to be safe.

When I returned to the bedside, Mira was already curled up on the bed and seemed to have dozed off. I carefully removed her boots, untied the corset and loosened it, and then set to work removing my own boots and leathers before I crawled into bed beside her.

Feeding would've been the smarter decision, but I didn't have the heart to wake her to demand she feed instead of sleep. She would be fine to feed in the morning, or whenever she woke up. There was absolutely nothing that would make me pull her out of an obviously peaceful sleep when she rarely had the pleasure of that.

Chapter 30

Mira

I groaned and rubbed my face as a monster of a headache hit me the moment I woke up. It was dark in the room, which told me it was probably the middle of the night. Deiric moved his arm up toward my face.

"I didn't have the heart to wake you to insist that you feed, but you're not going to get rid of that headache until you do." He mumbled, his voice a bit groggy with sleep.

I felt guilty for waking him, then for worrying him *again*. His patience seemed to know no bounds.

"I could just go back to sleep and sleep it off." I offered, although I wasn't sure I *could* sleep with the throbbing in my head.

"You won't, though." He whispered, his lips barely grazing the back of my neck. "And if you're planning to, you should at least take off your corset and dress."

I begrudgingly took his offered arm and brought his wrist to my lips. He didn't shift closer to me when I bit him, nor did he seem to react much at all, which was unusual. I drank just until the headache seemed to dissipate, then released him and moved to get out of bed and take off my clothes.

"You didn't take nearly enough." He grumbled, but did not rise from the bed.

"I'm fine." I insisted, letting my corset drop to the floor and pushing my dress down to follow it. "You're acting like a mother hen."

He scoffed and gave me a mocking look. "Most mother hens actually don't care much about their chicks once they've hatched, so I'm not sure that insult fits."

"Hmm." I hummed and climbed back into bed with him. I rested my head on the pillow and smiled at him. "A mother bear then?"

He cracked a smile. "At least you haven't lost your humor." His gaze darted around my face for a few seconds like he was memorizing the look. "I was starting to worry you had there for a second."

The concern was clear in his eyes, even though the smile still lingered on his face. I had to look away. I hated that everyone had that look lately. Pity, or concern, whatever it fell under. I was broken, likely beyond repair, but that didn't mean I wanted everyone to look at me that way.

I thought I'd shielded my thoughts from him, but it seemed like he heard it, because he pulled me into his arms.

"I'm sorry, love. I just don't know how to help you and I can *feel* how miserable you are."

"You didn't seem to notice my emotions at first. What's changed?" It was a dumb question, I suppose, because I felt his too, more and more each day, but I had to ask.

"There isn't really a 'guide to mated vampires' I can read up on to understand. I just assumed the longer we're together and mated the more connected we'd become."

It is the same for dragons. Gaisgeach's voice was quiet, but I could tell he'd spoken to both of us.

"I guess that answers that." I could hear the slight smile in Deiric's voice. "Get some sleep."

I slipped my arm around his waist, nuzzled my face into the crook of his neck, and took in a deep breath. Breathing in the scent of him. The scent of home. I didn't think anything else could help me fall asleep faster.

*

When I woke again it had to be midday. I was still securely in Deiric's arms, with his chin resting on the top of my head. He was gently running his fingers through my hair while I slept, and seemed like he'd been awake a while.

"You didn't have to lay here until I finally woke up." I mumbled a little bit apologetically.

"You didn't seem to appreciate the last time I slipped away while you were sleeping. I didn't think it would be wise to repeat that."

I'd forgotten that I scolded him the last time he'd done that. Part of me was glad I had. I wasn't sure how I'd feel waking up here alone.

"Thank you."

He pulled away so he could look down at me. "You don't need to thank me for lying with you while you sleep.

It's not like it is a difficult task. I quite enjoy it actually." He smirked. "And it's adorable when you snore."

I jabbed him in the stomach and laughed. "I do *not* snore."

You absolutely do. Macha's voice made me jump and look toward the window. She was perched on the sill. I hadn't heard her land, so I wondered how long she'd been sitting there.

Not long. She turned her head toward me. *Just checking in.* She hopped around and flew back out the window.

"She appeared less than a minute before you woke up. I assume she knew, which is odd, but I didn't question it until you woke up."

I looked back at Deiric, and he had the slightest smile still lingering on his face.

"Anything important?"

I shook my head. "She was just checking in, apparently."

He huffed a laugh. "I didn't realize she cared so much." He glanced over his shoulder, then back at me. "She wasn't terribly helpful with finding you until the day I brought you home."

"Something tells me she knows far more than she lets on sometimes. Or she's just as much at the Morrigan's mercy as I am."

I suspect it's a little bit of both. Gaisgeach grumbled. *I don't like her much.*

Macha didn't deign to respond, though I didn't entirely expect her to.

Deiric gently squeezed my shoulder. "You do need to *actually* feed today. We can have Triss shift you to Aris' manor and see if he has someone there."

I shot him a glare and he smirked.

"You can't get nearly enough from just me. And even if I told you to, you wouldn't listen anyway." He traced his fingers down my arm. "I'm tempted to just have her shift us back to the dungeons under that castle and see who else Tellus feels like sacrificing, but I imagine you're not interested in that."

I frowned and shook my head. "I think we pushed their limits enough on that already." It wasn't that I had a problem with that in and of itself, but I didn't want to ruin what we had going with Solas by gorging myself on their prisoners.

"Then Aris' manor it is." He leaned in, pressed a quick and gentle kiss to my lips before he rolled away and stood from the bed. I followed suit slowly and dug out another dress and corset.

When we reached the bottom of the stairs I grumbled that I could shift us there myself, which earned me a hefty glare from Deiric as he stepped around the handrail to head toward the dining room.

"This isn't negotiable." He mumbled, then kept walking as if I hadn't said a word.

I had half a mind to do so anyway, but something told me that going on my own would likely be an awful idea.

Triss nearly collided with Deiric on her way out of the dining room, but managed to sidestep and avoid the collision at the same time as him. She gave him a look that could've killed him, but then shifted her attention to me.

"You look like hell." She blurted, before she could think the better of it.

"Thanks." I grumbled and stepped up so that I was next to Deiric, because as much as I hated him for suggesting I have *someone else* shift me, I had to acknowledge I absolutely did not feel like myself. I hadn't really since I'd come back. It seemed like I was continuously pushing the limits of what I was capable of lately.

"I was looking for you actually–" Deiric started, but Triss grabbed my wrist and pulled me along behind her.

"What the hell?" I nearly shouted. I didn't have the chance to brace myself against her, even though I absolutely should've, and found myself getting drug down the hallway toward one of the storage rooms we rarely used.

She yanked me in and was seconds from locking the door before Deiric pushed his way in as well.

"What on earth do you think you're doing?" He snarled at her. He yanked her hand off of me and, given her visible wince, I assumed he wasn't gentle about it at all and forgot his own strength. He released her almost immediately, but she snapped right back at him.

"Your mate is fucking famished. Unless you intend to find someone to feed her perhaps you should keep your fucking hands to yourself and let me help her."

He looked like he wanted to throttle her, but then he stumbled back a step and stared at her in disbelief, torn between ripping her head off and quiet confusion at what she'd said.

"Yes." She stepped up to him, stood taller and was nearly chest to chest with him. "I noticed. Hell, I'm sure half the fucking *manor* would've noticed if you'd gotten any further into the dining room." She gestured toward me.

"She's as pale as a fucking ghost with bags under her eyes that make her look *ill*."

"No fucking shit." He snarled. "I hadn't noticed." Irritated sarcasm dripped from his voice like venom. "I–"

"I don't care." Triss snapped, cutting him off before he could finish explaining himself. She spun to face me and I flinched back a step at the look in her eyes. "*You* are going to drink from me and *you*," she turned and pointed a threatening finger at Deiric, "are going to make sure she doesn't kill me. Understood?"

Deiric nodded, then she turned back to face me with a raised brow.

"I–"

"No isn't an answer I'm going to accept." She lifted her wrist and offered it out to me. "I'm certain I can take it. Normally, I would trust you not to kill me on your own, but right now I don't know what to think of you. If he hadn't stumbled in here I'd just have resorted to magic, but he's here, so he can hold you back."

I almost started to protest again, but before I got the chance she pulled one of Deiric's daggers from the strap across his chest and slid it across her outstretched wrist.

"Triss!" Deiric scolded, but that was all it took.

I cleared the space between us in less than a second and had taken her arm in my hands to feed. My instincts took over, and I barely even registered what I was doing.

She hissed when my fangs hit their mark, but relaxed and let out a shaky sigh when the venom from my bite overwhelmed her senses.

I felt Deiric behind me then. He had one hand firmly resting on my hip, and the other on my opposite shoulder.

Triss stumbled into me, sandwiching me between the two of them.

I heard Deiric softly say my name in warning, but it was so far away I was unsure if it really was him behind me. Triss seemed to tug weakly at her arm, and then there was a piercing pain in my head.

I released her and flung my hands up to grab at my hair as though that would stop the stabbing pain felt in every part of me. I stumbled backward into what I could only assume was Deiric.

Triss' mumbled curses only made the pain worse. When it finally subsided the sweet, yet metallic scent of her blood had dissipated, with the exception of the handful of drops that had reached the floor before I seized her arm.

"I told you to make sure she didn't kill me." Triss sounded like she was faint.

"I didn't want to rip her off of your arm." Deiric had a solid grip on me now, with one arm wrapped around my waist and the other across my chest, below my raised arms. I still clutched at my head as though the pain might resurface.

Triss scoffed, then I heard the door open and close.

I could've killed her, I realized, far too slowly. *She* stopped me, and if she hadn't she'd be dead. Because of me.

"It's alright, love." Deiric soothed, as my mind began to spiral and I collapsed back into him. "I wouldn't have let you kill her."

"You didn't stop me." I breathed.

"I would have, but she had it handled."

"I've never lost control before." I covered my face with my hands now. He spun me around in his arms, so I was facing him. "Gods." I mumbled. "I could've killed her and I didn't even know what I was doing."

"You are in survival mode." He said softly. He hooked one finger under my chin to lift my head so I would look at him.

I let my hands fall away, but did nothing to hide the grief from my expression. "I could have killed her."

He cupped my face in his hands now and gently brushed his thumb across my cheek. "You've never lost control before because you'd never been starved. You *were* starved. Now your instincts are in overdrive to prevent that from happening again. It's why you killed all three of the men we presented you with when you woke. You aren't going to have the control you had before. Not right away."

"And you wanted me to go to feed from one of the willing people Aris had?" I couldn't wrap my head around that. If he knew I'd be like this, so volatile and out of control, how could he take me to someone like that? I'd have surely killed them if he hadn't stayed with me.

"Admittedly, I didn't know you'd be *this* bad. Perhaps going for another one of Tellus' prisoners would've been a better idea, but I thought it would be alright."

I searched his face for a lie, knowing that I'd have noticed the change in his heartbeat, but it was the truth.

He frowned, then kissed my forehead and pulled my head down onto his chest. "We don't let fledgelings go too long without feeding. It helps them gain control if they're always well fed, but you were starved for three weeks. Tortured, as well."

The mention of it made me cringe.

"I had no idea what to expect." He finally mumbled after a few moments of silence. "Obviously, we can't let you go so long without feeding, and we need to make sure you don't overexert yourself again."

"And how the hell do you suggest we do that?" I mumbled into his chest.

"We could start by not intervening with the executions like I'm certain you intend to do."

"That's not an option."

He sighed and pulled away so he could look down at me. "Then we need to make sure you have enough help."

"Triss and Adriana had no issues helping me and I didn't overexert myself the last time." I reminded him and turned to open the door.

"This discussion isn't over." He took on a more argumentative tone and placed his hand over mine on the doorknob, effectively halting me in my tracks.

"It *is* actually." I spun the knob and pulled the door open anyway, only to be met by Lazarus on the other side.

"It isn't." He growled, barely sparing me a glance before locking eyes with Deiric. "You, however, aren't required for it." Lazarus stepped to the side to allow me to leave.

I crossed my arms and glared up at him with a raised brow. When I didn't leave he shifted his attention to me and waved me on.

"I'm not leaving." I glanced between the two of them. "Whatever you're about to go off on him about involves me too, I'm sure of it. You will *not* discuss what to do with me while I'm not present and involved in the conversation."

Lazarus opened his mouth to snarl something back at me, but was interrupted by my father who appeared on completely silent feet behind him.

"I've had about enough of that as well."

Lazarus spun to face him, but I caught his forearm before this entire situation could come to blows over something as simple as including me in the godsforsaken conversation they were determined to have.

"Enough." I snarled. "All of you. For fuck's sake. Calm down and just say whatever it is you came over here to say."

Lazarus turned on me now. "You're out of control. You nearly killed Triss. And you," He spun to Deiric. "You did absolutely *nothing* to help that situation."

"I would have stopped her–"

"And yet you didn't." He took a step closer to Deiric and my restraint snapped.

I retrieved a dagger from Deiric's bandolier, shoved him back against the door frame, and held the dagger to his throat before he could even see the move coming. Shock flashed across his features, and I was surprised to find he didn't even resist or fight back.

I bared my fangs at him in a snarl. "If you want to blame anyone, you blame me." I snapped, leaning up and as close as I could to his face to convey my point. "Do. Not. Lay a *single* hand on him for something that was *entirely* my own fault."

I was overwhelmed with a sense of pride that I quickly realized came from Deiric. It was still odd to me how much more I could feel *his* emotions with each passing day. I didn't miss the hint of amusement flash across my father's face out of the corner of my eye, while Lazarus stood preternaturally still behind my blade.

"I wasn't–" He started to say calmly.

"I don't fucking care." I pressed the flat side of the blade against his throat. "You threaten him, you're threatening me. Whether you intend to incite physical violence or just throw your seniority around, I will *end* you if you harm him. Do you understand?"

The slightest dip of his chin told me he got the message. I removed the blade, returned it to the sheath on Deiric's bandolier, and stepped around Lazarus into the hall. "Now if you'll excuse me. I have an execution to plan an intervention for, and you're in my way."

Deiric followed less than a step behind me. My father gave me an appreciative smile, then fell into step beside Deiric to follow me back to the training room where I knew I'd find Adriana to discuss our plan.

Chapter 31

Mira

A thud woke me and I nearly launched myself from the bed. Deiric's arms flew around me protectively as he was jerked from sleep as well. His eyes were wild, despite having just been asleep.

"What's wrong?" He asked, after a quick glance around the room, showed that nothing was amiss.

Wind blew in through the open window and we both looked over as the rustle of paper drew our attention to the floor. One of the grimoires I had brought back with me was laying in the middle of the floor next to the bed. A gust of wind blew it open, but then stopped as abruptly as it had begun.

"That's not creepy at all." Deiric muttered, releasing me as I started to push away from him to go look at the book.

A flame appeared in my hand as I approached so I could read it. I heard him get out of bed and walk over to crouch behind me.

The book had opened up to a curse. A blood bound curse. All that you needed was blood from the person you intended to curse, or the blood of a family member of the person you intended to curse, and a personal belonging. The curse was open to interpretation and had a few different versions, but the general idea behind it was that it gradually turned the person's blood into something that was poisonous to them.

They would have to be bled regularly to diminish the toxin only for it to build back up again. You could determine the timeframe for this, as well as any actions that would speed up the process. It was perfect. I had *both* of those things. I didn't want a curse that would kill him. I wanted the bastard to suffer.

"This kind of magic has been banned for years." Deiric said softly.

"I know, but it's perfect."

"You can't be serious."

"Do you think that this book flung itself off the dresser, landed here, and then opened on its own to this page for me to just ignore it?"

I turned to look at him and the concern of his face was overwhelming. "Mira. This magic was *banned*. If Devlon or one of the magisters found out, you'd be in a shitload of trouble."

"I'm not casting it on a mage in our covens. Hell, I'm not even casting it on someone from this *realm*."

He didn't appear convinced.

"You didn't have a problem with a curse when we were at the Solas castle. What changed? I'd be willing to bet that either the Morrigan, or a fucking spirit of some kind willed this to happen so I would see it. Are you really going to ask me to ignore that?"

"No, but I don't want you to be killed."

"No one is going to kill me." I smiled. "Not if our future queen specifically allows it."

"Adriana is not going to go for this."

I smiled even wider. "She had no problem with the plan to kill the guards, love. She'll have no problem with this."

"If you're certain, then I think this is the bare minimum punishment he deserves. But I *need* you to get her permission first. Please." He traced his fingers along my cheek and hooked a lock of hair behind my ear.

I picked up the grimoire and walked it back over to the dresser. I marked the page with a nearby dagger as I closed it. I spun around and walked back over to where he now stood.

"I promise, I will get her permission first." I kissed him. "I need her blood for it anyway."

*

I was sitting in our training room reviewing the curse and writing down the incantation I intended to use with my quill when Triss walked in and made her way around the table I was sitting at. She peered down over my shoulder at what I was working on.

"That kind of magic has been forbidden for centuries." She sounded a little shocked, which surprised me because I was certain she knew just how committed I was to this curse. She also sounded tired, like she hadn't fully recovered from our mutually terrifying experience yesterday.

"I don't intend to tell anyone about it." I mumbled, continuing to write the incantation down.

"Surely they will find out." She walked over to the bookshelves and cabinets behind us.

"Whether they do or not is irrelevant when the future queen will be giving me explicit permission to cast it."

She made a noise that suggested she doubted it would still go unpunished, but continued about her business. She collected the bottle of mugwort tincture and the bottle of a vervain tincture she had been preparing, then placed them on the table on the other side of the room.

Macha fluttered in through the open window and perched on the table next to me. *You will need to be very careful with this one. You don't want to cast it incorrectly.* She walked over to look down at my incantation.

And does that look correct to you?

She shook out her wings and then her head before looking over at me. *It appears correct to me. Have you collected the blood yet?*

No. I'll get that when I'm prepared to do the spell. It needs to be done on the next dark moon.

She tilted her head in what I assumed was a nod.

Footsteps sounded from down the hallway. I picked up the incantation, tucked it into the grimoire to mark the page and then closed it just before Adriana, Sorcha, and Aodh walked into the room.

I looked up and watched as they made their way to the table that Triss was setting up on.

For what it's worth, Gaisgeach began, *I'm not very keen on the idea of having Adriana participate in this test.*

Yes, well. She volunteered.

Cairbre is not happy either.

He'll get over it. I shut him out then and shifted my attention back to our test subjects.

"One of you has to be a control. Eventually, we'll bring one of the vampires into the mix, but for now, it will just be you three." She picked up the mugwort tincture and put a few drops into two very small glasses. She pushed one over to Sorcha and the other to Aodh. I suppose that made Adriana the control.

This is an awful idea. Gaisgeach butted in.

I ignored him.

Liala walked in now with a pitcher of water and three more cups.

"You'll drink the vervain mixed in with water. I don't exactly know how to dose it, so we'll have to see how this goes." Triss explained while Liala sat the cups in front of them. They all just silently listened, not seeming to bat an eye at the fact that they may all be without their magic for hours, if not a day. The first time I'd been dosed, it took nearly three days to fully wear off. The gods only knew how much he'd given me to take so long to get out of my system.

Triss put three drops of the vervain tincture in each cup before Liala added a little bit of water. "Sorcha." Triss pointed to the mugwort. "Drink that first."

Sorcha threw it back in one gulp. Her face scrunched up in disgust and Triss stifled a chuckle. I wondered what she mixed it with that caused that reaction. They sat in silence for a minute or two before Triss directed all three of them to drink their water.

"Alright." Triss looked at each of them carefully. "We'll give it another minute or two and then I want each of you to try to use your magic. Starting with Sorcha."

"You'll be able to tell you've lost your magic." I pointed out, and they all looked at me. "It's like a piece of yourself is missing. It's hard to explain, but you'll know it when you feel it."

They looked concerned for the first time during this entire ordeal, but nodded anyway.

When Sorcha finally gave her magic a go, a fire flickered to life in her palm like it would in any other circumstance. She smiled victoriously. "I think it worked!"

She glanced at me to get my approval, but I just stared at her blankly. I had very little faith it would be quite this simple. Still, I prayed that maybe it was. Kieran had stated they hadn't really experimented with an antidote, but assured me he would research as well. His sudden change of heart was still alarming, but I wasn't going to question it.

Aodh tried his magic next, drawing my mind back to the present before I dove too deep into the misery I experienced in that cell. He held out his hand and a flame sputtered, then disappeared. He frowned. Another try left him with nothing.

"Shit." He cursed.

Triss pushed the mugwort to him. "Drink this."

He took it and threw it back the same way that Sorcha did. He scowled a little bit less at the taste.

Adriana held up her hand now and shadows swirled around her arm. I narrowed my eyes at her, and she looked equally confused.

"Shouldn't I be unable to summon my magic?"

Triss, Liala, and I all nodded. She looked frustrated. "Do I need a heavier dose?"

"Maybe." Triss put a few more drops of the vervain into her cup and then Liala added more water. Adriana drank that, then patiently waited while we all kept monitoring Sorcha and Aodh.

Sorcha was still able to use her magic as though she hadn't consumed the vervain. Aodh struggled for a few more minutes before his magic returned. A small smile now rose to his lips.

"It's working." He mumbled, hesitantly.

"Liala," I looked over at her. "Would you go see if Xander and Zane would come in here?"

"You want to test it on them?"

I shrugged a shoulder. "I think they'll be the only two that Deiric won't grumble about me stealing for this test."

Liala made a face that suggested I had a fair point, sat the water on the table, and walked from the room to go collect them. At least she could sweet talk Zane into helping. Xander might complain, but I hoped he'd be willing. I wasn't planning on trying this myself until I saw it work.

While we waited for them, Adriana, Sorcha, and Aodh continued to use their magic. They tested it every so often to confirm it was still reachable.

"It doesn't seem to be working on me." Adriana reached for the vial of vervain. "Should we try more?"

"No." I spoke up before Triss had the chance.

Adriana glanced at me with an exasperated look on her face. "Don't we need to see what it takes to work on *me*?"

"I don't think it's going to work on you." I shrugged.

Her face scrunched in confusion, and she was about to ask what I meant, but we were interrupted by nearly *all* of the vampires walking into the room, led by Deiric.

He gave me a look that said he was less than pleased that I'd decided to test on *them* without asking him first, but then he stepped aside and Zane and Xander walked over to stand behind Sorcha and Aodh.

"We're here to be your test subjects, I guess." Xander smirked at me. "Which one of us will you be torturing first?"

I frowned and he winced.

"Sorry." He muttered, then shifted his focus back to Triss who was glaring at him with an intensity I had never seen from her before.

"Well, just for that comment," she started as the rest of the guys shuffled in to watch, including Lazarus and my father, "You get to go first."

She took Sorcha's glass, dripped some vervain into it, and then added water from the pitcher Liala left behind.

"Drink up, asshole."

Deiric huffed a laugh and crossed his arms over his chest with a smirk. Xander hesitantly took the cup and drank. He tried to pretend he didn't notice the vervain, but it didn't work. I could still see the slight grimace of pain as he swallowed.

Triss poured the mugwort into one of the small glasses and handed that to Zane. "You drink this."

Zane drank it and handed the cup back to her without a word.

"What's that?" Xander asked, seeming to sway a little.

"The antidote." Triss smiled.

"Shouldn't *I* be drinking that?"

Triss shrugged. Xander swayed again, this time much more obviously. Zane caught his arm. Triss quickly poured another shot of the mugwort tincture and handed it to him.

"Drink this." She urged. "Before you actually hit the floor."

Xander took it and threw it back quickly. He was leaning on Zane now, like he might genuinely hit the floor at any moment.

"Deiric," Triss motioned for him to move over to Xander, "You take him. Zane needs to drink the vervain next."

"Shouldn't we wait to see what happens with Xander first?" Deiric asked, but obeyed. He slipped his arm around him just under his shoulders and took his weight off of Zane.

"No." I said simply.

He glanced back at me like he couldn't believe I still thought this was a good idea, but held onto Xander while he slowly seemed to regain his balance.

Zane took the cup that Triss handed him and drank the vervain water. He still flinched a bit as he drank it, but several minutes passed and he didn't seem to become unsteady.

I was equally happy that we found this as I was frustrated that I'd never worked on this on my own. I suppose I never really had the time for such experiments with how quickly things escalated back then, but I should've revisited this much sooner. We'd danced around being careful to avoid drinking anything that could be contaminated when all we needed to do was be prepared with an antidote.

"I'm not sure why Adriana isn't affected." Triss finally spoke when Deiric released Xander completely. "But, I'd say we can call this experiment a temporary success.

We'll need to continue to see what the long term effects look like, and figure out how long the mugwort lasts, but it looks like it's working the way we hoped."

"I think I've got an idea, although I don't know what it means."

The entire room shifted to look at me. Even Macha glanced my way, like she didn't know the answer and wanted to hear my theory. Something told me, knowing the Morrigan knew everything, that Macha might know for sure, but I tried not to think too much on that.

"I managed to goad Azazel into getting close enough to me that I got a taste of him one day." I shrugged. "He didn't taste… *human*."

"He smelled kind of off too." Lazarus added.

I nodded, though I just thought he might smell that way because he came from another realm. "I suspect that whatever *he* is, also affects *you*." I looked at Adriana.

She didn't seem thrilled about that and crinkled her nose at the thought.

"Regardless, unlike the rest of us, I don't think you need to worry about vervain."

"Well that's convenient." She muttered, despite her obvious distaste for the idea.

"I'd say so."

"So what do we do now?" Aodh asked, eyeing what was left of the tinctures on the table.

"Triss will monitor you. We'll see how long it stays in your system, test out how much will counteract vervain and for how long, and go from there." I looked at Xander and Zane. "You two will do the same."

"And what if I needed them for something else?" Deiric mockingly asked. No one else picked up on it, but I did.

"You won't." The corner of my mouth tilted up in a slight smirk. "We have other things to worry about." Like the execution tomorrow that we planned to interrupt. I knew he would still fight me on it, but I wasn't taking no for an answer.

Chapter 32

Deiric

Mira was standing in the dining room overlooking where the mages were outside sparring. Triss was working with Stella, while Zemora and Sorcha were working on sparring with swords. Triss, I realized, had yet to learn how to handle a blade. I wondered when Mira was going to start that with her.

She huffed. "Eventually." She shrugged then and glanced over her shoulder at me. "Right now I need her to teach Stella how to do the crazy lightning she does."

I smirked at her, but she turned to watch them again. Normally, she'd have a glass of whiskey while she stood in here to watch. That had always been her way of relaxing when she wasn't directly responsible for their training. Something just seemed off since we'd come back home.

"I did get rid of the whiskey that he put the vervain in, love." I walked up behind her to watch them over her shoulder. I let my hands rest on her hips and leaned in to kiss her neck in the spot I knew would send shivers down her spine.

She relaxed back into me with a contented sigh. Her fingers intertwined with mine. "I know."

"Do you suddenly not like whiskey?"

"I don't trust that he hasn't put vervain into *all* of the whiskey we have."

"Lazarus has had some and gave it the all clear days ago."

She leaned her head back against my shoulder and frowned. "Still."

"You could always go get *more* whiskey." Lazarus offered as he walked into the dining room behind us.

Mira jumped, like she hadn't heard him coming. She was also more jumpy since we'd come home. She never mentioned it though, and it ate away at me. This was her home. A place she should have felt safe, and now she seemed so tortured by it.

I'm fine. She shot me a look.

You don't act fine. I shot her a look right back. *It is okay* not *to be okay. You know that.*

She scoffed.

"You know, the silent conversations still get on my nerves." Lazarus sat down at the table behind us.

Mira sighed, slipped one hand from mine and then spun around so she could look beyond me at Lazarus. "And where, exactly, might we get *more* whiskey?"

I glanced over my shoulder and Lazarus grinned. "I thought you'd never ask."

*

An hour later we were walking through the foyer of Lazarus' manor, following Darragh to the stairs that lead to the cellar. Mira had been skeptical when Lazarus said that we would go to *his* manor to collect more whiskey. Normally, I would just send Leo, and he'd come back with a bottle or two, but today it seemed like the perfect chance for Mira to get it straight from the source. Just to confirm for herself that no one other than vampires had handled it.

Darragh opened the door to the cellar and stepped to the side to allow Lazarus to walk down first. Mira followed him and I stayed close behind her. The cellar was lit with magic, similarly to how the Morrigan's temple was lit. The torches that hung throughout burned *forever* without ever actually burning away the wood that held them. It was a nifty little spell.

The cellar actually extended far beyond the edges of the manor, despite that you couldn't see it from above. There were barrels lined up carefully in rows, stacked nearly four high in some places. The other side of the room had distilling chambers. Lazarus took extra special care in distilling and storing all of the whiskey he made for us. He had several barrels that were specifically set aside for Silas, for me, and the other elders. We each had our own tastes.

"You can choose the barrel, if you'd like." Lazarus walked down the middle of the cellar and gestured toward the rows of stacked barrels. "Deiric knows which barrels are set aside specifically for him, but the rest are available to you if you'd rather. The oldest barrels are the closest to the front. We move them forward as we add more."

He stopped at one row toward the furthest part of the cellar from the stairs. "This one has been aging for twenty years." He patted the barrel. "You might like it."

Mira was gaping at the barrels, distilling chambers, and everything before her like she'd never seen such a thing before.

I had no idea he made whiskey, nor did I have any idea how it was made. She thought while she looked down the rows. "What's the difference?"

"The flavor mostly." Lazarus shrugged. "Each barrel is a little bit different, and the longer it ages the more it pulls in the flavor from the barrel itself. Some of these are blends, and some are barrels we've traded with other distillers to get."

I knew he'd have to explain it in far more detail for her to have any idea what the flavoring was like. I'd been the same way when he showed this to me, but I had also assisted with making several of these barrels before I moved to my manor. In fact, I probably distilled the whiskey in the twenty year old barrel he was standing next to.

You helped to distill some of this? She seemed genuinely shocked, and overwhelmed. *What one would you recommend?*

I pointed to the barrel he had indicated, but then also pointed to a group of barrels beyond it. "Those barrels are the ones he specifically sets aside for me. If you liked the whiskey you had with Silas, those," I gestured to the row in front of her, "are the ones that he likes."

"Would you like to try this one first?" Lazarus offered, grabbing a whiskey thief from the table next to the barrel.

Mira nodded hesitantly.

He tapped gently on either side of the bunghole on the barrel with a wooden mallet until it popped out. He placed the whiskey thief into the hole and then used that to put the whiskey into a glass for her.

The entire time, she looked both curious and perplexed. When he handed her the glass, she very hesitantly sniffed it, before swirling the glass and really evaluating it.

Lazarus chuckled. "At least I don't have to teach you how to properly taste it."

She shot him a look that would've made anyone else shrink away and brought the glass to her lips. It smelled incredible. There were hints of vanilla, caramel, and a bit of oak. She seemed pleased with it.

"And this isn't for anyone specifically?"

He smirked. "Technically, it's mine."

She arched a brow at him.

"I'll share it with you though, if you like it."

A mischievous smirk now rose to her lips too. "I guess I should be honored if you're willing to share your personal stash with me."

He shrugged. "I've got more."

"I *do* like this one."

He motioned Darragh over to begin to bottle it.

*

By the time Mira shifted us back home, she was already buzzed. She and Lazarus had had nearly two glasses in total while he showed her around and let her taste each different variation of whiskey he made. It was such a relief to see her perk up and seem genuinely happy again. Since she'd come home to me, she never seemed totally relaxed and herself. But in that whiskey cellar, she was more herself than she'd been in months.

Teron was sitting in the den when we arrived, and walked into the foyer before Mira could wander upstairs. I had both bottles Lazarus had given her under my arm. I was sure she was sober enough to hold them, but it didn't seem right to make her carry them. I stashed them up in our bedroom and was back by her side in less than two seconds.

"It's nice to see you smiling again." Teron said with a smile as he took in his visibly buzzed daughter. "I assume you got to taste a little bit of everything?" He seemed amused, rather than judgmental for once, and I was glad that Mira didn't seem offended by his question.

"Every barrel he *let* me taste." She quipped with a smile.

"She's got two bottles of my best whiskey I'm certain she's not planning to share." Lazarus walked around Mira and headed for the stairs.

Mira smiled after him. *He's right. I'll share with you but no one else is going to find those bottles.*

I put my hand on her hip and leaned in to whisper in her ear. "Don't worry, I hid them well."

"Good."

Teron simply shook his head. "Would you like to have another drink? The mages have a fire going and it's a beautiful night."

I had been looking forward to whisking her upstairs and having her all to myself, but the light in her eyes seemed to get a little brighter with his suggestion so I didn't say a word.

"I would love to." She glanced over at me with a more sultry smile. *But don't think that this means you're going miss out on whisking me upstairs after that.*

I hope the wait will be worth it.

She leaned in and pressed a brief and sweet kiss to my lips. *Isn't it always?*

Teron made a slightly disgruntled noise as he turned to go get his whiskey.

"We'll be right out." Mira called after him. "Well, would you like a glass of Lazarus' whiskey, or are you going to drink your own stash?"

I snorted. "I think I'll take a glass from *your* stash for a change."

Her smile only grew. "Fine. But you've got to go get it."

I rolled my eyes and smiled at her. "Of course I do."

Chapter 33

Mira

I cut off the experiments with Vervain two nights ago to make sure that Aodh was at his full strength for our next outing. If Deiric insisted that *I* wasn't to use as much power, we needed more mages, and he was one of the only two I would consider allowing to help us. Deiric, Lazarus, and my father also came with us, despite my complaints about the number of us versus the number of them for shifting.

Triss helped to create enchanted items for them to wear to alter their appearance. Although, it seemed entirely unnecessary when they weren't likely to see us before we intervened. We obviously couldn't use the same method of attack each time. They would catch on and likely find ways around it.

I stood alone in the sea of people gathering to watch. I knew Deiric refused to be farther than four steps from me, but with the volume of people around me it felt like he was much farther. I despised being clustered in so closely with all of these people, but it was crucial to remain as inconspicuous as possible.

I glanced around to note that Triss, Adrianna, and Aodh were all in position, much closer to the makeshift platform than I was. It was poorly constructed. I was a little surprised it would even hold the twelve people they were lining up along it now.

Mira? Triss' voice had a concerned undertone to it. *Any time now.* She was getting impatient, but I needed to be able to *see* all the guards. I was responsible for disabling them, in whatever way I saw fit.

Almost. I responded with half a thought as I watched the final noose be fitted around a woman's neck. This group was surprisingly somber, given the situation. The last one had been far more theatrical about it all. I vaguely recognized a few faces, though they weathered with age now, while others were entirely foreign to me.

A chorus of cracks echoed off of the buildings as the faint tendrils of shadow I sent out before me snapped the necks of each guard handling the execution. Chaos rang out as they dropped to the ground, then we all shifted together.

Lazarus yanked off the necklace Triss had given him and turned to snarl at me. "What the *fuck* was that?"

I turned to face him with a raised brow. "You're going to have to be more specific." I turned my gaze to Aodh. "Go get Tellus." He nodded and disappeared.

"You *killed* them." He stalked toward me. "Every last fucking one. Are you out of your mind?"

Tellus appeared with Aodh, looking far more annoyed than I anticipated. He shot me a glare before he turned to the rightfully confused men and women we'd brought.

I looked back at Lazarus now, just as Deiric removed his necklace and stepped between us. "I think you'll find that my mind is clearer now than it has ever been."

"You've gone mad." He gestured toward the prisoners we freed. "We *don't* do that. It was one thing when Deiric was looking for you. I went along with it then and everyone seemed to look the other way, but we have no reason to *kill* them now. Nor do we have any reason to believe they are all in agreement with the laws that have been passed."

I raised a brow at him, vaguely aware of *everyone* listening in on this far too loud discussion. "Anyone who willingly follows orders to effectively perform genocide deserves the fate they were dealt."

Tellus appeared beside Lazarus, the annoyance I saw moments ago reaching all new heights. "You killed *all* of them?" He snapped. "We are not killers. This goes against *everything* we agreed on when we made our treaty."

I stood a little taller and stepped closer to him. "We are at *war*, Tellus. The treaty was an agreement about members of our coven, and last I recall we reacted accordingly to the violence against our coven. Does this not follow those agreements? A life for a life, no?"

"They were following orders." He argued.

"And she was following mine." Adriana appeared beside me now.

"I beg your finest pardon." Tellus gasped and glanced at her. "You have no authority here."

"But I will." She stood taller and stepped up so she stood directly in front of him. "And you would do well to pay attention to who you're speaking to."

Tellus' face screwed up in anger and confusion. He was torn between continuing to argue with the future queen of Leinster or to bow down and accept defeat. I knew when they found out the amount of death I was leaving in our wake they would not be on board, but I hadn't really had the notion to care.

"That's enough." My father stepped between us. "What's done is done, and we can't do anything about it now. We will *try* to leave less bodies in our wake next time." He shot a glance at me that promised we'd discuss this later, but he *also* had no authority over me so I ignored it.

Tellus apparently marked the look, because he shifted his attention to me. "I want your word that you'll avoid killing the guards unless it is absolutely necessary, or I'll be forced to bring this up at the next meeting for discussion."

His threat fell on deaf ears. What was the worst they'd do? Execute me? It was a fate I was sure I'd have faced eventually anyway. It didn't hit me the same as I am sure he expected or hoped it would.

"She is following *my*–"

"Enough from you," Tellus snapped at Adriana. "I know damn well she was not following your orders today. Or at the very least, that they were open to interpretation if she was. You're not your brother."

"Interrupt your future queen again and you will find out just how open for interpretation her orders are." I snarled at him. I would've taken a step toward him to follow through on the threat, but Deiric had an unrelenting grip on my arm before I had the chance.

"I want your word." His voice was harder than I'd ever heard it. "Or you *will* face consequences."

I searched his face for any doubt, any hesitation, and found none.

Give him your word, Alesmira, and then do be sure you adhere to it. I would rather not die because your reckless vengeance was unquenchable.

Mira. Deiric warned.

"Fine." I snarled. "I will *do my best* not to kill anyone unless it is absolutely necessary."

"Getting out quickly does not make it necessary." Tellus pointed out.

"I will not kill anyone who has not done harm to us or the prisoners we intend to rescue." I growled through gritted teeth.

Tellus studied me for a few seconds before nodding and returning to the group of prisoners Aodh and Triss were freeing from their binds. That vow still left things open to interpretation enough that I could do as I damned well pleased.

"Seriously Mira." My father breathed, holding the bridge of his nose between his fingers, obviously frustrated. "Snapping all of their necks? It's efficient, but entirely unnecessary. You could've simply knocked them out."

"What's the fun in that?" I shrugged a shoulder and stared blankly at the relieved men and women rejoicing nearby.

"Oíche may not have faulted you for it, but Solas is entirely different." He released his face and looked at me with nothing more than genuine fatherly concern for my wellbeing. "They'd sooner kill you than allow you to keep doing this and you know it."

"At least my death would've meant something."

He opened his mouth to speak again, but Adriana spoke before he had the chance.

"She's right, you know." She glanced over toward Triss and the others, then turned to face all of us. "Anyone who willingly follows his orders deserves whatever fate they're dealt. It is war. War is messy. We can't stand for it."

She locked eyes with me. "If they want to make us out to be the villains, then it is about damned time we became them."

A small, but proud smile rose to my lips. Gone was the fragile princess we brought to our manor nearly a year ago. The woman before me was a monarch who would fight to the death for her people, and get her hands dirty if she had to. If I had any reservations about involving her in the curse on Azazel, that all fell away the moment she stood up to Tellus to point out that we were absolutely justified in our actions today.

"I'll toast to that." I lifted my hand, and two glasses appeared before us, with two fingers of whiskey in each.

Adriana smiled and took one while I grabbed the other.

"To becoming the monsters they thought we were." She lifted her glass.

I smiled a little wider as I clinked my glass with hers. "To embracing the darkness I've longed to let out."

We both brought the glasses to our lips and took a single sip. My father and Lazarus shook their heads. Deiric loosened his grip on my arm, and I caught the smirk on his lips out of the corner of my eye.

Adriana coughed and swore. "By the gods this shit is awful. How do you drink that?"

I huffed a laugh. “It’s more of an acquired taste. Perhaps you should stick to mead.”

“Yeah.” She agreed and poured what was left of her glass into mine. “That’s all you.”

“Let’s get going before you’re too drunk to function.” I smirked, then shifted the four of us home. Aodh and Triss would follow when they were ready.

Lazarus walked away while mumbling something under his breath. Adriana shook her head at me in disbelief or disapproval and then sauntered off herself, leaving Deiric and my father standing with me in the foyer of the manor.

“Killing them was a tad unnecessary.” My father mumbled.

“Are you suggesting you’d have done it differently?” The amusement from our impromptu toast was gone. I downed the rest of the whiskey in my glass.

“I’m suggesting that we need to tread carefully.” He said curtly.

“I can’t believe I’m saying this, but I agree.” Deiric mumbled behind me.

“Well.” I waved the empty glass around. “I’m so glad that you’ve made the decision for me.”

“Mira,” Deiric started, but I turned and headed for the stairs.

“I’m not really interested in discussing it. I gave the fucker my word that I will *try* not to kill anyone else. If that’s not enough for you, I’m not sure what else to say.”

I continued up the stairs to our bedroom without another word and was thankful they didn’t try to call after me.

Chapter 34

Deiric

I knew she was off, but her actions yesterday were far worse than I thought. First it was the blood curse that was absolutely forbidden and now she was killing indiscriminately.

You were exactly the same way when she was missing. Fiadh interrupted my thoughts. I thought I had them guarded, even from her, but it seemed I was wrong. Mira, thankfully, was entirely blocked from them or I was sure she would've risen from her seat at the table and throttled me by now.

They were holding members of both coven hostage. They could've helped us find Mira.

But they didn't. She pointed out.

Teron caught my eye from where he sat at the table and gave me a questioning look. Apparently my frustration with Fiadh was showing on my face. I sighed and rubbed my hand down my face, then up through my hair. This entire situation was driving me up a wall. Between worrying Mira would dig herself a hole she couldn't crawl back out of and wondering what the fuck was next with Ronan and Azazel I could hardly think straight.

Mira glanced at Teron, who looked at her just long enough to give her a look that I assumed told her to ignore me because she looked back down at the grimoire.

That was the other thing that drove me a bit mad. She had already decided on a curse. She was supposed to discuss it with Adriana tomorrow. Yet here she sat, still browsing the last of the grimoires she had brought home with us. It was arguably the oldest and I found myself praying to the gods that it didn't contain anything even *worse* than what she'd already decided on.

And what if it does? Fiadh asked. *What do you plan to do about it?*

She was annoyed, yet amused. I could hear it in her voice. The annoyance confused me. The amusement was not surprising. She continued when I didn't answer.

It is a double standard, really, and it bothers me greatly. She was silent for several breaths. Long enough that I nearly asked what she meant before she finally continued. Teron watched me warily, reading every expression that washed over my face as I conversed with Fiadh.

You. That warlock.

Mage. I corrected.

Warlock. She repeated, clearly reveling in the fact that it was more of an insult. *Her own father. Even the eldest of you all. The first. You all act like she hasn't earned the right to be less compassionate.*

I never said that.

You didn't have to. I swore I could *feel* her roll her eyes. *You all attacked her yesterday for doing the very same thing that I would have done in her situation. Killing is easy. Leaving them alive leaves loose ends. War is coming. She knows it. You all know it, actually. Every man left alive is one you might face on the battlefield.*

This does not give any of us the right to kill indiscriminately.

Yet you *did.*

I did not–

Every guard you encountered is dead. Even the ones who cooperated with you. You never faced consequences. I can only presume that was because they feared they'd lost their biggest weapon. That's all she is to them, after all. It's all she's ever been.

I was about to demand that was a damned lie, but I realized that I couldn't. I didn't know how they actually felt about her. They *seemed* to care.

They don't. She said it so plainly that there was no room for doubt. Like she knew it in her very bones. *They wouldn't kill her though. They need her. However, they will make threats. None of which she will heed. She's beyond obeying anyone now.*

I've noticed.

It makes her ruthless. That's a good feeling to have on the battlefield.

It makes her reckless.

Perhaps. I could picture her holding her head high with a condescending look in her eye. I was sure she'd be doing exactly that if we were face to face. *But it will make a difference when we find ourselves fighting. Believe me.* She chuffed. *Perhaps* I *should've bonded* her *instead.*

My jaw dropped and for a moment I didn't know what to respond with.

She is mine. Gaisgeach snarled.

This prompted Mira to jump because Gaisgeach did *not* block her out. Her head spun around, and she gave me a questioning look.

She could've been mine. Fiadh pointed out.

It was never an option. The threat laced into his words quickly quieted Fiadh. I felt her frustration, but she went silent after that.

Mira raised a brow. I shrugged. She looked me over once, twice, then turned her attention back to the book. Not two seconds passed before the front door banged open and just as quickly slammed shut.

We were all on our feet in an instant and rushed into the foyer. Eimear stood braced against the door and gasping for air. The scent of her panic and fear filled the room. I could tell it provoked Mira, but she took every bit of the self-control she had to hold herself in place.

"What is going on?" Teron demanded. I heard some of the others emerging from their rooms upstairs to see what all the fuss was about. It was late. Most of them likely had already been sleeping.

"I–" Eimear gasped. "I– I don't know." She dropped the basket she was holding and mugwort scattered across the ground in front of her. "I– lost track of time." She stammered. "I was collecting mugwort so we could make more of the tincture and–" She looked down at the mess she'd made.

"And what?" Mira snarled. It was harsher than she intended, I could tell, but she was dancing a fine line of control at the moment, and anything could make her snap.

"I thought one of the mages called out to me. I followed their voice and–"

Mira seemed to reach the same realization as me the moment the words left Eimear's lips. I *felt* the shift in her. She went from borderline feral to calm and deadly focused so quickly that I almost couldn't believe it. She cut off Eimear's explanation when she shoved her aside and flew out the front door.

"Shit." Teron grumbled, drawing his sword and running after her. I followed suit less than two steps behind him.

A wendigo shouldn't be able to breach the wards, but she cleared that barrier in seconds. Zane was not far behind me, urging Eimear to calm down and keep everyone inside before he headed off in another direction into the woods.

I followed the scent of her until I had to stop to take in my surroundings. I could track her, yes, but it would be far more helpful to track the creature. I came up beside Teron, who obviously had the same idea as me.

"I don't know where she's gone, but we split up. It isn't going to come after us if we're all together."

"Obviously," I replied dryly.

He shot me a glare, but then headed off to the left. I headed right, assuming that she had gone straight. A stick cracked off to my right not far ahead of me, but when I looked there was nothing there.

The forest was silent. *Too* silent.

"Mira!" My voice rang out in the same direction as the stick had sounded, but it sounded far too close, which meant it was *very* far into the woods.

I took off toward the sound, knowing that Mira would do the same. I could see Teron closing in from the left as well. She could defend herself. She could kill it.

I knew that and yet I couldn't stop my heart from racing as I ran out to find her. To find *it*.

There was a scream that sounded *far* too much like Mira. It could've been the beast, I supposed, but I didn't care. I would let it manipulate me if it brought me to it instead of her.

The scent of her blood hit me just before I came upon them both. She had healed, but blood dripped from where it had sliced her abdomen. She snarled and it charged her again.

It all happened far too quickly. She ducked to the right and swiped her sword while it swung at her, severing the beasts arm clean off without much effort at all. It shrieked and she spun to swing again. This time she cleaved off its other arm. She was toying with it. Letting her aggression out even if it only lasted a few breaths.

Her last swipe of her sword took its head clean off, but she still stabbed it in the heart for good measure before it even hit the ground. She withdrew her sword and what was left of it thudded to the ground.

When she turned to face me and Teron, who walked up next to me and sheathed his weapon, she was splattered in rancid black blood. Her face, her body, nearly every part of her really. With her eyes still as black as night she looked like death incarnate.

"Well." Teron smirked. "That's one way to do it I guess."

A rueful smile rose to Mira's lips. "If I'm going to do it, I might as well do it with a bit of flair, don't you think?"

"Fuck's sake." Zane appeared to my right. "What did you do? Bathe in its blood?"

Mira snorted a laugh and began to walk back toward us and the manor. "It nearly took off my fucking arm. I thought I'd return the favor *twice* before I killed it." She shrugged her shoulder and stopped in front of me.

I knew I liked her. Fiadh commented. Mira's smile only grew.

Chapter 35

Mira

"Where are we going?" Adriana asked as I led the way up the side of the mountain on Draga. She followed closely behind on Velor.

I could have shifted us, but I needed to sneak away quietly for this and shifting would have wasted energy I didn't know if I had. I felt more like myself with each passing day, but I *had* burned myself out a few too many times lately.

"Somewhere no one but Deiric would find us." I replied cryptically.

Her indignant scoff earned her a glare over my shoulder. "You could at least tell me what this is all about. You just said you needed my help with something and threw me on the damned horse."

"I'll explain *why* we're going up here when we get there." I was irritable for a million reasons, but I had to remind myself not to be *too* angry with her. This wasn't her fault. Not really. I mean, yes it all stemmed from the magic she inherited and some sick and twisted past that I still wasn't privy to, but I knew that *she* didn't cause this directly. I wasn't sure if we'd ever know why it all happened.

She finally quieted, thank the gods. The remainder of the ride up to our secluded little cliff was silent. I dismounted when we reached the slightly wider part of the path and Adriana quickly followed suit.

I walked without a word through the overgrown weeds, leaving the horses to graze and occupy themselves. She was less than a step behind me.

"Will you tell me now?"

I sighed as I came through the weeds and finally walked out onto the cliff Deiric, and I had spent countless hours on. It was peaceful and quiet up here. The only sound was the horses munching on the grass a few feet away and their occasional stomp when a fly landed on their legs.

"We're going to cast a curse." I said simply. I turned to face her and then sat down on the ground cross legged.

She eyed me cautiously, but sat down with me. "And we had to come all the way up here because?"

"No one can know about it. Far too many people already do."

"Such as?" She raised a brow.

"Triss and Deiric."

She snorted. "Well, seeing as Deiric is your mate and I am fairly certain has access to your thoughts at all times I don't see how he would've gone without knowing."

"I can block him out if I choose to. If you recall, I did exactly that when we stopped that first execution."

She gave me an impressed look that said she had in fact forgotten that, but then shrugged. "Well, Triss knowing also doesn't surprise me. She was privy to far more of your plans than even I was. Speaking of that, why *do* you trust her so much?" She looked intrigued and cocked her head to the side when she asked.

"Who's to say that I trust her at all?" I challenged with a raised brow.

She rolled her eyes. "You wouldn't have gone to her for help if you didn't. I'm young, but I'm not stupid."

"It is entirely possible to use someone without actually trusting them. I *knew* she was still irritated with Deiric, though she didn't show it. It was something I could exploit, even if she questioned why I would go to her for help. She likely thought that helping me would be her last jab at him. It was convenient that it seems she decided she liked me." I shrugged a shoulder.

"That said, I *do* actually trust her, so you aren't wrong. The first thing you need to learn though is not to trust anyone too quickly. Especially with your royal status."

"I thought we were casting a curse, not learning life lessons."

Her indignant retort nearly made me snap at her, but I reined myself in. "Yes."

I pulled the dagger from my thigh and retrieved the paper with the incantation as well. She stared at the dagger.

"What is that for?" She pointed at it as she spoke.

"Are you going to let me explain or will you be interrupting me the entire time?"

She frowned but motioned for me to continue.

"We're cursing Azazel. It's a blood curse, designed to turn his blood to poison. He'll feel weak and ill, which will progress into a searing pain that feels like his blood is burning him from the inside out. He will have to be bled regularly to negate the effects, but just as quickly as his body replenishes the blood, it will begin to turn to poison once more. When he uses his magic it will expedite the process."

Her eyes grew wider as I spoke, but there wasn't a single ounce of hesitation in her thoughts as she processed what I'd said. She eventually nodded.

"What do we have to do?"

"*I* just need your blood and a personal item from him. I will take care of the rest."

"I'd like to–"

"No."

"But–"

"You're *not* helping me with this. If this goes wrong, it goes *very* wrong and backfires on the castor. *You* cannot afford for that to happen. *I* am cursed with immortal life, and I'm fairly certain that the healing abilities that came with that would negate the curse if it were to take effect on me. That would not be the case for you."

She opened her mouth like she might protest, but reality sunk in and she closed it and nodded instead.

"Now, the personal item will have to be your mother's ring. I am going to set up a small ward around us that should block any tracking spell he's placed on it. Once I've done so, I need you to retrieve it and give it to me. Do you understand?"

She nodded.

I closed my eyes, took in a deep centering breath, and then created and sent out a shield and ward around us. "The ring." I held out my hand to her.

The ring appeared in my hand. I closed my fist around it and then turned my attention to the ground between us. I drew the symbols I saw in the grimoire from memory. A symbol meaning transformation first, followed by one for gradual progress, then finally a symbol signifying fire. Layered on top of one another, they made little sense, but it looked just like the drawing in the book.

I placed the ring in the center of the part that resembled an 'x' then held out my hand to Adriana again, this time with the dagger resting in it, hilt toward her.

"I'll need you to bleed over it. I don't need much." I studied her as I spoke and caught just the slightest scent of fear from her. "You can cut your hand or arm yourself, or I can do it."

In truth, I would rather not be the one to do it, given my lack of self-control around *human* blood lately, but I had a feeling her blood would smell enough like his that this wouldn't become an issue.

She swallowed, then reached out to take the dagger. She sat up on her knees and leaned over the symbol and ring. "Just bleed over it?"

"The ring, yes."

She took a deep breath and drew the dagger across her palm. My instincts kicked in, but were quickly staunched when the faint sweet scent I recognized from Azazel's blood hit me. I breathed a shaky sigh of relief.

"That's enough." I instructed and she healed her hand before she handed the dagger back to me. I sheathed it on my thigh again and reviewed my incantation one last time.

"Will he know?"

My eyes shot up to meet her gaze.

"Will he know this was you and come after you again?"

I considered that for a moment. "I'm sure he'll know, but he won't be able to get to me."

"How can you be certain?"

"I know the ward I placed on our manor. He will not be able to come to us no matter how hard he tries."

She didn't seem convinced, but she nodded.

I took a few moments to center myself, held my hands over the ring, blood, and symbols, then mumbled the incantation three times. I felt the fire erupt the moment that the spell set in. There was no burning or searing pain for me, and Adriana didn't flinch, which told me that it worked as I expected. I watched as the fire burned out all of the blood that littered the ground, then burned out leaving the ring slightly glowing.

We both stared at it until the hot glow on the ring began to fade. "Send it back to the manor before I drop the ward." She did as I asked.

"That's it then?" She asked.

"That's it. Now we just need to go do our offering to the Morrigan."

She stood up and reached down to help me to my feet. "We should get moving then."

*

Leo walked into the manor shortly after Adriana, Deiric, and I had come back inside. Adriana had already gone upstairs, while I was lingering with Deiric and my father in the den for a few minutes before we were also turning in for the evening.

"We need to talk." He leaned against the threshold between the den and the foyer. He looked exhausted, and like he'd been in a fight. His leathers were torn in a few places, and his normally neat hair was a mess.

Deiric spun to face him, and my father did the same. I remained leaning against the cabinets at the base of the bookshelves and raised a brow expectantly.

"There's another execution scheduled for tomorrow, but I managed to get my hands on a list of people this time." He pulled a folded up piece of parchment out of the small pouch on his belt.

"Do I want to know how you managed to get that?" I asked, eyeing him cautiously.

"No." He held out the parchment and Deiric took it from him. He opened it and skimmed the list before handing it to me.

"And?" He asked him.

"Not a single name on that list is associated with either of our covens. They're all completely and utterly human." He crossed his arms over his chest and rested his head against the threshold as well. He *was* exhausted.

"That must be some mistake." I skimmed the list myself, but didn't recognize a single name. I passed it along to my father and he did the same.

"There's no mistake. They aren't doing any real investigation. If someone says, 'they're a mage' that's all the evidence they need." He sighed and pushed off the wall. "If you have other questions, I'd rather discuss them in the morning, but the details of when and where is on the back of the piece of parchment."

Deiric almost asked him another question before I cut him off. "Get some rest." I waved him off toward the stairs. "I'm sure any questions we have can wait till the morning."

He lifted his head and nodded at me appreciatively before he pushed off the wall and headed toward the stairs.

"I had several questions that I would've preferred he answered tonight." Deiric turned to me with a furrowed brow.

"Yes, well he was practically ready to fall to the ground. I'm sure it can wait. He's not just a spymaster. He needs rest too."

Deiric shot me a look that said he was offended that I thought he didn't care for the man, but I ignored him and glanced over at my father.

He shook his head and folded the parchment back up. When he handed it back to me he sighed. "I'm not terribly surprised. There were a handful in the last group that also weren't magic wielders."

"At least he hasn't managed to get any of us yet." I mumbled.

"Which is not a surprise." Deiric leaned against the cabinets next to me. "The handful of us that still go outside of the wards are good enough at blending in that they'd never know."

"That doesn't mean that we should keep pushing the limits of what they'll notice. He looked like he was in a fight. Someone must've found him out." I pointed out, crossing my arms indignantly.

"And yet he made it back here, so whatever or whoever it was didn't get any real blows in."

"That doesn't make me feel better about it." I frowned at him, but he shrugged.

"We can discuss it more in the morning. You and Adriana can make a plan, but we'll need to do something that won't involve killing any guards or Tellus will have your head."

"Well-the fuck-aware." I grumbled and pushed off the cabinets to head upstairs.

"We're just looking out for you." My father pointed out, handing the parchment back to Deiric.

I waved my hand dismissively and walked toward the stairs.

Chapter 36

Mira

We agreed that given the fact there were no members of either coven we had no intention to pull these people out of the town, however we couldn't just stand by while they died. I'd been to Deilginis before, and it was probably the largest of the three towns we'd gone to so far. That also meant there were more places for guards to hide in plain sight.

Adriana, Aodh, Sorcha, Deiric, Lazarus, and my father came along this time. Adriana was there solely to assist with shifting, but I didn't want her magic to be displayed otherwise. While I was sure they assumed that she and I were involved, we didn't need any outwardly obvious signs of us here.

Aodh and Sorcha would help to confine several of the guards in fire while I addressed the crowd. Lazarus, Deiric, and my father were supposed to guard my back while I did so. I didn't exactly have a speech prepared, but it wasn't my first time dealing with this town, and I was shocked to find that they had twelve *humans* up on the gallows today.

We shifted to various places along the edge of town, with Deiric, Lazarus, my father and I arriving in the same place we'd come when Deiric killed the Lanzani. They spread out around me and while they wove their way through buildings I walked directly down the street toward the town square.

The voices of the townsfolk grew louder as I approached. It was a beautiful sunny day, which meant that, much to their chagrin, the dragons were not able to offer aerial support today.

I still think this is an awful idea. Gaisgeach grumbled in my head.

I rolled my eyes despite the fact that he couldn't see me and proceeded ahead as planned. I slipped through the crowd unnoticed, my disguise working seamlessly to blend me with the residents. I could sense Deiric, Lazarus, and my father branching out around me through the crowd and toward the front.

I didn't understand why such crowds seemed to gather for these. I couldn't imagine that watching people die was such an exciting thing to witness. It seemed sickening to me, but I suppose that when you fear something enough anything can be made into entertainment. Even death.

I marked the handful of guards around the gallows, as well as the guards dispersed through the crowd. It was frustratingly easy to spot them. Most *normal* townsfolk didn't have swords hidden under their cloaks, nor were they wearing a cloak at all with the nice weather.

The caw of a raven was our signal, and we moved quickly. The mages shifted while we ran so quickly that it would appear as though we had. I ended up in the center of the platform with my sword drawn across a guard's throat, but I stood off to the side so the people could *see* me.

Deiric was off to my left, holding two guards on either side of him, one at the point of the blade of his sword and the other he had by the neck with a dagger. My father had the guard off to my right in a headlock with a dagger at his throat, and Lazarus stood at the stairs on that side blocking the guards from coming up to us. That only left the stairs behind me unguarded, and I hoped Adriana was watching that well enough from her position.

The crowd had gone almost silent after we appeared, then shouts of panic and alarm began to ring out.

"They've come to kill us all!" A male voice shouted.

"Gods help us." A female shrieked.

This town. The town that had welcomed us willingly when we killed the Lanzani was now horrified of us again. How? Little more than a year and a half had passed. It made me wonder what ungodly awful things Ronan must have said to these people to make them believe us to be something so horrid so quickly.

"We are not here to kill you." I projected out over the crowd. There were murmurs and other noises of dismay among them, but otherwise they quieted enough to hear me.

The guard at the edge of my sword moved to grab his weapon. I turned my head to the side and growled, "don't even try it." He, surprisingly, lifted his hand in surrender.

"We're here," I started and turned to face the crowd again. "Because we cannot stand by while you senselessly murder our brethren, nor can we stand idly by while you execute *humans*."

"Demons! The lot of you!" An elderly man toward the front of the crowd shouted. "We've heard what you did to the king. What you did to the princess."

Lies then. He won them over with lies. I should've seen that coming. As amused as I was, I had no intention of hearing whatever hatred he spewed. It was irrelevant to our cause. Then again, killing him likely wasn't the right move now either.

"While I'd love to hear the thrilling lies you've been told, I'd rather not spend more than a few minutes in this shit hole town, so I'll start with this." I gestured to the people bound and standing on either side of me.

"Every single person on this platform is nothing more than a powerless human. These are your neighbors. Your family. Your friends. And you've cast them off to die for what?" I looked around at the crowd and the murmuring got louder.

"You all are the *demons* for falsely claiming that these people belonged to our covens. They have no such affiliation."

I heard movement behind me. Light footsteps that would've been entirely too quiet if I didn't have supernatural hearing. I reached out with my senses and his thoughts hit me next.

He was inexperienced, assumed I was merely a mage and intended to run me through with his sword. I gathered enough about his plan to know that he wouldn't cause any serious harm.

Before I opened my mouth to speak again he'd cleared the distance between us, driven his sword through me, and shouted a battle cry that silenced the entirety of the town square.

The blade had veered just millimeters to the left of my spine and missed my heart. It did however, go straight through my lung, which is the only thing that prompted a reaction as it caused my breathing to falter. Gaisgeach's vengeful growl filled my head.

I glanced down at the blade, now bloody and sticking out beneath my breasts. I could smell his fear then. He knew what he'd done, and he knew what was coming.

"Rude." I mumbled, then spun and cleaved his head off with my sword. The motion caused the blade to shift, because he did not let go immediately, but it was nothing close to the pain I'd experienced in the dungeons and was surprisingly manageable.

His body and head hit the platform at nearly the same moment with two heavy thuds. I shifted my attention back to the crowd.

"Where was I?" My voice was clipped, but steady, as breathing had now become more of a challenge. The blood had drained from most of their faces, and the guard next to me stepped back, raising his hands even higher in surrender.

I could *feel* Deiric's rage and concern, though he hadn't moved a muscle. He held his ground with the guards he was in charge of and I didn't dare to look his way.

"You'll release these people, or you will find that you won't live to see tomorrow. Is that clear?" I raised a brow and wiped my bloody sword on the cloak hanging off my shoulders.

"You– You said you weren't– weren't here to kill us." A man toward the front managed to stammer.

I smiled at him as the sound of hundreds of soft wingbeats began to fill the air around us. "Oh, it won't be us that will kill you."

I gestured toward the sky as Macha came down to perch on my shoulder and the murder of ravens she had with her began to flutter down to land on the tops of the buildings around us.

"My friends though are quite famished, and wouldn't mind a midday snack." I sheathed my sword, which was an awkward act given the blade still sticking out of my abdomen. I did my best to avoid showing my discomfort on my face.

"The choice is yours."

Another caw was our second signal, and we all shifted back to the manor. The guys lowered their weapons, while Adriana, Aodh, and Sorcha came running toward me.

"Gods, Mira." Adriana ran up behind me while I blew out a shaky breath. "What do I–"

"Pull it out." I snarled through gritted teeth and glanced over my shoulder at her. She was as pale as a ghost and looked between the hilt and my face trying to decide what to do.

My father was behind me in an instant and yanked the blade out. I hissed and reached up to cover the hole in my corset and dress with my hand. By the time my hand had made contact, my body had stitched itself back together as though the blade had never been there.

"Did you not hear him coming?" Lazarus was in front of me now, looking both concerned and furious at the same time.

"I did."

“And you didn’t do a damned thing to stop it?” My father snarled now, hurling the blade at the ground behind him.

I rolled my eyes and waved them both off as I turned to walk into the front doors of the manor. “Relax.” I grumbled. “I’m fine. We got the point across.”

Macha flew up off of my shoulder to her usual perch on the front of the house.

“You were *stabbed.*” Lazarus nearly shouted.

I glanced back over my shoulder while I pushed open the front door. “And?” I raised a brow, then continued through the door, swinging it shut behind me to effectively end that conversation before it could turn into another argument I didn’t have the energy or motivation to deal with today.

“Is everything…” Liala asked as I walked past her to the stairs. Her voice trailed off when she saw the bloody hole in my clothes. “Gods.” She whispered. “Are you–”

“Fine.” I replied quickly. “I’m fine.” Then I continued on up the stairs and into the bedroom without speaking to anyone else.

*

I was halfway through removing my corset when Deiric walked into our bedroom. I was already in a foul mood, because the bastard had ruined my favorite corset, between the blood and the gaping hole in it. I wasn’t sure if I was interested in hearing whatever he had to say at the moment. The look on his face said this wouldn’t be a quick conversation, nor one I would enjoy.

His gaze fell to the corset as I dropped it to the floor beside me and the ghost of a frown tugged at his lips.

Talk to him. Gaisgeach snapped.

I nearly snapped back at him when Deiric walked over to me and picked up the corset, but stopped when he stood up and toyed with the hole in it. “You didn’t even flinch.” His gaze shifted to the hole in my dress and the deep red stain around it.

“Neither did you.” I pointed out.

His eyes met mine and annoyance flickered in them before they softened. “I was a little preoccupied, and a little bit too stunned.”

I fought the urge to roll my eyes. “That was my favorite corset.”

A muscle ticked in his jaw, like that comment only further annoyed him. It was the truth though. I was pissed about that, not really pissed at him. I was just as pissed now at Gaisgeach knowing that the look on Deiric’s face likely stemmed from Gaisgeach sending him up here to console me.

He is not there to console you. Gaisgeach snarled. *He is there because we are worried about you.*

I’ve told you, I’m fine.

Someone who is fine would’ve at least flinched as a sword was driven through them.

It was an excellent display though. It really got those fuckers to shut up and listen.

Gaisgeach only snarled, and the look on Deiric’s face said he also didn’t agree with it. I heard his thoughts before he lunged at me with that sword. I knew he wasn’t going to go for my head, and a sword through the chest wouldn’t kill me. It would have needed to be wood.

"It was careless." Deiric tried to keep the angry edge from his voice, but it didn't work.

"It was effective."

"At what?" He snapped. "Giving me more reason to be concerned that you'll seek your revenge at the expense of your own life?"

There was no stopping the anger he felt now. It was a combination of grief and anger, I realized. I could feel it emanating off of him.

"I won't let it get that far."

"And how the fuck can I trust that, Mira?" He shouted, which was entirely unlike him.

"You don't trust me?" I raised my voice in return and was more than a little bit insulted.

A myriad of emotions flashed across his face now. It was like he couldn't decide how to feel. I could hear his thoughts spiral. He trusted me, of course he trusted me, but he thought I was suicidal, and I had to wonder what the fuck had given him that idea.

Kieran did.

What?

Adriana demanded that he compel Kieran to show them his memories and he showed them everything. Everything that I *also saw in your memories when we found you.*

I staggered back a step like I'd been dealt a physical blow.

"Mira." Deiric's voice was softer now. Timid. He almost sounded hurt.

I looked up at him again, and it was indeed hurt I saw in his eyes. Like he was upset I couldn't or didn't want to share this with him. It wasn't personal. I didn't want to share it with anyone. I hadn't even wanted Gaisgeach to know about that. They weren't there. They had no idea the desperation I felt. They had no idea how utterly alone I was.

I made an attempt to move around Deiric to leave the room but he was in front of me in the blink of an eye. He grabbed my arms and stopped me.

"Mira." He pressed. "Just talk to me, please."

I couldn't look at him. There were so many emotions stirring in me right now I didn't think I could talk to anyone.

His hands moved from my arms to my face, forcing me to look at him. "You can talk to me about *anything*, love. You know that."

"Not. This." I forced out, and stared at his chest rather than his face.

"I can't lose you." He said firmly, and that made me look at him. "You considered ending your life. *Permanently*." He studied me for a few heartbeats. "You can't expect me not to worry. You are my *mate*." He emphasized the word, really leaning into it. "My entire fucking *world* revolves around you. We are bound in more ways than one. When you die, I will go with you. I can't exist in this world without you in it. Don't you understand that?"

I was barely holding myself together. I cried shortly after I escaped, but I bottled *everything* up after that, allowing only the rage and vengeance to slip through the tightly locked box in my chest. I was broken, left in hundreds of thousands of pieces. I'd given up hope of escape after maybe the fifth torture session. I stopped keeping track after that. It was hard to get my timeline straight.

I was avoiding facing it because I didn't think I could. I certainly couldn't describe what happened to me. I would completely lose it if he made me do that.

"You can't bottle up everything. You don't have to. Seek vengeance. I'm not telling you to abandon it, but please, for the love of the gods, do not sacrifice yourself on the way there. I couldn't *breathe* while they had you. I couldn't even think straight, let alone be the leader everyone here needed.

"And I just saw you run through with a sword, acting as though the weapon wasn't inches from your heart. What if it had been a stake? Did you even consider what that would've done to *any* of the people there with you today?"

"I knew it wasn't a stake." I forced as much bite into my voice as I could, but it was futile. I didn't have much fight in me at the moment.

"Fine." His reply was laced with annoyance once more. "I still need you to *talk to me*." He urged. "You were planning to stake yourself, love. You begged someone else to do it when you didn't see another way out. Our souls are bound together. Our *lives* are bound together. If you died, it would have killed me. There's no pain greater than losing a mate."

"I'm not going to kill myself." My voice was probably too hesitant, but I meant it. Despite how fucking tired I was of dealing with all this gods damned bullshit, I had no intention of actually driving a stake through my heart.

"Then talk to me." He stepped closer and pressed a kiss to my forehead. The tears and emotions I worked so hard to pack away were nearly bursting at the seams. I tried to blink them away. "Please."

I drew in a shaky breath. "I'm tired, Deiric." I met his gaze again as the first tear finally streaked down my face. "I'm so fucking tired. I didn't ask for any of this. I didn't *ask* to be born a dhampir, to be blessed with this fucking power. I thought I was tired of running when we met, but this is even worse. I only agreed to work with you and fight because I thought that would be the end of it.

"Yes, I came up with the title I have, but I didn't *want* a title. I *wanted* to be invisible and left alone. I thought once we set up the treaty that would be the end of it. I could come back here and spend an eternity with you, never having to worry that someone would come for me again.

"Now, here we are, hiding, fighting, and miserable again because of a power hungry bastard who planned to use his sister for his own personal gain. I thought all the time I was on the run was because of what I am. I thought it was *my* fault that my family and so many others were dead. The whole fucking coven thought that.

"But in reality, they wanted my mother. I was just an unfortunate last resort. They wanted *me* to train her to use abilities I barely understood because they thought my mother would've passed that knowledge down to me.

"And I'm far too entangled with Adriana and the fucking royal drama thanks to my deal with the Morrigan. I guess that was probably her intention all along, but I am exhausted. I'm over it. If she knows everything that's going to happen, why the fuck can't I catch a break for once?"

He let out a heavy sigh and pulled me into him until my head rested against his chest.

"I don't know, love." He mumbled, pressing a kiss to the top of my head. "But no matter what happens, no matter what our next move is, I'm with you. Please don't shut me out and put me on the other side of your masks. I'm here for you."

"There's not much you can do."

"I can listen."

"I don't want to talk."

"I can be *here.*"

"Okay, fine." I mastered myself enough to look up at him. "And if I tell you that I plan to torture Azazel until he's begging me for mercy, then keep him alive to continue that torture over several days even after that?"

"I'll hold him down for you."

I laughed, and he gave me a slight smile that didn't reach his eyes.

"I never said I didn't agree with your need for vengeance, love. I just don't want you to get yourself hurt any further in the process." His eyes danced around my face, like he was confirming I was really listening to him and processing what he said.

"Please don't make me watch as you're run through with a sword again. Just kill the bastard. The theatrics aren't necessary, even if they manage to shut people up. You have suffered enough."

I would tend to agree. Gaisgeach added.

"What would you have proposed I do instead?" It was an honest question. Tellus would've had my head if I killed him without just cause.

"You could've dodged him."

"That would have given the rest of the guards the chance to try to fight back."

He hesitated a second, like he hadn't thought through the consequences of that.

"They would've viewed it as a weakness. An opening to make a final stand. You know that."

"And then we would've had to kill them all." He closed his eyes and shook his head, admitting defeat.

"While I didn't enjoy the outcome we got, I think it was the best case scenario for the hand we were dealt."

He opened his eyes, and a small smirk rose to his lips. "And the ravens?"

I shrugged and smiled. "An effective negotiation tool."

"I'm not sure Tellus will see it that way."

"Nobody died. But they know the consequences of not following my demands."

"Nobody died *yet*."

"And no one will die if they come to their senses."

He considered that and shook his head again. He approached me and traced the hole in my dress. "I'm sure that Liala could clean and patch this up for you."

"It is just a dress." I shrugged. "I will mourn the corset though." I looked at the discarded leather on the floor. It may have been patchable, but it wouldn't have looked the same.

He slid his hand up to cup the side of my face and make me look at him. "Are you sure you're alright?"

I studied him for a few moments. It was a combination of worry and grief now. The anger from moments ago completely subsided. I gave him a half hearted smile. "I'm getting there."

Chapter 37

Mira

I was busying myself with braiding my hair when Deiric walked back into our bedroom.

"Are you sure you're ready to go to a meeting?"

I stopped mid-movement and caught his gaze in the mirror. "What makes you ask that?"

"You've been a little…" He paused and looked away while he searched for the right word. "On edge lately." He finally finished and met my gaze again.

I raised a brow, then returned my attention to the braid.

He came up behind me and rested his hand on my hip. "I'm just saying that I want to make sure that you can handle keeping yourself composed if they disagree with you or address the… somewhat excessive bloodshed from our recent outings."

He grabbed the piece of leather I intended to use to tie off the braid and handed it to me when I was ready for it. I finished tying the braid before I turned to face him and leaned back against the dresser.

"You want to make sure I'm not going to snap on one of them."

He searched my face for a few moments before his eyes met mine. "You were ready to throttle Tellus the last time we saw him. I'm just trying to make sure you're not going to do anything rash and get yourself in *more* trouble with Solas. I'm not terribly concerned about Oíche."

"They'll just have to get over it." I traced my fingers down one of the sheathes of a dagger on his chest.

"Yes, well we both know that it isn't just going to blow over, so I will ask again. Are you sure you're ready?"

I gave him a withering look, but he just smirked.

"I'll take that as the only *yes* I'm going to get."

We should include Adriana. Gaisgeach interjected.

"He's right." Deiric agreed. "I'm not sure why we hadn't thought of that for the last one."

"Perhaps because she's just a kid."

A kid *who will rule the country when her brother falls.* Macha added.

I narrowed my eyes as though I could scowl at her, despite that she wasn't even in the room with us.

"What?" Deiric looked puzzled.

"Macha, pointing out that Adriana will rule the country one day and that Gaisgeach is right." I slipped out of his grasp and headed toward the door. "I'll get her."

She's already on her way to the foyer.

Of course she would be. If Gaisgeach suggested bringing her, Cairbre already knew.

"Shall we?" Deiric smiled, and slipped past me to open the door for me. I rolled my eyes at him but walked out and headed down the stairs to the foyer. Adriana and Lazarus stood waiting for us.

"You should plan to stay quiet unless someone speaks to you." I instructed Adriana. She just nodded. I suppose she was probably more accustomed to these sorts of meetings than even we would be. I assumed she would have witnessed several of them during her time in the palace.

I shifted us directly into the room we typically met in. There was no sense in arriving in the foyer and walking there. Quinn and Tellus jolted when we arrived, as though they hadn't been expecting us.

"You're early." Tellus pointed out, and then turned away from Quinn so he was facing us. "With one more than we anticipated."

"It seemed important that she should be here given her stature."

Tellus seemed to consider that, then nodded his head. "I suppose it's not a bad idea, since we are in direct opposition of her brother."

"Half-brother." Adriana clarified.

I shot her a look that pointed out she wasn't supposed to speak up, and she shot an indignant one back at me. I rolled my eyes for what felt like the fifth time today. *Fine*. She could interject whenever she pleased. She would be Queen one day after all.

"She can speak freely here." Tellus declared. "I'll find another chair." His sudden acceptance of her wholeheartedly felt off, given their last interaction with one another, but I wasn't going to question it.

"That won't be necessary." I stopped him before he could turn to find one. "She can have my seat. I can stand."

He gave me a suspicious look, but shrugged a shoulder and turned back to finish whatever conversation he was having with Quinn. Quinn was still looking at me with a hint of pity in her eyes, but she didn't say anything other than giving me a curt nod to acknowledge my presence.

When the rest of the group had arrived, we all took our seats. I stood behind Adriana. Her presence, and my lack of a seat seemed to catch everyone's attention, but they didn't say a word. Their thoughts told me enough. Some of them were suspicious of her sudden inclusion, and others were just perplexed at the fact that she took my chair.

You're causing quite the stir, love. Deiric pointed out.

That's on purpose. If they're going to question me, I'll be looking down on them when I answer.

I didn't miss the smirk that he tried to hide.

Devlon spoke first, and the look on his face was hard to decipher. "It's interesting that you've decided to bring her today." His tone said it was anything but. "I finally heard from Vivian."

There were several gasps and murmurings among the Solas magisters. We all believed her imprisoned or dead.

"She was released, with a message." Now he looked absolutely disgusted.

"Is she alright?" I asked, before I could stop myself. Dread coiled in my stomach, nearly making me sick. I couldn't imagine what she might've been through.

"She wasn't tortured." I could've sagged in relief. "But… She was poisoned and she only survived long enough to relay the message."

I gripped the back of Adriana's chair for support. Something told me that was my fault.

"What was the message?" Adriana asked. Devlon's gaze fell to her.

"If we remove the curse from Azazel and return *you* to the palace, they will stop the executions."

Neither Adriana, nor I spoke. The room was so quiet you could have heard a pin drop, and the tension was so thick I could've cut it with my sword.

"The funny thing is," Devlon looked up at me. "I don't recall anything about a curse."

This is not good. Deiric thought, but kept his face impassive. I did my best to do the same with mine.

"I will not remove the curse." Adriana said without an ounce of hesitation.

Devlon couldn't hide his surprise as his gaze fell to Adriana. "Excuse me?"

"I cast the curse, and I will *not* be removing it. We'll handle the executions like we have been and save as many of our people as we can."

"Our people?" Quinn asked, the insinuation behind her words was obvious. Adriana was not a part of Solas.

Adriana kept her shoulders and head held high as she shifted her gaze to Quinn. "Yes." A hint of rage laced every word. "Our people."

"And what exactly is the nature of this curse?" Quinn wasn't going to let it go and her words got angrier by the second.

"The curse is none of your concern." Adriana said it with such regal finality that she left no room for argument. "The executions will not stop, even if we decide to meet his demands. My half-brother is not a man of his word. If you don't listen to anything else I say today, at least trust that. He's a bastard who never should've ascended the throne."

Quinn was left speechless. Garrick had a smirk on his face that he was trying desperately to hide. Devlon's amusement was evident in his eyes, even if his face didn't show it.

"For the sake of keeping us informed, your highness." Devlon shot Quinn a pointed look that said he was not thrilled about her lack of respect and formalities with Adriana. "Would you mind at least sharing what the curse is *doing* to Azazel?"

I didn't have to see Adriana's face to know she was smiling. The uncomfortable shuffling that several of the magisters did before she spoke told me enough.

"Let's just say, he's finding it increasingly uncomfortable to use his magic lately and leave it at that."

Even I raised my brows at her explanation, which likely only confirmed that she was the one to have cast it to everyone sitting at the table. My surprise of course, was solely because of how she said it and how she was holding herself for this meeting. I *knew* how much he would be suffering.

She was *made* to be a queen, I realized. Yes, she was a young mage who had only just mastered her magic. She had seemed sweet and innocent when she came to us, but beneath that innocence was a confident and capable ruler. Why else would the Morrigan have such an interest in her?

I'm starting to see why Gaisgeach insisted that we bring her. Deiric thought.

Me too.

You'll owe her for that. Gaisgeach interjected. *She's banking on that.*

I didn't know how to interpret that, so I decided to ignore it for now.

"Interesting." Devlon finally spoke when the initial shock wore off. "It's settled then." He moved on without any further questions. They went around the table to get everyone else's updates. There were mentions of a few upcoming executions, which I made note of, including one at the capital.

We will not *be intervening in that one.* Gaisgeach snarled.

It is far too risky. Fiadh added.

Agreed. Deiric added before I could interject. It was three on one, and I imagined Cairbre had the same feelings, so even if Adriana took my side we were still outnumbered four to two.

If you so much as attempt to intervene with that one, Gaisgeach's rage laced each and every word he spoke to me, *I will fry you myself.*

I refrained from pointing out that he would die too. I heard a chuffing noise, which meant he heard my thought anyway and found it rather amusing that I decided not to project it toward him. The bastard.

"There is, of course, another matter to discuss." Tellus started and his gaze, along with several other Solas magisters shifted to me.

Adriana leaned forward and placed both elbows on the table. Shadows danced around her. Tellus and the rest of the table looked at her. He raised a brow.

"If you mean the executions that we've stopped, then I'm not really sure what there is to discuss." A shadow slipped through her fingers like a snake before wrapping around her arm. "People died." She shrugged. "That happens when you're at war."

"We are *not* at war." Quinn pointed out.

"Aren't we?" Garrick asked and Quinn looked over at him. "Our entire existence has been outlawed by Leinster. Does that not constitute war?"

"They have not launched attacks–"

"They have nearly executed hoards of our people." Liam slammed his fist down on the table. "They have rounded them up like cattle and thrown them in dungeons across the country. And you claim that it isn't war?"

Quinn opened her mouth to speak, but Devlon stopped her.

"Enough." He nearly shouted. "The *problem*," he looked directly at me, "has been dealt with."

"You can't be serious." Quinn breathed.

"I am." His gaze fell on her now. "They are only *killing* people when it is required. Isn't that right, Mira?" He glanced my way again.

I nodded.

"See?" He gestured toward me. "They're showing far more restraint."

"She beheaded a man just two days ago." Quinn argued.

"He ran her through with a fucking sword." Adriana snapped. "Would you not call that just cause?"

"She's immortal." She shrugged a shoulder. "That was hardly more than an inconvenience."

"Shall we run you through with a sword and see how you handle it?" Deiric snarled while not so casually reaching up to grab the sword strapped to his back.

"I am not–"

"You can be healed."

And you said I couldn't handle it.

He shot me a look that could've killed me and I did my best to hide my smirk with my hand and a feigned cough.

Quinn scoffed and looked at Devlon for help.

"I'm sorry, but he has a point." Devlon shrugged. "Again, it's been handled. Yes, people died, but there's nothing we can do about it now."

"So you're all just fine with the fact that they kill for sport and use blood magic?" Quinn nearly shouted.

"No one mentioned blood magic." Garrick pointed out.

"The curse–"

"Was sanctioned by the crown." Adriana cut her off. "Azazel is a sadistic bastard and deserves far worse punishment than the blood curse that *I* placed on him. Since we are not in a position to punish him now, we're just taking precautions to ensure he doesn't cause the same amount of harm he did to Mira to anyone else. Surely that should be deemed acceptable in times like these, should it not?"

"Yes." Devlon answered. "If you have further questions or concerns, Quinn, I'm happy to discuss them after this meeting, but this discussion is over." He looked around the table. "Who's next?"

There was an uncomfortable silence before Liam spoke up. "Perhaps we should simply consider leaving Leinster altogether?"

"What?" Garrick snapped.

"I'm just suggesting it because they're determined to kill us all. Is there any reason to stay?"

"He won't stop at just banning magic in Leinster." Adriana spoke louder than everyone else who tried to protest or speak on the topic. “I can promise you this is bigger than just pushing us out of this territory.”

“And how exactly would you know anyway?” Quinn jumped in now, obviously still irritated from their earlier interaction.

“I’ve been informed that Ronan’s forces are gathering near our western borders. It would stand to reason that she has a point.” Garrick pointed out before Adriana could spit something nasty back at Quinn.

Adriana stared her down now.

“He could be doing that for any reason.” Quinn tried to argue.

“Maybe, but we should likely prepare for anything.” Garrick continued. “I have my suspicions about his plans, but only time will tell.”

I didn’t like the sound of that. The table fell into an uncomfortable silence again before Devlon coaxed the rest of the magisters into giving their updates. The rest of the meeting passed without excitement.

The moment we shifted back into the foyer at home Adriana started to walk away, like she couldn’t escape us fast enough. I caught her by her shoulder and spun her around to face me.

“Why the *fuck* did you tell them you cast the curse?” It was a combination of worry and rage bubbling up in me from the moment she made that declaration in the meeting, and I was near boiling over.

She looked at me casually assessing the conflicting emotions she saw in me and smirked. Her gaze flicked from me, to Deiric, and back again before she shrugged. “They can’t kill the future queen.”

I stared at her blankly for a few seconds until she spared one final glance at Deiric and walked away. I had a dagger in my hand and had him backing up a step with his hands raised in surrender in the blink of an eye.

"You son of a bitch." I snarled at him. He rightfully looked concerned, but didn't back up any further, even with the blade lightly pressed against his neck.

"Easy," he coaxed, his hands flexing with the word. "I had nothing to do with it. I was just as surprised as you."

It was my idea. Gaisgeach snapped. *Remove the blade from your mate's throat and calm the fuck down.*

"You fucking bastard." I flung the dagger at the floor and stormed off up the stairs to our bedroom. The dagger slammed into the floor with a loud thud, stabbing directly into the otherwise pristine wood floors. I was acutely aware of the audience we'd gathered, namely my father and Lazarus, who both struggled to hold in their amusement. I heard my father ask if there was 'trouble in paradise' as I crested the stairs.

I knew how it must've looked. I had directed the insult at Gaisgeach, but no one else knew that. I walked straight to my dresser, where the remaining bottle of whiskey sat. Gods, I'd finished an entire bottle already. I couldn't wait for this all to end. No matter how it turned out, at this point.

I had no sooner poured myself a glass and started to lift it to my lips that Deiric appeared behind me. He rested one hand on my hip and wrapped the other around my neck in a firm but gentle hold. He tilted my head to the side, leaned in, and nipped at my neck. "You are *so* fucking sexy when you threaten me. Did you know that?"

I gasped and nearly dropped the glass. My body reacted instantaneously and so vehemently that it was entirely out of my control.

He slid the hand on my hip lower, and it was only then that I realized he also held my dagger, because he parted my skirt and slipped it back into the sheath on my thigh.

"I think you dropped this." His breath tickled my neck. His fingers trailed under my skirt around to the inside of my leg and the sensation had me pressing myself back into him to try to escape it. The movement did nothing but encourage him. I could feel his lips part in a smile.

"Not so threatening now, are you, love?" His lips grazed up my neck as he spoke until he was just below my ear, while his hand continued its journey up my thigh, and he toyed with the hem of my underwear.

I didn't answer him. Couldn't. I sat the glass on the dresser in front of me, forgotten. I simply melted into him instead as my eyes fluttered closed.

He chuckled and nibbled at my ear. "Look at you." He breathed. "Melting into me with just the right touch." He hooked his finger under the thin fabric and dipped it down between my thighs.

I let out a shaky breath. His grip on my neck tightened ever so slightly and the smile returned to his lips as he turned his head and spoke directly against the side of my neck now. Leaning entirely into my space.

"And so wet, so *ready* for me already."

I found myself wondering exactly how I'd ended up here, entirely at his mercy. A *threat*. I was angry with him. I was *still* angry–

He circled my clit with two fingers, sending a jolt through me that had me forgetting all about why I was angry at him and melting away the tension I'd managed to drum up in the two seconds I remembered *why* I was standing here just now.

"As thrilling as I think it would be to fuck you while you're angry, I much prefer you this way." He continued moving his fingers in lazy circles, short circuiting my brain each time.

He spun me around so quickly I was a bit dizzy, then hoisted me up onto the edge of the dresser. I tried to pull him into a kiss, hooking my hands into his hair and pulling his face to mine. He obliged me for only a second or two before pulling away and dropping to his knees between my legs.

He slipped under my skirt, shredded the panties I was wearing, forcefully ripping them off of me, and then his mouth was on me. I nearly fell backwards into the mirror before I caught myself. I gripped the edge of the dresser like my life depended on it.

"Gods, Deiric." I managed to breathe, nearly on the precipice of an orgasm far too quickly for me to process what was happening. Never, in my entire existence, had I been with someone who could push me this close so quickly. Never had I known someone who *knew* me so well that barely a minute was all that it took.

And yet this man. *This fucking man* worked me like he'd been made solely for that purpose. This man *worshipped* my body like I was a goddess, and he was desperate for my favor. How did I get so lucky?

It was with that thought that I crashed over the edge of ecstasy and cried out his name with as much fervor as he was currently ravaging my body. He pulled back then, seeming to take a breath for the first time since he descended upon me only to lift me from the dresser and spin us around with me on his shoulders.

I panicked for a half a second, only for him to drop me onto the bed as he fell right down with me. It didn't knock the wind out of me, given that it was a very soft landing, but it startled me. I was still catching my breath as he prowled up the bed now.

His lips met mine, still tasting of *me*, in a suffocating kiss. Then he slid himself into me and I moaned into his lips. I hadn't even noticed him undo his pants. I could feel the leather against my thighs, so he obviously had not bothered to remove them.

He moved with an expert precision, as he'd done with his mouth. I rocked my hips up to meet him with each thrust and buried my hands in his hair. He slid one of his hands up into mine and pulled my head to the side before he sank his fangs into my neck.

I soared over the edge again, crying out his name as he continued to pound into me until he followed me over it too.

*

A knock came at the door, interrupting me as I kissed down Deiric's chest. A low growl rumbled from me and Deiric's responding dark chuckle made me want to ignore it completely.

The knock came again, louder and more insistent this time. "If you two can pull yourselves apart from one another, I need to speak with you." Lazarus impatiently called from the other side of the door.

I pulled the sheets up over my bare chest and looked toward the door. "Fine." I called through our sound shield. "Enter." Deiric shifted himself and the blankets to cover *him* as well.

Lazarus slipped into our bedroom and promptly shut the door behind him, as though he was concerned anyone in the hallway might peek beyond him and see what he was interrupting as well. He took one glance toward us before he averted his eyes and found the floor of our bedroom far too interesting. Aris and Silas never gave us that courtesy, so it was surprising to see it from Lazarus.

"Leo let me know that Rosalind is ready to be around humans. I know there are very few crystals left, but I'd like to ask your permission to give one to her while I'm staying here."

I blinked at him. I'd completely forgotten about the pretty little nightmage that he'd shared the night following the party with months ago. I hadn't even asked him about her after that evening. I knew she'd gone to his manor, hell, I had delivered her there, but that was the last I'd heard of her.

The question that was driving me mad was why he felt that was so important he had to interrupt Deiric and I *in bed.* And that, I was still a little angry about. I was quiet long enough that he finally looked up and met my gaze.

"You thought interrupting us was the best way to win my favor for that?"

There was a war waging in his eyes, and I still couldn't quite process what that meant. "I will not wait until you tire of fucking each other to ask it. You could be in here all night." There was a ferocity to the way he said it that told me he was close to snapping. I'd never seen that level of rage from him aside from the times that *I* was threatened.

As much as the comment built up rage inside me, and I could tell it did the same to Deiric, there was something about it that made me pause. “What is she to you, anyway?” I asked carefully.

He tensed like he was poised to strike me, but reined himself in. *That* told me everything I needed to know.

I laughed. “Well I’ll be damned.”

“I don’t find this even the slightest bit entertaining.” He snarled.

“I didn’t just get you a one night hook up did I?” I teased, taking pleasure in this despite his rage fueled posture. “I set you up with your *mate*.” I smirked.

He just stared at me, with a scowl on his face.

I rolled my eyes and sighed. “Fine.” I called a silk robe to my hand and carefully wrapped that around me as I slipped off the bed. “I’ll take you to retrieve your mate.” I walked over and handed him a crystal for her. “But, you’ll let me put a sound shield around your room before you can wake half the house with whatever it is the two of you do, and you won’t bother us for the rest of the evening, is that clear?”

He nodded, taking the crystal from my hand and crossing his arms to wait patiently for me to get ready to shift us there.

“Oh, I’m not getting dressed.” I smirked. “So you had better make this quick.”

I only took another second to process the shock on his face before I shifted us into the foyer of his manor. I startled several vampires who were lounging about the space when we popped in. He still looked at me incredulously. “Isn’t Deiric going to–”

“Deiric will get over it. I think he’s far more frustrated by your interruption than I was.”

Understanding flashed on his face before he disappeared to collect Rosalind. I waited patiently in the foyer while all of the current residents of his manor eyed me cautiously, clearly perplexed as to why I stood in the foyer in nothing but a silk robe.

They reappeared after less than five minutes with a bag slung over Lazarus' shoulder. She wore fighting leathers and had her hair tied neatly back in a braid. I hardly recognized her.

"You're sure she's ready to be around humans?" I asked Lazarus.

He merely nodded. "If she isn't, I'll handle it."

I gave her one more hesitant glance before I shifted us back to my manor and into the main hallway. I pushed open the door to Lazarus' room, put my hand on the wall, created the shield and then walked back out.

"No one will hear anything inside your room if the door is closed." I smirked. "Make all the noise you want." Then I left them alone and slipped back into my bedroom to finish what I'd started with Deiric.

Chapter 38

Mira

I was up bright and early the next morning. Before the sun, for once. Deiric merely rolled over when I slipped out of bed, reluctant to wake before the sun. I couldn't say I blamed him. I slipped on a nightgown and the silk robe I'd worn to Lazarus' manor before I walked into the hallway. I started to make my way down the stairs to prepare some tea, but was cut short on my mission by Rosalind.

"Mira." She appeared in front of me halfway down the stairs.

I jolted. "Fuck's sake, Rosalind."

She moved down a step. "Apologies. I forget how quickly I move sometimes."

I gave her a look that suggested she should sort that out before bombarding me first thing in the morning and she shrunk back another step.

"I wanted to speak with you, if that's alright?"

I didn't hide my annoyance from my face as I stepped around her and continued on my way. "You don't have to ask permission to speak to me. You can just do it."

She turned and followed me down the stairs. "I know I'm new. *Very* new." She started while I prepared a kettle for tea.

"Yes. I'm aware." I said dismissively as I placed the kettle over the fire in the kitchen and tossed another piece of wood on it.

She huffed and I turned to look at her. "You know, you were far nicer when you were trying to hook me up with Lazarus."

I gaped at her, taken aback not only by the comment, but by her brazenness in saying it.

"I'm sorry." She shrunk back again. "That was rude." She let out a disgruntled sigh. "Gods, I feel like I'm a mess now. My emotions are all over the fucking place."

I stood silently and let her sort herself out. I assumed Lazarus had kept her up all night. Or rather, they'd probably kept *each other* up all night. I smiled a little at the thought. I hadn't intended *this* but I certainly wasn't bothered by it. At least he found someone he could be happy with. He deserved as much.

"I'll just get right to the point."

I snapped my attention back to her. "That would be nice."

She gave me a look that reaffirmed she liked me better at the party. "I was wondering if I might be able to bother you for a daylight ring?"

Oh. Right. *Fuck*. I hadn't even considered that. Neither had Lazarus, apparently. Or he had just not cared when he decided he was bringing her here. The sun would be up soon and she'd be doomed to stay in his room with the curtains and shutters drawn all day.

"Of course, love." I spun and pulled the kettle off the fire now that it screamed. "I'll work on that during the next full moon. There's not much I can do until then though."

After I placed the tea ball in the pot to steep, I turned to see her staring at me like I'd just lost my damned mind.

"What?"

She nearly laughed. "I'm sorry. You just went from seeming like you wanted nothing to do with me to calling me love and nonchalantly agreeing to create a daylight ring when I was almost certain you'd make me wait a few years."

I couldn't lie and say that I said that to everyone. I didn't. I couldn't even lie and say I said that only to women. Deiric, clearly, was rubbing off on me, but I did occasionally use that as a term of endearment to the women I'd flirted and slept with. And I just called Lazarus' mate *love*. I would never live this down.

As if she saw the conflict and panic in my face she finally relaxed and actually laughed at me. "You didn't pick me because you thought he'd like me, did you? You picked me because *you* liked me."

"I–" I mean, I picked her because she showed an interest in him, but she hadn't been the only one. I noticed *he* had an interest in her and that helped my case, but there had been another reason she'd caught my attention in the first place.

"Okay." I relented. "Fine. Yes, I found you attractive. Can we just avoid sharing that with any of *them*?" I gestured toward where I hoped everyone else was still sleeping in the rest of the house.

"Too late." Xander mused as he walked into the dining room. "Deiric is going to lose his shit." He laughed, the bastard.

I don't personally think Deiric will care. Fiadh chimed in, and I wanted to scream. She rarely popped in my head, but I suppose this moment was fitting. Gaisgeach was frustratingly quiet.

I won't care about what exactly? Deiric's voice in my head was groggy with sleep, and now I was wishing I'd never woken up to come down here.

I'll let Mira tell you.

You're enjoying this far too much. I snapped at her.

There was an amused snort. *Consider this payback for the day you nearly burned your mate.*

Fuck you.

Mira. Deiric warned. I only sensed amusement from the dragon though. There was no animosity.

I shifted my focus back to Rosalind, now that my tea was ready. "I'll get you your ring as soon as I can."

"Thank you." She nodded her thanks and then wandered back up the stairs.

When I spun around with my tea Xander was still smiling like a child, giddy with his newfound discovery. "What is it you find so funny?"

He leaned back against the wall on the far end of the dining room and crossed his arms over his chest. "It's rare that I have anything to hold against you. This is probably the *best* thing I'll ever get."

I rolled my eyes. "You already knew I was attracted to women. I don't see how this is groundbreaking."

"You sent a woman *you* were attracted to to Lazarus. That's something I never saw coming."

"What, did you think I'd take her for myself instead? I have a mate. That is entirely off the table."

"Your mate wouldn't enjoy a woman joining the two of you?"

I glared at him. "*I* wouldn't enjoy *sharing* my mate with another woman. So *no*."

Well this is one hell of a way to wake up. Deiric chimed in, the hint of laughter edging his voice.

Fuck you, too.

I felt his amusement, rather than hearing his laugh. I'd only been awake for twenty minutes and I already wanted to stab two men, my mate included. This was not a good start to the day.

Relax, love. Deiric's voice floated to me again. *Come back to bed and we can start the day properly.*

I snorted. If I came back to bed now, we'd never leave it. I needed to do something productive today. We had another execution to deal with in two days. That would take careful planning.

Fine. He grumbled. *But you'll have to come back up here anyway to put on something more suitable to wear all day.*

*

Hours later I swung my sword at Deiric, but he ducked low in a dodge and countered my strike with one of his own. I barely managed to block that in time, but he nearly struck me anyway because my hand seemed to spasm and I lost the grip on the hilt.

He halted his swing with mind boggling swiftness to avoid actually striking me and stepped back when he noticed the confused look on my face. I opened and closed my hand, testing it out again because I'd never experienced such a spasm before.

"Everything alright?" I heard Lazarus ask from where he stood behind me.

"I think so." I bent down to pick up my sword again and my entire arm seemed to have a mind of its own. "What the fuck?" I muttered under my breath.

Are you alright? Gaisgeach's voice took on a worried tone that I rarely heard from him, as if he could sense or feel whatever it was that seemed to be going wrong with me.

I don't know.

I tried again to use my hand and arm to no avail just as my other arm seemed to become entirely useless to me. A strange feeling seemed to be creeping over my entire body, as though it was no longer my own.

A deep laugh cackled through my head, one that chilled me to my very bones. *Did you really think you could escape without consequences?* Azazel's voice in my head sent a wave of fear through me. He had my blood, and the gods only knew what he was doing with it to do *this.*

I looked up at Deiric. "Run," was all I managed to say before I lost control completely. Trapped like a prisoner in my own body.

Chapter 39

Deiric

Fear, true fear, was not something that I was accustomed to scenting on Mira. Nor was it something that I was used to seeing in her eyes. She'd been tense, anxious even, a number of times, but this was vastly different. She told me to run, but there was no way in hell I was going to run off and let her handle whatever it was that was happening to her on her own.

"Get *everyone* inside." I snarled at Lazarus when I saw *Mira* disappear from her eyes. Only cold and murderous rage appeared in her gaze now, and it was directly wholly at me. I didn't look to see if he obeyed.

A sinister smile spread across her lips as she stepped toward me. A ball of lightning sparked to life in her right hand.

I let her back me up a few steps.

"I forgot she was rumored to have various magic types." It was her voice, but the inflection and cold tone were *not* her. "I'm going to thoroughly enjoy killing you."

"What have you done to her?" I snarled. It had to be Azazel. No one else would have a reason to kill me or have a vendetta against her that would get them to make *her* hands be the one that did it. Then again, I was fairly certain that with our blood oath and bond to one another if I died, so would she.

I wondered if he knew that.

"Two birds, one stone." The smile on her face widened. "These gifts she has are quite interesting."

I backed up a few more steps before the ball of lightning came flying at me. "Sciath," I mumbled, and a transparent shield appeared in front of my closed fist, blocking the attack momentarily and disappearing seconds after.

The sinister look in her eyes faltered for just a second and was replaced by the briefest moment of genuine confusion. Then another attack came, this time shadows stretched toward me.

A wall of shadow appeared in front of me, and I glanced to my left to see Adriana standing on the front porch with a horrified look on her face, hand extended to shield me. I gave her a curt nod before redirecting my attention back to Mira. *Azazel.*

A rapid succession of attacks followed. Some were blocked by Adriana; some I blocked on my own. At some point she picked her sword back up and took a few swings with that. Each time she nearly landed a blow or *did* land a blow I could visibly see a wince, which told me she was still in there, watching *all* of this.

It struck me as odd that he wasn't attempting to go after anyone else, but I guessed this was about revenge, not about actually getting what they wanted anymore. She did curse him after all. At some point either the curse should force him to stop, or she should be able to break free of it. I hoped, anyway.

She nearly took my head off after three consecutive attacks, magical and otherwise. It was at that moment Lazarus appeared behind her and snapped her neck with a trained precision that even I would have had to admire, if it hadn't been my mate's neck.

She crumpled lifeless to the ground in front of him, and I launched myself at him with animalistic rage. Before I even registered that he was defending himself, I was on the ground, he was on top of me, and had me by the throat.

"Calm the fuck down or you're next." He snarled, barely seeming to struggle to hold me while I thrashed beneath him. "You know she'll wake up. We don't have time for this, and I couldn't stand by and let her kill you."

He looked over toward the house. "Adriana, we're taking her to Tellus' castle and locking her up there until we can sort this out. Can you shift us?"

"Like fucking hell," I snarled up at him. "We are *not* locking her up somewhere."

"Do you have a better idea?"

I opened my mouth to reply, but I didn't have any better ideas. We couldn't restrain her in any other way. She outmatched us power-wise in all aspects except physical strength, but we wouldn't be able to touch her.

I don't have any ideas either. I'm sorry. Fiadh's voice was somber, like she was just as upset about the idea as me.

"You'll break her." I hadn't noticed Teron come outside, but he at least was on my side.

Lazarus released me and stood up. "Better that she's upset than dead, is it not?"

I was on my feet in less than a second. Adriana came over to Mira and frowned down at her. "I didn't realize that you could *die* without dying."

"It's not pleasant." I grumbled and scooped Mira gently into my arms.

Adriana shifted us before Teron could say anything else. While I appreciated that he was on my side, I doubted he had any ideas either. We arrived in Tellus' office, startling him from whatever he was working on at his desk.

"We need a cell." Lazarus demanded.

*

Lazarus had Adriana shift him back after we had Mira secured in one of the cells with magic blocking shackles. I refused to return to the manor until she woke up, Tellus refused to leave me with her, and Adriana came back the moment she deposited Lazarus at our manor to keep an eye on Mira.

"She was *finally* acting like herself again." Adriana leaned against the wall across from me. "If she wakes up and she's… *her* she'll be a mess."

"I'm aware." I was leaning right next to the door to her cell, listening intently for any indication that she'd wake up. It didn't take all that long to heal from. A few minutes, at most, but it varied by the vampire and their age. I had no idea what to expect from her.

"Are you certain it was Azazel?" Tellus asked.

I barely spared him a glance. "I can't think of anyone else who *has* magic that would have a reason to kill me."

"I'm sure it had nothing to do with the guards you killed while he was torturing her." He grumbled sarcastically.

I glared at Tellus now. He put his hands up in defeat. "Look, all I'm saying is you didn't give him any reason to *like* you."

I stopped listening to him when I heard Mira's sharp inhale. The chains holding her rattled as she moved.

"No." Her voice was barely audible, but I knew it was *her*. "No. no. no. no."

I couldn't stand outside and listen to the panic rising in her voice. I moved to open the door and Tellus tried to step in my way. I grabbed him by the collar and slammed him against the wall.

"If you think you are going to stand in my way while my mate is in there *falling apart* because we didn't have any choice but to restrain her I will kill you where you stand without a second thought."

He looked at me with wide eyes and put his hands up by his head. I didn't wait for him to say another word before I released him and flung the door open to run to her.

I was only vaguely aware of Adriana saying she'd make sure that Mira didn't kill me.

I was on my knees before her with my arms around her faster than she could blink. She dug her hands into my leathers and sobbed. Her breath was erratic, and at moments she didn't seem to breathe at all.

"I'm so sorry, love." She only held me tighter.

“We didn’t have any other choice.” Adriana added from where she stood behind us.

“It’s alright. I’ve got you. You’re safe.” I ran my hand up and down her back, trying to calm her. It didn’t seem to do much for her. She was already deep in the throws of a panic attack. She would just have to work her way through it.

It took several agonizing minutes for her breathing to return to normal again. Adriana stood quietly at the front of the cell while Tellus lurked in the corridor.

“I’m so sorry.” Mira mumbled into my chest.

“It’s alright, love.”

“I tried to fight him.”

“I know.”

“Lazarus isn’t going to let us take you home until we figure out a way to prevent him from taking control of you again. Do you know what kind of spell could do that?”

Mira went completely still. “He has my blood. He could have done any number of spells. I’m not familiar with one that does what he did.”

“What about a way to block it?”

Mira’s silence told me she had no idea, but I had a feeling she wasn’t thinking well enough to come up with one yet anyway.

As if on cue, Triss appeared in the cell next to us. “Oh good, she’s back.” She glanced out toward the cell door. “Tellus, bring me the keys.”

Mira pulled away from me to look up at her. She looked miserable. Her eyes were still red from the tears she shed before she calmed down.

“Rosalind made this,” Triss leaned down and put a spell jar around her neck. “It should do the trick.”

"That seems far too simple a solution." Mira mumbled.

Triss shrugged. "If it doesn't work, we'll deal with it, and this time we're not bringing you back to this cell."

"Thank the gods." Mira held up her wrists to Tellus while he worked on unlocking them.

"For what it's worth," Adriana started and stepped forward toward us, "none of us wanted to bring you here. Lazarus demanded it. He was worried you'd kill Deiric."

Mira didn't reply. I helped her to her feet. Adriana thanked Tellus and then shifted us all home.

Mira looked me over and frowned. "I'm sorry."

"I'm fine, love. It wasn't anything I couldn't handle."

That didn't seem to make her feel any better. Teron appeared at the entrance to the den and eyed her carefully. I gave him a look that I hoped conveyed that she needed time.

He gave me a curt nod and disappeared back into the den. I guided Mira up the stairs to our bedroom before Lazarus could try to intercept us either. She didn't need to deal with anyone right now.

Chapter 40

Mira

I was jolted from sleep when Deiric moved suddenly next to me. It took me a moment or two to get my bearings and realize that *he* was having a nightmare for a change. While I hadn't had very restful sleep myself, I'd managed to escape that fate this evening somehow.

I propped myself up on my elbow and gently shook him. "Deiric," I tried, but that didn't seem to stir him.

I sat all the way up and more firmly grasped his shoulder to shake him. "Deiric."

He moved like he was fighting against an invisible force, and panic gripped me harder than I expected at the thought. Surely this wasn't magically induced. I straddled him now and shook him violently, nearly shouting his name this time.

In a blink, I was beneath him, and he held me down by my throat. He bared his fangs at me in a snarl. My breath was caught in my throat with how tightly he held me. I couldn't speak, couldn't reassure him that he was alright, and we were *safe*.

Two seconds passed. Three, before he finally relaxed his grip and his eyes returned to their normal blue.

"Mira." He breathed. "I'm so sorry, I–"

"Don't." I croaked out, finally taking in a real breath when his grip fully relaxed. "I'm fine."

His eyes searched my face, like he was looking for the lie, but found nothing.

"It's alright." I reached up and gently brushed my thumb across his cheek. "Do you want to talk about it?" In truth, I didn't know what to do for him. I knew what he did for me, but I'd never *attacked* him coming out of a dream, so this was new to me.

His entire body seemed to deflate, and he shifted so he was lying next to me, but rested his head between my breasts with a sigh. "I'm not sure talking it through will help much."

"Admittedly it doesn't help me much either." I mumbled while I ran my fingers through his hair. We fell into silence for several minutes, while both of our still racing hearts began to slow.

"He'd taken you again," Deiric said softly. "This time though, he took me too and made me watch while he tore you to pieces."

My fingers stilled in his hair, the rest of me along with them. The thought of him having to watch, even though I knew now that he'd seen it from Kieran's point of view made me sick. It was enough to experience it first hand, but if

I had to watch them do the same to him I would be inconsolable.

It explained his reaction to being woken out of it, at least. I resisted the urge to apologize, catching myself a second before the words escaped me. He'd told me that I was not allowed to apologize at all when it wasn't actually my fault.

He huffed a sad laugh. "At least you stopped yourself this time."

I smacked his shoulder, then went back to running my fingers through his hair. He let out a noise that almost sounded like a purr. His arm around my waist tightened against me.

"I'm sorry that I woke you."

I gently gathered a fistful of his hair and lifted his head to force him to look at me. "If I'm not allowed to apologize," I scolded, "Neither are you."

The corner of his mouth quirked up into the slightest smirk. "Fine." He mumbled, then lowered his head back down onto my chest when I loosened my hold on his hair. "But only if you don't stop doing *that* until I fall asleep again." He barely whispered when my fingers began their work in his hair again.

It was my turn to huff out a little laugh, but I just grumbled, "deal," and continued to toy with his hair until he fell back asleep.

I, however, was wide awake and confident at that point that sleep wasn't going to find me again.

*

Deiric stirred with an exhausted sigh as the sun was breaking over the horizon. He reached up and slipped his hand over mine, intertwining our fingers and forcing me to stop mindlessly running my fingers through his hair like I'd done for hours now. He propped himself up on his elbow and looked down at me.

"Did you sleep at all?"

I met his gaze and shrugged a shoulder. "I couldn't quiet my mind enough to fall back asleep."

"I'm–"

I silenced him with a kiss. "We made a deal," I whispered against his lips.

"Hmm," I felt his smirk. "Funny, I don't recall that. I must've been half asleep if I made such a promise."

I rolled my eyes.

He chuckled and kissed my cheek as he pushed himself up and slipped from the bed. "I'll make you some tea." He started to rummage through his drawers to get dressed.

"I can make my own tea." I pushed myself up and walked over to do the same.

"I think you should stay in bed and get some rest."

I could feel him watching me, even without looking. "I can't very well hide away all day when I have *things* to attend to."

"And what *things* might those be?" He stood behind me now, only partly dressed. His breath coasted along the back of my neck and had me seriously considering staying in bed, but it had nothing to do with getting any rest.

I glanced over my shoulder at him. "I have hardly done anything to help train Zemora, Stella, and Sorcha. I also need to come up with the plan for how we'll handle the execution tomorrow. I can't rely on Liala, Eimear, and Triss to take care of everything." I spun around to face him, putting us nearly chest to chest.

He brushed a stray piece of my hair back behind my ear. "Actually," he smiled. "You can."

I raised a brow and gave him a look that suggested he should elaborate.

He huffed a laugh. "Triss has basically taken over as an archmage. You might as well let her assume the title."

I stared at him incredulously. Doing so would make her temporary stay here permanent. It was something I'd sworn I would *never* do. And yet…

"Think about it." He turned and started to walk toward the door as he pulled his tunic on. "It isn't like you still *hate* her, unless I've read your interactions lately entirely incorrectly."

I scowled at him, which only made his smug smile grow. He leaned back against his dresser and crossed his arms over his chest.

I didn't even have to respond. He knew he'd made a point I couldn't deny. Which for all intents and purposes means he won this small argument. He wasn't, however, going to convince me to go back to bed.

I slipped on a blouse, skirt, and corset. He appeared behind me to tighten it for me without prompting, despite that he knew I didn't actually need him to help me. We silently made our way downstairs to discover a handful of the others already up and about. I walked straight to the tea kettle, which was already sitting near the fire to keep it warm.

Deiric followed me, never straying more than two steps behind me as I went. While he didn't look nearly as exhausted as me, I was certain he wasn't entirely recovered either.

A loud set of footsteps thudded down the stairs. Lazarus, if I had to guess, although some of them sounded the same. I didn't care enough to reach out with my magic and determine who. A second set of footsteps reached the stairs, one I couldn't pinpoint.

Teron. Deiric supplied.

I gave him a sideways glance and he shrugged.

You don't recognize his footsteps?

I frowned and poured myself a cup of tea. I may have recognized them at one time. Whether they were the same now as they'd always been or heavier with all of the shit he'd been through, I couldn't tell.

Lazarus hesitated at the threshold. The only thing that confirmed that was who had come down without looking. None of the other guys would've hesitated at the sight of me, regardless of how yesterday had gone.

My father cleared his throat and Lazarus must've thought the better of coming into the dining room because he walked toward the front door instead. My father walked up beside me. I passed him the tea kettle.

The look in his eyes asked the question, 'are you okay' which I ignored. It was a ridiculous question to ask, I began to realize. Yes is never an accurate answer. No is the obvious answer that no one knows how to react to, so why ask the question at all?

The sudden realization of the idiocy of such an interaction left me a little hollow and I turned away to go take a seat at the table across from Adriana and Esme. Deiric took the spot right next to me. A lighter set of steps descended the stairs and headed toward us.

"You're up early." Triss' voice was far too perky for how early it was in the morning and a stark contrast to the sullen silence our presence seemed to bring into the room.

I took a sip of my tea before I responded. "There's no sense in staying in bed if sleep is going to be so evasive to me." The words held a little more bite than I intended, but she paid them no mind as she swiped the kettle from my father and poured herself a cup.

She spun around and surveyed me. "You look like hell."

"Thanks." I mumbled dryly.

She looked around the room at everyone else. I didn't need to do the same to know that they were all watching Deiric and I like we were caged animals who might simply explode if someone said the wrong thing. Everyone, of course, except my father, who only seemed to look at me with a bit of concern furrowing his brow.

"Well," she started and made her way over to stand beside the table. "I'm going to keep working with Zemora and Stella today. Stella has been making steady progress. Zemora still struggles some, but she's getting there."

She squeezed herself in next to Adriana and sat down, so she was almost directly in front of me.

"I believe that Sorcha is ready to be given her marks, but I'll leave that decision to you, if you feel up to evaluating her today."

I searched her face for a few seconds, trying to determine if she was saying this to get a reaction out of me or if she actually meant it. There was nothing in her thoughts or body language that indicated she was anything but sincere.

I glanced down at my cup, then met her gaze again. "I trust your judgement." I took a sip of my tea and the wave of genuine surprise I felt from Deiric nearly made me choke on it. "Would you like to give them to her, or do you want me to take care of it?"

Triss' jaw nearly came unhinged, but she composed herself quickly. "I– Uh, sure." She cleared her throat and sipped her own tea. "I can take care of it."

"In fact," I continued, barely letting her finish her sentence. "You've been doing quite well with them. Perhaps you'd be better suited to be our archmage, if you're open to it."

She stared at me blankly for long enough that I raised a brow and shrugged. "Think it over."

You're welcome. Deiric thought.

I shot him a glare.

You're just angry you didn't think of it yourself.

I scoffed.

"This is another one of those silent conversations, isn't it?" My father asked as he walked over to take a seat on the other side of Deiric.

"Real annoying, isn't it?" Zane remarked.

"Entertaining, yes. Annoying, no."

Chapter 41

Deiric

Triss had finished her instruction with Zemora and Stella and everyone else had finished sparring for the day, but Mira had yet to move from where she sat at the edge of the front porch. She was staring off at the woods and seemed lost in thought. I stood behind her, leaning against the front wall of the house doing the same thing until I realized we were entirely alone. Now, my focus was on her.

Teron silently walked over until he was nearly standing next to her. He acknowledged me with a nod.

"I know that look." He mumbled, looking down at her.

She nearly jumped out of her skin, apparently entirely oblivious to his approach, then brought the glass of whiskey she'd been holding to her lips. "What look?"

He walked around her to sit on the opposite side of the column she was leaning against. "The mile long stare." He said simply. "The look you get when you're just trying to see past the misery you can't seem to shake."

She barely glanced at him. "What of it?"

"Did I ever tell you how I was turned? Or why?"

She went as still as a statue, then finally turned to look at him fully. He wasn't looking at her, though. He was looking out at the trees like she had been.

"No. You've never told me." She turned to look at the trees again. "I never thought to ask."

I didn't understand where this was coming from, or why he thought that now was the time to share this with her, but I wasn't about to interrupt.

Perhaps he thinks it will help her open up to him? Fiadh commented. *He has known her far longer than you have.*

He knew her when she was a child. I would hardly consider that knowing her better than I do now.

She chuffed at me, but made no further comment.

Teron huffed a laugh. "No one would think to ask. Not with the way we do things now."

A beat of silence passed between them, then she looked over at him. "How were you turned?"

"It was a lot like this actually," he started, with a half-smile as he glanced at her. "I was sitting in a bar and Lazarus approached me. He said, 'I recognize that look' and it all went downhill from there."

She summoned another glass of whiskey and handed it over to him. He took it without really looking.

"You and your mother weren't the first family I had."

He said it so nonchalantly that it shouldn't have hit as hard as it did. Mira wasn't shielding her emotions from me at all, so the horror and guilt hit me like a blow to the gut. Her mind whirled.

"I had a wife and two children before I transitioned."

She took the time to really look at him now and I did the same. I'd noted that he appeared older than most of us. Like he'd lived a longer life before the transition occurred. It was rare, but not entirely unusual. Lazarus also looked a little older. Closer to his forties.

"What happened?" She pushed when he sat in silence for a while.

He glanced at her briefly before his gaze shifted back to the trees again. He took a long sip of the whiskey before he continued. The gesture itself made me dread the full story.

"We had a small farmhouse a mile outside of town. Mirabel went into town that day with our children. She needed a few items and I needed to tend to the fields. Isabel and Jacob loved following her into town.

"She should've come home before nightfall. I waited up until nearly midnight before I finally went out to look for them. I hoped that maybe they just got caught up in something in town and were on their way, but what I found when I went to find them was nothing short of a nightmare."

He paused and got quiet for a few moments, like he couldn't bear to say the rest. He took another sip of the whiskey. She watched him intently, like looking away or speaking up would stop him. I was sure if either of us moved or made a single sound he'd shut down and not finish the story. It was hard to wrap my head around the fact that he had once just been a farmer. It seemed entirely unlike him.

"There was so much blood. I only knew it was from them because I recognized the fabric from my Isabel's dress." He grimaced and looked away. "I saw it then, a long way away through the trees. A beast with a lion's head and serpent's tail. A chimera, although I didn't know that at the time."

Fate was a sick bitch. Connecting me with Mira after she slayed the very same type of beast that set the wheels in motion for her to come to be.

"Not a single person in town believed me. I buried what was left of them the next morning. I tried to warn them all, but it wasn't until other people started to disappear that they started to believe what I'd claimed. I spent many nights at the tavern drowning my sorrows in shitty ale and taking my chances on the walk home. For some ungodly reason, the beast never came for me."

He shook his head and finished off his glass. Mira refilled it with a flick of her wrist.

"That's when Lazarus approached me. I was sitting at the bar for the fourth night in a row when the barkeep told someone that I was the man they were looking for. Lazarus came up, threw down a few gold pieces and told the barkeep to keep the ale coming so long as I would talk to him. I remember thinking how absurd it was to throw that sort of money around. Even the barkeep hesitated, but then he started with the questions.

"He asked me about my family and what I saw. At first I'd told him to fuck off, but he persisted. Eventually I gave in and explained it. If he was going to cover my tab, I figured I at least owed him a few answers. When I finished my explanation, he told the barkeep to keep the gold, forget the drinks, and then he demanded I go with him. I was a belligerent drunk, but he promised me that he'd help me kill the fucking thing that killed my family, so I agreed.

"He took me to an inn, told me to drink some potion he handed me, and the next thing I knew, I was waking up no longer feeling like myself. The bastard had bottled his own blood to give to me like it was some magic strengthening potion.

"In my drunken state I believed him. I didn't have any control over whether or not I drank to finish the transition. He threw a wanted man at me who was already bleeding and my instincts took over."

He paused again, staring out at the trees and taking two sips of his drink. Knowing Lazarus, I didn't put this sort of thing past him, but it was still a shit hand to deal to someone without explaining all of the details first. I wondered if he would've accepted it either way. I guess given that he was still here with us today, he probably would've.

"I didn't really know what had happened to me until the following day." He continued. "I was so blind to the hunger and the rage I felt in those moments that as soon as we took down the chimera he had to knock me out and drag me back to his manor."

He let out a humorless laugh. "Well, shit. He probably snapped my neck like he did to you I guess. I never found out. I just know the world went dark and I woke up in one of the rooms at his place." He shrugged and then turned to meet Mira's gaze.

"Long story short, there's a reason that I was so hard on you, and worked so hard to make sure that if I couldn't protect you, you could protect yourself. It's also why I never let your mother leave the manor. A lot of good that did." He shook his head. "I thought if I pushed you hard enough that no one would ever be able to hurt you."

She held his gaze for what felt like an eternity while she processed everything he'd told her. It was a gods damned tragedy, and made so much about him make sense. What she'd told me of him, anyway. He lost *everything* and Lazarus turned him into a fucking monster to get his revenge. Mira looked toward the ground and took a hefty sip of her whiskey.

"I don't really like to talk about it." Mira said softly. "My time in that cell I mean." She barely glanced at him before her gaze fell to her hands and she emptied her glass of whiskey.

Teron picked up the decanter and poured more whiskey in her glass. It was his unspoken gesture to encourage her to keep talking. I couldn't believe that his story had even prompted her, but I wasn't going to speak up now, nor was I going to walk away.

She sighed. "I gave up." She took a shaky sip from her glass. "I couldn't feel Gaisgeach's presence at all. I couldn't communicate with him. I was certain no one would ever find me, and I accepted that."

She shrugged a shoulder and lifted her gaze back to the tree line. "I knew that so long as Azazel was in there torturing *me* that he wasn't out here hurting anyone I cared about. So I just shut up and took it.

"When he mentioned Deiric…" Her voice nearly broke as she struggled to hold back a wave of emotions that I felt like they were my own. Dread, misery, fear. It nearly made my knees buckle.

"I didn't even flinch because I knew. I *knew* he didn't have him there. It was just to get a rise out of me and it would only make it worse if I reacted. But it fucking broke me. I prayed Deiric would stop looking for me. I knew he wouldn't, but I prayed he would because if he found me… Azazel would've killed him without a second thought."

She shook her head. "I knew it in my very bones. It was a certainty I can't quite explain." She took another sip of her whiskey and must have shoved the emotions back into a box inside herself, because they ebbed back a little.

"I begged Kieran to stake me. I thought that was the only way I thought I'd get out. I knew it would kill Gaisgeach, hurt Fiadh, and by the gods it would probably fucking kill Deiric too with the way we were bonded but I just couldn't do it anymore."

The flood gates opened and this time the emotions that washed over her hit me so hard I had to lock my knees to hold myself up. I had never felt such despair. Nothing even close.

"I was so tired." She breathed. It was barely audible, but we both heard it.

He moved so he was sitting next to her, without the pole between them, in the blink of an eye. He took her glass from her, pulled her into his arms, and held her as she shattered into a million pieces. I had to physically restrain myself to keep from trying to do so myself.

"You are the strongest woman I've ever had the privilege of knowing and I can't even say I helped you get that way." He held Mira like he might be able to hold all the broken parts of her together if he tried hard enough. "You're allowed to be tired. You're allowed to give up if you want to. But I would be lying if I didn't say that I'm glad he said no and brought you back to us instead."

I would have to agree with him. Gaisgeach added.

A full conversation that I was no longer a part of must have passed between them in the few moments of silence that passed, because eventually she grumbled something under her breath and Teron loosened his hold on her.

"I get the feeling that wasn't directed at me."

"It wasn't." She mumbled into his chest.

He chuckled. "I guess the dragon had something to say too?"

"Gaisgeach." She pulled away and began to wipe her eyes as the tears finally slowed. "His name is Gaisgeach."

"Right." He gave her a halfhearted smile. "Gaisgeach."

"I'm–"

"Don't you dare apologize to me." He scolded. "I wouldn't have come over here to talk to you if I wasn't prepared to listen too."

A rustling in the trees caught all of our attention, and we looked that way to see Leo emerging from the woods. He stopped dead in his tracks when he glanced up and saw the three of us. He looked like he'd been through hell. His leathers were torn and bloody in several places, his hair was disheveled, and he looked like he hadn't slept in a day or two. It was far worse than the last time he'd come back this way.

Mira was in front of him in a heartbeat, and I was less than a second behind her.

"Are you alright?" She demanded, before he could say a word.

He blinked in surprise and looked her over. "I could ask you the same thing."

"It's a long story," I cut in for her. "What happened?" Telling him what happened with us wasn't all that important. I did, however, want to know what had happened to *him*.

"An ambush." The bite in his tone told me he was more irritated about it than anything, thank the gods. "Humans attacked me when I left the shop."

He pulled a small pouch out of the satchel on his belt and offered it to Mira.

"Apparently they figured out *what* I am and thought they'd kill me." He shrugged a shoulder. "They got a few good blows in, because there were probably fifteen of them in total, but I managed to block any death blows."

Mira opened the pouch and poured it into her palm. A dozen rings of various sizes and stones glittered in the dying sunlight.

"They'll do just fine." Her voice was clipped. "Go inside and get yourself cleaned up." She poured them back into the pouch, pulled the drawstring on it, then looked up at him. "Whether Deiric likes it or not, you can consider yourself on an extended vacation."

"Excuse me–" I cut in.

She held up a hand to silence me. "You've done quite enough for him over the last couple months. You've more than earned some time to hang around here and relax for a while."

He tried and failed to stifle a laugh. His thoughts were not nearly as guarded. Suggesting she had me by the balls.

I stepped forward with a growl, but Mira stepped between us and smiled up at me. "Ah!" She scolded. "He didn't say it out loud." She shrugged. "And even if he did, he's not wrong."

I glared down at her, which only made her smile grow.

"You should probably get inside if you want to keep your head attached to your body." She spoke to Leo, but her eyes never left mine. There was a promise there. One that made me rein myself in *just* slightly.

Leo sprinted inside.

Teron laughed. “Happy wife, happy life.” He disappeared before I spun around to glare at him.

“You know, I can’t believe I’m saying this, but I don’t think I’d mind if he stuck around after this is all over.”

There was a lightness to her voice that hadn’t been there in a long time even with the heavy cloud that hung over us today. I spun to look at her and there was a genuinely happy smile on her face for the first time today. Every single argument I had about sending Leo back out when he recovered died before it could leave my lips and I smiled back at her instead.

Chapter 42

Mira

We barely made it three steps in the front door when Adriana stopped me in my tracks. She shifted in front of me, so close that I nearly walked right into her. If it hadn't been for my inhuman reflexes we would've collided. I stepped back and raised a brow at her.

"I'd like to help you make the daylight rings, if that's alright?"

I was certain that for a half a second my annoyance was clear from my expression, but I smoothed it out as quickly as I could manage. It *would* help, given that I was already exhausted. I had hoped to sneak off and get a few hours of sleep before I did the spell, but I couldn't ask her to wait up for me.

The sun had begun to set as we were walking inside, so the sooner we could get it over with the better. I looked behind her to find the rest of the mages congregating there with hopeful looks on their faces.

Triss rounded the corner from the dining room into the foyer and crossed her arms over her chest. "I did tell them not to bother you, but they were very insistent on learning how to make the rings."

"Why?"

Triss opened her mouth and took a breath to reply, but Sorcha spoke before she could.

"Teron said that your mother was the only mage who knew the spell well enough to do it without a spellbook. The only one who was ever willing to *do* it in general in the last hundred years or so, actually. Aside from you of course."

I shot a glare in my father's direction. He'd taken up a spot leaning against the threshold to the den.

"What?" He asked, a slight smirk rising to his lips. "They asked. I wasn't going to lie to them."

My frustration wasn't in that I didn't want to teach them. It was actually exciting to have this many mages *want* to grant vampires the ability to walk in the sun. But of all of the times for me to have to show this to them, today was the worst day they could've chosen to ask.

I summoned my mother's grimoire, which contained a copy of the spell, and let it hover in the air in front of them. It opened directly to the page that went over the process and listed out the enchantment. An enchantment I knew by heart, not because of the number of times we performed it together, but because I'd spent years committing the words to memory in case I would ever get the chance to help her with it.

"Study that. Meet me outside in twenty minutes."

With that, I turned around and headed back outside into the slowly cooling night air. Sleep would just have to wait. Deiric followed, still less than two steps behind me.

"Worried that this will end as badly as the last time I did this for you?" I tossed over my shoulder as I walked down the steps and into the grass.

"That is not even remotely funny."

I stopped and glanced back at him. "I didn't say it was funny."

He studied me for a few moments. "I'm not concerned something will go wrong within the wards with this *spell*. But I'm not leaving you out of my sight."

"You'll drive yourself mad trying to stay within two steps of me all the time, you know."

"Perhaps I'm already there." He shrugged and stepped up beside me. "I would gladly dance at the edge of madness if it means you're with me, and you're safe." He held out his hand to me and I took it with a smile. "And you do make an incredible dance partner."

*

The mages came out sooner than I requested, as was to be expected by this point. Everyone but Adriana stood a few paces away while Adriana sat on her knees across from me, waiting to get started. Deiric stood behind me, carefully watching.

A sudden and frustrating wave of emotion hit me, as I lifted my hands over the rings and Adriana mimicked the motion. This was *supposed* to be my mother and I years ago. The opportunity to do the spell with her for the first time that never came to fruition. For Deiric, ironically, though I didn't know that at the time.

Deiric's hand lightly brushed my shoulder. I cleared my throat and shook the thought from my head. I couldn't think about that right now. That grief needed to stay buried.

I guided Adriana through the process of pulling the power from the moon, mumbling the enchantments, and sending the magic into the rings. She took to the process quickly and without hesitation. Not even ten minutes passed, and the rings were ready.

The mages murmured amongst themselves about how simple the process was. They thought it odd that no one else would do this. I'd felt the same when my mother had told me. I'd never met a vampire who was anything less than kind, courteous, and loyal enough to give their own life for the very mages that looked down on them.

Things were very different then. Perhaps it was the contention before the attacks that drove the general distaste for them. I never did find out. The attitude toward them shifted so drastically by the time Deiric introduced me to Garrick that I hadn't known what to think, but the situation then didn't lend much time to question it.

Once again, I pulled myself back to the present, gathered the rings in front of me, but kept the pile of them in my fist to offer them to Rosalind when I went inside. I didn't give the mages the chance to ask me questions.

I thanked Adriana for her help and quickly excused myself to head inside with Deiric while they conversed amongst themselves. Triss took over answering their questions, thank the gods. Rosalind stood at the bottom of the stairs, nervously picking at her fingers when I walked in the front door again.

She lit up when she saw me and immediately seemed to look for the rings. I stopped in front of her and held out my hand. “Take whichever one you’d like.”

She looked them over and quickly took one of the more dainty rings Leo commissioned. “Thank you.” She tested it out on her fingers, deciding to place it on the middle one on her right hand, as that is where it fit the best.

I nodded. “Don’t make me regret it.” I placed the rest of the rings back in the pouch and headed up the stairs.

Deiric had us in the bedroom, the door closed, me pinned against it, and his lips on mine before I could blink. Sometimes, I still had to marvel at how quickly he could move. Substantially quicker than me sometimes, it seemed.

I dropped the pouch of rings on the dresser next to us and entangled my fingers in his hair. *Getting straight to the point I take it?*

His fangs nicked my lower lip as he moved to kiss down my jawline and my neck. *Have you ever known me to wait?*

I hummed. *You’ve been known to make me wait, occasionally, while you take your sweet old time.*

He slipped his hand into the slit in my skirt and hiked my right leg up until my thigh rested against his hip. He pressed his hips against me, and I let out a low moan.

He grazed his fangs along the sensitive skin between my neck and shoulder and I couldn’t hold *myself* back anymore. I moved without warning, and sank my own teeth into his neck.

He gasped, the only sign that it surprised him. *There she is.* He cooed, then he bit me, and my entire body nearly exploded in euphoria. I knew I shouldn’t drink from him as much as I needed to. As much as I *desperately* wanted to. I struck him several times with my sword yesterday and he hadn't done anything to recover from it.

I stopped myself and let my head rest back against the door, perfectly content to ride the waves of pleasure his feeding brought me. I licked the blood from my lips, but not before a stray drop had begun to run down my chin.

It was then that I *felt* someone shift into the room. My entire body tensed and Deiric let out an animalistic growl unlike anything I'd ever heard before. His head whipped around, and he bared his fangs at the unexpected guest.

Devlon stood by our bed, looking rightfully horrified.

I rolled my eyes. "For fuck's sake Devlon. You couldn't have shifted *anywhere* else?" I let my hands fall from Deiric's hair and tapped the hand that held my leg. He begrudgingly released me. I stepped around him and brushed the blood from my chin with my thumb.

"I'm sorry." He shuffled awkwardly on his feet, not taking his eyes off of Deiric. "I haven't shifted here before. I just shifted *to* you. You know that's not exactly a guarantee that I'll appear on the other side of a door from you. And I obviously had no idea you'd be… indisposed."

I crossed my arms over my chest. "Well?" I lifted one arm in an annoyed gesture. "What was so gods damned important that you've appeared in our bedroom this late at night?" It made me seriously regret and reconsider giving him a crystal to have access to get here in the first place.

He cleared his throat and finally looked at me. "There's been an incident at the border. We're moving the meeting to tomorrow morning, one hour after sunrise."

"What kind of incident?" Deiric seemed to get himself reined back in and turned so he fully faced Devlon now.

"I haven't gotten many details yet. Quinn is supposed to fill us in tomorrow, but her missive said it was absolutely urgent that we meet."

I don't like the sound of that. Gaisgeach observed.

I don't either. I replied.

"Is that all?" I asked, a little hesitantly.

He nodded. "For now." Then he was gone.

I glanced at Deiric. His face said everything I had yet to vocalize.

War. This felt like *war.*

Chapter 43

Mira

Lazarus was waiting outside of our bedroom door the following morning. I assumed that Adriana had told him about the meeting. Deiric hadn't gone out to tell him and Adriana was the only other person who knew thanks to the dragons. I barely spared him a glance as I stepped around him and headed down the stairs to the foyer where Adriana stood patiently waiting for us.

"I'll be accompanying you to the meeting." He said rather forcefully, like he expected me to turn him away.

"I assumed as much."

Deiric kept pace with me, walking right next to me as I descended the stairs. I could *feel* his lingering anger, but he kept his mouth shut.

"You assumed, yet you didn't come to tell me that there *was* a meeting yourself?" He was annoyed. As though he had any right to be. He'd broken my neck and tossed me in a dungeon. I couldn't say I *blamed* him, but it still pissed me off.

"Adriana obviously took care of that."

"You didn't ask her to."

I stopped on the last step and spun around to face him. "If you're going to act like an asshole to me after you dumped me in a dungeon until your *mate*," I slung the word like an insult, "figured out what to do with me, I will gladly have my father attend this meeting with us instead. He's perfectly capable of watching my back without growling at me for not telling him the moment that I knew about this gods-forsaken meeting."

He reeled back like I'd struck him and stared at me like he barely knew me.

"I would have come to collect you this morning if you hadn't been standing outside my door, but I knew you were there from the moment I woke up. There was no sense in rushing along to come out and tell you when you so clearly were already informed."

He blinked, the only sign of the remainder of his surprise by my actions.

"Now, if you're quite finished acting like an angry overgrown fucking toddler, we should be on our way before we're late."

Amusement flooded my senses and it obviously wasn't mine, but Deiric's mind was empty. He didn't utter a word. Even Gaisgeach was silent. I don't know if my outburst toward Lazarus stunned them all into silence or if they just decided not to poke the bear this morning, but when they all remained silent for a few beats I turned and took the last step off the stairs.

I shifted us to the Solas castle. Most of the other magisters, from both sides, were already there. Everyone except Quinn, actually.

This time they had a chair prepared for Adriana. She sat to my left, with Lazarus taking up the spot next to her and Deiric sitting to my right. It made the end of the table quite crowded, but we made it work. It was eerily quiet when we arrived. Garrick nodded his hello to me, but everyone else seemed to just be patiently waiting on Quinn.

The anxiety swirling around the room was palpable. I suddenly had no desire to be anywhere close to this discussion, but knew that I couldn't leave even if I wanted to. Macha had been frustratingly quiet lately too, which didn't seem to bode well.

Quinn shifted in and the smell of smoke, blood, and sweat flooded my senses. She was out of breath and her clothes were covered with blood that didn't appear to be hers. Chaos erupted as people realized what state she was in. A chorus of, 'what the hell is going on' and 'are you alright' rang out from various magisters on both sides of the table.

It was pandemonium until Quinn finally shouted, "Enough! Fuck." She slammed her hands on the table in front of where she would normally sit. "I am fine. They've sent a massive army to the border. We'd been keeping an eye on the group of them that seemed to steadily be growing, but then more troops arrived overnight, and they attacked before sunrise this morning."

She looked at Adriana, who was sitting as still as a statue and had yet to utter a single word. "Did you know anything about this?" She demanded.

Adriana blinked and cocked her head to the side. "I've been with Mira this entire time, with no contact to my bastard of a brother. How would I have known this was coming?"

"You alluded to him not stopping with the executions, the laws," she began. "Did you know of his plans this whole time?"

Adriana didn't shrink under the scrutiny. If anything, she seemed to sit taller. "I know him. I did not know his plans. I made *assumptions* given how he has always been. I expected this to happen, but I couldn't have predicted where or when. Nor would you have listened if I tried to warn you. The other kingdoms were already preparing for a battle because of his presence at the border. You've just stated as much yourself. There was nothing more my warning would've given you even if you had chosen to listen to me."

The anger that flashed over Quinn's face was unmistakable, but Liam spoke up before she could further push her arguments. "She's right."

Quinn's gaze snapped to him.

"She could've pointed out more explicitly that she expected him to push his borders, but all that would have done was cause us to do what they were doing anyway. Nothing can be done until war has officially begun."

"Bullshit." Quinn snarled. "We could've found out what he wanted. We could've helped the other kings broker for peace."

"No, you couldn't have." Adriana said simply.

Every gaze in the room shot to her.

"He wants to eradicate mages and vampires. He wants this entire world to be *his*. Don't you see that? I would go out on a limb and assume he killed the king. If not him, I wouldn't put it past Azazel at this point."

No one spoke. They all stared at her. She paused for several moments, giving them the chance to speak up, but still the silence stretched.

"What do we know about his forces after the attack?" Adriana met Quinn's gaze again.

"All we've seen thus far is his men on the ground. We don't have any idea what else he's working with or what he's brought to the front. We know that *he* is there, but we don't know where."

Adriana considered this and nodded. "Then we need to prepare for their next attack. Are they still attacking now?"

"No." Quinn stood up, no longer bracing her weight against the table as her breathing returned to normal. "They've pulled back for now and are allowing us to collect the dead and wounded."

"They want to draw us out." Lazarus cut in. "They were testing your defenses. They caught you off guard and now they know what you've got to defend those borders with. They'll be expecting you to call in backup. To call in *us*." He gestured toward Adriana and me. "Were there any mages on the front lines on our side?"

"No." Quinn looked unsure now. Concerned even, rather than angry.

"We shouldn't give them what they want." Adriana glanced at Lazarus with what I thought was an appreciative look. "Don't send any mages yet. And *we* won't bring in our backup yet."

"And what is *your* backup?" Quinn asked.

"Dragons." Devlon answered and everyone looked at him. "It's our best kept secret. Even from most of you."

Quinn sputtered. “But– Dragons have been gone for–”

“Centuries, yes.” Devlon shrugged. “Apparently they came back and are bonded to several people. Vampires and humans alike.”

“So we bring them in and roast his armies.” Quinn insisted.

“No.” Garrick stood up. “Adriana and Lazarus are correct. They *want* that. They likely could’ve taken out your entire force of soldiers this morning if they wanted to, right?”

Quinn looked around desperately, her mind racing to put the pieces together. “I– I mean I suppose they could’ve.”

“And they didn’t.” Tellus pointed out.

“They didn’t.” She repeated.

“Because your army wasn’t what they wanted.” Devlon added, staring directly at Adriana.

“Right.” Quinn sank into her chair.

“You will tell the King of Osraige to hold his ground on his own for now. We will provide mages for healing, but we will not send our forces yet.”

“They’ll slaughter them.” Quinn breathed.

“They won’t.”

“How can you be so sure?” She demanded.

Devlon shrugged a shoulder. “I can’t, but I can tell you that if we send our forces now, they’ll be more ready for us than you think. They’ll be *expecting* it. We need to weaken them first.”

“He doesn’t have the manpower to weaken them.”

“Then he’ll need to try and pull in forces from Munster. We are not his army. We will offer aid, but we will not send our entire force to his rescue.”

“This is insanity.” Quinn rested her head in her hands. “He’ll cast us out just like Ronan is doing.”

"If he has any understanding of battle strategy, he won't." Lazarus spoke up again. "He will see what they're doing. Have you spoken to him about it?"

Quinn looked at him now. "I– Well, no. I have been healing all morning."

"Speak to him about it." Devlon took over again. "If things get too drastic and they *are* just slaughtering his people we will come. Until then, he will need to fight this battle on his own."

Lazarus nodded approvingly. Adriana gave her curt nod of approval as well. Quinn frowned, but shifted away before waiting to be dismissed.

"Send out a call to all of the mages, vampires, and forces in the other kingdoms. We *will* have to fight them. All we've done is bought ourselves time to organize." Devlon instructed the rest of them. He was met with silence, and one by one each of them shifted to their respective manors to begin the process of preparing for the war we were about to find ourselves in.

"I trust the dragons are prepared to fight for us?" He looked at Deiric now.

Deiric nodded.

"Good. Let's hope we still have the element of surprise with them."

Something told me that we didn't, but I tried to ignore the lingering dread that was building with every passing second. I nearly jumped when Deiric placed his hand on my thigh under the table.

Your heart is racing.

I glanced at him out of the corner of my eye. He was still looking toward Devlon, as though he hadn't said anything to me at all. *Forgive me if this makes me a little anxious. I don't have a good feeling about any of this.*

I don't think anyone does.

We'll burn their forces to a crisp. Calm yourself. Gaisgeach's voice was quiet, as it usually was when we were this far away.

And if they're expecting you?

Do you really intend to make me repeat myself?

I rolled my eyes.

"You'll let us know when we're needed?" Adriana asked, but it sounded more like a demand.

Devlon nodded. "You'll be the first to know." He stood from his chair, and we followed suit. I shifted us home.

*

Sparring seemed like the best course of action to resolve the lingering anxiety I had after the meeting this morning. However, unfortunately, all it did was get some aggression out. The anxiety only continued to fester as I looked around and saw the mages sparring alongside us and *severely* lacking any genuine battle skills.

We trained. We trained quite a lot. And yet, as I looked around at them between blocking the blows that Deiric sent my way, I realized that while they know how to handle a blade, they don't have any idea how to fight someone who is genuinely going for the kill. There's *nothing* I can do at this point to help them either.

War is already here, and we are sorely underprepared. Gaisgeach has gone silent, likely because whether he will admit it or not he's started to realize the same thing. The dragons can burn everything, sure, but is that *really* how we should end this battle? Excessive bloodshed is never the answer. Right?

I was pulled from my thoughts at the high pitched shriek that left Adriana, followed by the sweet tang of her blood filling the air. Apparently Sorcha *was* going for blood today.

The blur of movement from Rosalind caught my eye, and I was moving before I could think through what I was doing. I threw myself in front of her as she charged toward Adriana. We collided, toppled over, and rolled across the ground.

When we came to a stop, she was on top of me. Somewhere along the way she'd bit my neck, ripping into me savagely, but the venom hit me seconds later and the conflicting feeling of pain, far worse than anytime Deiric bit me, and ecstasy was incredibly disorienting.

I flipped us over, yanking her from my neck and holding her by her throat on the ground. She squirmed and snarled up at me for a half a second, before her senses came back to her as the smell of Adriana's blood lessened. She blinked up at me in surprise now.

The venom won out now, sending waves of ecstasy through me despite that she was *not* my mate. I couldn't stop myself from tracing my fingers up her side toward her chest. Couldn't help the overwhelming urge to take her inside and show her precisely how I could pleasure her.

"I'm not sure that you're prepared to deal with the consequences of your little outburst." I leaned down into her as though I might bite her myself. I tilted her head to the side and tightened the grip I had on her neck just a fraction as I cupped her breast with my other hand.

The shift in her scent was unmistakable, despite the confusion swirling in her eyes.

Lazarus growled behind me and I was reminded that we had an audience. Deiric held him back with everything he had.

Mira. Deiric warned.

"I could leave you *begging*." I whispered, making sure I was close enough that my breath tickled her neck.

"Mira!" Deiric scolded me out loud now as Lazarus turned to throttle him to get free and come to retrieve his mate from me. I caught him with shadow, halting him in his tracks and keeping him from hurting Deiric.

"Gods, you really are a cranky old bastard aren't you." I shot toward Lazarus as I released Rosalind and rose to my feet again. Deiric released Lazarus and stepped back.

"She's all yours." I subsequently released him from my hold as well. They both disappeared in a heartbeat. Hopefully she would feed on anything other than my mages.

I wonder if she handles Deiric like that in the bedroom. It was Xander's thought, loud and clear, that I heard without prompting.

I spun and launched myself at Xander without considering the repercussions of ripping his fucking throat out for that comment, only to be stopped short by Deiric.

He caught me by the throat with surprising gentleness. His other arm wrapped around my arms and chest, effectively pinning me to him with my back against his front.

"Easy, love. He didn't say it out loud." He spoke right next to my ear, knowing damn well that the way he held me and the way he lowered his voice would only spur the desire the venom sparked in me to new heights. Consequently calming my rage and replacing it with lust instead.

I still scowled at Xander, who's face quickly paled when he realized what he'd done.

Of course, the way Deiric held me and the way I immediately quieted into the embrace dispelled his misguided thought, because even though it did absolutely seem to turn Deiric on when I took control or threatened him, he obviously was just as bothered by them knowing that as me.

"Let the venom run its course and let's get back to sparring, shall we?" He whispered a little quieter now. His hold on me loosened and I managed a deep breath and a nod. "Good–"

I elbowed him in the gut and he grunted as he nearly doubled over into me.

"I deserved that." He gasped after a moment.

"You think?" I quipped, stepping away from him and summoning my sword back to my hand.

"I take it the venom wore off then."

"No." I responded out loud. *But I'll gut you if you praise me in front of your men. Let alone my fucking father.*

His mischievous grin as he picked up his sword and turned to face me nearly made me want to gut him anyway.

"I feel like we missed something important." Leo commented quietly.

I shot him a look that could've killed him.

"I feel like you should go back to sparring before one of the two of them rips your head off." Triss pointed out from where she sat on the porch with a very entertained smile on her lips.

Chapter 44

Deiric

Sleeping had proven to be far more of a challenge than I anticipated following the meeting and everything that transpired afterward. We were all on edge, and nearly at each other's throats without Rosalind's outburst shaking things up. Mira, surprisingly, was not nearly as shaken by it as I had expected, but she had a rather fitful sleep as well.

I followed her out of our bedroom and started down the stairs behind her when Rosalind appeared in front of her without prompting. Mira, rightfully, jolted and came to an abrupt halt in front of me. I had to resist the sudden urge to throw myself between them.

"I'm so sorry about what happened yesterday," Rosalind started. "I was–"

Mira raised a hand to stop her from continuing and interrupted. "It happened. It's over. We can just move on."

"Yes, but I just–"

"Respectfully, Rosalind, I don't care why it happened. I stopped you from doing any real harm. It is fine." Mira made a move to step around her and Rosalind reached out to grab her arm and stop her. I was just as surprised as the two of them at the growl that escaped me and the rage I suddenly found entirely overwhelming.

Rosalind stopped mid reach and yanked her hand back as though she'd been burned. Her eyes shot to me and a combination of shock and confusion passed over her face.

"Lay a hand on her again and I can assure you, regardless of who you are mated to, you will lose your head before you've had the chance to realize what's happened to you."

If Mira was upset with what I said, she didn't show it, nor did I sense any apprehension from her. Rosalind searched my face, though I can't imagine what she was hoping to find. When she came up empty she opened her mouth to speak, but Mira sighed and spoke first.

"If it had been anyone other than Adriana who had been injured yesterday, I would have been in the same situation as you, but thankfully Adriana smells like *him* and just the scent turns my stomach."

"Him?" Rosalind's attention shifted back to Mira now, and she wrinkled her nose as she tried to think of who Mira was referring to.

"Azazel." I answered for her.

She still appeared confused, but mumbled a quiet 'oh' and looked away.

"What I'm trying to say is I forgive you." Mira shot me a look. "And apparently, keep your distance." She stepped around Rosalind now and continued down the stairs. I followed closely behind, sending one final glare at Rosalind to push the issue before I shifted my focus to Mira once more.

She headed toward the dining room and Adriana met her at the threshold with a steaming cup of tea in her hands. It seemed odd that *this* didn't seem to startle Mira, but she accepted the cup with a smile.

"You know," Adriana started as she turned to walk back over to her seat at the table. "Since Ronan is at the border, we probably *could* go stop the execution that's scheduled at the capitol today."

"Absolutely not." I said.

"That sounds like a fantastic idea." Mira said at the exact same moment as me.

We looked at one another. She raised her brows at me, while I narrowed my eyes at her and scowled.

"I don't think I was asking you." Adriana cut in.

I looked at her now with an exasperated look. "Well I'm sure as hell not letting the two of you go on your own, and I still don't think this is a good idea."

"They wouldn't be alone." Triss pointed out as she filed into the room behind us. I hadn't even heard her come down the stairs. I whipped my head around to look at her as she also now made her way toward the fireplace to get some tea.

"Lazarus already agreed to it." I snapped my attention back to Adriana who had a victorious smile on her lips. "I spoke to him earlier."

I was about to snap at her again, but Mira gently placed her hand on my thigh under the table. *Relax, love. Macha will make sure that Ronan and Azazel aren't there.*

I turned to her now, but she was sipping her tea as if they all hadn't just suggested going to do quite possibly one of the most absurd things while we were on the cusp of war.

We haven't been called to the front yet. Fiadh joined in now.

And you're on their side?

I am just pointing out that there is no danger and there's no sense in letting those mages die right before the real battle begins.

I sighed, leaned my elbows onto the table, and rested my head in my hands. *The two of you will be the death of me.*

I sincerely doubt that. Fiadh's condescending tone grated my nerves, but I bit back any retort.

*

Hours later, we were filtering through the crowd toward the gallows. This was not their first public execution here and I was certain it would not be the last. It was far more organized than any of the others we had come across, and also far more guarded.

It was another frustratingly clear day, which meant that Fiadh and Gaisgeach wouldn't be providing any aerial support *again*. That made me even more uneasy, but Mira assured me it would all be fine.

Somehow Macha managed to not only make sure that Ronan and Azazel were not here, but she also had a list of the prisoners up for execution and the vast majority of them were from Solas. That fact didn't surprise me. They were too stubborn to seek refuge elsewhere.

Have they all come out? Mira asked Triss.

Last one is coming up now. She responded.

Mira had to stand up on her tiptoes to see the platform. We were surrounded by city folk who apparently quite enjoy these spectacles. They were shouting all sorts of horrendous insults at the men and women, as well as loads of rotten fruit. It smelled awful.

Let's move then. Mira instructed.

They shifted all of the prisoners with us to the Solas castle. Tellus, to my surprise, was waiting there for us. The people we'd saved seemed confused at first. I would wager that many of them recognized the building and suspected that the change in scenery probably startled them.

We removed the enchanted jewelry we wore and Tellus stepped forward to begin to explain where they had spare clothing for them, and they could get cleaned up.

The moment that Mira turned to face me, one of the men summoned a cross bow and aimed it right at her chest. He fired and I moved to spin Mira and I out of the way. A piercing and stinging pain sliced into my back as the stake hit its mark in me instead of her, narrowly missing my heart.

"Deiric!" Mira screeched. The color drained from her face, and she was behind me instantaneously. I didn't look to see if anyone else had moved to confine the man who shot at us. I couldn't. Despite the mugwort that I took to prevent being *poisoned* by the vervain, it didn't take away the way it fried my flesh anywhere it touched me.

She pulled the stake out so quickly I hardly registered the movement. The relief I felt when she began to heal me was enough to allow me to draw a shaky breath and mumble a curse. The relief was short lived though, when she grabbed a handful of my hair and turned my head so I was looking at her.

"If you *ever* put yourself in front of a stake for me again I will kill you myself." She snarled, and then she was gone.

I sat up and turned to see Lazarus holding the man back, Tellus still a bit too stunned to speak, and all the other prisoners putting as much space between themselves and that man as they could.

Mira was in front of him now, and judging by the pained look on his face, I assumed she'd already struck him somehow. The scent of his blood hit me next, only affirming my assumption.

"I hope it was worth it." She snarled. She yanked her arm back and dropped his heart onto the ground.

It was pandemonium now. Someone had fainted. Another had vomited. Tellus just stared at them as Lazarus dropped him to the ground.

"We could have questioned him." Lazarus said cautiously.

Mira growled loud enough that Lazarus visibly retreated. Blood dripped from her hand, which curled into a fist as she stepped toward him. "He nearly killed Deiric *and* me. I am in no mood for questioning."

Tellus cleared his throat. "Well, on that note, please see yourselves out. I'd like to get this cleaned up and get the remaining people taken care of. As far as his death–" He paused when Mira turned to face him and even I would've shrunk away at the look on her face. "I'll see to it that the coven is aware it was justified." His voice only slightly trembled.

Mira scoffed, but visibly relaxed and turned to walk back over to me. I pushed myself up to my feet. Adriana reached me at the same time as Mira.

"Are you alright?" She nearly shouted while Mira stepped around me to examine the hole in my leathers.

"I'm fine." I shrugged my other shoulder. "Nothing I can't handle."

"If he convinced one of the people they intended to execute to hold onto a cross bow and try to kill us, then we have two problems." Mira mumbled and came back around to stand in front of me. "He knew we would come, *and* he might very well have mages with him."

"I doubt he'd be able to convince anyone to work with him." Triss walked over now and looked skeptical. "Surely they're smarter than that."

"He wasn't." Lazarus pointed out, gesturing toward the dead man.

Triss shrugged. "Okay, Oíche members would be smarter than that."

"You are giving people who may have been imprisoned for more than a month *far* too much credit." Mira said, almost too softly. She shifted us back home, but we arrived outside instead of in the foyer. "However, let's not dwell on something so depressing." She turned on her heel and walked toward the front door. "We have a birthday to celebrate, after all."

"What?" I hurried after her.

The front door opened, and Silas leaned on the threshold with a smug grin on his face. "Why is it that I've known you for six hundred and eighteen years and I've only just *now* found out when your birthday is? Honestly it's quite rude if you ask me. I had to find out from your mate's *father* of all people."

I stopped in my tracks and blinked, entirely taken aback by the fact that he was here, let alone what he had said.

He laughed then, a full doubling over laugh. "Oh, for fuck's sake. He's even forgotten his own birthday."

"I don't know why you're surprised." Leo came up to stand beside him as Mira crested the stairs. "He didn't tell any of *us* either."

Silas' laughter finally quieted, and he righted himself. "He's known you all for what, a century at best?" He scoffed. "We spent several centuries living with that gods damned prick." He gestured toward Lazarus. "You'd think he'd have told one of us."

"He didn't tell me either." Lazarus commented as he walked around me with a smirk on his face. It was surprising to see him jovial even when being insulted.

Mira turned back around and smiled at me. "Are you going to come inside, or are you going to stand there and stare at us in disbelief for the rest of the day?"

I closed my gaping mouth and finally walked toward them all with Triss and Adriana following behind me.

You're going to pay for this. I thought with a mischievous smirk.

Mira's smile grew a bit wicked. *Oh, I'm counting on it.* She hooked her elbow with mine when I reached her and drug me inside.

Killian emerged from the den with a bottle in his hand. "I heard we're celebrating… wait, how old are you anyway?"

"Six hundred and fifty." Mira responded excitedly.

"Hell of a milestone." Teron quipped and I wanted to throttle him. He huffed a laugh at my expression.

Killian walked over, handed me a glass, and poured from the bottle in his hand. "My personal reserve. I think you'll like it."

"Thanks." I mumbled.

Mira released my arm and walked over to Silas. "Were you able to get it in time?" She whispered, quietly enough that I was sure she hoped I didn't hear her.

Silas snorted. "I assumed you'd have my head if I didn't." He gestured toward the den with a nod of his head. "It's in there."

"Relax." Teron clapped a hand on my shoulder. "It's just a gift and I'm pretty sure you'll appreciate it."

I glanced over at him. "I wasn't aware you knew of anything I might like."

He met my gaze. "*I* may not know much about you, but I am fairly certain Mira knows precisely what to get anyone she cares about, and she's rarely ever been known to give gifts that lack thought or meaning."

I gave him a confused look.

Mira walked back into the foyer now with a satisfied smile on her face. "It's perfect." She said softly to Silas, who nodded in acknowledgement, and then she turned and walked toward me. She held what I was almost certain was a sword of some kind that was carefully wrapped in black cloth.

"I realize that it's pretty obvious what it is, but." A slim tendril of shadow stole my drink from me as she held out the sword. I took it from her. "I think you'll find this to be a bit more unique than it may seem."

I eyed her curiously for a moment. She unwrapped the hilt before I had the chance to readjust my grip and do so myself. My eyebrows nearly shot to my hairline. The hilt was adorned with tiny blue scales, which were strikingly similar to Fiadh. In fact, I could have sworn that I caught her scent on it.

"I would like it to be known," Silas cut in. "While it was *her* idea, and *she* had to collect the scales from that terrifying dragon of yours, it was an interesting challenge for one of the mages at my manor to help the blacksmith adorn that hilt."

Mira rolled her eyes and shook her head. "You know, if I'd have known you would be so worried about making sure he knew how much effort *you* put into this I might have asked someone else instead."

Silas scoffed. "As though you knew anyone else who had such a skilled blacksmith on staff."

I'm going to kill him. She thought, but there was a levity to her words that told me she didn't mean it.

"I don't know what to say." I shifted my grip so I could grasp the hilt and slide it from the sheath that was still wrapped in the cloth. The blade itself was plain, but perfectly balanced with the weight of the hilt. I couldn't see myself ever using this for anything other than to put on display.

She did not have it made for you to hang it on your gods damned wall. Fiadh snarled. *I did not give her the scales I shed to make you an ornament.*

Mira chuckled. "I think she'll be a bit offended if you don't use it."

Very.

I slid it back into the sheath. "Thank you." I smiled at Mira. "It's perfect." *And thank you too, before you bite my head off for leaving you out.*

Fiadh huffed, but went silent again.

Mira shifted it out of my hands and returned the glass to me. “Now,” she smiled and took the glass Killian offered. “Let’s get on with the festivities.”

Chapter 45

Mira

Macha's caw startled me awake. Deiric groaned and covered his head with the pillow. It was late into the morning, but I was thankful to find that I didn't have a hangover, despite how much we all collectively drank. I didn't think Deiric did either, he was just irritated to have woken up when I think the two of us had our first *real* sleep in a very long time.

I glanced over to see a sealed note on the table beside the bed. I sighed and reached over to slide it off the table and read it.

It's time. Macha said cryptically.

I glanced up right after I popped the wax seal and raised a brow.

They're calling for you to go to the front.

"I thought they were waiting until they had to?"

Macha stared at me unblinking. I flipped open the paper and skimmed through it. They apparently continued to obliterate Osraige's defenses. They'd pushed the borders significantly and even with the small amount of aid they received from Munster, they were not able to halt their advances.

"Fuck."

I will inform the others. Gaisgeach grumbled.

Deiric lifted the pillow from his head. "I take it that they've called us in?"

"It would seem so." I handed him the note. He read through it quickly.

"Fuck."

"Yeah."

Macha flew off the windowsill and back out into the trees.

*

"We'd like to come and fight." Aodh said, with Sorcha, Zemora, and Stella standing behind him.

"Absolutely not." I snapped without hesitation. There was no way I was letting them anywhere near the battlefield. "None of you have any battle or real fighting experience. You will stay here where you'll be safe."

"We're masters. Most of us, anyway. We can handle ourselves." Sorcha spoke up next. "We won't just stand around and let you all fight for us."

"Like hell." I snarled. "You're not leaving, and if I have to lock you here in chains and bind your magic I will."

Their faces blanched and they stared at me like they barely recognized me.

"You wouldn't." Zemora gasped.

"I would." I glanced around at each of them. "Zane, Xander, and Eimear will be staying with you. If anything happens to us, they'll make sure you're safe."

"I am *not* staying behind and hiding like I'm completely useless." Eimear walked into the foyer now, dressed for battle, sword and knives strapped to her. "I'm not invincible, but this is my home too and I'm going to fight for it."

"Eimear, they will need you if things go to hell." I tried to reason with her, but she shook her head.

"I am through with hiding. If I die, at least I'll have died fighting this time." There was no question in her tone. She was ready for this fight, and nothing I could do, aside from chaining her as I'd threatened to do to the mages would change her mind.

"Fine." I said through gritted teeth, then spun around to go stand with Deiric while he finished speaking with Zane and Xander. I walked over just in time to catch the end of what he was telling them.

"If we don't come back," He placed a hand on Zane's shoulder. "You're in charge."

The look that rose to Zane's face at that statement was hard to describe. It was a mixture of grief and pride. Like he was glad to have been chosen to be the one to take over, but the thought of losing Deiric was nearly too much to bear.

"Do me a favor and come back." He tried to force a smile. "I'm not sure I could handle all these idiots by myself."

"Asshole." Xander muttered under his breath with an elbow to Zane's ribs.

"We'll do our best." Deiric turned to face me. "Are we ready?"

"Not yet." I turned toward Triss, who stood with Lazarus, Leo, Renwick, Eimear, Rosalind, Liala, and my father. "Triss," I gestured for her to follow me outside. "A word?"

She looked at me hesitantly, but followed me outside, where everyone but prying vampire ears wouldn't hear us.

I stopped before I reached the stairs and turned to face her. "I know we had a rocky start, but I wanted to tell you that I appreciate everything you've done, both for me and for the mages, since you've come here." She nodded and opened her mouth to speak but I silenced her by raising my hand. "Let me finish."

"I'm sorry for how I reacted when I first met you. If anything happens to me, *you* are in charge. If you see that the battle is not leaning in our favor I need you to leave. Grab Eimear and bring her back here. Keep the mages safe. Leave and move to another country if you have to, but don't let any harm come to them."

"Mira…" She stared at me like I'd just ripped her heart out. "I can't just leave you all there to–"

"Promise me." I insisted. "Promise me that you'll leave and protect them."

She studied me for a few moments before she finally gave in and nodded. "I promise."

"Thank you." I stepped around her and walked back inside. I got a few cautious looks from Lazarus, Deiric, and my father. No one else seemed to want to look at me. Eimear hadn't heard anything I said. I looked at Zane and he just nodded, a slight frown on his lips.

Triss walked back in behind me. I glanced over my shoulder at her. "Can you shift all of them?" She nodded. "Good. Let's go then."

Triss shifted Lazarus, Rosalind, Leo, Liala, Eimear, Renwick, and my father to the front lines. I shifted Adriana, Deiric, and myself out to our dragons, who were gathering behind the front lines as well.

Are you ready for this? I asked Gaisgeach, who barely seemed to notice me climbing onto his back. He glanced back at me with a look that said he was annoyed with the question. I should have known better than to ask. He always seemed ready for anything.

You will not die today, was his response. As though he could see the future and see the outcome of the battle. It was a novel idea, but the gods only knew how this would go today. I was prepared or anything.

His annoyed grumble brought me back to focusing on what was in front of us. *I will not allow* you *to die today.*

I glared at him slightly. *You will not prevent me from shifting off of you to help on the ground if I'm needed.*

He angled his head so he could stare at me with his large golden eye. *If you die, I will die. I will not allow you to fight to the death.* His gaze flicked down to the metal armor on my chest. *If that is damaged, you will shift back to me and not leave my back no matter what.*

I nodded. That seemed like a fair agreement, although I had no room to argue. He could swoop down and pick me up whether I wanted him to or not. He seemed pleased that I gave in, so he turned his head back to face forward.

Ronan's armies began to rise over the hill in the distance. Hundreds of soldiers in white and gold tunics and armor spread across as far as I could see. It was hard not to marvel at the size of his army. I wasn't even aware that the country *contained* so many people. And after all the work we'd done to convince the people in those towns that we weren't the enemy; it was insane to me to see so many gathered to fight for a king who wanted to kill us all.

There was no sign of Ronan himself, nor of Azazel. That part didn't surprise me. I half expected the bastard to hide in his palace while his people fought for him. He hardly seemed like the type to get his hands dirty. They were here though. I was sure of it.

"If he's here, I'm going to kill him." Adriana announced, her voice cold and devoid of any emotion. I glanced at her, and she sat tall on Cairbre's back with her shoulders squared. She was the epitome of a queen braced for battle in her armor.

We had not had time to prepare armor for all of our men. In hindsight, we should have done that much sooner. Not even my father had the armor that we wore. That meant that they were all at risk, but I hoped that the soldiers attacking us were only using metal weapons and didn't go for the head. I doubted they would have worn the armor even if we had it made. It would have annoyed them with how restrictive and stuffy it felt, no matter how much safer it made them.

"Are you sure you'll be able to handle that?" I asked gently. I knew she'd said on several occasions that he deserved death, but it was odd to hear her say that *she* would be the one to bring him the killing blow.

Her golden eyes shifted to me, and there was a cold resolve in them that shook any doubt from me. "He deserves a fate worse than death for what he had Azazel do to you." She looked ahead again. "And if I come across that bastard on the field today, I'll kill him too. I don't care if you've staked claim on him or not."

I didn't reply. I wanted to be the one to torture him and rip his fucking heart out while it was still beating, but death by anyone's hands was still alright by me. Especially in battle. I looked to my left to find Deiric staring forward just as regally as she was.

Getting nervous, love? He looked over at me.

No.

A slight smile rose to his lips. *That was a little too fast to be convincing.*

Well, I'm not nervous. I snapped. *I'm concerned for your men. For the mages that haven't seen real combat.*

His smile fell. *Our men.* He clarified. *Have a little bit more faith in them, love. They'll be fine.*

I hoped that was true. However, a sinking feeling had taken residence in my gut and something told me we were not all going home alive today. Macha had neither confirmed nor denied my suspicion when I parted ways with her this morning. It hadn't left me feeling very positive.

I looked forward again. Ronan's armies were now in full view of us. The valley between us suddenly felt so small. The rows of soldiers only solidified that sinking feeling in my gut.

"Magical attacks first." I shouted. I glanced over at Adriana. "Ready?"

She gave me a sinister smile, and nodded.

I pulled in as much energy as I was capable of. The Morrigan's energy signature flooded me as well. I raised my hands up, held them out toward Ronan's men, and with nothing more than a thought to send the energy their way, half of their front lines turned to a fine mist. Effectively ceasing to exist. Adriana's blast hit next, taking out another section of the front line.

Triss and another lightning mage unleashed a storm upon them that struck the remainder of the front line of soldiers and part of the second. Before more magical attacks could diminish their lines, they surged forward with a thunderous roar.

Let's fly. Deiric commanded Fiadh. With a roar that was echoed by every other dragon on the field, she launched to the sky. The deafening sound of wingbeats echoed across the valley as all of the bonded dragons took off in unison. There were only twenty of us, which now seemed far too little for the might of what we were facing.

When we leveled out in the sky, I got an even better vantage point of what we were up against. Beyond the wall of soldiers stood a line of catapults already prepared with blazing balls of fire. What they were made of, I wasn't sure, but I knew their purpose. They were to knock us out of the sky.

It will take a lot more than a ball of fire to knock a dragon out of the sky. Deiric tried to remind me. *Don't worry too much about that.*

However, his tone didn't give me the encouragement he hoped for, because I could hear the slight tinge of fear at the edge of his voice. He didn't like it either.

Our soldiers surged forward now. The armies of Osraige, combined with the forces sent through from Munster matched their numbers almost equally. With our death dealers and mages, we outnumbered them, but numbers weren't everything. The soldiers from Munster were exhausted from traveling, and the remaining soldiers from Osraige were already worn down from the first attacks.

Focus, Mira. Gaisgeach snarled. *We cannot win this battle if your mind plays out all the ways in which we lose.*

I love you. I threw the words at Deiric before I put up a mental wall to cut him out. I couldn't focus on the ways we'd lose, and I couldn't focus on what could go wrong with him either. I needed to focus solely on Gaisgeach and the battle in front of me.

Gaisgeach swooped toward the ground and blew fire on the enemy lines, just as several other dragons did the same. The catapults fired, flinging the flaming projectiles up into the air at random. There was no aim, not yet. These were just to keep us from staying on track with our attacks.

Once the lines intermingled with our own, we would have to fly further behind the enemy lines to do damage. They'd be able to aim at us then.

I scanned the men fighting beneath us as they merged with our own lines. There was at least one mage we had yet to find that could've been working with Ronan. Oisin. Devlon had given me a detailed description of him. Although, he shouldn't be hard to find. He was a water mage. I was sure I'd see his magic before I would see him.

Gaisgeach dipped toward the ground again with another blast of fire, and I threw some of my own. A flash of steam alerted me to Oisin. I squinted at him, mumbling an incantation Gaisgeach had told me about to see through his eyes.

There he was, surrounded by Ronan's soldiers, headed straight for Devlon, Tellus, and the group of mages aiding in the advancing of the right flank.

I found Oisin. I said to Gaisgeach, before I shifted from his back and into the swarm of men.

Mira! Gaisgeach shouted, but I was already on the ground, directly in front of Oisin.

He was taller and broader than Deiric. Even though I suspected he didn't have any skill whatsoever with a weapon, his size alone was enough to give me pause. I didn't know why. My speed and strength far outweighed any advantage he would have had over me when I was human. Or, dhampir, anyway.

His gray eyes gave me one quick look over before his lips curled up into a smile. "Oh, I'm going to enjoy this."

"As am I." I gave him a wicked smile back as I drew my sword.

He scoffed at the idea that he would fight me with a weapon, but drew his own sword anyway. The soldiers behind him advanced around him and swung at me.

I dodged left, then right, away from their blades, moving at a speed too quickly for them to process. Soldiers behind me spun around and began to attack as well, leaving hardly any room for Oisin to approach with his weapon.

A sharp sting radiated from my arm as one soldier's weapon hit its mark, despite my dodging and blocking.

Mira. Another snarl from Gaisgeach somewhere above me told me he did not approve of how close I was letting them get to me.

I blasted ten men back with a wall of shadow before advancing finally on Oisin. Misting him would've been easy, but that drew far too much power. I would need that power later.

I ran at him and swung for his face. He blocked me with ease, but I swung again before he could attack and severed his sword arm.

He cursed, and I swung around with my blade, severing the heads and various body parts of other advancing soldiers. Oisin sent shards of ice flying for me, which I melted with a fire I drew from Gaisgeach. I got a half a second to appreciate the fear in his eyes before my sword severed his head. It hit the grass next to him with a sickening thud before his body followed and I shifted back to Gaisgeach.

That was unnecessary. You could've ended that much faster.

Would you rather I use all my magic now?

His scoff was obnoxious, but he banked us so that we would fly further behind enemy lines. *We need to take out the catapults.* He explained.

Then get us there.

He didn't reply, but instead tucked his wings and pushed us faster, sending us rocketing further beyond enemy lines. Arrows and spears flew up at us, some too quickly for me to track and deflect.

A few hit their target in his wings, but he barely seemed to notice their presence. I was vaguely aware of Fiadh and another dragon trailing us into the fray. I still had a wall up, blocking out both Fiadh and Deiric. I was almost certain that Fiadh would be far more adept at dodging than Gaisgeach, just given her smaller size.

I could feel Gaisgeach's disdain for that thought the moment it crossed my mind. It was true though, and he couldn't deny it. His mate was far more agile than he was. The catapults sent another grouping of fire balls at us, this time nearly hitting him several times. He twisted and spun to avoid them, nearly unseating me and flinging me toward the ground in the process.

Some warning would've been nice.

Forgive me, I was too busy trying to keep us from getting shot out of the sky. Pay closer attention next time.

I rolled my eyes at him, then fixed my gaze on the catapults ahead. Several of them were being shifted and moved to aim toward us.

Gaisgeach.

I see them.

We're right in their line of fire.

I know.

We're not going to get close enough to take them out before they fire.

Just trust me.

I held on tighter to the spike that I'd been using to keep myself seated and leaned in closer to him. *I hope you know what you're doing.*

I didn't survive this long to die this soon into a battle.

Then fly faster.

I've got this under–

The first catapult shot toward us.

Shit. We both thought simultaneously.

Gaisgeach banked left. I ducked with him. The fireball whirled right past my head.

Gaisgeach.

He didn't have the chance to reply before seven more catapults fired.

Oh gods.

We were too close. There was no way to dodge them all.

Hold on, was all he got out before we were caught in the fray. He tried to set us into a spin, but one hit his right wing before he could. It sent us spiraling without control directly into two more. One hit his chest and the other hit his left wing.

I held onto him with everything I had as he roared in pain. They couldn't have been just fireballs. Dragons were *fireproof.* I lost track of what hit us and where we were headed. The world blew by in a blur while he flailed to keep us in the air.

Shift away. He demanded. *Get yourself clear.*

Absolutely not. I pressed myself against him. We were spinning, I could tell because the force of it threatened to pull me from him even if I didn't want us to be separated.

Mira. His voice was weaker. I managed to lift my head enough to see where we were, to see the condition he was in, and realize we were seconds from crashing into the ground.

No. I pressed myself into him again. *I will not leave you. You will not die today.*

He stretched out his battered and broken wings one last time to try and slow our descent, but it was too late. He landed on his left wing, crashing through soldiers before the momentum had him flipping over.

I was launched from his back. I hit the ground shoulder and headfirst with a piercing pain shooting from my shoulder through my body before the momentum threw me into a roll that flipped me several times. I skidded to a stop a few meters from where he finally landed as well.

I took several deep breaths through the pain as my body stitched itself back together. All except my dislocated shoulder, which I had to shove back in myself. I grunted as I righted it and lifted myself to my knees. I looked toward Gaisgeach. His chest rose and fell slowly. *Too fucking slowly.*

I scrambled to my feet and was next to him in a single heartbeat. His large golden eyes fell onto me and he huffed a wavering breath.

Go. He demanded. *Get out of here and keep fighting. Go to Deiric.*

"Like fucking hell." I said out loud.

I turned toward him to evaluate his injuries. He had been ripped to shreds, like the fireballs they shot at us were made of a thousand blades. His wings were in tatters, one tucked underneath him and bent at an awkward angle.

"Shit." I grumbled, tears welling in my eyes. "Shit. Shit. Shit."

Go.

"Shut the fuck up." I snapped at him. "I am not leaving you here to die."

No one came near us. I could tell that the soldiers we'd killed in our descent were enough to prevent the others from coming toward us. I tried to heal him, called on all my power, but it was futile. I couldn't heal everything fast enough to save him. Not by myself.

"Fuck." My mind raced as his breathing slowed by the second.

It hit me then. My blood. I could give him my blood. It healed a human instantly, perhaps it would do the same for a dragon.

No. He seethed. His eyes were heavy. I could see he was struggling to keep them open.

I didn't hesitate. I ran to his face, opened his mouth and sliced my arm open on his teeth. "Drink. Damn you."

He couldn't resist me. He didn't have the energy to move away. He had no choice but to allow my blood to pool in his mouth, and I prayed that he might swallow it. That it might be enough to heal him.

Mira. His voice was so quiet in my head. I could feel the bond between us fraying.

"No." I yelled at him. "No. No. I will *not* lose you." I looked up and stared directly into his eye, which was now half closed. "Please." I begged him, opening the wound on my arm again to give him everything I had. "Please drink."

I saw his throat move while he attempted to swallow.

"There." I urged. "Keep drinking." Again, I sliced my arm. Gods damn my healing.

I'd nearly given him every last fucking drop I had before I pulled my arm out of his mouth and let his jaw close. I collapsed against him.

I'm sorry. He mumbled.

I lifted my head. Stars spun in my vision, but I looked back at him. None of his wounds had healed. He continued to bleed out before me.

"No."

You are everything I knew you would be, and more. He said, straining to take another breath and letting his eyes close. *I am honored to have had the chance to bond with you.*

His chest fell and didn't rise again.

"Gaisgeach," I shouted, tears now streaming down my face. It was useless. He was gone. The bond we'd had left an empty feeling in my chest, like a part of my soul had left with him.

A rustling behind me caught my attention and I spun around so fast I nearly hit the dirt. I cursed myself. We were still mid-battle, and I was sobbing over my lost dragon. I was an easy target for any soldier within striking distance.

I froze at what I saw next, and another piece of me splintered apart. My father stood less than twenty paces from me, but that wasn't what stopped me in my tracks. No. That wasn't it at all.

It was the stake protruding from his chest.

Chapter 46

Deiric

Fiadh slammed down onto the ground next to her way too still mate. My own mate was out of sight, and I wasted no time dismounting and sprinting around to check on her. What I found when I reached Gaisgeach's head stopped me in my tracks.

Rosalind stood with her sword through Azazel. Mira was on her knees and looking at the two of them in abject horror. Lazarus was a few paces behind his mate and the look on his face was indescribable.

A pile of ash lay at Azazel's feet, that along with the stake in his hand told me enough, though I couldn't be sure which one of us fell. My gaze shifted back to Mira, and she just looked shell shocked, like she couldn't believe her eyes. Tears streamed down her face freely.

Azazel shifted away, an issue we'd have to deal with later. A single soldier came sprinting for Mira. Before I could step in, she'd cleared the distance between them, disarmed him, and sank her fangs into his neck.

He struggled for only a few seconds before he hung limp in her arms. I felt her rage before I saw it. It was nearly overwhelming. She dropped the soldier in a heap on the ground and glanced my way with a viscous smile. Blood covered nearly half her face and ran down her neck. She looked like the demons they made us out to be.

Her focus shifted back to the remaining charging soldiers who had paused just a few feet beyond Lazarus.

She sank into a fighting stance, summoned more fire than I'd ever witnessed her produce and sent it flying forward into Ronan's ranks. People turned to ash in seconds. The fire stretched back through several rows, too many to count.

She stood and started forward one *slow* step at a time, making her movements all the more terrifying. Lazarus snarled at her for nearly hitting him and she stopped to look in his direction.

"Stay the fuck out of my way then."

I barely recognized her voice when it was coated with so much unending rage. Her focus shifted left, and she moved again, shooting hundreds of ice shards flying into another group of men. They all fell.

She glanced over at Fiadh. "Guard him." She demanded.

To my surprise, Fiadh agreed without hesitation and stood guard over Gaisgeach's body. I didn't have the heart to tell her that he was gone, and there was nothing we could do.

Those dark eyes shifted to me. "He's not gone yet." She snarled, then began to move forward again. Shadows shot out to her right, slicing through more enemies as she walked.

I ran up behind her and guarded her back when people who survived the onslaught of her magic began running at her. She caught one, ripped his throat out and carried on as though he was nothing more than a minor inconvenience. I hadn't ever seen this side of her. I was both impressed and a little bit terrified.

She didn't make it too far from Gaisgeach when I saw him draw in a breath. His eyes opened and rather than their normal gold they were blood red. I looked back at Mira to find a feral grin plastered on her face, made more horrifying by the fresh blood running down her chin from her most recent victim.

"Told you." She said, to me I assumed.

Gaisgeach rose to his feet and let out a roar that shook the ground around us. Fiadh took a few steps back, like she didn't recognize him. I could feel her shock flowing down the bond we shared mixed with a little bit of fear.

Mira sent a few soldiers flying toward Gaisgeach, and he caught them midair. The crunching of their bodies as he ate them made me cringe. I didn't think I'd ever forget it. I could handle blood and gore, but this was… disturbing.

With another roar he shot to the skies to complete the mission he'd set out on in the first place. He raced toward the line of catapults with a preternatural speed. Without having to worry about Mira on his back, he did far more wild and dangerous maneuvers to avoid the fireballs they sent up at him.

Mira continued forward, battering their defenses with fire, ice, shadow, and lightning. Wherever she sent her magic, no one survived. She also blocked several fireballs from Gaisgeach, now that she could focus on him from the ground.

Fiadh fought from the ground behind us. She swung her tail out as soldiers approached her from behind and breathed fire on those that came toward her head.

I fought off anyone who turned to run at Mira from behind, striking them down with practiced precision. Gaisgeach reached the catapults and blue flame poured from his mouth as he decimated the line. The resulting fire and chaos gave the other dragons and dragon riders the opening they needed to push forward beyond where our lines clashed with one another and take out the army in droves.

A glint of gold above our heads caught both Mira and I's attention. We watched as Cairbre carried Adriana to the back of the enemy lines. I could see Ronan there now, watching as we ripped apart his army. It was hard not to smile at the look of shock on his face as his half-sister ran down off her dragon, landed on the ground, and sprinted at him.

He didn't react quickly enough, and before he could block her advance her sword hit its mark. She stopped a few steps beyond him, and we all watched as his head fell from his body and the rest of him crumpled to the ground.

Cairbre let out a roar, which was echoed by the rest of the dragons, both in the air and on the ground. Adriana turned toward the field where we all fought and projected her voice out for all to hear.

"Your king is dead. Surrender now and live. Continue to fight and we will slaughter you without mercy."

The soldiers that had been advancing halted in their tracks. I glanced over at Mira to see the feral grin still sitting on her lips and for a moment I wasn't sure she would hold back despite their obvious surrender when swords clattered to the ground. She raised her hand as though she intended to send another blast of magic at them.

She was practically bathed in blood. It still dripped from her chin, from her clothing. It was splattered up most of her face by now. She'd torn soldiers apart without mercy, and I was certain she'd abandoned every last shred of humanity within her to rip them all apart and succumb to the rage I still felt from her.

I put myself in front of her without a second thought, catching her hand and placing it over my heart. A viscous snarl ripped from her throat as she tried to pull away, but I held her hand steady and held my ground.

"Mira." I pleaded with her.

Silas appeared behind her with a far too amused look on his face. "What fresh hell have you–"

"Don't." Lazarus interrupted. I could tell by his tone he knew exactly what I was dealing with.

Mira almost managed to overpower me and turn her rage on Silas. *Almost.*

I had my hand in her hair and held her forehead against mine. It took every ounce of strength I had to continue to hold her there, facing me, with her hand held firmly against my chest.

"Mira, love. It's over." I stared into the cold black depths of her eyes. She was out of breath and nearly vibrating with rage.

I could see Silas in my peripheral. He glanced around and when he seemed to make sense of what happened, his face had gone ashen. Aris appeared seconds later and, taking in the scene, disappeared just as quickly as he came. Killian appeared too and looked to Lazarus for an explanation.

"Fuck." Silas breathed.

"He didn't see it coming." Lazarus said quietly.

Mira was still lost to me, but at least seemed rooted to the spot.

"Mira," I whispered.

She didn't reply. Gaisgeach and Fiadh slammed to the ground behind us. I was sure they nearly smashed the soldiers that had been standing there.

"Anamchara." I stepped a little closer to her, so we were nearly chest to chest. "It's over. Come back to me please."

She closed her eyes and took a breath, but only slightly relaxed. I lifted her hand from my chest and kissed the back of it, then the inside of her wrist, hoping the more intimate touch might coax her to calm down.

I knew she blocked me out mentally the moment she'd thrown those three words at me when we took to the sky. Nothing I could say or think mentally would bring her back.

"We're safe now. You can breathe." I stroked my thumb across her cheek.

Her nose scrunched up and she pinched her eyes shut tighter. A frown ghosted her lips before she finally opened her eyes, and they were their normal brilliant violet once more.

Except they were empty. Entirely devoid of emotion. She'd brought herself back from bloodlust, but she had yet to allow herself to *feel* anything. Everything that kept us *tame.* That kept us from becoming monsters. Her humanity was so far buried that I wasn't sure if she could bring it back in that moment.

Leo walked up now. His leathers were torn and tattered. He was coated in blood, though it was not nearly as much as I knew was now caked on Mira.

She met my gaze and dropped the wall she built up in her mind enough for me to confirm that she was in fact *calm*. She spun around now, without warning and took stock of everyone around us. Rosalind looked at her with pity. Lazarus was staring off at the ground before him. Silas and Killian observed Mira skeptically, while Leo seemed to be glancing around us to take stock on the situation.

"Where's Renwick?" Mira demanded. "Liala, Eimear, and Triss?"

"Eimear was injured. He healed her, but…"

"She went down fighting like hell." Silas finished for him. "Triss shifted both her and Renwick back to your manor. I imagine she's *still* with them now to make sure Eimear doesn't kill all your mages."

I grumbled a curse.

"Liala?" Mira snarled.

She appeared now, as though Mira's snarl had summoned her. She rivaled Mira with the amount of blood on her, but Mira still took the cake where that was concerned.

"Fine." Liala grumbled. "Although I fear I may need to burn these." She scowled down at her leathers. "Looks like you might suffer the same fate." She looked Mira up and down.

"I need to get a count of my men." Silas mumbled. He disappeared before any of us had the chance to say anything else.

Adriana? Mira asked the dragons.

She's got it covered. No one will harm her with Cairbre at her side. Gaisgeach replied. His composure and control surprised me, but being the first of his kind, I didn't know what it must feel like for him. *Much like your mate*, he snarled at me. *I am quite competent with maintaining my composure and control when I desire to.*

I didn't turn to look at him. I knew that would only anger him further.

"We should get back." Lazarus looked up at Mira. "The gods only know what state Eimear is in by now. The mages–"

Mira shifted us without warning. The dragons as well, much to their frustration. I felt the annoyance from Fiadh almost instantaneously. If Mira cared, she didn't give any indication. Instead, she took off into the manor and I followed right after her.

She hesitated in the foyer where her sudden appearance startled Sorcha, Aodh, Zane and Xander. Blood trailed up the stairs. Eimear's blood, by the scent of it.

"She's–" Zane started, but Mira took off again before he could finish, and I trailed right behind her. She was in no condition to be alone.

I can handle myself just fine. Her curt thought hit me like a slap to the face.

I halted behind her as she slammed open Renwick's bedroom door. I took in the scene before us and quickly shut and locked the door behind me. The room was lit only with candles. The curtains and shutters were drawn. Eimear lay on the bed, now completely whole again. Renwick was distraught, breathing raggedly and pacing.

Triss stood near the door with her arms crossed over her chest and a relatively unamused look on her face.

"I realize you said only to leave if things had gone to shit," Triss began, "but I figured getting her back here before she burned to death in the sun would've also been on the top of my priorities. So I left."

Mira didn't spare her a glance. She walked right up to Renwick and stopped him in his tracks. "Did you ever ask her if she wanted to turn?"

"No." He nearly shouted. "I didn't ever really think to. I just acted out there. She was dying. I had to save her. I didn't think she'd rush back to fighting and get herself killed."

Mira frowned and shook her head. "She'll need to feed if she decides to proceed with turning."

"She can feed from me, if she wants to." Triss didn't move, but looked between the three of us. "Just make sure she doesn't drain me, would you?" She spoke to Mira this time, rather than me.

Mira didn't even hesitate before she nodded, and it was a good thing too, because Eimear shot up in bed.

"What the fuck." She scrambled backwards toward the headboard. "How am I here? What happened?" She looked down at herself, nostrils flaring. "Oh gods."

"I'm so sorry–" Renwick apologized, but Mira cut him off.

"You died." She said bluntly. "You're transitioning, as I'm sure you've figured out."

Eimear stared at her in disbelief.

"You can either feed or you can die." Mira shrugged. "Your choice."

That's a little harsh, don't you think? Mira looked at me. *You could've been a little more gentle about it.*

Mira snorted. *I'm sorry, I'm not in a gentle mood. If he hadn't fed her his blood to save her the first time she'd just be dead. I did tell her to* stay here.

Still.

She shrugged at me.

“I don’t want to die.” Eimear finally said, looking between all of us. “I don’t know that I want to live forever either, but I don’t feel like I’ve got much choice.”

Triss stepped forward and without hesitation slid a dagger across her now exposed wrist. “Then feed.” She held out her arm.

Eimear only hesitated for a moment. Triss had to know that was a stupid idea and that even if Eimear didn’t want to turn, slicing her wrist would’ve forced it on her. Eimear cleared the distance between them quickly and Mira was behind her, holding her before I had the chance to step in myself.

Mira let her drink until Triss swayed just slightly and braced herself on the counter. Then she yanked her back. Eimear was nearly rabid in her arms.

“Renwick.” Mira snarled. “A little fucking help here?”

That seemed to snap him out of his daze, and he launched forward to grab ahold of Eimear and take her from Mira. Mira stepped around so she was in front of her while Triss healed her wrist.

“Calm the *fuck* down.” Mira shouted at Eimear.

She visibly flinched and reached up to her ears. She tried to take a deep breath, which only resulted in her thrashing against Renwick’s hold again. I stepped in front of Triss.

“Get the fuck out of here.” I snapped over my shoulder.

Triss shifted away.

"Breathe through your mouth you idiot." Mira snapped. "Breathing through your nose only makes it worse right now."

Eimear glared at her, but did as she asked. After a few seconds, her eyes returned to normal and her breathing steadied.

"Fuck." She gasped. "How the hell did you stand being within twenty feet of me when you first turned?"

"Self-control." Mira said nonchalantly. "Learn to have some."

"Easy for you to say." Eimear snapped back at her.

Mira disappeared, then returned less than a second later. She held out a ring. "I made extras, because like I said, I had a gut feeling." She smirked at Eimear and handed it to her. "She's your problem now." She looked at Renwick. "Don't let her kill anyone, please."

She stormed out the door and into the hallway. I caught up with her and caught her by the elbow the moment she shifted away. It was jarring, especially when she hadn't meant to take me with her, but we stood on the cliffside now. She yanked her arm out of my grip and took a few more steps.

Grief like I'd never experienced crashed over me like a tidal wave. Mira dropped to her knees as she stared out at the landscape before us. I was by her side in an instant and pulled her into my arms.

Gaisgeach and Fiadh, perched on the cliff next to us, sat and watched silently.

Chapter 47

Adriana

It was a weird feeling, staring down at my brother's beheaded corpse. Yes, I wanted to do it. There was no hesitation in my mind. I didn't think I felt regret. No, this wasn't regret at all. This was a numbness I hadn't ever felt before. It was what he deserved, but I felt no relief. No happiness.

Azazel was nowhere to be found. I looked around the field ahead of me. Cairbre walked over so he stood directly behind me. It was a bloodbath. The earth was scorched in nearly a hundred places. Several of the spots still burned.

It had not taken me long to realize that he had a group of fire mages helping them with those catapults. I didn't know if anyone else had noticed, because none of them fought with the soldiers and it would've been easy to assume they were lighting them with torches. They weren't though. I watched the mages light them and maintain that flame as they soared through the sky and crashed into Gaisgeach and Mira.

I watched as Fiadh banked away from the ones that came for her and Deiric. Her smaller size made her a much harder target to hit, thank the gods. But that pit in my stomach when Gaisgeach and Mira hurtled toward the ground had yet to subside. Even when he rose up and continued on his own. Even when he burned the mages and catapults they operated to a fine crisp. I couldn't erase that memory from my mind.

Mira had been flung like a rag doll. If she were one of the human riders she'd most certainly be dead.

You should not dwell on those thoughts. Cairbre interrupted my spiraling mind. *Your mentor lives.*

Gaisgeach isn't exactly himself. I pointed out.

A huff of steam hit my back. *He is also alive, or whatever you might call the curse she's placed on him to keep him with her.*

What will happen with him? I knew nothing of dragon politics, if there even was such a thing.

He has always been the strongest among us all. We do not exactly have a court like humans might, but he was who we all looked up to. I imagine that will remain, despite his... changes.

I turned and faced him. He looked down at me contemplatively, with his head cocked to the side.

You worry for him?

Of course I do. I worry for all the dragons. The vampires. Even the other mages. Why would I have come to this fight if I didn't care?

He seemed to consider that, then looked out at the field once more. *Humans do many things I do not understand.*

I shook my head and followed his gaze. *I could say the same.*

"Your highness!" Captain O'Byrne shouted as he came scrambling up toward me. His uniform was disheveled, but he appeared unharmed. He bowed at the waist. "How can I be of assistance?"

I raised a brow at him. He did not rise from the bow. It took me far too long to realize it was because I had not yet given him permission to rise.

"I'm sorry, you may rise." I mumbled a bit clumsily.

He finally stood to his full height and looked me over. "Please forgive my delay in reaching you. I had to get the royal guard under control. The general will be here any moment, I'm certain. I'm happy to advise you if you'd like. He will need to know what you'd like the army to do now."

Right. I would have to jump in immediately and make these decisions. My head spun. I knew *some* about military strategy from the meetings I once eavesdropped on, but I didn't know how to direct them after a war.

"Would you direct them to clean up, tend to the wounded, and then prepare to head…" I trailed off when I realized I didn't know where to tell them to go. Home? To the barracks? What *did* we do?

"I will direct him to have them tend to the wounded, prepare to clean up our camps and return to their stations." He nodded. "Is there anything else I can assist you with?"

"Can I trust you?" The question left my lips before I had the chance to consider the brazenness of it.

He blinked, the only sign of his surprise. "Of course, your majesty." I didn't miss the change in title. "I am bound by my position to serve you to the best of my ability, whether I agree with your decisions or not."

I raised a brow at him. This seemed to prompt him to explain.

"Forgive me, your majesty. I should've explained that better. I was *forced* to follow along with King Ronan's decrees whether or not I agreed with them. I will be honored to serve you and hopefully lead this country to a far brighter future."

I see no indication of a lie. Cairbre interjected. *He is being sincere, though he is incredibly nervous.*

He's standing before a golden dragon who could fry him where he stands. I wouldn't expect him not *to be nervous.*

"Thank you, Captain. I believe that will be all. When we've gotten everything situated, I'd like to shift you and the royal guard back to the palace so we can quickly revoke the laws banning magic and vampires."

"We'll need to assemble the court for that."

I nodded. "Then I will trust you to assist me in doing just that."

*

The following morning I found myself still numb, processing what had happened. It was the first time I'd slept in the palace since I met Mira, Deiric, and the rest of a group of people I now considered more family to me than my own mother. What I found upon arrival with Captain O'Byrne was nothing short of horrifying.

The dungeons beneath the palace were filled to the brim with everyone that had been jailed during Ronan's magic ban. No vampires, of course. They were killed on sight, though I had yet to find out if they had found any. Mira never mentioned it. While not officially crowned, I was able to demand their immediate release and appoint guards to oversee that they were properly clothed and prepared to return to their homes.

My mother was among them, and she was absolutely traumatized. How he'd managed to keep her hidden right under Azazel's nose, I wasn't completely sure, but she had yet to come out of her quarters.

I had yet to leave my rooms either. Esme was still with Mira. I had not sent for her. I couldn't bear the thought of bringing her here until I knew for myself that it was safe. Devlon and Garrick sent two mages with me upon my return, and they were assigned to guard my door.

I barely slept. This room still felt like a prison to me. I couldn't wait until they cleared out and prepared the proper royal chambers for me. It was not quite sunrise yet, and here I sat, staring at the door to the hallway where I knew that the mages and likely two royal guards still stood.

I wondered if he would have sent mages to relieve them. Perhaps they did. I didn't have the energy to look. I rose from the bed only to walk to my desk, pick up my quill, and pen a note to Mira. It would mean the world to me if she attended my coronation. And I had plans. Many, many plans that I stayed up half the night considering.

Cairbre confirmed they were the right political moves to make. The best way to assert that magic users were safe here. However, I was certain if I explained it to Mira she would refuse. I didn't plan to give her the option. She owed me, after all.

I completed the note, folded it up, and, upon finally getting the wax hot enough to seal it, I took the ring that the captain had passed to me last evening and I stamped it with the royal seal. Before anyone could wake to notice my absence, I shifted to Mira and Deiric.

I was not entirely surprised to find them asleep. I shifted in silence, and aside from my breathing and heartbeat, I was certain they couldn't have heard me. Shadows further silenced my steps as I approached the bedside table and placed the parchment on it.

I couldn't stop myself from watching them for a few moments. They were covered up with the sheets, much to my relief. Deiric's cheek rested on top of Mira's head, which was tucked between his neck and shoulder. Her arm was splayed across his stomach and his arms were loosely looped around her, like the thought of her moving away, even in sleep, was too much for him.

It was odd to see both of them so relaxed. Deiric's brow was not slightly furrowed in concern as it often was when he was awake, trailing behind Mira like she might break apart at any moment and he had to be close enough to catch the pieces.

Mira's face was similarly peaceful. She hadn't donned a single one of her masks. She looked so much younger when she was like this. So much lighter. I hoped that now that this was all over, they might get to look like this even in their waking hours.

I shifted myself to Silas next. He was awake sipping a glass of whiskey in his office and startled when I appeared before him.

"By the gods. The sun has hardly risen." He grumbled.

"You know, you *could* show at least a modicum of respect and conclude that exclamation with 'your majesty'." I arched a brow at him and placed a hand on my hip.

He snorted. "You, my dear, are not *my* queen, and have not even officially been crowned." He looked me up and down. "You also have never been one for formalities, unless I've misinterpreted our handful of interactions with one another."

"I don't recall running into you much, aside from less than pleasant situations, but I'll let it slide. On one condition."

He arched a brow at me now. "Oh, do go on." He set his glass down on the desk before him, leaned forward, and rested his elbows on his desk, letting his head sit on his hands.

"How quickly can your master of a seamstress work?"

He huffed a laugh, leaned back in his chair, and scooped up his glass again to take a sip. I swore all the vampires drank enough to single handedly keep the whiskey market alive for all eternity.

"That depends." He swirled the glass and stared at the small amount of amber liquid that remained in it. "What exactly is it that you need?"

His piercing hazel eyes met mine and I smiled a bit deviously. "Several items, actually. Most of which, you should already have the measurements for."

Chapter 48

Mira

Deiric's fingers tracing along my arm was the sensation I woke to. It had to be midmorning, judging by the light of the room. I took a deep breath and wiggled myself closer to him. When I lifted my head to look up at him I found him smiling down at me.

"I'm not sure I've ever found you to be sleeping so peacefully." He whispered.

I studied his face for a few moments. "I'm not sure I've ever felt like the conflict's we've found ourselves in have ever been resolved until now."

"You think it's finally over?" He looked genuinely surprised.

"I think it's as *over* as it's ever going to get. And we survived." My throat tightened as I said the last word and I looked away. *We* survived. Many were lost. Including–

"Hey." He caught my chin and turned my face back to him. "You can grieve, but don't let yourself get stuck in it."

I was not able to stop the two tears that escaped, but did my best to blink away the rest. He gently wiped them away with his thumb.

"I–"

He stopped me with a single finger on my lips. "And don't you *dare* apologize to me."

I couldn't help the slight smile that rose to my lips. The grief dissipated just as quickly as it had risen, thank the gods. I thought I had cried as much as I was realistically capable of already, but apparently I still had more to give.

His gaze flicked behind me. "What's that?"

I extricated myself from his hold and turned to see a folded piece of parchment with a royal seal on the table next to our bed. I picked it up quickly and broke the seal faster than I probably should've. He moved behind me so that he could read it over my shoulder with one arm wrapped around my waist and the other holding him up.

"It's from Adriana." I mumbled as I read through her beautiful script. It was an invitation to her coronation and a promise that she would provide us with the proper attire to attend by tomorrow morning.

The anxiety that I *thought* I'd moved past settled in my stomach once more.

Cairbre assures us that it will be safe. We are to make an appearance as well. Gaisgeach chimed in.

I glanced over my shoulder at Deiric, who's brow was furrowed with confusion when he read it. "What could she possibly want us at the court meeting for?"

"Your guess is as good as mine." I set the piece of parchment back on the table beside us.

He seemed to be thinking, or communicating with Fiadh and blocking me from it. I couldn't quite tell. He arched a brow, then seemed to be relieved as he smiled at me. "I'm sure that it will be alright."

I narrowed my eyes at him. "There's something you're not telling me."

"I suppose you'll just have to trust me and Adriana then." He leaned in and pressed a light kiss to my lips, then trailed kisses down my jaw to my neck.

My breath hitched when he nipped me.

"But we don't have to worry about that until tomorrow. *For now…"* He practically purred as his hand slid up into my hair and he held my head to the side. He trailed his lips up my neck and stopped just below my ear. "I am absolutely ravenous, and you are *exactly* what I need."

I hummed and angled my neck to grant him better access, effectively giving him the permission he was asking for. I slipped my hands up into his hair and slid my leg up until my thigh rested against his when he bit me. My entire body sparked with the need for him.

He rolled us so I was on my back, and he was between my legs hovering over me. He grabbed my ass with his free hand and lifted my hips up into him as he guided himself to my entrance.

I gasped and he moaned against my neck as he slid himself into me. *Gods, I will never grow tired of this.* He thought to me. *The way you taste.* He ran his tongue along my neck as he drank. Each pull heightening the ecstasy I already felt.

The way you feel. He slid out slowly and then slammed back into me. I moaned and pulled at his hair. *The beautiful little sounds you make.*

I hooked my legs around his waist and he slid his hand to my breast now, palming it and teasing it with his fingers while I squirmed beneath him and desperately tried to grind my hips in a rhythm that would offer me some kind of release.

He let out a dark chuckle, but thank the gods, he started to move and settled into a pace that would bring me to the edge within a handful of breaths. Just when I was on the brink of my orgasm, he withdrew his fangs and pulled back to watch me.

"Look at you." He breathed as I came with his name on my lips. "Perfect." He brought his lips back to mine and drove into me through every wave of pleasure that followed.

I flipped us over before he could stop me. He smiled up at me, like I'd played right into his little game. "And you," I started, then leaned down to kiss him and pull his lower lip between my teeth. "So eager to watch me that you don't see this coming." I whispered against his lips.

I slipped my hand up around his throat and rocked my hips against him. I tightened my grip when he breathed my name. Shadows slipped from me and encircled his wrists, pulling his hands from where they now rested on my hips and restraining them above his head.

"It's my turn, love." I peppered kisses down his jaw, skipping over where my thumb held firmly against his neck before I nipped my way down to where his neck met his shoulder. He tried to squirm beneath me and rock his hips, but I held him firmly in place.

Patience, love. Don't make me make you beg.

He growled, but I silenced him when I sank my fangs into him. The growl turned to a moan as I began to move my hips against him.

"Fuck." He choked out. I loosened my grip for a moment to give him the chance to catch his breath before I pulled back and smiled down at him, our lips nearly touching.

"Give in to it." I breathed against his lips. "Don't try to hold out for me." I claimed his mouth then, stealing his breath with a kiss.

He struggled against the hold my magic had on him while I slid my hand down his chest. He trembled beneath me, like he was still desperately trying to make himself last longer for me, when the very *feel* of him getting off would be precisely what would send me over the edge again too.

I tightened my hold on his throat again, and he shuddered as the release rocked through him. My own climax followed, and I rocked my hips against him until he stilled. I released him from the shadow restraints and loosened my grip on his neck so he could catch his breath.

I pulled back just enough to catch my breath myself and rested my forehead against his.

"Perfect." He breathed. "You're just… perfect."

I smiled down at him. "I know."

*

I wandered back into our bedroom from our bathing room in a silk robe to examine the gown Adriana left for me. I felt far more comfortable attending this summons in my armor, but Adriana had seemed *very* insistent on this gown for some reason.

It was exquisite. The fabric was thicker than any of the other gowns I typically wore. It had long flowing sleeves and a stiff high collar with a deep v neck in the front of it. The navy color was accented by shimmering streaks of lighter blues and silvers. There was no slit on the leg like I preferred, though I did notice that there was a small, armored patch in the front and back, directly above where my heart would be.

Deiric stopped in the threshold between the bathing room and the bedroom, nothing but a towel on his hips. I could feel his eyes on me, as though he could see through the robe I wore.

"It would look stunning on you." He walked up behind me and slipped his arms around my waist. "Perhaps you should listen to her and wear it."

"You trust her to ensure that no one will try to kill me?"

He took one hand off of my waist to move my hair over my right shoulder so he could kiss down my neck. "I trust that the Morrigan wouldn't have had us win that battle to kill you two days later when our new queen is likely preparing to recognize your efforts in the battle."

I arched a brow and traced my hand down the sleeve of the gown once more. "I suppose that's a good point." I placed my hands over his where they rested on my hips. "Are you going to release me long enough to put it on?"

His fangs grazed my neck. "I suppose I'll have to, won't I?"

"I'm not sure I want you to."

He chuckled, his breath tickling my neck. "We can't be late, love." He traced his hands up my sides and slipped them over my shoulders to pull off the robe.

I spun around to face him, and he turned me around again. "No, love. You need to get dressed."

"I won't be able to concentrate on that with you so close to me."

Another half laugh, and he was across the room. "I will keep my distance then."

"You know something."

"I might."

I turned and gave him a slightly amused and slightly annoyed look.

"Get dressed, love. You have nothing to worry about today."

He gathered his armor and disappeared into the bathing room, shutting the door behind him. Alone at last, and regaining at least some semblance of self-control, I lifted the gown off of the bed.

You should have far better self-control than that. Gaisgeach grumbled in my mind. *You've done nothing but bed your mate all night. It's excessive.*

I scoffed at him. *As if you and Fiadh are no better when left to your own defenses.*

He growled at me, only confirming I was not wrong in my observation.

Macha fluttered into the room next and perched on the dresser. She observed me silently as I loosened the ties on the dress and then slipped it on. It fit me like a glove, and was just as imperial looking as I suspected.

The collar rose above the nape of my neck, and was stiff enough that it would not fall or fold. I would need to tie my hair up so as to do it justice. The v of the neckline dipped down to just above my breasts, and the bodice concealed the plated armor hidden there.

I had to wonder when she'd had the time to have this made. Surely a tailor even working through the night would not have had the time to complete this already today. The skirt was hemmed perfectly, to allow me to wear my usual boots with a slight heel and just graze the ground as I walked. It hugged my curves until it reached my hips and flared out just slightly, but the weight of the fabric kept it subtle and sleek.

Deiric appeared behind me again and began to tie up the back of the dress, neatly tucking the strands within the bodice itself so it was nearly seamless.

"Just as stunning as I expected." He whispered. "I'm sure Triss would help you tie up your hair."

I snorted. "I can handle my hair myself."

He spun me around and lifted my chin so I looked directly in his eyes. "You're appearing at court today, love. Let her help you."

I stared at him incredulously, like I barely recognized the man before me. In addition to his normal leather armor he had a navy cape strung from his shoulders with a pin that held the royal crest. It had been laying with the dress she'd sent me, but I didn't understand its purpose until I saw it on him. He only smiled.

"I *was* appointed to a court before Lazarus found me. They take these things rather seriously, and you should absolutely look your best." He tucked a section of my hair behind my ear. "Just trust me."

"You never told me you were assigned on a court before."

"You never asked."

"What were you?"

"Just a guard."

"That's where you learned to fight?"

"That's why Lazarus sought me out, actually. Yes."

"Interesting."

"It took him a few years to finally convince me. When Fiadh left, I finally gave in and went with him." He shrugged, then grabbed the armor off of the bed. "We should get moving. Find Triss."

He slipped out the door and left it open for me. I followed right behind him, and wandered down to find Triss.

*

As Adriana suspected, her armor fit Rosalind nearly perfectly. Triss had managed to twist up my hair in a high ponytail, held in place by a twisted braid. It was elegant, and yet simple. I was thankful it wasn't terribly different from how I preferred to wear it normally.

I shifted Lazarus, Rosalind, Deiric, and myself into the foyer of the palace. It was decorated far more elaborately than I had ever seen it. Flowers adorned nearly every available surface, and parts of the palace were blocked by an excessive amount of royal guards to lead all visitors to the throne room.

We followed the same hallway we'd gone down during our first visit here to get to the throne room. It wasn't terribly crowded, but I spotted Devlon and Garrick rather quickly. Devlon stood at the front of the room, near the throne, while Garrick was a part of the group on the left side. My eyes landed on each magister, except two. Quinn and

Liam. When I locked eyes with Garrick again, his sad smile told me everything I needed to know about their absence.

We were directed over to the left side of the room with them, and quickly filed into the alcove with the magisters.

"Glad to see you're alright." Garrick leaned in and whispered into my ear when I stepped up in front of him.

I almost asked why he would say that, until I recalled that *everyone* must have seen Gaisgeach and I fall out of the sky. I was sure that had been quite hard to miss.

"Terribly sorry to hear about your father." He added.

Deiric grabbed and gently squeezed my hand, his only way of subtly offering comfort in this cramped and far too public space.

"Thank you." I mumbled over my shoulder. "I didn't expect *all* of the magisters to be here."

He met my gaze and smiled. "We were requested, or, more like demanded, by Adriana. Apparently she really didn't want any of us left out."

I arched a brow. He shrugged. A familiar scent hit my nose and I spun my head around so quickly I nearly saw stars at the edge of my vision. Silas strode into the throne room and smiled my way, before he walked over to stand between Deiric and Lazarus.

"I see my seamstress matched your measurements quite perfectly once again." He muttered quietly with a knowing smirk rising to his lips.

I had to pick my jaw up off of the floor while Deiric elbowed him in the ribs.

"What? You can't tell me that dress wasn't perfectly made for her."

Deiric's low growl just made Silas' smile grow. I found a slight smirk rising to my own lips at their continued chess match when it came to me. It was pointless, but never failed to be entertaining.

They both quieted as it was clear the ceremony was about to begin. Everyone who had been sitting rose as we were directed to by the herald who was to announce her entrance.

"Presenting, her highness, the crowned princess of Leinster, Adriana MacMurrough." He gestured toward the large doors that lead into the throne room.

Adriana strode in slowly and confidently. She wore a surprisingly modest gown, though it was still adorned in gold, and a very simple tiara that fully circled her head. Her hair was braided intricately, with smaller braids framing her face and a large thick braid trailing down her back, framed with smaller artful pieces.

She did not look our way. Her focus was entirely on the throne laid out at the other end of the room. She strode forward with her shoulders back and a neutral expression on her face, like she'd been preparing for this very day for years and not just a handful of weeks or months.

When she reached the throne, she spun on her heel and flung the dress she wore behind her, so it settled perfectly around her.

Devlon stepped forward, followed by the captain of the guard. Devlon bowed in front of Adriana briefly, before stepping forward and placing a beautifully adorned torc around her neck. He was then passed a ceremonial blade by the captain of the guard. He held it out to Adriana, the hilt in one hand and the blade carefully poised in the other.

"Do you, Adriana MacMurrough, swear to protect and guard the land, honor our gods, and uphold the truth and justice of our people?"

She reached out and placed her right hand on the hilt of the blade. "I do." She took the blade from his grasp and held it up before her.

Another man, dressed in long robes, walked up and held out a pillow containing an elaborately adorned crown, with golden trim and a white velvet cap, to Devlon.

"It is with great honor that I appoint you as our Queen." Devlon said regally as he placed the crown atop her head. He stepped to the side.

The herald shouted now. "I now present to you, Adriana MacMurrough, Queen of Leinster."

A wild cheer and chant rose up among the gathered crowd. "Fadó gan deireadh, ár mbanríon!" We shouted and clapped along with the rest of the crowd.

Adriana gave Devlon a knowing look and a smile. He nodded and stepped forward.

"Our new queen now calls forth her mentor, Alesmira and her mate Deiric." Devlon called out, nearly as loud as the Herald had shouted Adriana's name just moments prior.

I was certain my face drained of all color. Deiric merely chuckled. I knew he knew something that he refused to tell me, but this was not what I expected.

He hooked his elbow with mine and led me forward into the center of the room and up the long carpet they laid out for Adriana to walk to her throne, smiling all the way. I tried to school my features into a neutral expression, but it was futile. I had never been more terrified. Battles, I could handle. Being presented in front of a crowd of people I didn't know? That was not what I was prepared for today.

I followed Deiric's lead and bowed when we reached the bottom of the stairs leading to the dais.

"Rise." Adriana commanded and we did.

I heard her think that she was thankful I listened and wore the gown, but then her attention shifted to Deiric. She rose from her throne and beckoned him forward. I stood frozen to the spot and feeling far too alone when he dropped my arm and left my side.

She stopped him when he reached the top of the stairs and stood before her. "Kneel."

He did as she asked.

"Lords and ladies gathered here today, I present to you Deiric O'Conner. A man whose unwavering dedication and loyalty to our country has been proven time and time again. Most recently in the battle at Osraige where he led the dragon riders against the former king of this land when his tyrannical reign resulted in the deaths of countless innocent people."

I tried to blink back my surprise as I watched, but it was more of a struggle than I thought. That, combined with the fact that I'd never cared to learn his family name, left me entirely speechless. The O'Conners were the royal family that ruled Connacht. My husband, my mate, was a former royal and I had never known.

"In recognition of his service, I, Adriana, by the grace of the gods and the will of the people, do hereby appoint him as a General of our armies and leader of the dragon riders." She looked down at him now. "Do you accept this title and swear your loyalty to the crown and the people of Leinster? To protect and to serve this country for as long as you shall live?"

"I do." He said without hesitation. She lightly tapped the flat side of her sword on either of his shoulders.

"Then rise, General, knowing that you carry with you not only my trust, but the hopes of our people as well. Let it be known to all present, and to all corners of this realm, that Deiric O'Conner now serves as my general and leader of the dragon riders. May the gods watch over him and guide him in all that he does for our realm and our people."

He rose to his feet and descended the stairs walking backward toward me with his head lowered before he reached my side and finally stood tall next to me. I didn't have a moment to spare him a glance before Adriana's attention shifted to me. She handed the sword back to Devlon.

"Alesmira." She used my full name as she called upon me. "Please approach the dais."

I snapped myself out of my confused daze and forced my feet to bring me up the stairs to her.

"Kneel."

I did as she asked.

"Lords and ladies, we will now recognize Alesmira O'Conner, whose loyalty and service to the realm are also deserving of high honor."

"Through steadfast devotion and commendable actions, Alesmira has proven herself a true servant of the kingdom. Upholding honor, integrity, and loyalty despite facing ruthless brutality from the former monarch. She protected our people, regardless of the consequences to herself."

I should have kept my head bowed. That was the proper honorable thing to do in this situation, but I found myself glancing up at her. Her eyes glistened with unshed tears, but she held her composure and kept her voice steady.

"It is my honor as sovereign, to recognize those virtues and hereby declare you Lady O'Conner of our vampires, and grant you all of the rights, privileges, and responsibilities of your new title. Do you hereby swear to serve as Lady of Vampires, to protect the orders of the crown and uphold the laws and traditions of this country?"

"I do." I spoke before I could think the better of it. Without even fully comprehending what exactly that might mean for me.

Adriana smiled. "Please accept this sword as a token of my gratitude for your service to the crown."

A sword appeared in her hands, and she held it out to me. It was battle worn, still dirty, and without a sheath, but I would have recognized it anywhere. It was the sword my father carried into battle just days ago.

The very sight of it nearly broke me, and if I had not already been on one knee, I would have fallen to it. I drew in a shaky breath as she laid it in my hands.

The Captain found it as he was walking the field. He recognized it as an elder's blade and brought it to me immediately. She spoke into my mind. *He was the only elder to fall.*

I choked back a sob. Deiric appeared beside me and gently rested his hand on my shoulder.

"Lords and Ladies, please join me in welcoming General O'Conner and Lady Alesmira O'Conner to their rightful titles among us. Let us celebrate their titles along with my own in the banquet to follow."

Applause rang out through the crowd, but the ringing in my ears and the grief nearly overwhelming me practically drowned it out. Adriana knelt down in front of me and locked eyes with me. She lowered her voice so that only we could hear her.

"You are dismissed, but please return here this evening to assist me in creating a ward similar to the one on your manor around my chambers. I cannot sleep here another night without knowing that no one but those I allow may enter."

I managed a nod. She turned to Deiric. "Please bring Silas, Lazarus, Rosalind, and Aris with you. You will all be blood bound to the warding to allow you entry no matter what. Very few others aside from my maids will be allowed entry, and I would like it to be done exactly as the Morrigan did it for you. If they wish me harm, they will spontaneously combust."

We both nodded, despite that I had no idea if I could replicate the Morrigan's additions to the spell that warded our manor. Deiric practically lifted me to my feet, then guided me back down the stairs to rejoin Lazarus and Rosalind. The moment we reached them, I shifted us home. I was in no condition to handle the banquet at that very moment, and I hoped that Adriana would understand.

Epilogue

Mira

I shifted Deiric and I to the Morrigan's temple. I was still surprised that it survived all of the time that magic was banned by Ronan without any damage whatsoever. If I didn't have a far more pressing question to ask the Morrigan today, I would've asked that. I had no idea whether she'd show, and I'd get the chance to ask, but I had to try.

Deiric walked with me up to her altar. The sun had already fallen below the horizon, leaving us in darkness except for the eternally lit torches hung around the circular space.

"Are you sure you would like to confront her about this?"

I could feel Deiric's anxiety. He feared her, and rightfully so, but I felt at this point I had built up enough of a repertoire with her that I *could* ask questions.

"I'm sure that if I don't ask, it will drive me mad for the rest of my life."

His sigh echoed through the empty chamber as we reached the altar.

"Are you sure you still want to give an offering with me?"

"Of course, love." He responded without hesitation.

I drew my sword and sliced my palm over the offering bowl, then passed it to him. He sliced his palm and bled into it with me. I began my prayers quietly and he joined in. I hadn't realized he'd paid attention to them enough to memorize them as well.

When we finished the prayers, we bowed our heads. The usual rush of energy didn't seem to flow through the space this time. Nothing but silence greeted us. I glanced at him, and he at me, before we both looked up.

We stepped back together, surprised at her sudden and silent appearance. She stood before us at the altar, cloaked as usual, with shadows swirling around her.

"You are angry." Her ethereal voice echoed around us.

The sound of it shook me out of my shock. "You knew my father would be killed." I knew it. I didn't have to ask.

I'd read all the lore on her before I prayed to her that first day. She knew the outcome of all battles. She knew everything until the end of time. She'd known I would be captured and tortured, that I would take those three stakes to the chest. She knew *everything* and she let me walk around blindly.

"I did."

"You could have warned me." I snarled. "I could have saved him."

"No."

"Yes." I stepped forward into the altar. "I could have done *something.*"

She shook her head. "You could not have saved him."

"Someone could have."

"No, my child." She stepped through the altar as though it didn't exist at all, and I was now close enough to see her face beneath that large hood. She was beautiful. Far more so than any human being I'd ever seen. Her depthless eyes glowed and I could have sworn the universe swirled around in them. Deiric stood next to me, frozen in place and watching in mute horror while I challenged the very goddess who blessed my creation.

"There will come a time when magic is no longer welcome in this world. Everything that has happened, and everything that will come to pass is happening exactly as it needs to be to ensure that magic will live on, even if it doesn't remain here."

"What the fuck does that mean?"

She smiled, and the look of it sent chills down my spine. "You will understand when the time comes."

Pronunciation Guide:

Eimear - ee-mur
Oíche - ee-ha
Aris - air-iss
Gaisgeach - Gay-z-gee-ack
Fiadh - Fee-ad
Cairbre - Kay-rr-br-eh
Azazel - Ah-zay-zelle

Acknowledgements

I can't believe that I've reached the end of this series. Genuinely, I never thought the day would come that I'd publish my first book, let alone the next, and then this one. It has probably been one of the most fun things I've ever been lucky enough to do. Yes, riding my horses is a thrill. Training them up to get through the levels of Eventing will never not be what I would love to do every single day, but this? Writing out these stories? This is such an incredible ride.

I found myself in tears, reading the final few words as I finished my second to last round of editing. There are so many people who helped to make this possible that I struggle to even list them all. First and foremost, I have to thank my friend Mandie, who was an absolute champion in pushing me to move forward with this project when I shared with her that I was writing it. She was the first person I felt confident enough to send the manuscript to. Closely followed by my friend Abbey. Both of whom thoroughly enjoyed the first book and were more than supportive of reading through subsequent books when they were ready.

Since then I have had so many incredible friends who have read the books, listened to me talk about the fun I had working on them, writing them, and hearing others' reactions to them. Truly, what I enjoy even more than writing these stories, is seeing the reactions that my readers have to each twist and turn in the plot.

I recognize that not every reader will love my books. It's something I've had to learn over time. "You can't please everyone." And that has been one of the biggest challenges. Not reading those initial reviews and getting discouraged. But it brought me to tears when there were a handful of reviews from people I'd never met and they were five stars, four even, and going on about how much they enjoyed the story.

These books have been an incredibly therapeutic experience for me too. I've left a lot on the page. Mental health is a *serious* concern for many people. Anxiety is crippling. Depression even more so. PTSD, no matter what it is from, is real and valid. We all handle our trauma differently. Whether you're a combat veteran or you've simply had a traumatic experience in your everyday life, we all go through it. Just know that you are not alone. Your feelings are valid. You *belong* here. You are loved. Don't give up. You never know when that hard day will be followed by one that is better than you ever dreamed of. I will leave you with my dedication…

Our darkest days remind us to appreciate the brightest ones. Don't lose yourself in the dark. The light will always find its way through.

www.ingramcontent.com/pod-product-compliance
Lightning Source LLC
Chambersburg PA
CBHW030809310726
48980CB00006B/439/J

9798992918274